BART AND THE COMPASS ROSE

Copyright 2014 by Kevin Saulnier.
Cover by Courtney Lopes
ISBN: 978-1497306462

For the greatest girls in the world
Anne, Emma & Lily

CHAPTER 1: THE ISLAND

"It's only an island if you look at it from the water."
—*Chief Brody, from the movie Jaws*

There isn't a place on this earth you should want to be but on the south coast of New England in the summertime. The winter—well, that's another story. When people ask what exactly makes New England so special, you have to take them back to the Pleistocene epoch, which was the last great ice age, sixty thousand years ago; that's when glaciers covered this entire region. With the warming temperatures these great glacial masses started to recede, and in doing so they deposited the sand, clay, and rocks they picked up along their ten-thousand-year journey. When all was said and done this little ice age ended up creating Cape Cod, Nantucket, Martha's Vineyard, and all the bays and harbors of the south coast of New England. But one island in particular seemed to garner a little more attention than the others. It's set farther down the New England coast, sixty miles west of famed Nantucket and Martha's Vineyard, those islands where the rich and famous buy million-dollar homes thinking they can now call themselves New Englanders. Not so fast. The *real* New Englanders live on this special island, with a great salt pond, beautiful cliffs, and rolling hills—this is a true New England island. But the most important feature you will find here is an area so rich in fish that to come here and not fish would be to commit a sin of gargantuan proportion, a sin so great that some think it should be a mortal one.

This was just a sampling of how Nathaniel West would enlighten his clients. It was part of what he called his "total package." The first part of this so-called package was his God-given ability to catch fish, accompanied by history lessons about New England, which, Nate believed, kept them coming back for more. And he needed them coming back for more, because he was a charter boat fishing captain, and they were tourists visiting his home, which was Old Harbor, on the island known as Block, part of that little state of Rhode Island. Hopefully well-paying customers, wanting to catch a fish or two and hear speeches about glaciers.

This particular time, though, there were no speeches about New England, no fishing, no well-paying customers. At this particular time his thirty-foot boat was hauling ass across Block Island Sound as he tried desperately to get his female companion back to shore before he could no longer resist the urge to throw her, or himself for that matter, overboard.

The bluffs of Block Island were finally coming into view, and his mind started to wander. His daydream was always the same: what it would have been like to see all of this for the first time. To be an explorer, at the helm of his vessel, watching the newly discovered land grow larger, wondering what adventures or riches lay in wait for him. He knew that what lay in wait for many of those early explorers were Indian wars, the spread of smallpox, land speculation, and bankruptcy, but he always left that out of the tour; nothing like the thought of thousands dead from disease and wars to bum out a well-paying customer.

When the condos along the beach came into view his daydream was broken, and his attention returned to his companion. Nate's boat crossed the wake of a high-speed ferry coming from the mainland, bringing those sought-after but at the same time dreaded tourists to what could fast become a very small island.

The boat handled the wake with ease except for a little bump that made Charlene look up from the magazine she was trying to read. If looks could indeed kill, at that very moment Nate's head, with surgical precision, would have slid clean off his tan shoulders.

"We're almost there," he told her.

"We better be," she said, emphasizing each word.

Man, things looked so promising this time, he thought. Then again they all started off that way.

Block Island was only around nine square miles and had a population, off season, of around one thousand or so. Most islanders like Nate had exhausted their search for a soul mate from the island residents by their early teens. So off island was his only real chance, and since he didn't own a computer, or even a cell phone, the whole internet dating scene was completely lost on him. He had to rely on the girls coming to him, but trying to find that special someone from the thousands that called Block Island home in the summer for only a week at a time never worked out the way he wanted.

He tried, though, season after season. Now in his early thirties, he met girls the old-school way, at a bar or the beach. But not all girls visiting the island were tourists, some were hired help here for the summer. And since most young Americans found being a waitress or a shopkeeper below them, most businesses in New England had to go global and recruit foreigners for this so-called menial work.

It was hard enough to foster a real long-term relationship with someone from the mainland, but a girl from one of the former Russian republics, that was actually impossible. But if Nate ignored these fundamental flaws in dating and indeed found somebody he would like to spend time with, then he would give it one more island try.

It started off with the usual: drinks and dancing, add some small talk, which covered the basics—likes, dislikes—and then, if it looked like things might progress further, the dreaded three-day boat test. Since Nate spent about every waking moment on his thirty-foot boat and made what some thought barely a living, the boat and the girl, in that order, had to be compatible. His current companion, Charlene, hadn't lasted half a day.

He met her at the bar his friends Jack and Josh owned, the Sign Post. It was the hotspot for the island, with great bands that packed in so many people that finding room to tie your shoes was rare, and by midnight people were very fond of dancing on the tables. This was the place to meet someone fast. So a night of dancing, drinking, and groping led to a day of sightseeing, which led to more groping and then finally the test. They made plans for a ride on Nate's boat, the *Legacy*, up to Cape Cod, which would bring them through the Cape Cod Canal with a couple of nights in Plymouth, Massachusetts.

One bit of information he didn't take into consideration was that Charlene hailed from western Massachusetts—not a lot of ocean out there in the western mountains of the Berkshires.

The boat ride from Block to Plymouth would be about three hours. An hour and a half into the test, upon entering Buzzards Bay, the seas kicked up to about three- to four-footers and the fog made its traditional early summer appearance. This was the exact moment Charlene stopped talking to him. Undaunted by her silence, he made a decision to pull into Cuttyhunk Island, which was one of twelve islands known as the Elizabeth Islands that lay between the coast of New Bedford, Massachusetts, and the island of Martha's Vineyard.

As the boat was pulling into the harbor she went below to get her overnight bag. Nate explained that there were no hotels or inns, or restaurants for that matter, on the island. He then proceeded to tell her, even though he was pretty sure she had stopped listening, that they were going to just grab a mooring in the middle of the harbor, till the weather broke, and while he guided the boat through the mooring field, he told her she would be the one grabbing the mooring. He handed her a boat hook and pointed to the bow. That was the first of what Nate would come to know as the "just die, boat boy" looks.

Nate had named his boat to remind himself of the legacy of making a living on the water, just as his father had done. In its prior life, twenty years ago, The *Legacy* was a lobster boat. It was all deck, with very little interior accommodations, so an air mattress and a pop-up tent had to be set up on the deck for sleeping. The weather never broke that day, so they stayed a very long night in a very small tent. That look she gave him after he set up the sleeping accommodations defied description. Finally, at first light, he fired up The *Legacy's* engine and pushed the throttle up a little faster than he would have liked, put a Jimmy Buffet CD on, a little louder than normal, and tried to make record time back to Block.

Old Harbor lay on the east side of Block and was the oldest part of the island. The giant National Hotel sat up high overlooking the harbor. Ice cream shops and gift shops made up Main Street, with motor scooters and bike rentals every two feet. Down along the north side was where the new high-speed ferries docked every two and a half hours. From this point the docks began. This was where the lobster boats and the fishing charter boats tied up. Following the main dock past the working boats, there was room for the pleasure boats, where they could tie up and spend some fun-filled nights, as long as they didn't mind a whiff of fish and lobster bait.

To continue along the dock you had to turn left, heading out to another row of charter boats. But to continue straight you entered the Beach Bar. Located smack dab on the beach, it encompassed the entire end of the docks and you would have to pass through its doors to get to the beach. With bands playing and alcohol served to you on the beach, this was the place everybody came to during the day, before heading over to the Sign Post.

Nate pulled his boat into his slip, which was in the middle of the last row of charter boats. Not a lot of foot traffic this far down the dock, and he liked it that way. He always maneuvered his boat seamlessly and this time was no exception.

After a quick tie-up of the lines he returned to the deck and Charlene already had her bags lined up at the stern. Nate jumped from the deck to the side gunwale of the boat and then to the dock in one swift movement. Charlene was not so agile; she slipped, and Nate, with cat-like reflexes, grabbed her arm and saved her from a sure swim. Her sunglasses were not as lucky, flying six feet in the air from the sudden change of momentum when Nate grabbed her.

"You shit-head!" Charlene blurted out.

This brought Nate's boat neighbor, Lou, to pop his head up from the engine compartment he was in. "Very salty language you mastered, for only one day at sea," Lou said.

Lou now received that patented look she'd perfected probably long before Nate and Lou had come into the picture. Nate started to help her with her bags, and when she resisted his help he just put his hands up in the sign of surrender and shrugged.

With the music from the Beach Bar echoing down the docks, Nate just stood there and watched her walk down the dock. Once again a failed test, a bitter goodbye, and the ever increasing possibility that he would spend another summer alone.

"I think you set a new three-day boat test record," Lou said from behind.

Still watching her walk away, Nate said, "Actually no, there was that one that showed up with her boyfriend."

"I think you need to revamp your testing, Nate."

Nate looked back to Lou. "This coming from a man who's never been married."

"Yeah, what do you know about it?"

"Well I guess I'll just die alone—hey, just like you."

"I loved many, Nate, a few have even loved me back," said Lou, looking away. "I think. Anyways, I'll tell you this much about it, the sea and women don't mix, never have."

Nate stopped watching Charlene walk down the dock. "I give up; this island is a relationship hell."

"You'll find love on this island yet."

"I honestly don't think so. This island is getting smaller the older I get. Maybe it's time."

"Time? Time for what?" Lou was laughing. "You can't leave; you've been here too long. If you go live on the mainland now you would be like a feral cat once you bring it inside. You'd end up scratching everybody you met and peeing in the corners."

"You should have your own advice column, you know that?"

Nate picked up his backpack. It was red in its heyday but now had some semblance of its former color only in some of its corners. Saying it was well worn would be describing it from years ago. As he slung it over his shoulder he raised an arm in farewell and started to walk down the dock.

"Hey, Lou?" he said, stopping. "Come to think of it, didn't you have a charter today? The one I gave you, the Pelletiers?"

"Had to cancel," Lou told him, getting back to work in the engine compartment.

"You're kidding me, right? That's twice in one week. Your boat hasn't had that much trouble in two years," Nate said, looking down at Lou. "What now?"

"Clogged fuel filter again. Must have gotten some bad fuel."

"We all get our fuel from the same place. Stop covering for them."

"What?" Lou said.

"You lie like shit, man."

"Let it go, Nate. I can't prove it, and even if I did, what good would it do?"

"Well for starters it might stop him from stealing other people's charters."

"That's the only way he knows how to get them, so why deprive him of that?"

"You should stop letting them make you their whipping boy, Lou." Nate knew the second it left his lips that he should not have said this.

Lou stood up and jumped onto the dock, wiping his hands with a rag. He looked into Nate's eyes. "I'm seventy-eight years old, fought in two wars, been around the world twice. Seen and done things that I'm not proud of and others that I'm very proud of. Worked and fished this island for forty years. Nobody could ever make me do anything that I was not willing to do of my own free will. Do I make myself clear?"

"Yes, sir," Nate replied.

Lou put his hand on Nate's shoulder. "Don't worry, they'll get theirs someday." He started back down to his engine compartment. "You can't send out that much bad karma and not have it smack you square in the ass at sometime or another. I've seen it happen."

"You should really think about that advice column," Nate said.

"Anything else there, sunshine?" Lou asked.

"I suppose you wouldn't want to tell me the whereabouts of my lobster pots."

"Keep working on it, you'll get it, you always do," Lou said, smiling.

Nate threw his hands up again and walked down the west side of the dock to the road or bulkhead that ran along the marina. This was the hub of the harbor, where several of the main streets that flowed from the center of town came to an abrupt end, dumping a bucket-load of people who were walking, biking, or riding one of those crazy scooters onto the main dock. They mixed in with the people coming to and from the bar or beach or from their boats which were tied up along the bulkhead with their sterns facing the street.

This was where the fun was, the fun for the pleasure-boaters. If you didn't come by ferry then you came by a pleasure craft of some sort, be it Jet Ski or boat. The partiers all wanted to dock up in Old Harbor.

There were mainly two types of boaters on Block: the commercial guys, like Nate and Lou, who made a living with their boats, and the pleasure-boaters, who came for a weekend of fun and had more amenities on their boats than most people had in their homes. They docked their boats for the weekend, sometimes rafting them out five deep. Their sole purpose, some believed, was to drink, and they were good at it. Their beer cans were stuck in their foam cozies for no other reason than looks, because their beer never had time to get warm. They stood on the sterns of their boats watching all the people go by, convincing themselves that just because they had a boat, they were somehow better than most. They were not successful at maintaining this illusion. Once you noticed the beer guts that went along with the cans they were holding, you saw that they took better care of their boats than they did their bodies.

With the music blaring and the endless laughter, Nate walked by these weekenders and thought that as much trouble as they were, they were the summer and this sound was his life. When it all faded with the colors of the trees, he actually missed it.

As he walked along the dock the dominant sound was coming from David Cavarlo, who was the harbor master for Old Harbor. David wore his utter distaste for the job on his head like a birthday hat, the kind with glitter and a tassel. So anybody not following the rules of the harbor as set forth by David Cavarlo would bring upon them a bucket-load of trouble. He was explaining in more detail than was probably necessary to a boat of Long Island guys—the name *CHICK MAGNET* was stenciled on the stern—that not everyone around them and on the other side of the island for that matter loved Duran Duran, or even remembered who they were, so maybe they could be so kind as to turn the music down.

Nate walked down past the harbor master's office and gave a nod to old Pat Veary, probably the oldest former harbor master in the free world. Nobody had the nerve to tell Veary that he was too old for the job, so they just let him show up and called him the assistant—which was a sore subject with David Cavarlo. Nate continued past the weekenders, even recognized some, mainly from their boats, though.

One of the last four boat slips before the parking lot to the ferry was Darren Saucier's. His was the first you would see coming off the ferry. These slips and Darren's in particular were the most coveted spots for a charter boat captain in Old Harbor. If some unsuspecting tourist happened upon the docks in need of a fishing charter, Darren and his gang of misfit toys usually didn't let them get all the way down to Nate. This didn't really hurt Nate or Lou because Darren had the reputation of not being able to catch a fish if he were to fall into a trawl net. It was Darren's father who had this spot, and since he was taking in some quality time at the Rhode Island House of Correction, he had by default given Darren the right to run a shaky charter business into absolute ruin.

As Nate passed Darren he didn't give him the satisfaction that he was occupying space on this island.

"Nate?"

Nate didn't even flinch, just kept walking; he was a mere foot from the end of the dock.

"Thank Lou for the charter, will ya?" Laughter from Darren and his misfit friends echoed in Nate's ears.

He stopped dead in his tracks and turned around, walked the short distance to Darren's boat, and still not making any sign that Darren and the boys were there, bent down, picked up a hose, and squeezed the handle all the way, sending out a jet of water that was going to leave a mark. The shouts of surprise and anger were barely audible since Nate was hitting most of them in the face. Nate just dropped the hose, turned, and continued on his way. *Lou will understand*, he told himself.

As two of the misfits tried to climb off the boat in a rage, the sound they made slipping and landing ass-first on the deck of the boat could be heard all the way down the dock.

Continuing to walk to the visitor's booth, Nate made it halfway across the parking lot when a hand grabbed his shoulder and spun him around. Nate was six-one and Darren five-seven, so this was a very bold move on Darren's part. He looked up at Nate and right away gave off the look of someone who had just made a very bad move.

"*Hey*, you two," someone yelled while trying to keep his voice down at the same time. It was Harbor Master Cavarlo, who caught up with the two of them.

"Chief," Nate said, not taking his eyes off Darren.

"David," Darren said, not taking his eyes off Nate.

"What seems to be the problem this time?"

"Nate started it."

"What are you, five years old? Can we not start beating the shit out of each other on the first day of the season, huh?"

"Why you looking at me?" Darren asked.

"I don't know, just a hunch." David stared down Darren. "Take a walk."

But Darren stood there a moment too long for David.

"Get out of here," David yelled.

Reluctantly Darren turned and walked back, his soaking wet sneakers making a squishy sound as he walked.

"By the way, Darren," David said, "you should know, there might be some bad fuel going around, so you better be careful when you fuel up your boat."

Darren slowly turned upon David and gave him a puzzled look.

"Something needs to be done about him," Nate said.

"Are you telling me how to do my job?"

It was Nate's turn to stare down David.

"Look, Nate, you're the smart one here," David said, nodding back over his shoulder in the direction of the docks. "Can you maybe try—"

Nate cut him off: "You're not telling me how to do *my* job, are you, Chief? Because all I do is fish. Which is getting increasingly harder the way Darren runs his business. Now you, on the other hand, have to deal with all these people coming to our docks … add the fact you had someone stealing Lou's electronics off his boat last month, and now sabotaging his fuel, all this shit makes you quite busy, so I don't know what I can try and do for you … Because all I do is fish."

They both stood there for a moment.

"Maybe it's time," Nate said softly.

"What?"

"Nothing. Look, I have to go see Rebecca," Nate said, pointing to the visitor's booth.

"Yeah, go. And stop calling me Chief."

"You used to like it."

David turned back and headed toward the docks.

Nate knocked on the back door of the visitor's booth, which was not really a booth, at least not any more. It started out a booth, at best five feet by five feet, but as the tourist industry started to pay off in the eighties it became an actual small building, with somewhat clean bathrooms and even lockers. Rebecca Preston had been running the info center with her mom since the days of the shed. Her mom was now semi-retired and drove a cab, leaving her only daughter in charge, and Rebecca took this facility seriously.

A short blonde girl answered the door and just stared at Nate. He took a step and her hand went up, stopping him. He didn't know how to react.

"Beck," he yelled out.

Rebecca turned in mid-conversation and waved to the girl stopping him; the girl's eyes went down to the floor and she let him pass.

Nate walked over to Rebecca. "You can't treat the summer help like servants, Beck."

"Yesterday afternoon I left for a couple of hours and they had a party in here. All that was missing was a band and a cover charge."

"Ah, man, I love those visitor's booth parties. What time was this?"

"Not funny, Nate."

"You're drunk with power."

"I told you she would only last a day," Rebecca said.

"Don't change the subject; technically she lasted half a day with the boat test. I just didn't take her back till today."

"So you don't want to talk about it?"

"Do I ever?" It was Nate's turn to try and change the subject. "What have you got for me, Beck?"

"Two half-day charters tomorrow, and three full-day ones after that," Rebecca said while she handed him his schedule book.

"What would I do without you?"

"Book your own charters like everybody else. Hey, I know: you could get a cell phone."

"That's crazy talk. Plus I need that extra edge, and you're it."

"It's rather unethical," Rebecca said.

"Says who? There are more tourists than charters most of the time. Who's going to complain?"

"You know who. Speaking of you know who, did you get into something with him on the docks?"

"It happened two minutes ago, how would you know that already?"

"You can't fart on this island without me knowing."

Nate moved his hands all around. "It's all your little foreign spies you have."

"It's all about the edge," Rebecca said.

Nate walked out the back door and turned to the little blonde girl. "Run for your life."

"Katrina, you better not be smiling," Rebecca yelled to her. "I'm serious."

Nate was now at the front window. "Do you think it's Darren screwing with Lou's boat?"

"I told you before: no. He's a good guy, Nate, you just forgot that."

"I don't know," Nate said.

"Well you do remember that you, Darren, and David were friends once, right?"

"That was a long time ago. I don't know why we even hung out with them."

Rebecca looked around with her hands up. "It's an island, Nate. Not a lot of choices." Nate shrugged as Rebecca continued, "Look, I can understand David and you with that shit that happened years ago, but leave Darren out of it."

"Between you and Lou, nothing but advice ..."

"You find your pots yet?" she said, smirking.

"If anybody comes by for a charter around dusk, pass. This early season heat has to break at some point and I don't want to be out at night in a thunderstorm."

The late afternoon sky to the north was starting to turn black, and the sea was showing signs of white caps. A once beautiful day was turning to crap fast.

"What, are you scared?"

"I'm the captain, and you know what that means."

Reluctantly Rebecca said, "Yes."

"Say it."

"The captain is always right. You know I don't believe that ... right?"

A large clap of thunder rang out.

"Man, I love being right," Nate chuckled to her as he walked off.

Chapter 2: The Wreck, Part 1

Like all the demons loosed at last
Whistling and shrieking, wild and wide,
The mad wind raged, while strong and fast
Rolled in the rising tide.

—Celia Thaxter, from *"The Wreck of the Pocahontas"*

The winds were blowing forty knots, give or take. At that point it was nothing but a mere technicality—they were in trouble.

"Captain, you must wake up, sir," the second mate pleaded, standing outside the captain's cabin door knocking.

"Enter. I am not sleeping."

The second mate entered and saw the captain hunched over his desk looking at a chart.

"How far has it pushed us, Christopher?"

"Hard to say."

"If you had to take a guess?" the captain said, very agitated.

"Twenty, maybe thirty miles."

The captain stared back down at his charts, and compass in hand, plotted out their possible position.

"Block Island." The captain rubbed the back of his neck and took a deep breath. "What do you know about this Block Island, Christopher?"

"Well, sir, those islanders … they're once removed from pirates. It's not a place we want to port, Captain."

"That's not what I'm worried about." He moved out from behind the desk and out of the cabin, Christopher close on his heels. As he climbed up the stairs to the topside the wind and waves were deafening. The captain opened the hatch to the deck and was hit with the wind and rain. He grasped the door frame and fought his way out onto the deck and up to the helm. Jonathan, his first mate for a decade, was at the wheel.

"Are you holding track?" the captain shouted against the wind.

Jonathan shook his head.

The four-master ship, a hundred and ten feet long, was holding her own, for now. The rigging was fraying in places, sails were ripped, and one of the masts, made of the heart of an oak, was under considerable stress; if it were to go, so would they all. Keeping this from happening, and keeping the ship off the reef, was something only a few were capable of doing. Captain Jacob Mayhew hoped he was one of them.

"Take the wheel, Christopher."

Without question Christopher ran to the wheel and took over for Jonathan.

"Hold her straight as you can, we have some time."

The captain walked down from the helm to the main deck. The crew, twenty in all, had been through a lot in the last five years, and the oldest—maybe eighteen at the time of their departure—had the look of a well-worn sailor. They were New England whale men, down to their bones, every last one of them.

"KEEP YOUR EYES AND EARS SHARP," the captain cried. "YOU KNOW WHAT WE ARE LOOKING FOR. LET'S PRAY TO OUR GOD WE DON'T FIND IT."

The crew yelled in unison, "AYE, AYE, SIR," and scurried off.

The captain and Jonathan headed back down to the captain's cabin; the door slamming with the wind made them both jump.

"We've been through worse, but not much," Jonathan said.

"We are off Block Island."

"Captain … Jacob … if we wreck off this island, the wreckers can't find this cargo."

The captain placed a hand on Jonathan's shoulder. The sinking of the *Gosnold*, one of the greatest whale ships of its day, was the foremost thought on Jonathan's mind, along with their secret cargo.

"If we can make it round the reef, to deeper water, then I think we'll make it," Captain Mayhew said.

"I hope you're right, Captain."

"If we don't, I will take the remaining whale oil and set her ablaze, keep the wreakers away, and let her sink to the bottom—a chance to recover the cargo some other day."

Jonathan stared at the captain and wondered why, why did he take on this fool's errand?

CHAPTER 3: A DAY IN A LIFE

If I have to have a religion, it may as well be fishing,
Because it will be the closest I'll get to heaven.

—Michael McCloud, from the song "Fishing Fool"

The thunderstorm that threatened to bring in cooler, drier air never fully materialized that night, so the early morning fog still had its hold on the island, which made it hard for Nate to see the road as he walked. As he rounded the last corner, just before his house was swallowed by the fog, he turned and glanced back to it. The house had been his parents', back when all was right in his world. A mile or two from the center of town, it was tucked away on a small piece of land that was once a large farm. Other than the ocean, his home was his favorite place to be. He liked the solitude of the fields that surrounded his house. This was the theme that ran through Nate's life.

He had been walking to his boat for so many years he could sense his impending doom in just enough time to jump out of the way of one of those ridiculous scooters as it blasted by from out of the fog. He started the song he'd been singing in his head from the beginning and headed toward the center of town.

The early morning chatter of birds tried to make a bid to drown out the sound of the ocean as he neared the beach. He walked up a hill and entered a breakfast shop.

"Good morning, Helen," he said as she handed him his coffee and he dropped a couple of bucks on the counter.

"Working today, Nathaniel?"

"Fishing is not working, Helen."

"You always say that, but do you mean it?"

Nate smiled. "Get outside today, Helen, it is going to be a beauty."

On his way to his boat, he walked past the shops and bars that were not yet opened. The ferry was warming up at the dock, making a low vibrating rumble, and the visitor's booth was shut tight.

As he approached the docks there was a scattering of people milling around, coming back from a morning run or swim. One should not expect customers to be waiting for a charter with Darren so early in the morning—that would have been a sure sign of the apocalypse. The weekenders were all still tucked in nicely in their boats, sleeping off something or another, which was just fine with Nate.

"Chief," he said as he walked by the harbor master's office.

"West," David said without looking up from his logbook. The summer ritual had begun and Nate was smiling from ear to ear.

Just as he finished wiping the morning dew off his boat and warming up the diesel engine, his charter arrived, right on time.

The Ellises were repeat customers, which was always good. Their two kids, around ten years old, were still at that age to find this family fishing stuff fun, unlike after the age of hormonal infusion, when there were a bucket-load of things more interesting than fishing with mom and dad.

"Mr. and Mrs. Ellis, and I believe we have Jake, Sammy." The Ellises smiled at Nate for remembering their names, a quality he'd learned from Lou, who was now walking down the dock to his own boat.

"Hey, sunshine," Lou said with his usual smirk.

"Morning," Nate said, smiling back.

"Fog should be gone around ten, should make for a hot, sunny day, five to ten knots out of the south." Even though Nate studied the weather each and every day like a good captain, Lou was compelled to tell him every morning what that day's weather would be.

"Thanks, Lou." And with that Nate threw off his dock lines and headed out into the fog to try to impress the shit out of his clients.

Every good charter captain had his secret spots, places where only he knew when and on what the fish would bite. There were popular spots that every fisherman or would-be fisherman went to, even Nate when the time was right. But that secret spot was the key; this special spot would hold tons of fish just asking to be caught. Others had followed captains out to their spots; after all, it was a free ocean. But the good ones, the exceptional ones, like Nate, would let a competitor or a recreational fisherman fish five feet away, and he would out-fish them ten to one.

The spot he picked for the Ellises, the all-important repeat customers, produced six forty-pound stripers by ten o'clock.

The family was laughing, taking pictures, and having a ball.

"Nate, I was wondering," Mr. Ellis said. "We caught six of the biggest stripers I have ever seen and threw back ten. How do you do it? I've chartered people all over New England and nobody catches fish like you do, and you seem to enjoy it more than us."

"Well, my secret is to love it, but also"—he leaned in closer to the family—"you have to have secret spots that only I know. These spots were discovered by the Wampanoag Indians, who told it to my great-great-grandfather, and then were handed down to me."

"Really?" Mr. Ellis said, surprised.

"Nah … I'm just lucky."

"I somehow doubt that."

Nate raised his eyebrows and returned the smile.

"How about once around the island," Mr. Ellis said.

"It's your charter. Now that the fog has lifted, it would be a great tour." Nate looked down at his watch. Ten o'clock. *Damn that Lou.*

Nate started the tour at the Southeast lighthouse. He explained when it was built, and all about the time they had to have it moved farther back from the cliff. He couldn't help but tell the story of the Orlando, a ship that wrecked at Southeast lighthouse and now lay under forty feet of water. The wreck itself was no captivating story, just a tanker running aground in the late fifties. But he'd already used the forming of New England speech with the Ellises, so he had to dig a little deeper into his total package arsenal.

"Now take a look at my fish finder screen," he said when they slowly cruised over the wreck. "The sonar sends a signal from a sensor called a transducer, on the bottom of the boat, it bounces the signal off the structure and gives us an interpretation of the image on the bottom of the sea floor. See, you can make out the hull." Nate's fingers traced the hull on the screen. "She's lying upright, but she's in half."

Mr. Ellis looked at Nate staring at the screen in silence. "It's got you mesmerized."

"Huh? Oh … yeah. This wreck is where I learned to scuba dive as a kid, with my dad." Nate's eyes lingered on the image.

"He is gone now, isn't he?"

Nate nodded his head. "Twenty years now."

Mr. Ellis, feeling he might have traveled down a road he hadn't meant to, changed the subject. He pointed to the dash of the cockpit. "Is that a sextant?"

Nate nodded, smiling. "Yes."

"With all this electronics on your boat, you're telling me you use that?" Mr. Ellis said.

"Well, to give you the short version. You asked about my dad, well … I was only fifteen when he died, so a family friend, the guy telling me the weather this morning, that was Lou. He sort of looked after me. Since I could remember he would send me on these tests, he calls them Lou quests. These quests could be as simple as learning to tie different knots, or," pointing at the sextant, "a little more complicated."

Mr. Ellis picked up the sextant and examined it. "It's beautiful."

"Yeah, well … it's a complicated piece of equipment. The problem is that these quests sometimes have a larger importance. In this case Lou moved my lobster pots to new areas, then he gave me the celestial quadrants, and you need a sextant to determine the locations. I'll lose hundreds of dollars in lobsters if I can't find them in a week."

"Good luck to you."

"Unfortunately Lou always tells me luck has nothing to do with it."

He smiled and the boat continued on in silence.

The Ellises at this point were all sitting in the deck chairs. Since Nate's boat was also a lobster boat, it was all deck and very little cabin. The boat's forward area had an enclosed cockpit that led below to a small cabin that had only one place to sit, a toilet. He let them relax on the deck in silence and enjoy the ride around the beautiful island, a sight to behold even for the most jaded islander.

He spotted boats fishing here and there, most of them recreational guys just out for a good day on the water. As he stood there and drove he kept glancing down at the GPS and chart plotter mounted in front of him. In the age of satellites it showed exactly where you were, with a picture of the nautical charts all laid out on the screen. Boats had been using this technology before car makers jumped on the bandwagon. He also glanced down at his fish finder out of habit. Most new spots were found by just driving around till you saw the sonar image of fish, lots of fish, stacked up in a particular spot. He spotted a couple of potential spots to investigate later—with nobody around, of course. Nate may have been able to out-fish most, but that in no way meant you gave away your productive spots. Lou wouldn't even tell or show Nate all of his.

Halfway from Southeast Light and New Harbor Lou's theory of no such thing as luck was proven wrong. Nate spotted one of his lobster buoys. He slowed down and pulled alongside. The family joined him at the side to watch this process. After hooking the line, he pulled in a full pot of lobsters sixty feet from the sea floor. His arms were sore.

"These four will do you just fine." He stuffed four two-pound lobsters in a bag and placed them in a cooler.

"You just lucked out, didn't you?"

Nate smiled. "Sometimes I'd rather be lucky than good."

After pulling into his boat slip he helped the family off the *Legacy* and brought the fish they had caught down to the fillet tables at the end of his dock. He filleted the stripers like a surgeon and put them in plastic baggies and even packed them in the family's cooler along with the lobster. *It's the intangibles that keep them coming back for more, sunshine.* Nate heard Lou in his head as he handed the cooler to the family. They all took pictures of the lobsters and the bags of fish, and even of Nate, a ritual that had been repeated a hundred times over the years. The family walked away after the hugs and thank-yous. Nate put the hundred-dollar bill Mr. Ellis had insisted on him taking in his shorts and headed off to the visitor's booth to see Rebecca.

Once again he tried to enter the visitor's booth through the back door, but was rebuffed again from another foreign summer worker.

This time the young girl looked up at the wall that had several pictures of people tacked to it. The top right pictures had the heading ALLOWED and the left side NOT. Nate looked at his picture smiling down. She let him pass.

"You smell like fish," Rebecca said without looking back to him.

"You're out of control."

"You're lucky you made the right side of the wall, I could have gone either way." She smiled at the next tourist looking for a restaurant. "Good day?" she asked Nate.

"Yeah, good charter, they had fun. So did I."

"Your night charter canceled. They all got seasick on the ferry ride over."

"It's flat calm out there and it's a high-speed ferry—it's like a cruise ship. How the hell do four guys out for a fishing trip get seasick?"

"How the hell do I know," Rebecca stated.

"Well something's not right with them, I'll tell you."

"You always tell me ... why do you?" she asked while handing a brochure to a customer.

"I like to."

"Well, stop it."

"Well, that's not going to happen."

Rebecca just smiled at him. "No, I can see that."

"I'm going back to wash down the boat. Beach Bar at four for margaritas?"

"Yes, please," Rebecca giggled.

As he turned to leave, a woman dressed in a waitress apron came to the window. "Excuse me," she said in a British accent. This made Nate take notice. "Do you know of any jobs in these parts? I seem to have just lost mine."

"Usually one in these parts returns the apron when leaving," Rebecca sarcastically replied.

"Well if you were grabbed on the ass as many times as I was, one may forget the return of said apron."

On hearing that, Rebecca's attitude shifted gears quickly. "Mel's?"

"Yes, you know him?"

"Everyone does. There isn't an ass he doesn't like," Nate added, looking for a way in to the conversation.

"I am sorry about that, but we don't post jobs here," Rebecca said.

"But we do hear of things from time to time," Nate said.

"We do?" Rebecca asked him.

"We do indeed."

"Don't you have some washing to do?"

He whispered back to her, "Shut up."

"Well I'm a bartender by trade but apparently so is everyone else on this island."

Nate and Rebecca stared at each other and shook their heads no, when neither of them could think of a job opening.

"No, wait," Nate said. "You know what? Phil is back on the mainland for a wedding, won't be back for a couple of days. You could talk to Mark the manager at the Beach Bar. He might let you tend till he gets back."

She smiled and thanked them and walked off.

"My God she is absolutely stunning," Nate stated.

"Wow, you pulled that one out your ass for her. Way to go."

"Thank you, it's a gift."

"What, pulling stuff out of your ass?"

"You're going to hurt my feelings," Nate said, smiling.

"She's our age, not one of these young pups," Rebecca told him.

"Yeah, but a relationship with someone on the mainland has been proved, by me of course, to be an impossibility. But England. You would have to be a superhero to make that one work."

"Like a Superman or maybe the Green Hornet?"

"Nooo ... Aquaman."

They stopped in mid-conversation; the English girl was back at the window.

"I'm partial to Superman—you know, the flying," she said. "But look at it this way: England is an island also, so we already have something in common."

Nate's face heated up.

"Where's the Beach Bar?" she asked as she looked through the window.

"Aquaman was just heading that way," Rebecca said, smirking at him as he gave her his best evil eyes.

As the two walked down across the parking lot to the docks that led to the bar, Rebecca was half in, half out of the visitor's booth window, watching them walk away.

"Your friend is watching us."

"Until her spies take over."

"Spies?"

"Yeah, they're everywhere, watching, reporting back to their queen."

The Brit smiled and they continued in silence for a moment.

"Since you won't ask, my name is Kate. And I already know that you're Nate. Nice to meet you, Nate."

Nate smiled. "I'm sorry—nice to meet you, Kate."

"You're the strong, silent type, right?"

"Yeah, but when I start talking you can't shut me up."

"Something to look forward to."

"First time to the island?"

"Yes. My sister talks about it endlessly from about two years ago. Lived here your whole life?"

"Yes, ma'am."

"Yes, ma'am. You're a formal one."

"Yes, ma'am."

She laughed.

"How do you like it so far?" Nate asked, trying to keep the conversation going.

"The company or the island?" she said.

It was Nate's turn to laugh.

"Well, I'm older than most summer workers," she said.

"Really, I haven't noticed."

"Nice one."

"Thanks."

"Well let's see, I had my ass grabbed a dozen times on my first day of work, lost my job, I live with five girls, all of whom are only interested in getting drunk and laid, in that exact order, mind you. So I would have to say I am having a below-average time. But the last ten minutes have the potential to get me back in the positive. I mean it's not every day one meets Aquaman."

Nate smiled and stopped at the steps of the Beach Bar. The walk was short but the impression of her would be long-lasting. She stood out from every single summer girl he had met, but he also knew it always ended the same. They stood there for a moment watching the people walk by.

She looked up at the sign on the roof. "This is it, huh?"

"This is it," he replied back.

She smiled at him and he smiled back. "Come on, let's find Mark," he said. It wasn't hard to find him; he was behind the bar stumbling his way through the afternoon drunk crowd. Nate introduced them.

"It was nice talking to you," Nate said. "Good luck. Mark, take good care of her, she's had a bad day."

"I will, Nate."

She watched him walk out of the bar.

When he arrived at his boat Mike was there helping Lou unload lobsters. Mike was a nineteen-year-old who received all of his income from working for Nate and at times Lou. Be it washing the boats, helping Nate with clients, or simply staying out of the way, Mike was the go-to kid around the docks of Old Harbor. That's of course when he was not chasing girls around the island. He was unyielding and relentless in that pursuit.

"Mike, my lad, when you're done here, wash my boat down and button her up, too."

"Okay, Nate," Mike said.

"Then come see me at the bar," Nate said to Mike.

"Hey, sunshine, lobster at my house around eight?"

"Oh man … are those from one of my pots?"

Lou grinned. "Bring your English friend if you like." Mike and Lou started laughing like little girls.

"How the hell?" Nate looked around wildly for any sign of the spies. He walked off shaking his head.

Four o'clock and the crew was assembled at the Beach Bar for their end-of-the-day ritual of bullshitting and margaritas, which started years ago and took on a life of its own, making it a summer-long tradition.

Nate was the last to arrive and took the only remaining seat, with Rebecca to his right. Rounding out the table were Jack and Josh, a tag-team brother act who moved to the island when they were twelve to live with their hardnosed aunt after getting kicked out of every private school Rhode Island had to offer. This group—plus or minus a stray girlfriend or boyfriend at any given time—had been friends for over fifteen years. When a group such as this found common ground a bond was formed and for good or bad it could not, and would not, be broken. Island life bonded this group. With so many people they met coming and going, they found comfort in familiar faces they could trust at the end of the day and especially at the end of the season.

Soon as Nate took his seat, a tray of margaritas arrived, like they were sent from heaven. As the waitress finished passing out the last one to Nate she bent down and kissed him on the cheek. Startled, he looked up and saw Kate smiling back.

"Just wanted to thank you for the job. And the good news is it might be for the whole summer."

"Hey, that's great. I wish you could join us," Nate exclaimed.

"Me too, I make damn good margaritas."

"Everybody, this is Kate."

"We know, Rebecca filled us in," Josh said.

Everyone at the table held up their glasses and at the same time shouted, "TO KATE."

"Hey, wait a minute, I was instrumental in the job thing, too," Rebecca told them with a hint of a whine in her voice.

"Yeah, you should kiss her, too," Jack said, gesturing to both of them.

"Rebecca, I thank you, too. This round is on me for Rebecca."

"To Rebecca!" they all shouted.

"Hey, that's right, I heard the wedding Phil is off to is actually his own," Jack recalled to the stunned table. "He ran off with a twenty-year-old he met last summer."

Nate turned to Rebecca and gave her a quizzical look.

"I can't be on top of everything," she defended.

"His wife can't be too happy," Josh half-joked.

"She hasn't been back on island since last summer," Rebecca said. "I heard she is already living with some male model in Newport."

"So you knew about the male model thing but not the whole Phil running off to get married?" Nate smiled.

"I chose not to divulge that for his wife's sake," she said.

"What are you talking about? You didn't even like her."

"I liked her, you must be confused—she didn't like you."

"I knew she didn't like somebody," Nate finally determined.

"I use my powers for good, not for evil, you would take care to remember that," Rebecca stated.

"Your ego must be continually fed, huh?" Nate laughed.

Rebecca flipped him off.

"Should we toast Phil?" Jack asked.

"Bullshit," Rebecca said. "He ran off with a Russian girl half his age. No way."

"Oh she's really broken up with it, male model and all," Josh said. "I mean where do you even find a male model anyways …? Uhhh …"

"Apparently Newport," Jack said. "Looking for one, bro?"

Josh flipped Jack off.

A muffled scratchy voice came out of Nate's backpack, which broke up the Phil discussion. He reached into it and pulled out a handheld VHF marine radio. In the high-tech world of cell phones and Blackberries on the island, nothing was more durable and free than a marine radio.

"Hey, Nate, did you want to save this bait?" Mike's voice asked squawking out of the marine radio. Nate picked up the radio and adjusted the volume knob on the top.

"Yeah, Mike, go ahead and dump it. I'm done for the night. Over."

The radio squeaked back, *"Okey-dokey. Over and out."*

A couple of hours rolled by with the telling of old stories and some new ones even though it was early into the tourist season. Mike finally showed up and reported to Nate that everything he wanted was done and Lou had been taken care of.

"It's margarita time," Mike stated while rubbing his hands together and taking a seat.

"Yeah, in about three years," Rebecca told him, assuming her mother role.

"Wicked uncool, Rebecca."

Kate showed up and started to clean the table. "Another round?" Everyone, with the exception of Mike, moved their hands to signal no. Mike raised his and Kate took off with the empty glasses.

David walked down the dock, which was visible from their vantage point at the outside tables, and glanced over to the group. When Nate and Rebecca noticed him, he quickly looked away. David and Nate had worn out their friendship long before the tradition of this group. It had transpired soon after the death of Nate's father. A major fight ensued from Nate accusing David of stealing something from someone; he would never give specifics, so their time spent together as friends ended not as enemies but more simply as two people who didn't like each other very much. When David finished high school and joined the Guard, nobody seemed to notice. Then, for some undisclosed reason, he left the Coast Guard Academy after one year and returned to the island with that famous chip on his shoulder. Nate attributed this to David's father, a rich businessman and town manager, the closest thing to a mayor on the island. Nate and a lot of other people thought of David Cavarlo Sr. as a major asshole. Maybe the nut didn't fall far after all. Rebecca thought he was simply unhappy with his lot in life, in particular the part of being an islander. Nate and Rebecca looked back to each other and shrugged. Kate came back with a drink for Mike, but when she placed a glass of milk in front of him the table exploded with laughter.

"Wicked uncool," Mike stated.

The twins were the first to get up and leave. "Have to start ramping up the club; half the help doesn't show up on any given night." At this everyone got up and threw money down at Nate for the tab. Since he was a kid Nate had been pegged as the smart one, so figuring out the bill always fell to him. This time he didn't mind; it gave him more time with Kate. Mike was still lingering around the table. Nate reached into his pocket and pulled out the hundred Mr. Ellis had given him and handed it to Mike. "You're going out with me tomorrow. I have a group of seniors." Mike grabbed the hundred, downed the milk like a shot, hugged Kate, and ran off toward town.

"I hope you tip that well, too."

Nate smiled as he counted up the money. He had just enough, so he reached into his pocket and pulled out a twenty and added it to the pile.

"Thanks again, Nate."

"Don't thank me; it wasn't that big of a deal."

"It was to me."

She had more substance just standing there than all the summer girls he'd met in years. He wanted to see her again but he didn't want to be disappointed again, at least not this early in the season. Even so, he pressed forward. "Maybe when I don't have a charter I could take you fishing."

"I would love that. That is, if you don't mind the company."

With that, Nate started to laugh.

"What's so funny?"

"Nothing, just an inside joke about fishing alone."

"Tell me," she demanded in her adorable accent.

"Maybe on our trip around the island."

They said their casual goodbyes and as Nate headed down the dock he turned and there she was, watching him, so he simply smiled and waved, which she eagerly returned.

As he walked home with his backpack over his shoulder, he started to hum a Jimmy Buffet song in his head. A trip around the island, sort of like a pop quiz, before the three-day boat test, he thought. Lou was right: a revamping of his screening process was in order.

CHAPTER 4: LOU'S WALL

And the walls that won't come down
we can decorate or climb or find some way to get around,
because I'm still on your side.

—Jimmy Buffet

A short walk home and a shower only helped improve Nate's already idyllic mood. The buzz from the margaritas was partly to blame.

From his house to Lou's was about two miles. This time he decided to take his mountain bike, his favorite mode of transportation, even though the Jeep was in fine working order. The island foliage rushed by him as his bike headed down Freemont Street. The hum of the tires on the road changed when they hit Lou's crushed-seashell driveway.

As he walked up to the screen door he could hear Lou's raised voice. He was in the office at the back of the house, and the conversation was one-sided; apparently he was on the phone. Nate couldn't exactly make out what he was talking about, only a word or two. Words like *never* and *go to hell*. Leaning in a little closer to the door he caught himself—this was none of his business. He decided to walk out into the front lawn and wait for him to get off the phone.

He stopped at Lou's stone wall, or rock pile as his neighbors called it. He had been working on this wall in one form or another for as long as Nate could remember. In total it was about forty feet long. It started off as a double-faced dry wall, a front and a back with interlocking rocks to hold its form. Then it deviated to a wet wall, rocks held together with cement. The trick or skill was to put just enough cement to hold the rocks together, but not enough that the cement would become too noticeable. At first he seemed to have the knack, but then there was a ten-foot section where the cement seemed not to work, then another five- to ten-foot section where the cement seemed to be as cement should be, hard and unyielding. Then the last ten feet again started to crumble. He had asked Lou about the wall over the years but Lou would just shrug and say that kids kept knocking it down. The one major thing when it came to understanding Lou was, if he didn't freely give you the information you were seeking, don't ask, because it was none of your business there, sunshine. *At arm's length, that's what he does,* Nate thought, *he keeps me at arm's length. This close … but no more. Shiiiit.*

"Been out here long?"

Nate turned from the wall. "No, I knocked, there was no answer. I thought you might have gone out for a walk."

Lou smiled, knowing the courtesy he had been given. "You know the story of this wall?" Now Nate smiled, letting him know that he'd never talked about the wall before. They both let this sink in for a time. "My family, when they came here, were stone masons. Built everything you see on this island made of brick and stone—well, the ones still around—and probably a few miles of stone walls. Made their own cement, from the products on this island, not easy to do. Too much salt—in the air, in the sand—breaks down the lime in the cement, makes it crumble. My grandfather taught my father and my father tried to teach me. But the sea called me, not cement. But I don't know …" He was lost in thought for a moment. "Years later, when they were all gone, I felt that I let them down. That I didn't let them teach me something." He laughed a little. "That's important for us old-timers, to feel needed, to know that we taught the next generation a skill." Lou looked down at the wall. "Bankers, lawyers, and Wall Street wizards—that's not work. Work is done with your back and with your hands, what we do, what my family did, that's work. Creating a life from your environment, that's a skill. One day I felt the need to learn to do this, for them, but mainly for myself. As you can see I'm not too good at it."

"Lou," Nate said. He looked up from the wall. "You taught me how to fish and dive, to earn a living out there."

"Your dad had a large part in that."

"I know, but every day the memory of him, what he looked like, the way he talked, fades. But you ... you have been in my life longer than him at this point. No disrespect of his memory, but you're my family ... my father. Please tell me you're proud of that, of what I've become."

Standing before Nate was the single toughest man he had ever known ... and he could just make out, if he looked really closely, a glassy look to his eyes.

"We taught you well," Lou said. "Come on, let's cook some bugs."

As soon as the first glimpse into the inner workings of Lou appeared, just as quickly they were gone, leaving Nate to wonder what had caused this conversation.

Lou's house or at least the property had been in his family for over one hundred years. The house had burned down about that many times, too, if you believed Lou; he had built its current structure back during one of the wars and it was still in fine shape, with that old farmhouse, weather-beaten quality to it. The windows were all open, letting the gentle night breeze move the curtains around. Nate sat in a worn-out armchair with busted springs that he had called his years ago.

"I'm going to throw the bugs in. Want a beer?"

"Yes, sir." Nate stared around the familiar room from his usual position. Some of the contents of the drawers were out on top of the end tables and the couch had been dragged from its longtime position, leaving scuff marks on the old painted wood floor. He looked down to the floor on his right and picked up an old photo album. Lou came in and handed him an ice-cold Corona. "Just doing some spring cleaning, sorry for the mess."

"It's July," Nate stated, and Lou gave him a shrug.

He started to look at the pictures and was instantly amazed. They weren't just random pictures of the island; they were the history of the building of the island, starting around the turn of the century. The album contained pictures of the North Light and the Southeast Light in their early stages of construction.

He shouted to Lou in the kitchen, "Is this your family in this photo album?"

"Where'd you find that?" Lou shouted from the kitchen.

"It was sticking out from under my chair."

Lou walked into the room. "I've been looking for that."

"Some spring cleaning there," Nate joked.

Lou took the album from him and stood there turning the pages slowly. "I haven't thought of these people for years." He threw the album onto Nate's lap and pointed to a picture. "That's my three uncles, my grandfather's brothers." The picture was of three young men standing in front of a stone foundation of some sort; there were still rocks piled up at their feet.

"This is incredible stuff; it's the history of the island."

"Not all those pictures are of this island. It's just photos, sunshine, nothing all that incredible. What's the big deal?"

"Big deal? It is a big deal. Why haven't you ever showed me this before?" "What could these pictures do for you, huh? Would it help you in school, would it help you earn a better living or even be a better person? They are just pictures."

"And they have stories," Nate said.

"Well those people are gone, along with whatever story they had."

"That's a sad commentary on history."

"Ah, history, that's something entirely different there, sunshine. History contains the shadows of the past that surround us and the stories it tells are important even today. Something that could make an impact on your life, like the Mayflower Compact or the Declaration of Independence."

Nate just sat there taking in Lou's rant. He'd learned as a child that when Lou started one of his rants, you had to just let him go. But as he got older he started to push back a bit, to challenge him.

"It's all the same, Lou—history, stories, these pictures. It's all history."

"No it's not, sunshine. Okay, look, for example." He pointed to a picture on his wall of a large three-masted ship in a terrible storm with cliffs in the background, the ship looking like she was about to lose the fight with the sea. "Who painted that picture?"

Nate looked up at it and shook his head. "I haven't got a clue."

"A guy named Maurice, use to live in a tent out back of the Bayberry Inn, sold paintings on the side of the road. I had him paint it for ten bucks back in eighty-three. Big deal, right, like I was saying. What could you possible care about Maurice's painting? Won't impact your life, it won't help you make a living, it will just give you a funny story to tell one of your friends as you throw it into a dumpster when I'm gone. But now ... what if I told you it was painted by John Thomas, one of only two survivors of the pirate ship called the Inferno," Lou said looking up at the picture.

"I would say that in the background that's the north side of the island. A pirate ship off Block?" Nate asked looking back at Lou.

"Ahh ... now is it just a story or is it history? Only the shadows that surround it can tell us."

"Was there gold on her?"

"So you're saying this could have a repercussion for us today?" Lou asked.

"Well if it has gold, yeah, that's a positive impact. That would sure help me make a living."

Nate got up and walked over to the picture and looked in the corner for the name. When he saw the name "Maurice" scribbled in the lower right corner, his shoulders slumped.

"What, disappointed? You see, Nate, what we learn about the past is only relevant to those who find an interest in it; to everyone else it's just useless information. The vast majority of history is lost on most people, they have no idea what has taken place to get us where we are today. When you learned of Maurice's dabbling in oil paintings before he ran off to marry his dog, you thought, big deal, ha ha, funny story. But when you learned about a pirate ship off Block, you thought, I need to learn more.

We all need something to pique our interest. These pictures in this album mean nothing, it's not relevant."

"To you, but what about me? The only way to find out is to tell me all you know. Tell me your mistakes, your successes, show me your past, let me decide what piques my interest."

"That was your father's job. He believed in history."

"What do you believe in, then?"

Lou looked down to the floor, then into Nate's eyes. "I believe in nothing ... I believe it's all for nothing."

"Jesus, Lou."

"Besides, I just gave you some history, I told you about Maurice."

Trying to lighten things up a bit, Nate said, "Did he really marry his dog?"

"Yep, black Lab; maybe you saw his tee shirts." Nate laughed. "Come on, let's eat out on the deck. It's a beautiful night."

Nate stared at the painting a little longer. He noticed it was a whale ship. *No gold on a whale ship*, he thought.

CHAPTER 5: ONE-DAY BOAT TEST

On his morning walk to work, another picture-perfect day was on the way, but he wasn't thinking of the perfect day or even singing any Jimmy Buffet songs in his head, he was obsessively going over his dinner with Lou. Something didn't seem right to Nate. And from all of that he was starting to think about his dad, and he hadn't done *that* in years. But Lou—Lou was his dad now, whether the old man liked it or not. He thought to himself. He tried to wrap his mind around their discussion last night, but couldn't seem to make that happen.

A crackled voice came from his backpack, stopping any further thoughts.

"Nate, come in—Nate, are you there? Over."

Nate jumped and spun his backpack off his shoulder and fumbled to get the marine radio.

"NATE. Where the hell are you, man?"

Nate put the radio up to his face. "Calm down, Mike, what's wrong?"

"Get down here right now."

"What's going on?"

"It's your charter. I guess they been here since five, and ... well ..."

"Well what?"

Mike wasn't calling back fast enough for Nate, so his pace through town quickened. Mike finally came on but didn't say anything, all you could hear was a lot of conversation going on in the background.

"What?" Nate repeated.

"It's Darren."

This time he heard that very clear. At the sound of that name, Nate's pace went to an all-out run. As he reached the fountain in the middle of the town square, he could almost make out a group of people walking from his boat to Darren's. He swung the backpack around both arms and radio in hand ran at breakneck speed down to the docks. People walking by stared at him as he flew by.

He made it to the group of seniors just as they were passing the harbor master's office. Darren was leading the pack of six seniors with Mike following like a lost dog in the rear. Nate tried to gain the party's attention, but could not for the life of him remember any of the seniors' names. Mike sensed this, ran up to him, and whispered, "Mr. Shea."

Nate called out his name a couple of times before Mr. Shea turned and waved at him. He called his name again. This time Mr. Shea turned and acknowledged Nate.

"Mr. Shea, is there a problem? You booked a charter with me for six o'clock. It is now a quarter to. I'm a little confused."

"Well, son, we were down here at five—you see, son, we are early birds—and while we were waiting, this nice gentleman told us he was ready and would take us for two hundred dollars less than you," Mr. Shea explained as Nate stared at Darren who stared at his feet. Mr. Shea continued to Darren's boat, and one of the misfits started to help them onboard. Nate grabbed Darren by the arm and led him out of earshot. With the seniors' advanced age, it was only about five feet.

"You can't run a business like this."

"You can't, but I can."

"I wasn't late," Nate argued.

"I never said you were. Still have that whole punctuality thing working, huh, Nate?"

He stood there staring at Darren.

"Look, it's too late now. If I tell them to go back to you, they'll leave." Nate shrugged.

"Well you might not need the work, but I do, and for the fucking record, Nate, they came to me while they were waiting for you," Darren said as he turned and left.

"I wasn't late!" he yelled down the dock. Darren gave him a wave without turning.

"I'm sorry, Nate," Mike said. "I tried to keep them there."

He looked at Mike and put a hand on his shoulder and nodded his head. They both *started to walk back to the Legacy.*

"Do I have to give the hundred back?"

"I'll find a way for you to earn it, don't worry."

"Actually, I am a little worried," Mike answered.

As they walked by the harbor master's office Nate saw David sitting at his desk doing the morning log sheet. He stared at him long enough for him to get the picture. Unaffected by his stare, David returned to his work, indifferent to what had just transpired.

They made it halfway down the dock when Nate noticed Lou's boat was gone.

"When did Lou leave?"

"He was gone before I got here and I was here around four."

Nate looked at Mike. "If you were here at four, how did they leave to Darren's?"

"Well ... ummm ... Sara was on the beach, running ... and I like to run, too ... ummm."

"The only thing I have seen you run is your mouth."

"It's all good, my brother."

"What do your parents say?"

"What? I tell them I'm with you."

"Great, real great there, my brother," Nate said with a sarcastic grin. "How much of that hundred do you have left?"

Nate just shook his head and looked back at Lou's empty slip. For the beginning part of the season, it had been anything but boring.

Mike was sitting on the stern of the *Legacy* with Nate's multi-tool, splicing some of the older boat lines. Nate sat in one of the deck chairs, reading the newspaper and facing Mike, sipping coffee and occasionally staring at the people walking by. Nate bolted up straight, because Kate was coming down the dock, and she was carrying a couple of coffees. He quickly opened the cooler by his feet and threw his coffee in it.

"What the hell you do that for?" Mike said. "You just sent me to get that."

"Say goodbye, Mike."

"What?"

"Good morning, boys," Kate said. "Thought you might need a coffee after the morning you're having."

Nate looked at Kate with that confused look.

"Your friend, Rebecca, I ran into her opening up the visitor's booth on my way back from a run. She told me you were late for a charter and were just sitting around, so I just thought you might need some company." Looking at Mike, she added, "But I don't want to interrupt you two."

"I wasn't late."

"What?" Kate asked.

"Never mind. Mike was just leaving—right?"

Mike got up. As he walked by, he leaned over Nate and said, "I just worked off that hundred, dude."

Even though the thought of being bested by Mike would bother him later, a chance to be with Kate, whom he had thought about a lot since yesterday, outweighed his pride. "Just go, please," Nate said.

"Wow … 'please.' You like her," Mike said and then climbed up to the dock. He smiled as he passed Kate and headed off to God knows where. Wherever it was, it would be a safe bet it would involve girls.

Nate reached up and took the coffees and put them down on the boat. He turned to help Kate on, but it was too late, with ease she went from dock to boat like a pro.

She walked around the boat, looking at everything; she went down below and back up, stood in the middle of the boat with her hands on her hips, and stated, "I'm ready to go fishing."

Nate smiled and walked over to the cockpit and started up the engine.

Five minutes later they passed the breakwater and headed south to one of Nate's secret fishing spots.

Once again the waters surrounding the island were mirror-like, just the ever-widening wake behind the boat to break the calm.

The heat that had engulfed New England was not going to let up today. The fog was lifting and the sun had only itself to contend with in the morning sky.

Within a half hour they had two rods in the water and were trolling around a couple of umbrella rigs about a hundred feet behind the boat.

"So we just drag these umbrella things around till we trick a fish?"

"Well, it's a little more complicated than that," Nate said, laughing.

"In what sense?"

"Well, you first have to know where to fish, and that depends on the tides, the seasons, time of day, and the weather. Then you have to decide what kind of fish you're going for. We have striper, also known as bass. You have black bass, which is not the same as the previous. You have flounder, not to be confused with summer flounder or fluke, don't make that mistake. And let's not forget cod, haddock, bonito, tuna, and my personal fave, tatoug."

Kate started to laugh.

"Wait, I'm not done. Once you decide on the species and where, you now have to decide what bait to use. You have squid, mackerel, sea worms, clams, eels, pogies, hickory shads, or about a million fake lures, each one having some unique quality that sets them apart from the next."

Kate threw her arms up in the sign of surrender. "Okay, mate, I am thoroughly convinced that there is far more than I first thought."

The port reel went off with a clicking sound as a fish started peeling off the line.

"Quick, take the rod," Nate said, laughing. "We tricked one."

Kate ran up to the rod, took it out of the rod holder, put it between her legs, and started cranking the handle. After a couple of minutes, when she was out of breath, she had herself a thirty-pound New England striper.

They trolled around and caught a couple more until the novelty wore off. At this point in the day the sun was up at its highest, the lines were all reeled in, and they were just sitting there with the sun beating down on their shoulders. The boat, just going wherever the tide wanted to take them.

Nate was about to give his total-package speech, probably starting with the whole thing about the glaciers. But he caught himself. *She's not a tourist, definitely not your typical summer girl, if I give her my bullshit she'll see right through me. My God, she stands out like an Audrey Hepburn movie.* Which left him speechless; the best he could do was to look at her and smile. She smiled back and got up and walked down to the little cabin. She returned with fewer clothes than she went down with, just shorts and a white tank top. She also put on a Red Sox baseball hat and had two Coronas in her hand.

"I hope it's not too early," she said as she offered him a beer.

"In the season or the day?"

"Does it matter?"

"Absolutely not," he said as he took a beer.

"How did you end up on Block this summer?"

"Wait just a minute, I'm the girl, I go first."

"I'm sorry, be my guest."

She nodded her head and continued, "How long have you been a fisherman?"

"My whole life, started with my dad by the age of five. Got my first boat when I was fourteen, and have been running a charter business ever since."

"You don't get sick of it, the people, smelling like fish and the such?"

"I love to fish; I don't think I ever even thought of doing anything else. You can't get sick of something you love."

"You actually believe that, or is it just something you tell people?"

He was caught off guard and stared at her for a moment.

"I really believe that," he told her, but for the first time in his life that statement felt real. It very rarely happened that someone or something could for the first time make you feel the truth in words you took as gospel. He stared out at the calm ocean for a moment.

Kate broke his silence. "What's wrong, am I prying?"

"No ... not at all, it's just the first time I've answered that question. I mean the ocean has always been my life, not part, but all of it, everything I am or do is connected to the sea. When the summer finally arrives in New England, it's indescribable. It is the only place I would ever want to be. I just never really thought about it this deeply till I answered your question."

"I have a penchant for getting people to spill their guts. But look on the bright side, your parents must be happy that you do something you love."

"I lost my mother when I was born and my father when I was fifteen."

"Oh my God I'm so sorry, it's a problem I have, prying and the such."

"Don't be sorry."

She smiled back at him. "Well then, since I've violated your privacy with my questions, I might as well ask the big three: no girlfriends or wives or ... boyfriends?"

"Well yeah, I have all of those, but I'm still taking applications," Nate stated.

"So that's it? All you do is fish and the such?"

"All I do is fish. I'm not a very complicated person, I live a simple life. 'And the such,' is that an English thing?"

"No, it's my trademark. What do you think?"

"Has anybody called you odd before?"

"Just my ex-boyfriends."

"Good to know," Nate told her. "Is it my turn yet?"

"By all means," Kate said.

Nate spread his hands out. "Come on, tell me your tale of how you ended up on my island."

"Well, my life is not a simple one. I never went to college, much to the disappointment of my dad. I became a photographer for the *London Times*. Good job, till it bored the shit out of me. Just up and quit, once again to the disappointment of me dad. Started bartending then got bored with that. And about five other jobs that ended up with the same result. Then there was a string of boyfriends that nobody liked."

"I'm starting to see a pattern," Nate said.

"So did my parents. My sis came here last year for her final summer before graduating college. All my sister did was talk about the beauty of this island, so I decided to take it on the lam and maybe when I get back my family will have given me a clean slate."

"Come on, this is Block Island. Nobody comes here to figure themselves out."

"Okay, okay, cute American guys and parties. You happy?" She got up from her seat and walked to the side of the boat and stared down to the water. "Do you realize that most people today spend ninety percent of their time trying to figure out what to do with the remaining ten percent? Don't let my cuteness fool you; I'm just fumbling around, throwing things at the wall to see what will stick. Hoping beyond all that I'm not one of those people."

"You seem happy, though," Nate said.

"Yeah, I am … always have been. I think that since I don't fit into a certain type of mold, some people—namely my parents—think that I'm not a success."

"Success is all relative. I mean if you're happy, I mean truly happy, then all the rest falls into place. I take out so many people who go on about how much they hate their jobs, most of them have lots of money, big fancy titles, everything other people would deem a success. But how does anybody truly define success?"

"Are you happy?" Kate asked.

"I live my life like I'm happy. Just don't look too close."

"Looking too close is where the fun is."

"What's next?" Nate asked.

"Don't really know; I'm hoping for a sign."

"Halfway around the world."

"Well yeah, I figure I'll take the summer to look for a sign. I hope it's in neon, I love neon."

A splash and a thud hit the side of the boat; they both quickly went to the side in time to see a shark thrashing about.

"Oh my God," Kate gasped.

"It's a mako shark, about three and a half feet."

"There are sharks in these waters?"

"There are sharks all over."

"Not like the movie *Jaws,* though, right?"

Nate was taken aback. "Ah … no, not that big."

"But wasn't the movie filmed around here?"

"Ah, yeah, about sixty miles away, on Martha's Vineyard," he said pointing south.

"Sixty miles in a center-console for a stupid movie." He shook the voice out of his head and looked out to sea. "We're about two miles out from the island, a lot of activity out here, lot of bait." He smiled at Kate. "Look at it closely, you can see the markings on its side." She bent down over the side a little bit and peered down at the shark. Nate straightened up and with a hand on each side of Kate's lower back goosed her sides and said, "GRRRR." She screamed and jumped at least two feet in the air. The shark splashed off into the blue water. She turned around and faced him; they were only about three inches from kissing. But when it involved the rules of flirting, sometimes even three inches was still an eternity. *At the end of the summer she's going to break my heart,* he thought.

"Do you want another beer?" She smiled and he nodded. She turned and walked to the front cockpit.

In the distance he spotted a boat on the horizon, a boat with the same outline as his and … Lou's. *But it can't be, can it? We are too close to the island for it to be anybody else. Even the ones from Point Judith I know and that's not any of them.*

"What are you staring at?"

"Nothing, just thought I recognized a boat."

She handed him a beer. He looked back at the horizon. *That's Lou's boat all right.* He reached for his binoculars and tried to take a better look. It was definitely his boat.

"We're going for a little ride, so hold on." He started the engine and throttled it up. That kiss he was so close to would have to wait.

After a few refits and custom engine work, the *Legacy* was still just a lobster boat, so she could only cruise around eighteen knots. She was doing all of that right now, and if sheer will could increase the speed, the boat would have been setting records.

Kate, sensing the urgency in their departure and the sudden speed, stood next to Nate and held on to the rail mounted to the cockpit dash. She glanced over to him quickly, trying to get a vibe off him. Nate looked quickly to her and then back to the horizon.

"The boat up ahead belongs to a family friend; he told me he was going to the mainland today, he was gone by four this morning. I don't know … I'm just a little paranoid." *Sixty miles in a center-console, to see a stupid movie.* Nate shook the memory out of his head again. Damn it, Lou.

They were about twenty yards from the boat and Lou was nowhere to be seen. Nate's heart rate stepped up; there was a knot in his stomach growing tighter by the moment. *Maybe he's diving. Lou is old-school, no dive flag, no dive buddy, after all his first set of diving gear came from Cousteau himself, with 'patent pending' stamped on it … the first in the area, the only one on the island back in the fifties. But this … this isn't right, I can feel it.*

"What can I do?" Kate quietly asked.

"Grab a couple of lines from the stern and put them around the cleats when I pull alongside." Kate headed to the stern and accomplished this task with ease. At a different time this would have impressed the shit out of him.

Nate revved the engine a couple of times. If he was indeed diving, that noise would be the signal that someone was above. Sound traveled for miles underwater, and with an engine revving right above, it was like thunder; if he was down there this would bring him up. He glanced to his depth finder and noticed the depth at sixty feet. It would only take Lou a minute or two to get to the surface.

Nate checked the lines Kate had tied and noticed Lou's anchor was indeed set out. The tide was still at ebb, all seemed calm. Except there was still no sign of Lou.

Nate swung his body over the sides of both boats and stood there in the middle of Lou's, afraid to move or to even investigate further. He just kept looking around in the water for air bubbles rising to the surface, a sure indicator that he was in fact down there. Not only the lack of rising bubbles gave him a bad feeling, but there was no sign of dive gear out on the deck either, and that drove the bad feeling home, right to his heart.

Kate was standing by the side of Nate's boat, unsure of her role. Nate finally and reluctantly took a step closer to the cockpit. And he saw it: blood splattered all over the cockpit dash. His breath skipped. He took the last two steps needed to see into the cabin and the two steps that, like his own boat, led into the small interior. There Lou lay in a heap, his head covered in blood. Nate stood there draped head to toe in denial.

He lunged at the body of his longtime friend and mentor and turned him over to face him. Lou's eyes were open, but there was no life in them. Nate didn't have the mental capacity to handle what was laid out in front of him. He had been calm and cool his whole life, getting through situations that most would run from, but this was something entirely different. Kate entered the small cabin and gasped with her hand over her mouth.

Nate looked up to her.

"Help me," he said weakly.

Kneeling down next to them, she looked to him. "A pulse—did you try to take a pulse?"

Nate shook his head no, a technicality he thought, but the thought of hope snapped him back to reality. He lay Lou back down. His hands were shaking badly, making this hard to do. Kate leaned over and placed her two fingers on Lou's neck. After a couple of tries her hand fell away. "I'm sorry, Nate."

Nate fell back off his knees and stared.

"What do we do, Nate?"

He looked up at her. Her simple beauty lost to the moment, he didn't know how to answer her. He just stared down at Lou. He knew he would not want Nate to cry or show any kind of weakness in the face of adversity. As he sat there in the small cabin, water was steadily flowing in from the holes in the cabin wall down at floor level; these holes were there to allow water to flow to the back of the boat under the deck, to be pumped by the bilge pump overboard.

"We're taking on water."

"What?" Kate asked.

Nate stood up and headed out of the cabin. Covered in blood he ran to an access hatch cut into the deck of the boat. There were two hatches, one forward, one aft. The hatch was an oval shape about two feet in length and flush with the deck. He lifted the handle on the hatch and turned it to unlock. As soon as he lifted the two-inch-thick aluminum hatch, water started to pour out onto the deck.

"Holy shit."

He placed the hatch back down and had to use all his weight to stop the water from coming out. "Oh shit ... shit ... shit," he said, trying to secure the hatch. When he finally accomplished this he ran over to the cockpit. No lights on the dash, batteries shorted out, pumps not working. Kate was by his side now.

"Get back on my boat."

Kate didn't have to be told twice, she moved quickly and jumped over to the *Legacy*. Nate was right on her heels.

"I'm going to drive my boat with Lou's still tied up to us, it should slow the water a bit from entering his boat. I'll try to beach it on a sand bar."

All of this was fine with Kate as she forced a nod. Before he reached for the key to start his boat he remembered Lou's anchor was set. He started to head to the bow of Lou's boat but stopped—it was too late. Lou's boat had reached the swamping stage; water was coming in over the starboard side. Nate jumped back on Lou's boat and in knee-deep water headed to the cabin. Moments later he was backing out of the cabin with his arms under Lou's, dragging him. Kate jumped over and helped him with Lou's body. The boat was now leaning so much that they couldn't possibly get Lou over to the *Legacy*. Nate's boat was now at an angle that in mere moments would start bringing water over into his boat.

"We are not going to make it, get back on my boat."

Kate grabbed hold of the side and pulled uphill to get on Nate's boat.

He didn't want to let go of Lou. The lines were creaking under the strain of the sinking boat.

"NATE!"

The angle of Nate's boat was such that Kate stood at least five feet higher than he did. He looked up to Kate and slowly let go of Lou. *A captain going down with his ship is bullshit*, he thought. Kate grabbed his outstretched hand and he straddled both boats. He reached into his pocket to get the multi-tool knife he always carried, but he came up empty. He never got it back from Mike.

"There is a knife under the side, right behind you, behind you!" he screamed, pointing at the stern of his boat. Kate looked frantically around the boat and finally saw it. She grabbed the fillet knife and started to cut the rear line from the top with both hands in a sawing motion. Lou's boat at this point was three quarters under now and the *Legacy* was going to swamp in a few seconds. Nate was trying to make his way to Kate; she was struggling to cut the tight lines.

"NATE ... help me!"

The water was only an inch from flowing into Nate's boat. Kate managed to cut the rear line and the stern raised up several feet, but the mid-section, still attached, now had water coming over its side. Trying to make it to the midline Kate slipped and reached for it. Water poured into the *Legacy*. Nate was straddling both boats; he was sitting on the line that needed to be cut. He reached out to Kate. "Here!" In a diving motion she managed to get him the knife but she sliced his arm. She screamed. He got the knife and put it under the straining line and with an upward motion cut through it. The *Legacy* snapped back upright with a bang, sending Kate flying across to the other side, where she banged her head against the bulwark. She fell in a heap. Nate got sent in the opposite direction, into the water. Lou's boat quickly and quietly left the surface of the ocean, heading sixty feet to the bottom of Block Island Sound.

Nate treaded water for a few seconds and gained his wits, then started to swim to the stern of the boat, to the small ladder.

He made quick time getting onto the boat and raced to Kate. The two or more feet of water that had entered his boat were now pouring out through the small openings in the back wall. Known as scuppers, they were designed for this very purpose. The bilge pumps were also running, pumping the remaining water overboard.

On his knees he rolled Kate to face him. For a split second he was rolling Lou over again, but the image quickly disappeared when Kate moaned, slowly opening her eyes. She bolted upright. "We okay?"

Nate stood and looked around. If a passing boat had happened on them nothing would have indicated what they'd just gone through.

"Yeah ... holy shit." Nate rubbed his forehead. The cut from his arm was starting to clot. He helped Kate to her feet.

"I cut ..." She looked over his shoulder and pointed. "Nate."

He turned and saw Lou's body float to the surface for a brief moment, about thirty feet from the boat. Without hesitation Nate dove over and swam as fast as he could to that location. He stopped and treaded, looking around from side to side. Kate had climbed up on the side of the boat, one hand holding the top of the cockpit, for a better view. Nate dove down under water and looked around. The stinging of the seawater in his eyes was nothing new for him and he could make out shapes quite easily. He saw a shape about ten feet down and dove deeper to reach it. His hands grasped a denim work-shirt and he pulled and kicked to get them both back to the surface.

He put Lou's body in a rescue swimmer's hold and started to kick back to the drifting boat. For some reason Kate was still pointing at him. The look of fear on her face also had him a little puzzled, and when he reached up with his arm waving, to show that he was all right, he saw the blood pour from his arm again. In that moment, without turning around, he knew—the mako was back.

Most sharks do not just attack when they sense blood or prey in distress. Most, like people, will have a look around first. See if it's something they want, bump it a couple of times, and take a few sniffs, like checking a cantaloupe. The problem Nate was facing was that in all this confusion, all of these things could already have been checked off the mako's list.

At three and a half feet, it wouldn't sever a limb, but a bite would surely allow one to bleed out in a matter of minutes. But there was no way in hell he was going to let Lou go again, shark or no shark.

The fin of the shark passed by them again about a foot to his right. He started to kick faster and then suddenly stopped. *Can't make a lot of movement, no signs of distress, let it think I'm just a floating log, or something … a bleeding something?* He started to kick harder to the boat again.

The tide had finally turned and was going out and was taking the boat with it and it was now forty feet away. That voice in his head was telling him that he was not going to make it to the boat before the shark had a taste. Nate looked out to the boat; Kate had a cover to the cooler in her hands and in the other the striper they had caught earlier, and she was slamming the cooler cover on the water, over and over. The shark was there by the boat now, one pass by the starboard and Kate followed it around to the port, smacking as she went. Then with all her strength she hurled the fish fifteen feet in the opposite direction of Nate, and with a splash the striper and shark were gone. He swam hard now and made it to the boat in little time. He climbed up and with Kate's help managed to get Lou's body in the boat.

Nate was sitting on the deck floor staring up; Kate flopped with sheer exhaustion next to him. She looked over to him. No words were spoken, just cold, frightened silence.

"We need to call somebody," Kate stated, still looking at anything but the body. "Nate."

He turned his head toward her.

"You need to call someone."

He nodded in agreement and slowly got up and walked to the cockpit. Kate followed.

"You don't have a cell phone, do you?" he asked her. She shook her head. "Me either." He reached for the marine radio and put the mike up to his face and hesitated. He tried again to say something into the mike and lowered it again. Kate rubbed his back in support. Nate looked back at the body of his friend and, related or not, the last of his family. He put the mike up again.

"United States Coast Guard, United States Coast Guard, Block Island, this is the *Legacy* … over."

Since a large population of the island had something to do with the sea, a large percentage of businesses had marine radios tuned to channel sixteen, which was the main channel. Bait shops, towboat companies, harbor masters, fishermen, and even the visitor's booth monitored the chatter. Right now every marine radio on the island was hearing this. And Nate knew it. *Tread carefully, sunshine,* Lou's voice rang in his head.

"This is the United States Coast Guard, *Legacy*, please turn to channel one-two, one-two … over."

"One-two," Nate answered. He reached up and turned to channel twelve. In doing so he hoped he had just lost half the people monitoring. Since he didn't declare an emergency or a mayday, most listeners would probably not follow to channel twelve. "Yes, Coast Guard, is Petty Officer Gilmore on duty?"

There was a pause; this was not proper protocol, but he had to try.

"This is Gilmore, *Legacy*," a very professional woman's voice answered.

Now what, Nate? The only help he hoped she could offer was to lessen the amount of trouble his next statement would bring.

"We have recovered a body and are en route to your station … over."

Another long pause. He shook his head and looked at Kate.

"What is your location, *Legacy*? Over." It was a new voice—a male voice.

Nate was still looking at Kate. "You're not supposed to recover a body," he told her. "You have to call the Coast Guard. Everything happened so fast back there, I just didn't want to lose him or leave him floating there waiting for the Coast Guard to pick him up. He belongs on my boat. I'll take him home." Kate just stared at Nate. This was his call and he knew it. That it was not his friend, Betsy, on the radio for the second transmission meant she had been outranked at the station this week—not good.

"*Legacy*, come in. What is your exact location? Over."

Nate decided to ignore the male voice and speak to Betsy, who he was sure was listening. "Betsy, I'm heading your way with …" He took a deep breath. "I have recovered the body of Lou Gauthier." He put the mike down, reached up and shut off the radio, and continued to drive to the other side of the island, to Great Salt Pond. *Sixty miles in a center-console for a stupid movie …*

CHAPTER 6: GOING TO THE MOVIES

"We're going to need a bigger boat."
—Chief Brody, from the movie *Jaws*

"Come on, Darren, we have to get an early start, you know that, man," Nate whined.

"Get off my back, man. If my dad finds out I skipped work, I'm dead—dead, do you hear me?"

"We all hear you, meatball, the whole island hears you."

Darren and Nate turned around at the sound of David's voice coming over the hill in the cemetery.

"Oh like your dad wouldn't flip a nut if he found out you skipped out on your lawn-mowing duties," Darren stated.

"Well we all can't be like Nate here and have a dad who is never around, and when he is really doesn't care what he does," David said, looking at no one in particular. Nate just shrugged and they continued to walk through the cemetery.

"You're late, David," Nate finally told him.

"Lighten up. But check it out: I won't be anymore." David raised his arm to show a new dive watch with a big chrome bezel and black rubber band—the type of watch nobody their age could afford or even say how much it would cost out loud.

"Jesus, where did you get that?" Darren asked.

"I saved up for it."

Nate looked at it again and shook his head. "No way, not that watch."

"What do you know about it, West?"

Nate just ignored him. Something was not right about him having that watch, but he wasn't in the mood for one of David's arguments today, because today was a watershed moment, an epic day in the life of these three boys, and it all had to do with a movie.

They made their way through the cemetery to the little inlet down off Neck Road that led out to Great Salt Pond. That's where Nate kept his twenty-one-foot center-console boat. The boat was a gift from his dad. The deal was that he had to earn enough money to pay for fuel and insurance, and that first year with the boat, he broke even.

As they crossed the street they kept their heads down, trying but not succeeding to look inconspicuous. But once they made it to Mr. Dushamps's yard, which ran along the inlet, they were home free; his boat was tied up to his dock. The good thing about Mr. Dushamps was that he was deaf and blind in one eye—or was it blind and deaf in one ear? The three boys could never seem to remember.

"What time does the movie start?" Darren asked.

"Noon," Nate said as he kicked over the Yamaha outboard motor. "It's sixty miles north-northeast, which if the weather conditions hold, should put us there around"—looking at his watch—"eleven."

"Aren't we the professional?"

"Bite it, David."

As the boat pulled out of the inlet into Great Salt Pond, Nate weaved around the larger boats in the mooring field and kept an eye out for anyone recognizing them. Their laughter could be heard at times over the rumbling of the outboard, but three friends heading out with the rising sun on a beautiful summer morning was nothing out of the ordinary on an island like this.

Their sixty-mile ride to Martha's Vineyard was perfect. Since the first voyages upon the seas there had always been feeling of adventure and accomplishment when you could successfully traverse the open ocean. The sight of tuna jumping out of crystal clear waters, and for a short time during their voyage, the inability to see land left a lump of pure excitement in their throats.

They made it to Menemsha Harbor on Martha's Vineyard by eleven fifteen. All their hair was windblown and their faces red from the combination of salt and sun. The harbor itself sat to the left after you passed the breakwater walls on either side of the opening. If you were to stay straight, you would continue down an ever-narrowing and increasingly shallow channel that led to Menemsha Pond. Before heading left to the docks, they headed down that channel.

"Where you goin', Nate?" Darren asked.

"Something my dad talked about. Look."

There to the right, sitting high and dry on the beach, was a beat-up boat, the color long gone, all that was left an empty hull.

"It's the boat from the film," Nate said. "My dad said that it was left there when the film was over." The three boys stared at the boat as if it were magical.

They doubled back to the harbor and Nate tied his boat up to a spot down at the end of the dock where the charter fishing guys holed up. His dad was friends with all these guys and just the mention of his father's name gave him instant approval to tie up there. The three teenage boys started their trek to the north side, to Oaks Bluff, where the movie theater was located on Circuit Avenue. It only took about ten minutes of walking for a pickup truck to pull up and offer a ride. They made it to the theater with twenty minutes to spare.

On the theater marquee was why they had traveled all that way. The ten-year anniversary of the motion picture *Jaws*. When it first came out they were only five years old, and every parent on Block held a secret meeting and agreed not to let the kids see a movie where a killer shark kills kids on a New England island. It would make for a very long summer. When the video age hit the island, somebody checked out the movie and never brought it back; most believed it to be the swimming instructor ensuring that his job would still be there next summer. So ten years after its release, a chance to see it for the first time—and on the big screen, on the island it was made on—was an opportunity that three enterprising teenagers were not going to let slip by. They bought their tickets and ran into the darkened theater.

When the movie ended and the lights came up they sat mesmerized at what they had just seen. They left the theater and started their walk back to Menemsha, going over every detail about the movie.

"So that's Quint's boat, the Orca, we saw?" Darren asked.

"Yeah," Nate said. "I can't wait to ask my dad. He did some dive work for the movie."

"Do you think sharks get that big?" David asked.

"I don't know," Darren said, "but I'll tell you this much: I don't think I'm going swimming or diving for a while."

The three boys imagined they were characters from the movie. David took the role of chief, Nate was Hooper, and Darren got stuck with the kid who got eaten on the raft at the beach.

It took a little longer to get a ride but they made it to Menemsha Harbor just before three.

Darren and David were too busy talking and laughing to notice. But Nate did the second he jumped out of the truck and saw the white caps out in Vineyard Sound. The wind was screaming. When the other two finally noticed, all three stared up at the flag on top of the little convenience store and then the two turned and looked to Nate.

"Twenty, maybe twenty-five knots," Nate stated as he started to bite the inside of his cheek. Darren turned to David and said, "Hooper drives the boat, Chief." A little nervous laughter was all Darren got from this quote from *Jaws*.

After fueling up they were heading home.

"How long, Nate?" David was the first to ask. Salt spray was already soaking them.

"It took about two and a half to get here, under perfect conditions. Around twenty-four knots. Now? We're doing eighteen knots in a head-on sea, which will be on our starboard side once we get out past Nomans

Island, which will slow us down a little more. I don't know but my guess is three and a half to four hours."

"Shit, if I'm not home by five, five-thirty, I'm in deep shitola."

"Yeah … that's an understatement," David said. Nate just stared ahead and continued to drive. The fact of the matter was that it bothered Nate sometimes that he didn't have a traditional family. Or at least a traditional father. Whenever he got home he got home. Besides, his father wasn't even on the island, he was off working as a commercial diver for a company out of Long Island; Lou was keeping somewhat of an eye on him. As much trouble as his two friends were going to get in, he in a strange way envied them.

The trip took more like four hours. With the sun setting so late in the summer months it was still daylight, but it was fading fast as the harbor came into sight. The wind had diminished and Nate had the throttle buried all the way up. Thinking it made sense to call Lou just to tell him he was still out on the water, he reached for the marine radio. "Oh shit," he said.

"What—what is it?" Darren half screamed, looking wildly from side to side.

Nate, half laughing, said, "Easy, fella."

Darren rubbed his hands through his dampened hair. "Yeah … man … just freaking out, you know, with the movie and shit … I mean it's getting late, and you know, dark."

"You still don't like going out on the ocean in the dark, huh?" David asked.

"No, I don't—Chief."

"That's just silly," David stated.

"Yeah, well, you weren't trapped out at sea overnight."

"Your rowboat hit a sand bar. You were in front of the National Hotel … in the freakin' harbor. The water was three feet deep—you could have walked to the beach."

"I was just a boy."

"Dude, it was two years ago."

"No, it wasn't."

"Hey, ladies," Nate said, "all I was trying to say was that in all the commotion I never turned on the marine radio." He reached to switch it on. Immediately they heard the broadcast.

"This is the United States Coast Guard hailing the boat ..." They didn't catch the name the first time.

"Shhh—shut up for a moment," Nate said. The broadcast started again. "Please don't let it be mine ..."

"Fish Head, Fish Head, Fish Head, come in please. Over."

"Shit." Nate went to answer it.

"Don't answer it!" Darren said as he slapped Nate's hand away.

"Ow—why did you do that?"

"Don't answer it."

"I have to. They're calling us."

"No, they're calling you. You're missing, not me."

"Darren," David interjected.

"Don't Darren me. Listen, it's the old man freaking out that Nate isn't home and his boat's gone. We can still sneak into the lagoon and be on our way, nobody has to be the wiser."

Nate shook his head and reached for the mike again. This time David slapped his hand.

"Hey, man," Nate said, shaking away the sting in his hand.

"Listen, meatball has a point."

"I'm answering it." Nate reached for it again and paused, trying to anticipate the slap. This time the one from Darren missed. And Nate reached the mike.

"NOOOOO—wait," David yelled. "Look, go ahead and answer, but tell them you're having radio trouble and you were out fishing, and drop us off on the beach. We'll hike it back to town."

Nate gave the boys a stare that had "you're shitting me" written all over it.

"United States Coast Guard, this is the Fish Head."

"Fish Head, switch to one-two, that's one-two, over."

"This is Fish Head, switching to one-two."

Here they go. Nate chewed the inside of his mouth again.

"Fish Head, is everything all right?"

"Yes, we had a little radio problem while we were fishing, but we fixed it." He paused. "Is there a problem? Over."

Darren and David started moaning. "Man ... you said 'we.'"

"I'm not dropping you off on the beach."

"That's just great, man—just great," Darren whined.

"Do you have Mr. Cavarlo and Mr. Saucier with you, over?"

"NO, NO, NO," the two boys screamed.

"Yes, I do, over."

"Man," Darren and David moaned. Nate shook his head at the two of them.

"What is your location, over?" The tone from the Coast Guard had changed; all three noticed it right away.

"About ten minutes from Great Salt Pond."

"You need to proceed directly to the Coast Guard Station, do I make myself clear? Over."

"Umm, yes, sir."

"Coast Guard out."

Nate felt his "yes sir" might have been a little too cocky for their liking but he didn't like being told what to do—*so too bad*, he thought.

As they rounded the breakwater they could just make out the group of people standing on the Coast Guard dock. Nate was getting the feeling that this was not going to be good. And that feeling started with David saying that it was just Lou over there reacting and looking for him. That's not it, he thought.

The Coast Guard station, located at New Harbor, was commissioned in 1936 and was consolidated from the old LSS, Life Saving Stations, which used to dot the island. It was made up of two buildings, a Roosevelt-style house and a building at the top of a ramp that led to the channel of the pond. It was Nate's estimation that there had to be thirty people standing on the dock staring at them pulling in. The three boys had the lines tied before any of the crowd could help them. As they walked down the dock, people were just standing there looking at them—mainly police, firemen, and harbormasters. David's father, being the town mayor—although he acted more like the governor of Rhode Island—always had to make a grand entrance, and this time was no exception as he started pushing people aside.

"Where are they? Let me through."

When he got through the crowd, Mr. Cavarlo stared at the boys, David and Darren stared down at their feet, but Nate had his eyes fixed on Mr. Cavarlo.

"Where the hell have you been? Half the island has been out looking for you three. Do you have any idea the trouble you caused today?"

Why is he directing this at me? It wasn't like I forced his son to go with me; actually it was his idea. Nate may have been thinking this but he continued to stare and said nothing. He turned to look at David for his reply but David's feet seemed to still have his full attention.

"We went to the Vineyard to see a movie," Nate finally said.

"You're kidding me, right? Sixty miles in a center-console for a stupid movie? Is that what you're telling me?"

"It was *Jaws*." After Nate said this he actually expected a little laughter from the crowd, which was slowly dispersing. When it didn't come he started to look around at the faces of the people. They all looked very uncomfortable. He saw Rebecca and her mom and Jack and Josh with their aunt and most of the charter guys as well.

He slowly and deliberately turned back to David's father. "Am I missing something?"

"Damn right you're missing something."

"Hold it right there, Mr. Cavarlo, if you don't mind." Chief Petty Officer Charlie Lester stepped up to Nate and put his arm around the boy and started to walk him down the dock away from the crowd.

Chief Petty Officer Lester was probably only ten years older than Nate, but he carried himself as someone much older. Getting him away from Mr. Cavarlo was something Nate regarded as an act of kindness, one that he would never forget. Since that day twenty years ago, on hundreds of occasions, Nate had tried to remember exactly the words spoken by Lester about the death of Nate's father. The words he spoke were of no consequence, just the point of them: his father was dead.

...

As Nate pulled up to the dock with Lou's body, he expected for a minute to see Lester standing there, but the personnel changed with great frequency at the station and Lester had left a decade ago. The faces in the group waiting for them on the Coast Guard dock had changed since that day twenty years ago, but then again, some had not. There was Rebecca and Jack and Josh, twenty years older but with the same looks on their faces. Apparently most of the island did switch their marine radios to channel twelve.

The four officers of the Coast Guard station were on the end of the dock along with the ever-present Cavarlo. Nate pulled up to the dock and tied up the *Legacy*. Up on the hill by the station was an ambulance. Doctor Spencer was making his way down to them. Two of the Coast Guard officers climbed onto the boat and lifted the blanket covering Lou. Kate turned and leaned on Nate. The doctor climbed down and examined the body and gestured for the paramedics to bring the stretcher. Everyone on the boat climbed off.

Nate's friend Betsy Gilmore walked up to Nate and rubbed his arm. "We need to talk to you," she said, and gesturing to Kate, "You, too." Nate didn't move until the body had been placed in a body bag, put on the stretcher, and rolled by. As the body passed he reached over and hugged Kate. At first she was surprised at the sudden show of emotion, but then it all became clear.

Nate whispered in her ear: "They're going to separate us in there. You need to tell them that while we were fishing on the south side, the side with the lighthouse, we saw something in the water. I thought it might be a sunfish or a shark so we went to take a closer look and that's how we found Lou, floating with no sign of his boat. Can you do that for me?"

Kate held Nate harder. "Absolutely."

They separated and continued to the station.

Rebecca ran up to Nate. "Oh my God, what happened, Nate?" she said, tears running down her face.

He leaned to her and hugged her. "Listen—and don't ask why right now—have Mike take my boat back to Old Harbor and get my dive gear out of my shed, and then you come back and pick us up in your car."

She looked at Nate confused; his eyes stared with all their power telling her not to question this now. She nodded her head in agreement.

"When the Coast Guard is through with you I would like to see you," Cavarlo boomed, walking out from behind Jack and Josh.

"Where's your son? He's the Harbor Master, has jurisdiction out there, not you," Nate stated.

"Don't you lecture me on jurisdiction on this island."

Nate stopped and turned to him. "Let me make myself perfectly clear, I have nothing to say to you." Nate entered the station.

An hour later Kate and Nate walked out into the summer air. The stars were out and the crickets almost deafening. Rebecca was sitting on the hood of her car; she slid off and walked over to them.

"What the hell is going on?"

Nate gestured. "In the car."

On the way back to town, while Rebecca drove speechless, they explained everything that had happened out on the boats.

"What did you tell the Coast Guard?"

Kate spoke first and recounted the story that Nate had told her to say. Rebecca looked over to Nate. "Jesus, Nate, you can't up and lie to the Coast Guard."

"Why not?"

"For one thing, they need to do an investigation."

"Look, Beck, if we didn't find him out there he would be missing right now. Maybe his body would have turned up later, but if it did, all the evidence would have been washed away and we probably wouldn't even have found his boat. So what can this possibly hurt? I mean, if they start an investigation, the entire island would know the next day, right?"

Rebecca nodded reluctantly. "This island is too small, too many people will get involved, mayor Cavarlo will muck it up. Things will get out of hand."

"So who's going to get to the bottom of this?" Rebecca asked.

Nate fell silent.

"You?" Rebecca continued, "Oh great, you. Are you shittin' me? Where are you going to start, tell me that?"

"I'm going to start on Lou's boat."

"Look, I'll support you, I'll even lie for you. But this is serious shit."

"Beck, look, I need you to go with it for now. If things get too complicated I'll bring all of this to the authorities. But I'll tell you this much, without a doubt, tomorrow the powers that be will state that Lou slipped on his boat and hit his head and fell overboard. They'll say that his boat drifted out to sea or got swamped by a wave and sank."

"Because that's what you led them to believe," Rebecca said.

"How can you be so sure that's what they are going to say?" Kate asked from the backseat.

As Nate stared out the side window, he replied, "Because that's what they want it to be, because it would be the best for the island."

"Answer me this," Rebecca said. "Who would want to murder Lou? Can you think of anybody that even disliked him a little bit?"

"Darren?"

"Nate, don't tell me you think Darren is capable of something like this."

"No, I don't."

"So what about Lou's boat?" Kate asked.

"I'm going to dive on it and find out why it sank. If it looks like sabotage, we'll know."

"And if not?" Kate asked.

"Then I'll bury all of this along with Lou."

"When are you going to do this?" Kate wondered.

"Right now."

"You're not going to dive at night," Kate stated.

"If I wait till morning there will be a bucket-load of people searching for Lou's boat, with salvage rights to a drifting boat being what they are. I need the darkness."

"Isn't diving at night dangerous?" Kate asked.

"The only thing that doesn't scare me about any of this is Nate diving at night. You're looking at a person who was trained to dive by two of the best in the country. By the age of ten," Rebecca explained to Kate.

Kate said, "Well, I'm going then."

Nate just kept staring out the passenger window.

CHAPTER 7: THE WRECK PART II

In your belly you can hold the treasures few have ever seen.
—Jimmy Buffet

The rain and wind were making it hard to stand on the bluff, but then again it was his job—not actually a job, but a way of life, a means to an end. Others started to gather around him now. The question was when, and the answer was different every time. The ship had to be in the right tack to the reef, the visibility had to be poor, and the tides had to be in their favor. All of this seemed to be working for them this night of nights. But this ship and her crew were making a remarkable attempt at escaping their demise.

"Light it now."

"Shut up, you wretched creature, before I throw you off the bluff."

He stared out to the ship and thought, Who is she? Where has she been? And most importantly, What does she have in her belly? "A little more ... a little more ... Forgive me, Father, for what I am about to do." He made the sign of the cross. "Light the fire," he said as the others laughed and rubbed their hands. This never sat well with him, but survival, survival on this island sometimes took drastic measures.

Christopher was holding the wheel as hard as possible, his hands numb. *Where is the captain and Jonathan? I can't keep this up much longer.* The crew was running around and up and down the rigging like ants.

Someone was yelling at him, yelling over and over, and he finally focused in on the yelling. "The light, I see the light," someone was saying, "we are around the reef!" And Christopher finally understood, he saw the light now, too. "Thank you, God," he said, "thank you, dear God." He let the wheel spin in his hands, the *Gosnold* turned twenty degrees to the south, and now the stress pressure was gone from the wheel and the mast eased its fight with the wind as the crew cheered.

"Why are we turning?" the captain asked. "What was that?"—hearing the drowning echoes of the crew's cheer. "Oh my God," he cried.

The captain and Jonathan stumbled in their mad dash topside. They got up and crashed up the stairs and pushed open the door. The crew was just standing there, crying, "WE DID IT, CAPTAIN, the light-keepers signaled us around the reef."

The captain had a look of horror on his face as he saw the fire on the bluffs.

He turned to Christopher, but Jonathan was already there, trying to turn the ship back to the north. He was screaming to Christopher for help.

"Captain, what's wrong?" Christopher asked, but the captain pushed him aside.

"IT'S A FALSE SIGNAL," he shouted. "THEY'RE TRYING TO WRECK US. BRING DOWN THE FORWARD SHEETS, FOR GOD'S SAKE—WE ARE HEADING STRAIGHT FOR THE REEF, YOU FOOLS."

"I don't understand—what have I done?"

"You possibly just killed all of us."

All the color drained from Christopher's face.

This was an unjust thing to say to him; most of the boys on board hadn't been around enough to know about people who make their living wrecking ships and waiting for the cargo and the bodies to wash up on the beach so they could take what the sea didn't claim.

The captain, still yelling, ran up to the wheel and helped Jonathan turn the ship. The sound of the hull scraping the reef was undeniable. The *Gosnold* listed to starboard and then straightened up again.

"We hit it," Jonathan said, and the captain nodded in agreement.

He turned to a crew member standing next to him. "Give me a sounding."

The captain stared at Jonathan, wondering if he could read his mind.

Jonathan turned to Christopher, who was kneeling down praying. "Go down below and check the hull, quick."

He got up off his knees and ran down the deck, out of sight. He opened the door and ran down the stairs. At this point he was at the doorway to the bottom decks, which included the storage decks and crew quarters. At this level no more than a foot of wood separated them from the ocean.

He got to the last step and his foot found cold ocean water. He turned and ran back, praying loudly as he went, and presented himself in front of the captain again. "A foot and rising … I'm so sorr—"

The captain raised his hand and stopped him. He turned to the crew member who had just run up to him.

"Three fathoms, Captain."

The captain sent him away.

"We need deeper," Jonathan said.

"We could just run her aground, keep them at bay with our guns."

"We traded a dozen or so muskets for beef in Tortola; we have one left."

The one thing in their favor was that they did manage to make it around the reef. The crew member ran back to the captain. "Six fathoms, sir."

The captain nodded and the crew member ran off again.

Now that they were around the southernmost point of the island and heading out to sea, the thought of her sinking was starting to take hold like a wet blanket.

"Take the wheel, Christopher, hold course," the captain commanded with a heavy tone. Crying, Christopher took the wheel.

The captain and Jonathan headed down below as the crew just stared at them. The rain relentlessly hammered down.

For these two oceangoing veterans, the feel of the *Gosnold* listing to port slightly was obvious well before it was to the others.

"There is no way out of this," the captain said, and his longtime friend nodded. "Set her ablaze."

"Damn it, five years and it comes to this."

"It's not over yet, there is a chance to recover it," the captain said.

"But how in the name of God do we locate her?"

The captain just smiled at his friend. "I want everyone off in the long boats before we set her."

CHAPTER 8: DIVER DOWN

Rebecca dropped Nate off at his house and agreed to meet at his boat around midnight. Nate waved to the two girls as they pulled away.

Kate and Rebecca drove in silence for a short time.

"How are you doing?" Rebecca finally asked. "Are you okay?"

"Well, I'm okay, but I'm thinking none of this has really sunk in yet."

"Did he give you any idea why he's doing this?" Rebecca asked.

Kate shook her head. "When he hugged me on the dock, he whispered in my ear what he wanted me to say. That was the first time I thought he was up to something. He seemed to have it all worked out by the time it took us to get back to the harbor."

"It was the way he was raised—on his own. He's always been like that. But to do this, he has to have a good reason. Nate's one major flaw is that he thinks he's smarter than everybody else. The problem with that is … well, he *is* smarter than everybody else. And he's absolutely right about how the investigation would go and the reaction on the island. But this is Lou, he watched over him after his father died; I just don't know if he is thinking rationally right now."

"So him going it alone outside of the authorities and the such is cool with you?"

"I love Nate, I would never do anything against him … I'll give him some time to put it all together. I'm hoping after the dive he'll come to his senses."

"So you and him …?" Kate weakly smiled at Rebecca.

"Friends since the age of five. Think of us as a brother-and-sister team. Nate, though, has never really let anybody else close. Which I believe to be a byproduct of being raised by men like Lou and Nate's father," Rebecca said.

"He told me that his mother and father died."

"Jesus, then you already got more insight with him than most people on this island. Listen, Kate, I know you have just met him, but Nate is a special person. He seems to have the ability to make people feel comfortable around him. He understands people better than anybody I have ever met. But he never lets people get too close, even me."

"Are you warning me not to get too close?"

"I'm just telling you a little about him. I just want him to be happy."

"So a girl from England who is on the island for two months doesn't have a chance?"

"I guess it depends on the two months."

"Well, so far it's been quite the ride," Kate said.

Rebecca pulled into Kate's driveway.

"I'm just a visitor here," Kate said. "I've overstepped my bounds."

"Look, I truly believe he wants you here, but I don't blame you for keeping your distance in all of this. Don't do anything you don't want to."

Kate opened the car door. "Thanks, Rebecca. I'll meet you guys at the boat around midnight?"

"You sure you want to go?"

"I've just been through hell; I'd like to see what's on the other side."

Rebecca smiled as Kate got out. She started to close the door but stopped and leaned in. "How did you know where I live?"

Rebecca just shrugged and smiled.

She pulled out into the dark street and as she drove away she started to cry, not only for Lou but for her lifelong friend, Nate. Life could change in a second, and she had seen this too often on the island. And with sudden change, wrecked souls were left in its wake. As she wiped the tears from her eyes she hoped that her best friend was not making a mistake that could bring him more tragedy.

At midnight the crew was assembled, Nate and Kate along with Rebecca and Mike. Jack and Josh were there only for support. The Sign Post was running shorthanded as usual and they had to get back. All the better, Nate thought. Jack and Josh would have dove with him, and he was not sure he wanted that; he was starting to feel that he needed to do the dive alone.

As they pulled out from the slip and headed out into the dark ocean that surrounded the island, Jack and Josh stared at each other and walked down the dock in silence.

The *Legacy* cruised through the darkness, the four occupants' faces illuminated by the glow of the GPS and the radar and sonar screens. The day was still running through Nate's head, playing over and over again, on a continuous loop. He stole a glimpse of Kate as she stared out the cockpit windshield. Rebecca and Mike walked out of the cockpit and started arranging Nate's dive gear like they had done hundreds of times over the years.

He hadn't marked the exact position on his GPS. To mark the position he would have had to punch the MOB—or "man overboard"—button and the corresponding latitude and longitude numbers would have been saved. But in this case all he had were the track lines or bread crumbs that were indicated by the GPS dotting the screen, retracing his past location. Luckily, he had never cleared the track lines.

The exact location would have to be found from years of training and searching for lost things underwater. As they got close, Nate and Mike started watching the sonar screen for the outline that would signify a boat. It took all of ten minutes of trolling around the last position of the GPS's track lines to come across it.

"I'll pull up past the boat heading into the current," Nate said to Mike. "Set the anchor and start letting out line; I'll tell you when."

"You got it, boss."

After about a hundred and fifty feet of anchor line they sat right on top of Lou's boat.

"Mike, take a look at this," Nate said, pointing to the sonar screen. "There is something else down there, maybe a reef?"

Mike was by his side leaning into the screen. "Lots of fish down there, too. Maybe this is one of his secret spots."

Nate hit the MOB button, leaving a blue dot on the screen exactly where they were sitting.

Twenty minutes later Nate was suited up and double-checking his gear. "Don't look at me like that, you two."

Rebecca and Kate looked at each other and back at Nate. "What?" Rebecca asked.

"First of all, Kate, I'll be fine, I have over two hundred hours of night bottom time logged, don't worry."

"Two hundred hours, wow. Now, if I knew what the frig that meant … I probably still wouldn't be impressed," Kate said.

Rebecca looked at Nate with a raised eyebrow.

"If I don't find something, I'll tell the Coast Guard where the boat is, okay?"

"I'm worried if you do find something," Rebecca flatly stated.

They all fell silent for a minute.

He sat on the side of his boat, the very spot that a mere twelve hours earlier had almost sunk along with Lou's. He flipped on his dive light and unceremoniously flopped over backward into the ink-black water.

He followed the anchor line down to the sea bottom. He made sure it was set in the sand and had a look from side to side. Sixty feet and dark.

Nate had entered a world that was not his to command, all five senses greatly diminished if not entirely lost to the underwater environment. His heart pumped faster, echoing in his ears, accompanied by the sound of air bubbles escaping his regulator as he breathed, filling his head with unrelenting noise. All of this had always gotten Nate excited; the feeling of being underwater was addictive. There had never been a time when it ceased to amaze him—even tonight he felt some form of excitement being underwater.

His vision was guided only by his dive light. Which even at a million-candle power only gave you a concentrated area to look at. The light illuminated a column straight out to about fifteen feet. You always seemed to notice more fish and sea life at night because of the dive light making your attention to be concentrated to one particular spot.

He looked at his compass and headed toward Lou's boat. Slowly the light began to reveal the hull and cabin. Fish were already seeking shelter inside of it. It sat there upright and leaning to the right due to the long keel on the bottom. He floated there for a moment and felt goose bumps rise all over his body. *Why am I doing this? Because Lou would do the exact same thing, for me … this I know. So shut up and get to work, sunshine.*

He entered the little cabin and looked around. There were still a few air pockets under the roof and anything that could float was pinned under the roof of the cabin screaming to get to the surface. He swam to the deck of the boat and opened one of the hatches built into the floor, the one he had to shut because of the rush of water. No such problem now. He discarded the hatch and managed to fit his arm with the light and his head under the deck floor. He found one of the through-hull seacocks, a fitting with a handle that was connected to a hose. When the handle was pulled open, water was allowed to be pumped into or out of a bait well or a holding tank. If the line were to be cut and the handle opened, then it would just be a hole in the bottom of your boat. And that would not aid in the whole flotation idea, which boaters seemed to like. The hose that fed the bait well on Lou's boat had been cut in half. Nate pulled his body out of the hatch, and as fast as he could manage under water, he wrested the other hatch off and threw it to the side. The second hose was cut as well.

It doesn't make any sense. Who wants you dead?

Nate pulled out of the second hatch and something hit him in the chest. He let out an underwater grunt and dropped his light, but being buoyant and tied to his wrist, the light bounced everywhere, the beam shooting wildly all over and not letting him get a clear look at what was attacking him. He got hit again; he lay flat on the deck of Lou's boat and gained control of the light. He focused the million-candle power above him and was mesmerized. Stripers, hundreds of them, swimming after smaller fish, bunker fish he thought. This was something few if any had ever seen, and he was a witness to this natural beauty in the middle of chaos and death. For a moment he forgot where he was, and why. As the last of the stripers swam by, he tried to follow them for about fifty feet until they were gone.

He shined his light around, looking for stragglers, and what he saw set him in momentary shock. Stretched out before him were the ribs and keel of a wooden ship, a large wooden ship. Ballast stone lay to either side and there were pieces of debris scattered about. This ship had been down here a very long time. Nate swam around surveying the wreck. There were stakes placed around the wreck and measuring tape from stake to stake. Gridding—someone had been investigating and archiving the wreck. The tape and stakes were covered in seaweed and deteriorated; this had been done some years ago. He swam along the outside of the wreck. From the stern to the bow he estimated to be about two hundred feet.

This has to be Lou's handiwork down here; nobody else could have done this.

Why didn't you tell me?

He swam down the center of the ship, like passing through the ribcage of a skeleton, and came to the stern. He could just make out Lou's boat, about thirty feet away. A cross member of the ship's timber, about a foot by a foot and ten feet long, came into his light. Sitting on the end of the timber, which was pointing to Lou's boat like a finger, was something he couldn't wrap his mind around. He floated closer to the object. He shook his head and reached out to touch it. He pulled his rubber-covered hand away as if the object were hot. He once again reached out and this time touched it. He picked it up; it was indeed real, so real in fact that he needed two hands to pick it up. It was all of fifteen pounds.

Lou … what is this all about? What in the name of God is going on?

He started to look around the wreck for more gold but stopped in his fins. There was no more. If this was indeed one of the secret spots, Lou was … had been … very thorough and would have seen to any secrets the wreck had been willing to give up.

This gold bar had been just sitting here, wanting, waiting to be found. Had it been put here deliberately ... by Lou? With the weight of these questions floating around in his head he shifted the weight of the bar to his right arm and with his left checked his air gauge: 800 out of 3,000 psi left. About ten minutes worth of air. Since the discovery of the gold bar, his breathing had been a little rapid to say the least. He floated back over to Lou's boat for a moment.

Call it momentary greed or just plain concern, but showing the gold bar to the group would complicate things, he convinced himself.

He swam into the cabin again and found one of Lou's tackle boxes. After emptying the contents he put the bar in the box and the box into his mesh catch-bag, and headed to the surface.

The light getting brighter brought the crew to the edge of the boat just in time to see Nate break the surface. He swam to the stern, and after taking off his gear and handing it to Mike, climbed aboard the *Legacy*. The three of them stared at Nate for his report.

He pulled off his dive hood and it made a sucking sound. "Both intake lines, the one for the bait well and the saltwater wash-down, were cut and the handles opened."

"Shit," Rebecca stated. "Now what?"

"We'll go home and get some rest," Nate said.

"Rest—this is your freakin' plan? You said—"

"I know what I said. I think some sleep would help in this thought process a bit. That's all."

Mike picked up the catch-bag with the tackle box in it.

"Mike, I'll take that," Nate said. "Some lures that Lou made. They mean a lot to me." He took the box and put it in his bait well, out of sight, out of mind, he hoped.

Rebecca paced around the deck, not looking at Nate.

Back at the dock they said their good-nights. The plan Nate had come up with, weak as it was, was to meet at Nate's house around eight in the morning and discuss options. At this point he was unsure how and when to bring up the gold thing.

Kate lingered behind with Nate. Rebecca was already at her car.

Turning to Nate, Kate said, "I can't help feeling that this shouldn't concern me. I'm not part of your group, your island."

"I wouldn't blame you if you ran for your life. I just wish we could have continued with a somewhat normal relationship," Nate said awkwardly.

"But what fun would normal be? We would probably have had sex by now, and then we would see each other around town and have that awkward moment where we wouldn't know what to say, then it would end up with each of us just nodding when we saw each other and then by Labor Day we wouldn't even do that."

"Yeah ... exactly ... this is way better," Nate laughed.

"I'll stick around for now, but when the indictments come down, I'm out of here."

"Deal." Nate walked her to the parking area. "Where's your car?"

"England."

"Ahhh."

"I was supposed to get a ride from Rebecca. I guess she left."

"She has a tendency to force my hand," Nate said.

"I don't think she is playing matchmaker, I think she's pissed," Kate told him.

He pulled into her driveway and put the Jeep in park. They sat there in silence from the sheer exhaustion of the day and the inability to take the next step in their potential relationship. Kate placed her hand on Nate's and smiled at him. He smiled back. This wasn't the time for a make-out session, with Lou lying in the morgue. He watched her walk into her house and then pulled away. *Damn it, Lou.*

He walked into the hallway of his house and noticed the drawer of the end table where his phone sat and where he put his mail was opened. He was trying to remember if he'd left it open when the blunt end of a four-cell metal flashlight came with great force into contact with the back of his head.

CHAPTER 9: THE DISCLOSURE

"This was no boating accident."
—Matt Hooper, from the movie *Jaws*

"Gold, I tell ya … gold," Walter Huston was shouting as he danced around Nate's house, doing that crazy dance he did in the movie *Treasure of the Sierra Madre*. Nate couldn't for the life of him figure out why Mr. Huston was in his house. *That pounding, what is that pounding?* Nate wondered.

"It's gold, I tell ya … GOLD!"

Nate opened his eyes and saw the legs of his end table and the dust that had accumulated on the wood floor. *I need to dust this place.*

"NATE, oh my God, NATE!"

Now he saw feet wearing flip-flops—oh there were some sneakers, too.

"NATE!"

He slowly rolled over and standing above him were Rebecca, Kate, Jack, and Josh.

Nate tried to stand but the best he could do was sit up. He rubbed the back of his head and felt an enormous lump that apparently had its own heartbeat.

"What the fuck happened?" Jack asked.

"Well, my best guess is that I got hit in the back of my head."

"By who?" Josh asked.

"I don't know, check around, maybe they left a business card," Nate said sharply to the group. "What time is it?" he asked.

"Eight," Rebecca answered.

Kate came in with ice wrapped in a dish towel. Nate placed it on the back of his head. "Man, that's the first time I ever got knocked out. Wow, does this suck."

"I got knocked out once from a beer bottle at my club," Josh said.

Everybody turned to him after he said this.

Jack came back into the hallway. "Hey, remember the time I got knocked out trying to run from old man Dushamps, when I ran into the tree …?" Now everybody looked at Jack.

"Is the class done sharing their stories?" Rebecca asked.

"Yes, ma'am," Jack and Josh replied at the same time.

"It looks like they ripped through the house in a hurry looking for something," Jack stated.

Nate tilted his head slightly. "Why do you say looking and not taking?"

"Oh, I guess … because your DVD player is still here and you have money on the kitchen table, too." They all looked at Jack for this surprising deduction. "What? I have my moments."

"Yeah, well, don't use them all up now; we might need some for later," Nate said.

Nate stood up and walked into his living room. The cushions were off his couch and drawers were pulled open everywhere. Nate looked around. "Does anybody hide anything under the cushions of their couch, really? I mean you see it in every movie, somebody tossing a house by flipping over all the cushions. Jesus, all you're going to find is change and some pretzels." They were all staring at Nate, except for Kate, who was putting the cushions back on the couch.

"Wait, Kate," Rebecca said, "you better leave the place the way we found it till the police show up and make out a report." She looked at Nate. "Right?"

"I think you know the answer to that."

"Well to be honest, we don't have any answers, do we, Nate? Just questions piling up."

"You're right, Beck, let's get out of the way of people like the mayor—and hey, I know, let's get the mainland involved while we're at it. Let's splash it all over the newspapers that this wasn't an accident so whoever did this to Lou can hightail it out of here on the next ferry. That way we can go back to fishing and handing out brochures about bike rentals, because I am starting to think that you think these things are more important."

He'd gone too far, and he knew it. Rebecca's eyes welled up; she walked up to him and whispered, "I know you didn't mean what you just said, because my whole life you have never hurt me, so I know you don't mean that. But you're a very smart guy, one of the smartest I have ever known. So let me ask you how you would feel if someone else died, maybe one of us in this very room. Do you think you could go on fishing?" She said this as tears ran down her face.

Nate leaned in and touched his forehead to hers and softly said, "I am sorry … I have my reasons, Beck, I beg you to trust me, and I'm asking you to let me do this for now. Can you do this for me?"

Rebecca nodded. "Then let's get to the bottom of this fast."

Nate kissed her on the forehead.

They all yielded to Nate's decision. They were going to split up. Jack and Josh were to go back to town and quietly sniff around the docks for anybody who might have spotted a boat out in the area of Lou's yesterday. Maybe check with the cab drivers and rental guys, people they could trust, and see if anybody had been bothering Lou. The girls were going to Lou's house with Nate to have a look around and wait for the police and medical examiner's report.

Since waking up on the floor, Nate had been in a quiet panic about the gold bar. Did whoever hit him have possession of it?

"Hold up a minute," he said as the girls were getting into his Jeep. He walked over to his shed out back. The shed held not lawn equipment, which was obvious from the landscaping Nate had decided on, but all his fishing and diving gear, which to say the least was very extensive.

On the back side of the shed was a large copper tub, recovered from a shipwreck—ironically, he thought now—which he used to rinse his dive gear. He'd fill it with fresh water and soak his gear until he could find some time to put it away. Late last night he had placed the tackle box in it, with his wet suit and the rest of his gear on top, before entering his hallway and his date with a flashlight.

All looked as it did last night. He dug to the bottom of the tub and pulled up the tackle box, which was extremely heavy for an ordinary tackle box. *Gold, I tell ya … gold.* He placed it on the table next to the tub. "I think I know what this might be all about," he said to the girls, who had followed him to the shed. They stared at him. He looked down at the tackle box. "I found something down at Lou's boat, a wreck of a very old ship, one that's probably been there for a hundred years or so." Nate opened the tackle box and water poured out. The girls were now leaning on him, trying to have a closer look. But that wasn't a problem because he pulled the brick of gold out of the box and held it up to them.

Kate was the first to reply: "Holy dear mother of God."

And then Rebecca: "Holy friggin' shit—I mean holy friggin' *shit.*"

"It was sitting down there on a beam of the old wreck, just sitting there out in the open, begging to be found."

"By you?" Rebecca said.

"I have no clue. I haven't even tried to comprehend that I was the one to find him out there. So I know I can't wrap my mind around the fact that he might have left that down there for me to find. But I have to believe it's his wreck down there. It's his handiwork all over it, and if that's true, then it has to be his gold. Can you think of a better motive for Lou's murder?"

They both shook their heads.

"We need to go to Lou's house and have a look around," Rebecca stated.

As the three of them walked to the Jeep Rebecca asked Nate, "Are you going to tell the others?"

He stopped and stared out to the distance, finally just shrugged and climbed in behind the wheel.

After the ten-minute drive they entered Lou's house and just stood there looking around. "What are we looking for?" Kate asked.

"More gold?" Nate said.

"Let me ask you guys something," Kate said. "You think Lou and the gold are connected, right? So you would think that his death had something to do with this."

"Yeah, I think so," Nate said. "I mean that bar is probably worth somewhere around a hundred thousand dollars."

"Then why hasn't Lou's house been tossed, too? This would be the first place to look," Kate explained.

Nate walked farther into the room and looked around.

"When I came over here for dinner the other night, the room was moved around a bit. And some pictures were off the wall. He said he was spring-cleaning. Maybe someone did toss his house three days ago?" Nate walked into Lou's office at the back of the house. There were books all over the floor. "I just thought he was cleaning out some shit."

"Anything missing?" Rebecca asked.

"Lou self-taught himself everything, he has books on every subject you can think of. He has machinery in the shed and garage, and the basement is full of artifacts recovered from dives over the last forty years. If he had more gold bars in the house, which I highly doubt, then how would we know if they were taken?" Nate asked.

"Well I think it's safe to say that if they found more bars here a few days ago, then they would not have killed Lou and tossed your house," Kate said.

Rebecca and Nate nodded in agreement.

"None of this is making sense," Nate said out of pure frustration.

Over an hour the three went through the house and gathered up bank books and checkbooks and some cash that Nate knew Lou hid. They would give it to the sheriff for safekeeping till Lou's family showed up. Lou had a couple of sisters and their kids. They lived just across Long Island Sound, in Connecticut, and to Lou, spending any time with them was equal to getting the bends while scuba diving—very painful and unnecessary to experience, something to be avoided at all costs.

The girls left to get some lunch and to find out how Jack and Josh were making out in town. Nate wasn't ready to leave Lou's house just yet. Down in the basement he looked over the amount of artifacts Lou and Nate's dad had recovered from the wrecks and salvage jobs they were involved in for years. *Finders keepers* was the general rule. Most of the stuff was crusted-over tools, china plates, brass props, and portholes. It seemed divers had a need to take something back up with them—a prize, if you will—to show people or just remind themselves that they had found something in a way only a few people could do. And the deeper and more dangerous, the bigger need to bring something back up. Now all that was left was a ton of shit someone would have to haul off in a dumpster.

Order, blind, simple order: this was how Lou ran his life, and all the artifacts in his basement held true to his mantra. They were all lined up on one side of the basement. On shelves or tables, all labeled with the name of the ship and the date it had sunk, along with the dates the artifacts had been brought back to the surface. There was no gold down here, simply no place to hide it. Besides, Nate thought as he looked around the basement, if the gold were here, Lou probably couldn't have resisted placing it on a shelf and labeling it.

But on the opposite side of the basement sat a group of artifacts that, though he hadn't been down here in years, Nate was sure he'd never seen. He took a closer look. They were some type of tools. Some were long and slender, cutting tools, and one was a large kettle—in total about ten artifacts. He noticed a brass nameplate, the same kind Lou had made for other artifacts on the other side of the basement. It read, simply, "New Bedford Whaling Museum."

There was a knock at the front door and he heard people enter the hallway upstairs. He slowly made his way up the cellar stairs and waited by the partially opened cellar door. Two men walked into the kitchen; it was Mayor Cavarlo and Dr. Spencer. "Hello," Cavarlo called out.

"Rebecca Preston said Nate was here," the doctor stated.

"NATE!" Cavarlo screamed. "I can't wait around for this little shit all day. You wait if you so choose, I have an island to run." He stormed out of the house. After the screen door swung back on its hinges, Nate popped out of the cellar doorway and startled the doctor.

"Oh, Nate, Mr. Cavarlo just left—maybe you can catch him?"

"Don't bother. I was waiting in the basement till his patience wore out."

"Not much of a wait, eh?"

"Never has been," Nate said.

"I have the medical report completed and filed this morning. Given the close nature of your relationship with Louis, I felt I should tell you personally before I notify his next of kin."

"That means a lot to me, Doctor."

The doctor nodded. "The cause of death was blunt trauma to the head."

"From what?"

"My determination is that it was something flat."

"From a slip and fall."

"That would be my determination, Nate."

Nate stared at the floor, rubbing the back of his neck.

"You have a problem with this determination? Nate?"

"Ahh, no ... well ... just Lou has been at sea his whole life; I just don't see him fumbling around on his boat like that."

"And your father was one of the best commercial divers in the area. We are not invincible, son. Things happen that aren't supposed to."

"Yeah, I guess. But I just can't accept that both these men died doing something that they were the best at."

"The cemetery is full of them. I guess they could have just sat behind a desk all the time, maybe then they would have lived to be a hundred. But that wouldn't have been them, now would it?"

Nate nodded in agreement.

"Well, if there is anything you need, please call me, okay?"

Nate smiled that smile of his.

Chapter 10: The Visitors

He that maketh haste to be rich shall not be innocent.
—Proverbs 28:20

The eleven o'clock ferry was pretty full for a Wednesday. It was the new high-speed one, from Providence. As the people disembarked, some went left, some right; from above it would have resembled ants running for cover from an overturned hill. Jimmy and Stu Ricci were not ants, or your typical summer tourists. They didn't have cameras or backpacks; they were not even wearing shorts.

Jimmy was dressed in black; he considered it his trademark. This time it was black jeans and a very tight v-neck short-sleeved shirt. Stu carried the look of someone who had just walked off a construction site: jeans, tan work-shirt, and boots. They looked around the ferry parking lot. Jimmy nodded to his brother and they headed to the dock area, moving along to an area near the back of a storage shed, where Jimmy made a call from his cell phone.

"We're here, where the fuck are you?" Jimmy screamed. "Don't give me this 'we shouldn't be seen together' bullshit. Did you get the info we need?" He pulled a piece of wrinkled yellow paper from his jeans and wrote something down. "Look, just tell me what boat is his, I'll handle the rest."

After sniffing around Lou's house for another hour or so, Nate made his way down to his boat. It looked lonely without Lou's to keep it company.

Nate just stared at it and wondered if life would ever return to normal, and if it did, would someone like Nate recognize it when it arrived. When he was finally ready to jump down onto his boat, he stopped dead in his sandals. He swung his backpack off his shoulder, and because of the twenty pounds of gold wrapped in a beach towel, had to place the backpack on the ground to retrieve the marine radio.

"Mike, Mike, Mike, are you there? Over."

The response was a tap on the shoulder, which Nate reacted to with a slight jump as he rushed to close the backpack.

"Hey, Mike, try not to sneak up on me."

"Sorry, I saw you heading down the dock. How's the head?"

"Did you leave my boat like this?"

Mike looked down at the *Legacy* and shook his head violently no.

"Are you sure?"

"Look, man, the last time I left footprints like that on your boat, you put a fish head in my bag. Which I left in a car with the windows shut. On a very hot day."

"Yes, Michael, I know what I did."

Nate stared at Mike a moment longer.

"Dude, I didn't even do that! But since you brought the subject up, you're a little neat-freak and it scares some of us."

"Mike, this means somebody has been on my boat."

Mike looked down at the boat with serious interest.

"They had to be on her since you washed her down and before the sun dried the morning dew."

"I washed the boat down after the dive, around two this morning. And the boat probably didn't dry till nine this morning," Mike said, looking up to the late morning sun.

Nate nodded in agreement.

They both climbed down onto the boat and looked around. Everything seemed to be in order. His marine radio and all his electronics were still bolted down to the boat's dash.

"Shit … shit … shit." Nate turned his attention to the GPS, which was on.

"What?" Mike asked.

"Shit."

"WHAT?"

"My GPS is on, and I didn't clear it since—since everything. My bread crumbs are still on it and my friggin' MOB position of the wreck is still in the memory."

He now believed that someone else on the island had the latitude and longitude of the wrecks, but who and why was unclear.

"Look, Mike, ask around, just the kids you know and trust, and see if anybody saw someone around here last night. Can you do that for me?"

"Yes, Nate, absolutely."

"Good … thanks," Nate said, patting him on the back—a reassurance more for himself than for Mike.

"Rebecca wants to see you at the booth," Mike finally told him.

After grabbing some lunch, Rebecca and Kate separated, Kate to the Beach Bar to find out about her schedule, and Rebecca to the visitor's booth to make an appearance.

The booth was quiet for midweek. Nate was alone with Rebecca. She had sent the summer help away and now they both sat there for a while, not really knowing what to say to each other or even what to do next.

Rebecca was reading the story about Lou's passing in the local paper. It was a nice write-up; the entire island would be at the funeral the next day. Nate was sitting up on the counter that ran the length of one wall with his feet on a file cabinet, listening to her read the obituary. When she finished, she turned to him.

"Lou's two sisters and their families are coming in tonight at five. My mom called from the airport. When Mrs. Hayworth from the town hall tracked them down in Connecticut, they said that they would make the funeral arrangements when they arrived."

"Of course," Nate said. "Why should the people who knew him best do it?"

"Play nice when they arrive, for Lou's sake," Rebecca told him.

"For Lou's sake I should kick them in the ass."

"Now that would fall under the category of not playing nice."

There was a knock at the back door and Mike came in.

"Ran into Josh and Jack. They said to tell you that they don't really know what they're looking for or who, for that matter, so they will meet up with you later tonight."

Rebecca and Nate exchanged glances.

"What are we doing, Nate?" Rebecca asked, defeated.

Ignoring her he turned to Mike. "Find them again and tell them tomorrow at my house at seven in the morning." Looking back to Rebecca: "We should all be together before the funeral."

She nodded at this idea.

"Any luck on the other thing?" Nate asked.

Mike started looking around the room. "What?" he asked the floor.

"What other thing?" Rebecca asked.

"Mike. Look at me." Mike reluctantly looked at him. "What did you find out?"

"My buddy who works on the ferry—well, he sleeps on the ferry sometimes instead of going home ... and I think there is a girl from the island, you know her," nodding to Rebecca, "the tall --"

Nate cut him off: "Get to the friggin' point."

"Around three this morning he was looking out from the wheelhouse and he saw someone on your boat. He thought it was me from earlier that night. But he got halfway down the dock and realized it wasn't."

"Oh for God's sake," Nate complained.

Mike was reluctant to answer. So Rebecca did. "Darren?"

Mike nodded. Nate jumped down off the counter and started for the door.

"Nate, wait," Rebecca said. He stopped but didn't turn to her. "You're not thinking clearly. You need to stop and think, if you truly want to get to the bottom of this. You need to be smarter. Going down and getting all manly on him is not the way to go about it. And if you do that, you'll never get the answers you are looking for."

Nate continued out the door.

"Getting all manly on him?" Mike said, putting his hands up. "What the hell does that even mean?" Rebecca gave him her evil eyes, which Mike would never admit scared him.

Nate walked down to Darren's slip, but his boat was gone. He wasn't really sure what he was going to do, anyway. He'd get manly with him later, he thought.

"Hey, Nate," Kate called from the end of the dock. He smiled and momentarily forgot what he was doing. They walked back to the *Legacy.*

"The other night you said you didn't think Darren was capable of doing this. Do you still think that way?"

"Yeah, but it has to be more than just a coincidence that he was on my boat. Lou was having problems with someone putting water and sand into his fuel tank, and a while back someone was stealing GPS coordinates for his secret fishing spots. We never caught who did it. Darren was always my bet."

"What did Lou think?"

"He never seemed to care. Said whoever did this would get theirs someday." He tried his best Lou voice: "*Good always prevails, sunshine.* Man, it's hard to see that now, though. The thing is that we were inseparable as kids, Darren and me. David, too—you know, the harbor master. Everything and everybody got so serious that Darren and I just stopped being inseparable. David ... well, he did something I can't forgive him for, and the fact is, he's a complete ass. But Darren just never seemed to get a handle on things, he just keeps stumbling around."

"And you? What is your problem?"

"Me? I don't think I have any problems. I like to think that I never changed, I'm still that fun-loving guy with boyish good looks. Who's mature yet in touch with his feelings and surroundings," Nate told her with a smile.

"Wow, you said that with a straight face," Kate said.

"Well I practice a lot in the mirror. Honestly, though … I think I just grew up too fast."

"Well that shouldn't stop you from being that fun-loving guy."

"Yeah, but it's getting increasingly harder to do on this island. Plus, at my age, I could break a hip"

He looked down at his watch, trying not to look like someone who wanted to know what time it was, as if he hadn't a care in the world. He was not good enough to pull off this technique.

"What time is it?" she asked.

Shit, she thinks I need to leave, which I do, but I don't want her to think I want to leave … Ah, shit, what am I, fourteen? "Almost five," he said.

"I have to bartend at five." She got up and kissed him on the lips—not the cheek, but smack on the lips. *Gold, I tell ya … gold.*

"What's the next step?"

"Well, I have to go meet Lou's family at his house."

"The funeral's tomorrow?"

"At ten."

"Can I get ready at your place?"

"Yeah. Everyone is meeting at my house at seven tomorrow morning to get ready and maybe try and figure out our next move."

"Oh … okay, great." She walked down the dock to the bar and looked back about halfway and smiled.

"Oh," she said, "oh," and what does "oh" mean in this context? "Oh, I was hoping to be alone with you in your home," or, "Oh, I feel like I'm intruding in your life, and should leave now"? Christ, I am fourteen.

Nate started to head over to Lou's house for the arrival of Lou's family and various members of the island. Whatever high he had being with Kate was gone. Furthermore, while he walked to Lou's, his mind was starting to skip, it was getting increasingly tougher to keep everything together. As he walked he started to bite the inside of his mouth. And they hadn't even had the funeral yet.

Just as Nate was rounding Main Street, a boat pulled around the breakwater, Darren's Black Watch thirty-five. She was old, and beat-up, and showed her age like the owner just didn't get it, too busy stumbling around to even think about refurbishing her, which she needed years ago. After he pulled her into his slip, two gentlemen jumped off, no fish, and no goodbyes. One dressed in black, the other in jeans. After they walked off the boat and made their way up the hill toward town, Darren's boat pulled out of the harbor in a rush and rounded the breakwater whence it came.

The visitors, Jimmy and Stu, needed to get some form of transportation. After roaming around Old Harbor for the better part of an hour they were pissed.

"Listen, shitball, I don't want to rent a moped," Jimmy said to the kid who rented out scooters on the island.

"Mopeds haven't been around since the eighties," the kid said proudly. "This is a scooter." He held his hand out like a game show model.

"Where can I rent a fuckin' car?"

"You can't. You need to reserve them weeks in advance."

The kid's name was Jeffery but his friends called him Bug, and he was getting the immediate impression that the man in black hadn't been told "you can't" a lot in his lifetime. And Bug's lifetime felt like it was coming to a close if he couldn't get these guys out of there fast.

"Look, it's a small island, and the scooters are a hundred a day. You can have them for fifty. And I even have one in black."

Jimmy stared at Bug a lot longer than he needed to in order to get the price down to twenty-five. He handed the kid a hundred for the two and they putted off. They pulled over to their hotel and Jimmy took out his phone. The veins in his neck were out and looking for a fight. When he dialed his cell he hit the numbers so hard it took him five tries to get the number.

The voice on the other end answered, "Hello?"

"Hey, fuckface, you just wasted our day, so you better start giving us the information we need."

"I didn't waste your day. As I explained before, that spot you just went out to is where the wreck is located. It is where the gold came from."

"But you said there was no gold there."

"Right, but as I explained before, to show you my determination in settling up with you with this matter, I gave you the whereabouts of the wreck, and if you don't believe me that I think all the gold has been retrieved, then now you can arrange for someone to dive on it and check it out for yourself. Plus, if you doubt my story of the wreck and the gold, then this should help close the gap of misunderstanding."

"The gap of misunderstanding," Jimmy said, rubbing his forehead, "right, right, right." He took a deep breath. "The only fucking gap is going to be between your fucking teeth." He was really screaming now and turning red. "You piece of SHIT! I want my money or at least the person who has it. Right the fuck now!"

"It's not that easy," the voice on the phone said. "The person you are looking for is here, he has one brick in his possession, and the others are an unknown at this point. Look, we both want the same thing. I have been working on this for sixteen years. We need to find out where the rest of the gold is. And we need to let this person lead us to it."

"Are you sure there is more?" Jimmy asked. There was silence on the other end of the cell. Jimmy was trying to calm down. "You said we were both looking for the same thing. If I don't leave this island with what I came for, the one thing I'm going to be looking for is your lifeless body at my feet."

The voice on the cell was silent for a minute. "You're going to have to go to a funeral tomorrow."

CHAPTER 11: ANNIE

A wise and understanding heart.
—1 Kings 3:12

When Nate's stress-walk finally led him to Lou's house, he noticed two cars in the yard, three people walking around the outside of the house, and several more inside. He recognized one of the people outside as Lou's younger sister. Lou called her the Wicked Witch of the West—unfortunately right to her face, if his memory served him right.

He didn't knock but walked into the house; he had never knocked and wasn't about to start now. When he entered the living room three people were sitting on the couch and Mr. Patterson, the funeral director, was standing just to the right of them, speaking in that *I'm very sorry for your loss* sort of way. One of the three on the couch was Lou's oldest sibling, Janet, which he only guessed from her flaming red hair. Lou had once described her as a redheaded bitch. The other two were his niece and her husband, whose ages and descriptions from Lou over the years seemed to fit. Nate wondered if they were even twenty-one yet. He stood there in the hallway, feeling like a visitor in a house that had been more his home than his own place.

Mr. Patterson caught Nate in the corner of his eye. "Ahh, Nathaniel, I was about to mention you. This is Janet and her daughter, Annie, and her husband, John."

Nate nodded at them and walked deeper into the room.

Mr. Patterson had no intention of shaking Nate's hand with that limp, apologetic handshake or even of telling him how sorry he was for his loss. If he did, he knew that Nate would probably walk out of the house without ever looking back. No way, Mr. Patterson needed him there. Janet was a tough customer. She was hammering him hard on the price for the funeral arrangements, while her sister was walking around the house with a realtor who had come with them from the mainland. Mr. Patterson had absolutely no problem identifying a train wreck in progress; he had seen his share of bickering families in his line of work, oh yes … This situation was a wreck that was minutes away from happening.

"We are making the final plans for the ceremony at the church," Mr. Patterson said. "We all agree that you should say a few things about Mr. Gauthier."

"Really, me? Gee, why don't you have Janet here speak about his past forty years on this island and the people he knew and loved."

Janet didn't back down but stared at Nate with uncaring eyes. Annie just looked down at her feet, her husband up at the ceiling. *A friggin' lively bunch,* thought Nate.

The front screen door creaked open and Lou's other sister and her son along with the realtor came in with smiles on their faces.

"Maria here thinks at least nine hundred thousand, maybe more if we clean up the yard and fix that god-awful wall."

Before Nate had a chance to register any of this, Annie jumped up from the couch. "Auntie, this is Nathaniel West, I'm sure you've heard me talk about him."

"Oh, sure honey, nice to meet you …"

"Nate."

"Nate," she said with a smile.

Mr. Patterson looked to Nate then to the group that was now assembled in Lou's living room and waited for Nate to digest the scene. The train was bearing down on the car sitting on the tracks. *Come on, Nate, don't let me down,* he thought. Nate didn't disappoint.

"Let me get this right," Nate said. "You brought a real estate agent with you. So after the call to tell you your brother was dead, your first call was to a real estate agent? Am I right here? Well that's just fantastic," he said, faking his enthusiasm. "Maybe all of you would like to see Lou's body up at the morgue—maybe you might want to see the cold, lifeless body, check it for a wallet, maybe he had some money in it, huh?"

Both sisters and the agent gasped.

"Oh, am I upsetting you? How do you think I felt when I fished your brother's dead body out of the Atlantic yesterday and held him in my arms? HUH? I can tell you this much, I wasn't thinking about what he left me in his will." The backpack over his shoulder seemed to get heavier with that last statement. "As I stand here I can't help but wonder what Lou would say at this moment. You know ... I mean from the one conversation I had with him in the last thirty years that even remotely pertained to either of you. If I recall, I believe he said that you two were like bloodsucking parasites—you know, like a tick. So I can say with pretty good authority that I think he would want me to say ..."

Wait for it ... wait ... Mr. Patterson thought.

"Get out of his fucking house right now. And by the way, if one thing is taken out of this house without my approval, then you and I, ladies, are going to have some real troubles."

They all stared at Nate with shock, except Annie, who appeared to be trying not to laugh. Lou never mentioned her, but she seemed not like her mother and aunt, Nate thought. After a moment longer he looked at all of them and loudly professed, "Get the fuck out of this house now!"

They all jumped and walked very fast out the front door. Nate turned to Patterson and smiled. "You liked that?" Mr. Patterson nervously smiled as he walked out. Nate hoped he did enjoy the show, because like it or not, Patterson would tell all who would listen, which was of course everyone, about what had transpired here today.

They all drove off, with the exception of Annie, who was lingering by the stone wall. He walked over to her. As he approached her, his first impression was that she was crying. As he got closer he saw that it was the opposite.

She stopped laughing as Nate walked up to her.

"That was some show in there," Annie said.

"Well, I had to do that for Lou. I hope you understand."

"You didn't direct it to me?"

"I don't know, should I have?"

"Just for the record, I hold as much disdain for my family as Uncle Louis did."

"I kind of got that feeling with you having trouble keeping a straight face. I'm sorry if I offended you … you were caught in the crossfire. But the real estate agent? My God, how cold can somebody be?"

"It's all about money, and they just don't care," Annie said, looking back at the uncompleted wall. "I do not share their attitude with the death of my uncle, so you don't have to apologize to me. They're my family, and I will not make excuses for them. The thing is, Uncle Louis and I have been writing and calling each other. We became very close over the past five years. I know a lot about him, especially what you meant to him."

Nate looked at her with a little hint of surprise.

"You didn't know that, did you?"

He shook his head.

"Well, Uncle Louis kept his cards close, didn't let anybody too close. Which I figure is why he never married, though I suspect there are a few girlfriends around here somewhere."

"I have my suspects," Nate teased.

"He loved you more than you can ever realize. Most of his letters were about you. He would tell me about what you did growing up on your own, how great a fisherman and a diver you were. That you were a special person of great intelligence and determination."

Nate just looked at her as if the words weren't about him.

"What's the problem with guys and expressing feelings to each other? It would make our job a lot easier." She looked into Nate's eyes, any form of lightness long gone. "I'm sorry if this is a bad time to tell you this," she went on, "but I'm not sticking around past the funeral. I'm moving to Florida; that's where my husband's from. So this is my only opportunity to tell you face to face. You see, Uncle Louis and I shared something else besides the dislike of our family. I also moved out when I was fifteen, moved in with friends. Family didn't seem to care—more for them. But that's the time he started writing me. Telling me how strong I was for leaving. And that you had lost your family, and mine were lost to me, around the same age, both on our own at a young age. He would tell me what he told you. That as much as it hurts, it will make you stronger."

Nate stared at the wall and kicked at a stone. The cement crumbled away and a rock fell to the lawn.

Annie stared at Nate until he smiled. "What?" he asked.

"There's more that I need to tell you."

"Well this can't be good if you need to ramp me up for it."

"Nate, he was sick, cancer."

"What?"

"He was diagnosed, a year ago. He wasn't going to take treatment. They didn't catch it in time. I guess he wasn't a big fan of going to doctors."

Nate shook his head and laughed in an awkward way. His eyes took him back in time, a memory that came flooding back; he looked up to the sky. "He cut his hand open once shucking oysters," he said. "Found a medical book and gave himself ten stitches."

"Well this time there was nothing he could do to fix it," Annie said.

"I don't understand why he didn't tell me any of this."

"He said that you had been through enough tragedy, that you'd had your fair share."

"There he goes again, presuming what is right for me without letting me decide for myself."

"What would you have done?"

Nate looked at her. "For the first time in my life, to have said goodbye to someone I loved before they were gone."

CHAPTER 12:
WHERE THE DAY WILL TAKE HIM

The lure of the sea is some strange
magic that makes men love what they
fear. The solitude of the desert is
more intimate than that of the sea.
Death on the shifting barren sands
seems less insupportable to the
boundless ocean, in the awful, windy
emptiness. Man's bones yearn for
dust.

—Zane Grey

To say that everyone on the island was going to turn out for Louis Gauthier's funeral was to state the obvious. Any business that could operate with a summer worker would do so, and any other business that couldn't would close its doors for the funeral. There would be no discussion about it. Lou, it seemed, had touched every single person on the island at least twice. He organized Fourth of July parades, started veterans' groups, taught every child how to fish, and tried to tell anybody and everybody how to do their jobs properly, especially those who would not want to heed his advice. You couldn't even look at a nautical chart of the waters surrounding the island without owing him a bit of thanks. For two years Nate's father and Lou subcontracted for the Army Corps of Engineers. They field-tested a new type of sonar that made reading the sea bottom easier. Lou even fixed several problems associated with the sonar array, which embarrassed a group of Navy-educated engineers. This without question was one of his proudest achievements: to watch a group of engineers admit that they were wrong and that a fisherman who had never graduated grammar school was right. It had to have been a sight to behold.

All of this was crashing through Nate's memory, but the one thing that was bothering him the most was that the simple act of tying a tie had never been a happy moment for him. He didn't say it out loud, but it showed in his face. He had worn one once before, and as he stood in the mirror that hung over his fireplace, he tried to push that memory out of his head. His fingers fumbled and he tried again, succeeded, the knot was right, but the business end of the tie was too short, Laurel and Hardy short. He started again from scratch. The memory came flooding back. He was just a boy of fifteen, and two callused and weather-beaten hands helped him tie it then, but this time there was no one left. Lou was gone.

It was still a couple of hours till the funeral, so he left the tie untied and hanging around his neck like a dead snake.

Jack and Josh were in the kitchen drinking Bloody Marys; it was summer after all. Rebecca was in the bathroom doing something or other; everyone was too scared to knock and ask what was taking so long.

There was a quick knock as Kate walked into the house, carrying her dress on a hanger and a backpack over her tan shoulders. She walked over to Nate and hugged and kissed him, and he smiled back.

"Where is everyone?" she asked.

"The boys are in the kitchen, and Beck is in the bathroom. I believe she is now living in there."

Kate walked over to the bathroom door and knocked.

"I wouldn't do that if I were you," Nate told her.

After some whisperings back and forth through the closed door, Kate opened the door and went into the bathroom. Talking and laughter could be heard from inside. He shook his head, and realized that he could better understand the inner workings of fish than of a woman, so he decided that it was Bloody Mary time. A short time later Mike showed up with clam chowder and an apple pie, homemade from his mom, Stella. Jack and Josh's eyes widened when they saw the apple pie.

"With Bloody Marys?" Nate asked.

"What, you think White Russians?" the boys asked, shrugging.

Mike looked at the pitcher of Marys on the table. "Hey, you guys think I could have a small drink?"

"Yeah, go ahead, but not too much, Stella would kill me." Nate paused. "Actually, I have a better idea."

Rebecca walked into the kitchen, wearing a black skirt and white blouse. Her hair, which was seldom without a baseball hat, was down and flowing around her shoulders. Being lifelong brother-and-sister-like friends, Nate and everyone else in the room had forgotten just how beautiful Rebecca was. When Kate followed right behind her, it made Nate's stomach go all loopy, in the good kind of way. The black dress Kate was wearing fit her like a work of art, like a Picasso or Monet. Maybe it was the grief, or the fact that she had been out there when he found Lou, or just that friggin' dress, but in that instant he knew without a speck of a doubt that he, Nathaniel West, might be falling hard for her.

Mike, Jack, and Josh applauded the girls. Then Kate took a bow, Rebecca held her hand out to be kissed by Jack, which he did, finishing off the scene perfectly. This gave Nate a moment to gather his wits.

"Okay, listen up, kiddies. We all know the story of Lou's famous bottle of rum, but for you new students … While playing poker in a bar in Shanghai, he drew a straight flush, and in doing so came into possession of a bottle of rum. A bottle of rum reportedly from the pirate Captain Kidd. A pirate, mind you, who has stepped foot on this very island, as the legend has it."

"I still don't think that he was ever a pirate," Jack said. "History is sketchy on him with regards to being a pirate. I even tried to Google him once."

"Google this," Josh said to his brother.

"Anyways, Lou always told me that I needed a real important occasion to drink it. I can't think of a more important one."

Nate opened the cabinet he always kept it in. The bottle was not there. The whole room opened all the cabinets in the kitchen, but no luck.

"He did give it to you, didn't he?" Jack asked.

"Yeah, about a year ago, told me to hold on to it for an important occasion." Nate shook his head. *He gave it to me a year ago ... a year ago. Damn it, Lou, you are playing me like a fish, aren't you?*

There was a knock on the front screen door, which interrupted the futile search. They all reached for the pitcher of Marys as Nate left the kitchen.

A minute later shouting began and then the sound of furniture being knocked over. They all ran out of the kitchen.

Nate had Darren by the cheap suit he was wearing, pinned up against the hallway wall.

"You got some fucking nerve coming here today," Nate shouted.

"If you just let me the FUCK go, maybe you can see the amount of nerve it took me to come here today."

At this point the boys had Nate off Darren and were holding him at bay.

"Just get out of here, Darren," Jack insisted.

Rebecca stood in between them. "Not today, I will not allow this here today!"

The boys let go of Nate.

"What are you doing here?" Rebecca asked.

"I came here today not just to pay my respects to you for the loss of Lou, but to--"

Nate cut him off. "What? What did you say? Did you say respect? You have never shown him one bit of respect."

"Stop it, Nate, just let him say what he came here for, and then he'll be on his way," Rebecca insisted.

"That's all I'm asking for," Darren said, looking right at Nate.

More sullen, Darren continued, "Since you seem to have a short memory, let me remind you that Lou saved my father's life ten years ago. Now I know most in this room might think my father's life might not have been worth it, but I happen to think it was, as much pain as he has given me. And needless to say, I owe Lou my father's life and will be indentured to him for the rest of mine."

Shit, Nate thought, *how the hell did I forget about that?*

"You and I, Nate, were once the best of friends, remember? If you can just think back to that time, a time when I was a part of this group, and if you can remember that time, then you can understand that I am truly sorry."

The hallway fell silent.

Finally Nate said, "I find it hard to believe you have the nerve to stand here the day after you were seen on my boat stealing GPS numbers."

Rebecca lowered and shook her head.

"You want to do this now? Bring all our problems out today?" Darren stared at them and continued, "Okay, I was off island the night before last, left on the four o'clock ferry and returned the following morning by eight for a charter—check it out. So to begin with, get your facts straight before the accusations."

Nate looked over to Mike.

"Whoever told you this is lying," Darren stated, looking at Mike. "May I continue?"

"By all means," Nate returned the sarcasm.

"The other reason I'm here is that my charter yesterday has something to do with Lou." If Nate had something more to say, this shut him up. "The charter I had yesterday was, to say the least, strange, and it led me to this." Darren reached for the bag he'd carried in and pulled out an orange lifejacket with the name *Sea Bounty* stenciled in black letters.

They all stared at it.

"Look, these two guys booked my boat for the day. When they got on board, one of them pulled out a crumpled piece of yellow paper and gave it to me, told me it was the location of a spot that he and his father fished and he wanted to go there to spread his old man's ashes. When we got there, they had me drive around the spot while they looked at my sonar screen. After they whispered to each other, they told me they forgot the ashes and wanted to go back. They paid me cash, so what did I care? After they left, I went back out to the spot, mainly because it showed something big down there, that wasn't on the charts—I'm thinking a reef, you know, maybe my own secret fishing spot. When I got back there, this floated to the surface, along with some other stuff while I was there. It's Lou's boat down there, isn't it?"

Some stared at the floor, others the ceiling, except Nate, who just stared at Darren.

"Okay, Nate, no comment?"

"I don't know what you're looking for from me."

"The truth."

Nate just shrugged at Darren's comment.

Darren continued. "I see. What would you say, then, when I go diving on the site to make sure it is his boat, then inform the sheriff and maybe the mayor about the location? Do you think they will realize that to put Lou's body off Southeast Point, where you reported to the Coast Guard you recovered it, it would have had to drift three miles *against* the tide and around Breton Reef without anybody seeing it? And that now that you mention it, Petty Officer Gilmore, I saw your friend Nate's boat about a quarter of a mile from the very site of the *Sea Bounty* when I heard him call you. Do you think any of this is a possibility, Nate? Look, I just want to know what's going on."

Nate walked into the living room and they all followed.

"I'm having trouble figuring you out here, Darren. I mean, since you took over the charter business from your father, you've seemed to be a thorn in Lou's side, stealing his charters and fucking with his boat. And now you come in here and think you deserve answers?"

"I never stole a charter, and I never touched his boat."

"Then who, who did all this to Lou over the past year?"

The past year rang in his head like an alarm. *He was diagnosed a year ago,* he could hear Annie's voice from yesterday. *All this started a year ago. All the problems with his boat, losing charters, it all started a year ago.*

"Do you even remember why we stopped hanging out, Nate?"

Nate's mind was racing around with thoughts of what Lou had been trying to do over this past year—and of course, the gold.

"It was David," Darren said. "When you traveled to the Cape for a year with your dad, David took it hard, never forgave you for leaving. When you moved back he kept talking shit, he poisoned our friendship. Every time he and I were alone he would tell me things you'd said about me, pretty shitty things, and I started to believe them. I didn't know what really happened between you and him, but the past is the past, as cliché as it sounds, and circumstances being as they are, you have to decide on what the truth is here. And the truth is I never did anything to hurt Lou."

"What are you going to do now with all this information?" Nate asked.

"Nothing. I'm not a big fan of the authorities, but I think you know that, so I'll just sit on it. But really, what the fuck is going on here?"

Nate sighed and walked around the room, shaking his head back and forth, trying to come to terms with all that Darren was telling him. "We really don't know, at this point. I found Lou's boat and it was sinking. He was dead when I found him." Darren stared at Nate for more, and reluctantly he continued. "I dove on it last night. His through-hull hoses were cut, by whom we have no idea. So I've also decided to sit on it."

Nate couldn't see the harm in telling him this. If Darren did have anything to do with it then he might feel the walls closing in, but he really didn't think that Darren had, and besides, with Darren's father's connection to Lou, Darren was not lying when he said that he owed Lou.

"Then what do we do now … you and me?" Darren asked.

"We have a drink," Nate said. "Then we bury Lou."

The seven stood around the table holding up their glasses. It might not be pirate rum, but Bloody Marys would have to do, for now. They all just stared at the glasses in their hands. They all knew it was Nate who needed to say something, but it was also Nate who had taken another loss, and what could they have said in his shoes? All he could come up with was, "Lou." They all drank.

"Jesus, we're going to be late," Jack said, looking up to the clock on the wall. They rushed like herded cattle for the front door. Nate stopped in front of the mirror again, to give the tie one more try. This time two beautiful, soft hands came around his neck and in a flash made a perfect tie, length and all.

They faced each other.

"Thanks."

"No worries."

Nate stared into her eyes.

"What?" Kate asked.

"It just seems like you have something on your mind. You keep squinting at me."

"I just feel a part of this group. I never felt this kind of friendship in my life before. And I know with the circumstances today this is not the right time … but … I just wanted to thank you for allowing me to be a part of this."

Nate looked into her brown eyes. "You were out there with me when we found Lou, so even if you left tomorrow, you would always be a part of me, of this, like it or not. But remember when you leave—which you will do, everybody leaves—we will haunt your dreams."

"Well that's the rub. I don't want to leave. I feel a part of this group. I know it's only been a few days, but I feel a part of something for the first time in a long time. I would really like to stay awhile … here … with all of you."

"Please do."

"But is it always like this around here?"

"You kidding me? Last year we had to fight off a two-hundred-foot octopus, and Beck was kidnapped by modern-day pirates."

"Great, then I'll stay to see if things start getting interesting."

They walked out of the house and made their short walk to the church. St. Peter's sat just to the right of Main and Center streets, built in

1930, ironically by some of Lou's family. It was made of a rich, deep wood from the rafters to the floor—an island church, not one of those stone castles on the mainland. And for Father Fitzgerald, it had been home for the last fifteen years. His first funeral service on the island had been for Nate's father.

The church could hold about one hundred people, and it was at full capacity to say the least, with a hundred more people outside, staring at it like somehow it could grow before their eyes to accommodate them. No loaves and fishes, no miracles, just a lot of people.

Nate and Kate walked up the center walkway to the entrance. The people outside were lining both sides of the walkway, sort of a funeral gauntlet, and they started whispering to each other as the two walked by. Some came up to Nate to tell him how sorry they were, but most were just acquaintances from the mainland or simply summer residents; because of the small size of the island, many had had dealings with Lou. These people, the casual acquaintances, were the ones doing the whispering.

When Nate entered the church the women's guild, led by Mrs. Fletcher and Miss Hobson, hugged him and walked him to the front pew. Lou's family was in the pew across the aisle and didn't bother a look in Nate's general direction as he walked in. Except for Annie, who was crying and mouthed "hi" to him.

There comes a time in all our lives when we realize the passage of time. Sitting there, Nate could feel the weight of the last fifteen years on his soul. Just like that, he was in his thirties and he was now the last of the little family he had. This weight tugged at him, unrelenting, unforgiving, leaving him alone to come to terms with it, to understand it and accept it as life. He looked around and saw what he considered his family now, no blood ties, simply friends who had been with him as he had been with them for well over thirty years. It was that comfort, this understanding that would let him get up again tomorrow and wonder where the day would take him. To see the adventure still left in this world. He could hear the old man in his head: *It's just life there, sunshine, you can't run from it, so when it's not looking, kick it in the teeth.* Kick it in the teeth, he thought. Lou kicked life hard, but this time it kicked back.

Rebecca nudged him. The readings and prayers had all been said; it was now his time to say something about the man who had raised him for the last fifteen years.

He stood at the lectern not afraid, not embarrassed, he had never been, no, he was firm in his dedication to the man who was Lou Gauthier, lying before him now in a wooden box. He stood up straight, no tear in his eye, no quiver in his voice—that would not have been allowed by the man lying before him, he'd learned that fifteen years ago. This was about pride and honor, and he would show what he'd learned from him and make the old man proud.

The procession to the cemetery seemed long only because of the jockeying of all the cars among a fair share of tourists who were biking or walking around. As they stood around the grave, Lou got the military-gun sendoff. They gave the flag to Annie. Nice call, Mrs. Fletcher. Patterson's story of Lou's family must have gotten to the women's guild. Sometimes the small-island mentality worked just fine, Nate thought. Final words were said and the crowd set off to the VFW, for the usual food and drinks.

Nate stood at the grave site, letting everyone slowly disperse. He turned upon hearing someone approach. Kate stood there at his side.

After a few minutes of silence he looked out to Great Salt Pond. "This is it, huh? Life."

Kate didn't know if she should answer, and when he continued, she realized he wasn't looking for an answer.

"The only thing we know, from the day we put our first thought together, is that we will die. And in knowing this undisputed fact, everything around us stops making sense when it happens. It's all for nothing."

This time Kate answered. "You can't mean that."

"At this moment I do."

"The grieving is for the living," Kate told him.

"Then the dead are getting off easy."

"Are you giving up on life?"

Surprised at the question, he answered, "No."

"Then the day will go on and tomorrow the sun will rise."

"I know. It will. But I don't have to like it," he answered.

"Hey you, with the pretty face, welcome to the human race," Kate told him.

Nate looked at her with a smile. Holding hands, they walked over to the gang.

"You just quoted the Electric Light Orchestra to me?" Nate asked.

Laughing, she said, "Yes, I did. Sometimes we don't feel a part of something until that thing changes. That song always seemed appropriate. I am very impressed that you knew it."

They all started walking down the hill to the cars. Darren was there and stopped them.

"Hey, Nate, umm … I'm sorry again. Nice service, though, huh?"

"Yeah, nice," he answered.

Darren stood there for a minute, uncomfortable.

"What's up, there, Darren?"

"Umm … There are a couple of things I neglected to tell you this morning that just became more apparent now."

"What is it?"

"The two guys who chartered me yesterday to Lou's boat?"

"Yeah," Nate said slowly.

"They weren't your typical guys. They're, like, from Providence. And I'll bet the little I have, connected."

"Connected?" Kate asked.

Darren tried to explain. "Well I guess you could say the mob—you know, organized crime. I don't think these two are too organized, but they are connected, I am damn sure of it. Maybe not too far up the mob food chain, but far enough to break your legs and start asking questions later. I asked them their names and they told me it was none of my fucking business. Who says that?"

"What the fuck would Lou have to do with the mob?" Jack asked, stunned.

Gold, I tell ya … gold, rang in Nate's head.

"Are you sure, Darren?" It was Rebecca's turn.

"Look, my father is in jail for the next two years because of associating with people just like that. I had the feeling when they were on my boat. I was thinking that they were after me for something my father did, so I had my gun tucked into my pants."

"Jesus, this is serious shit, Nate," Rebecca stated.

"It gets worse. See those two guys getting on the Vespas, the one in black and the one in jeans and work boots?"

"Yeah?" Nate said.

"Wait—those two?" Jack said.

"Yeah, those two," Darren said.

"Shiiiit, man … I saw those two at the church and then up on the hill back there." He pointed over Nate's shoulder. "Just before the crowd broke up. They were staring at us."

Nate started across the street toward them, but Darren stuck out his arm and stopped him. The two visitors pulled away on their scooters and didn't look back.

"You can't just walk up to them and start asking questions," Darren stated.

"Well what the hell do we do now?" Rebecca said. "I mean the fucking mob, Nate."

"The language, Beck … God," Nate said, pointing at the cemetery.

"That's all that's missing, a lecture from Saint Nathaniel."

Nate paced around the group for a moment. "Look, I have to go to the VFW to thank everybody. Why don't we meet at my house at two, all of us, and regroup. But listen, no boyfriends." He pointed to Rebecca. "And no girlfriends or the like," he said, looking at Mike. Darren was standing there, staring at his feet, not knowing his place in all of this.

"What about Darren here?" Jack asked.

Nate looked stunned at the group, who were nodding as if the question made perfect sense. "What? You're serious, you want Darren there?"

"Christ, I'm standing right here," Darren stated to the group.

"All of you were asking me yesterday if you thought he did this," Nate explained.

"You guys thought I did this?" Darren said, shocked.

Now everybody stared at their feet.

"Look, I'm out of here. I just thought you guys should know who you're dealing with."

He walked away, shaking his head.

"Darren," Nate called out to him. "If you are telling the truth with all of this, then you should be there. So come, if you want."

Looking at him, Darren said, "The truth is all I have. Yeah, I'll be there, but get your 'I'm sorrys' straight when I get there." He turned and walked away.

CHAPTER 13: SEE NATE RUN

Nate did a quick walkthrough with the mourners at the VFW. Most were just stuffing their faces with food and telling stories about Lou. As he expected, Lou's sisters were nowhere to be found, and that was just fine with him. But he couldn't take much more of this, the hugs and I'm sorrys were pushing him to the edge. And that damn gold brick, sitting there under the floorboards of his shed, was driving him mad, right out of a Poe story. He kept picturing the two guys from the funeral finding it.

He finally made a break for the bathroom and climbed out of the window and headed down over the small hill that led to the main road. Walking along the street with the VFW out of sight, he finally started to relax, until he heard his name being called. He ignored it the first couple of times. But when the person calling his name ran after him, he realized it was Annie calling him, so he stopped and waited for her to catch up.

"I was trying to see you all morning," she said.

"Sorry, being pulled five different ways."

"Pulled right out of the bathroom window?" she said, laughing.

"Well ... yeah."

"I was hiding behind the big oak tree, so ..."

"Nice choice."

"Thanks. Look, Nate. I had a meeting with Attorney Cooper. Uncle Louis made me executor of his will."

Nate laughed. "Wow, that must have gone over well."

"You have no idea. But it gets better. He left his house and the surrounding land to some island land trust. The contents of his house he left to me. But it just doesn't say anything about you. I don't understand, Nate," she said as she started to cry.

"Hey, hey, hey, Annie," he said, putting his hands on her shoulders. "Listen, that's okay, I had a feeling as much. Your uncle gave me so much over the years, I wouldn't expect anything more."

She handed an envelope to Nate. "He did leave you this. All I know about the letter is that it was given to the attorney the same time he drew the first will up, about fifteen years ago."

"The first will? There were others drawn?"

"Umm … yeah, the attorney said that Uncle Louis changed it about five years ago."

"Do you have any idea what he changed?"

"Well, he said that he wasn't supposed to tell me, but my mother and aunts berated him last night on the fact that Uncle Louis made me executor—of course I was sitting right there. After their grand exit, he told me my uncle took them out and put me in. Why do you care about the other wills?"

"I don't know, I'm just trying to figure the old man out," he told her.

"You knew him better than I did," she said.

"I'm starting to realize that I didn't know him as well as I thought."

"I'm sorry that he didn't leave you anything. Whatever you want, you can have."

"Answers, I need a few of those."

"I'm fresh out … sorry."

"You know all that stuff in the basement is not worth a fortune but might hold some value to the right people."

"Yeah, Uncle Louis has been schooling me since—well, since he found out."

"Good."

They both stared at each other. Knowing now that Lou had a family member like Annie made Nate feel better about this whole process. And besides, he really didn't want to clean up another loved one's life again.

"Nate, maybe you can help me figure something out? My uncle kept telling me that he was going to leave me a nest egg. Enough money to set John and me up in Florida. I mean I don't want anything, I mean it, I don't want a dime from anybody, but … He had a safe deposit box signed out in my name, and when I opened it, it was empty. I'm just worried I'm missing something."

"I don't know. But if you don't mind, I'll look around his house one more time, see if anything could relate to that."

"Of course, it's your home more than mine."

She hugged him and walked back up the hill.

He stared at the envelope. He walked over to the shade of an old tree and sat on the roots, which were busting through the ground from its hundred-year reign.

Now what? He stared at the letter. *Lou, I hope the fuck you explain everything in this letter, because all of this is starting to damage my calm.*

Two things were written in Lou's handwriting on the single page. The first was this:

The isle is full of noises, Sounds, and sweet airs, that give delight and hurt not. Sometimes a thousand twangling instruments Will hum about mine ears; and sometimes voices, that if I then had wak'd after long sleep, Will make me sleep again, and then in dreaming, The clouds methought would open, and show riches Ready to drop upon me, that when I wak'd I cried to dream again.

Beneath this were two words:

COMPASS ROSE

Nate read the letter again and then once more, for the simple reason that the third time's a charm. Also because the first two didn't give him any idea what the hell it meant. *Screw all this shit,* he thought. It was time to lay all his cards on the table. He sprang up from the roots as if his ass were on fire. His pace was quick as he walked home, biting the inside of his cheek until he tasted blood.

He was standing in the doorway that led to the kitchen. Jack, Josh, Rebecca, Kate, Mike, and the latest addition to their little group, Darren, were staring wide-eyed at the kitchen table—or not actually the table, but at what Nate had just placed on it.

"Can I touch it?" Jack was the first to ask.

"That's the best you can come up with?" Nate asked.

"Jesus, Nate, I never saw anything like it, that's all."

"Look, this is starting to get out of hand in a hurry. We need to have a plan."

"This has been out of hand from the start, Nate."

"Duly noted, Beck."

"How much do you think it's worth?" Josh asked.

"Just an estimate, I'd say close to a hundred and fifty thousand," Nate answered.

"No way, more like two hundred," Jack stated.

"Two hundred?" Josh answered his brother.

"Yeah, look, it weighs like sixteen pounds, and you have twelve ounces to a pound, times—what? Like six hundred dollars an ounce?"

"Uh, bro … it's sixteen ounces to a pound, and I think it's around nine hundred dollars an ounce," Josh told his brother.

"Is it that high?"

"HEY, can we get back on point?" Nate said, losing his patience.

Jack cleared his head by shaking it. "Okay, you found this where Lou's boat sank, just sitting there on the old wreck, and you think it was left by Lou for you to find. I mean, who else would have dove on Lou's boat?"

"That's if you believe that Lou thought he was in trouble and left it there, knowing that his boat was going to sink there," Mike said.

"Wait, that doesn't make any freakin' sense," Jack said.

"Oh, like you are?" Mike shot back.

"What do you think 'compass rose' means? Do you think it's the ship that's down there? Why wouldn't he just tell Nate what's going on?"

Rebecca said, trying to answer Mike, who was talking to Jack. It seemed everyone was talking at once, until finally one loud voice prevailed.

"Do you think there is more?" Nobody heard, so once again, with more volume: "DO YOU THINK THERE'S MORE?" Everybody stopped talking and stared at Darren, who was looking at the gold bar. Then he looked up and said, "Sorry."

"That is one of many questions I don't have an answer for," Nate said as they all turned to him. "This might be a little much to throw at you with all that's going down, but I talked to Lou's niece, Annie. They have been talking a lot over the years. She told me that Lou had cancer, untreatable." Stunned silence engulfed the kitchen. "I believe this gold bar here was not meant for me, but for Annie. Think this out with me. He left his house to the town with the contents going to whoever Annie decides, and any cash, bank accounts, and the such," he said, smiling toward Kate, "would go to her. But that might total fifteen grand, tops. His sisters get a big steaming pile of nothing. Annie told me that Lou said that when he was gone, he would leave her a nest egg, something for her and her husband's future. Fifteen grand won't pay for the funeral. Why would you leave the one family member you loved only fifteen grand?"

"Because you thought there was going to be more," Rebecca stated.

"Exactly," Nate said, pointing to her, "because you thought you were going to have more for her. He also left her an empty safe deposit box. I think, based on the gridding work on the wreck, that he found it years ago, salvaged whatever it was, and sat on it till he found out he was dying. Then he tried to cash in all of it, or maybe just some of it, without the help of legitimate means. In doing so, he tipped off the wrong kind of people and they came looking for him, for the gold. But he managed to get rid of it."

"You're talking about the mob," Jack said.

"Yeah."

"But how did he know you would find it?" Josh asked.

"I don't think I was supposed to find it or even know about it. Look, the letter has really nothing to do with the bar here, they're independent of each other. If you play it all out the way Lou might have really wanted it to go, he cashes in the gold, gives the money to his niece, and days later I get a letter. The letter and the clue I would have laughed at, probably looked at it now and again. I would have maybe started looking things up in some of his books, made a list of things that it might pertain to. The point is, it might have taken months or years before I figured it out. He has been doing this kind of shit since I was a kid—you have all been a part of some of them over the years. Lou's little challenges. And I would have thought, one last challenge."

"But somebody got involved, that changed his plan, and we found him," Kate said.

"Right, call it fate, or karma, divine intervention, or just dumb fucking luck. We found him caught up in some serious shit, and in doing so found the gold. Which probably screwed up the way he wanted it to play out, and now we have answers to questions we don't know. The letter might not even be about the gold. But either way, that poem and the words 'compass rose' are clues to whatever it is he wants me to find."

"Back to Darren's question, you said you think there's more."

"I just find it hard to believe that he uncovered only one brick of gold."

They all stared back at the table.

"So any idea why he was anchored up on the wreck to begin with?" Darren asked.

"I'm guessing here, but if you wanted to hide a gold bar in the ocean, where would you hide it so you could find it later?"

Kate answered, "Where you found it to begin with."

Nate looked from Kate to the rest of the group.

"You know she's smarter than all of you," Nate said, smiling.

Jack and Josh nodded and Rebecca gave her evil eyes.

"But ... but, the problem here is what do we do about Lou's death and our two visitors on the scooters?" Nate asked.

"Well, I know you've been saying this all along, but, if we come forward now with this gold and shit, you'll have two hundred boats diving and digging up this island like a reality show. And the news coverage.

It will be a nightmare," Jack explained. "Finding Lou's killer when this news breaks would be impossible."

"So I think we might try and find out the connection with Lou and our two visitors," Nate said. "And then without the gold, go to the police with what we find out."

"And tell them what?" Rebecca asked. "'Someone killed Lou—but we can't tell you why.'"

"Umm … yeah, something like that," Nate said.

"Great plan," Rebecca stated.

Darren pulled out his cell phone and looked at his watch. "I have to make a phone call and cancel a charter I'm late for—excuse me for a minute." He walked out to the front yard.

"The two guys rented the scooters from Bug, so I bet they're staying at the National, or Helen's place."

"Okay, good, Mike," Nate said. "Why don't you go into town and see if you can find them and try to follow them around a bit."

"Are you shittin' me, Nate? They're following *us* around!" Rebecca yelled.

"Good point," Josh answered.

"All right, I'll go to Lou's house and have another look around for anything about who he might have contacted. Look, just look around. If anything seems to fit into our little story, let me know. But don't take any chances."

"Don't take any chances? Are you listening to yourself? You're friggin' Columbo here, for Christ's sake," Rebecca screamed.

"Well I'm a little new to the whole investigative process here, Beck."

"Do you think these two killed Lou and tossed the houses?" Josh asked.

"I don't see why not, if Darren's right. Who else is capable of all this?"

"Greed makes people capable of anything, not just the obvious," Kate stated.

"Where the hell did Darren go?" Jack asked, looking around.

Mike came jogging into the kitchen. "Hey, just thought you should know, Darren just took off in his car doing about eighty down the street."

They all looked at Nate, who was shaking his head. "Shit, I knew it."

"What are you going to do with the gold?" Josh asked.

"I don't know—you want it?" Nate asked, smiling.

"Yeah."

"Nate, you know Josh and I will do anything to help you," Jack said, "but I need to head back to the club. We got a great band from L.A. in tonight; the place is going to be packed."

"Yeah, I know, go ahead. If anything comes up, I'll let you know. And thanks, guys."

They both patted Nate on the back on their way out. Mike was standing there, eager to help.

"All right there, Mike, go down to my boat and fuel her up, and check with your buddy from the ferry again to see if he knows about the two guys and when they came in."

Mike shook his head and headed out of the room, but then he came right back in, reaching for the gold bar. "I almost forgot this."

Nate got to the bar first. "Nice try, meatball."

Mike spun around again and headed out.

"Hey, Mike, when you talk to your friend, ask again about Darren the other night, and let me know," Nate yelled to him.

Now it was just Rebecca and Kate left. Rebecca had something on her mind and Nate could see it coming from a mile away.

"I have to ask one more time, do you really think we should be doing this?"

"I don't want you to think I'm being cold here," Nate said, "but Lou is dead, and cops or no cops, he would still be dead. I need to do this."

"But why? Why the need for any of this?"

"I never told you about this … but … after my dad died, the investigations from the state and the Long Island construction crew showed it was diver error that killed my dad. He got stuck and ran out of air, they said—part of the job—and that investigation lasted two months.

Lou went out there and re-interviewed the construction workers, the demo guys, and some of the federal investigators. Went diving down to the scene, under the same conditions as my dad, and at the end of one week proved that the demo guys screwed up the stability of the site and when my dad went down there that day, he'd found different conditions, creating a fatal error not on his part but on the construction crew's and the state's. Which the investigators agreed with. Lou's main problem with the way most people conduct themselves is that they're all, 'Why give a hundred percent when fifty will do?' When someone's heart and soul are not into it, if there is no connection for them, then the average will do. Lou deserves more than the average. It's not about the gold. He gave his all for my father, and I need to repay him."

Rebecca realized he was right, and she wouldn't argue with his logic right now. But she was not one hundred percent comfortable with it all just yet.

"Okay," she said, "what do you want me to do?"

"Go back to work. I'm going to Lou's house and grab a couple of books and maybe look for some phone bills, then take off."

She looked at her watch. "All right, I'll be at the booth till six." They hugged and kissed, and she waved to Kate on her way out.

"You, too," Nate said to Kate. "Go. I'm all right."

"Are you kidding me? All the speeches and the intrigue? I'm going with you, screw bartending."

"Okay, get your ass in the Jeep."

Jimmy's cell phone rang. He put his beer down on the bar and answered it.

"The group is at his house as we speak," said the voice coming from the phone. "He has one bar of gold with him now, still unclear on the rest."

"Look, I'm done doing things your way. I'm going to the old man's house first and have my own look around, then when he's alone, I'll have a little talk with our golden boy."

He didn't wait for a reply from the voice on the other end of the cell. No, that time had passed. It was Jimmy time now.

"Finish your beer," he said. "It's time to have some fun."

Stu downed his beer and rubbed his hands together. "Let's rock and roll, baby." They headed out of the bar and onto their scooters—not the image the boys back in Providence would find cool, but Jimmy and Stu had never been known even to drive by the neighborhood of cool.

Lou's house was empty, his family probably out buying tee shirts, getting sunburns, and laughing and taking pictures like good little tourists. Nate headed straight to the back office; books were still strewn everyplace. It was hard to tell what was Lou's mess and what was created by whoever toured through his house. Kate came into the office and started picking books up.

"You just love to clean things up," Nate told her.

"I like order."

"Yeah, I know what you mean."

"Really."

"Are you inferring that I don't?"

Kate smiled. "Looking for anything in particular?"

"Well, he kept a book on the dive sites and fishing spots he found, it has drawings and a bunch of numbers. Should be a very worn book, a brown leather cover."

They went thought all the books in the office, but no luck; the one book he'd seen the old man write was not there. He walked into the living room and found the photo album still sitting where Nate had left it. He picked it up and looked at the history of Lou's family once again. He placed it in his backpack. "This is mine," he said, simply, to the empty room. He knew Annie wouldn't mind. And the others—well, they could kiss his salty ass. He walked back into the office.

"Up for some tea?" Kate asked.

"Tea?"

"It's been a long day, it will help you settle down. Besides, you Americans should drink more, you might lighten up a bit."

"Tea it is, then."

He sat down and surveyed Lou's very neat desk. Lou may have let his collection of books pile in the corners, but his desk was another story. His filing system was as follows: get a bill, pay the bill, and throw it away. No receipts, no paper files. Lou collected relics stored in his garage and basement, but bills, letters, birthday cards—as far as Lou was concerned, these just took up space. So Nate knew heading in that he was not going to find a date book with mysterious names and phone numbers in it, with the words "meet bad guys at four" circled in red. And whatever quest Lou was trying to get him on was not in this house, either. Nate just needed to find that connection to Lou and the two large fellows on the scooters; the quest would have to wait.

Kate was standing in the doorway and cleared her throat. There, in her pretty little hands, was Lou's notebook.

Nate threw his palms up and shook his head.

"In the cupboard, with some cookbooks," she said. "The cover is labeled, 'Family Recipes.'"

"Brilliant, just brilliant."

He opened it. There had to be over a hundred longitudes and latitudes of the secret spots he'd found over the years. His dirty little book of secrets, he once heard Lou call it. He started to page through it and the amount of areas was overwhelming.

"Tea's ready."

He put the book in his backpack.

Sitting there at the kitchen table, they sipped their tea in silence, just like an old married couple worn down from years of conversation. But in this particular situation, they were just worn down from the last few days. They needed a different beginning to their story, to try to make this feel right again. The front screen door creaked open; Nate gave the face of disappointment for the return of the evil sisters.

"We're in the kitchen," he shouted, but no answer came back. "Hello?"

Still no answer. In a hushed voice, "Go out the back door—go now." She reluctantly started for the back door. Nate stood up and slowly started to walk to the front of the house as Kate opened the back door and headed out into the backyard.

He walked as quietly as he could, his back pressed up against the wall, heading into the living room. As he peeked around the corner, he came face to face with Jimmy, and in his hand, a very large gun. Nate didn't really care about the make or model, it was the kind that bullets came out of real fast and made holes in people—that much he knew.

"Hi, can I help you?" Nate asked him, trying to ignore the gun pressed up to his forehead.

"Look, dickhead, back into the kitchen, we need to have a little talk."

When they entered the kitchen Kate was already sitting at the table with Stu standing to her right.

"A lovely couple, don't you think?" Jimmy said.

"Beautiful," Stu replied.

"Let's cut to the point. We want the gold bar you have, and let's see … Oh, yeah! Where's the rest of it?"

"Who sent you?"

Jimmy punched Nate on the side of the face, knocking him to the floor.

"Wrong answer, dickhead."

Nate slowly got up and sat back down on the kitchen chair. There was a phone ringing, but he realized it was just in his head.

"Once again, and if you do not answer correctly this time, your girlfriend will be next."

Nate's blood was boiling in his veins, but he couldn't let her be hurt, not for this.

"Don't, Nate," she said.

"SHUT UP!" Stu screamed in her ear.

"Okay, okay, I'll get it." Nate got up and walked into the office and picked up his backpack. Jimmy was right on his heels. Back in the kitchen he put the backpack on the table.

"Open the bag slowly and give it to me."

As Nate reached down to the zipper he glanced up to Kate to make sure she was all right. Their eyes met and he saw Kate moving her eyes to the right, over and over, in the direction of Stu's crotch. *No way, she's got to be shittin' me. This can't be what I'm thinking; she doesn't have this kind of nerve, does she?* She gestured again, this time more adamantly. With his patience gone, and his head pounding for the second time this week, he was about to find out. He reached past the zipper and clutched the cup of tea and in a motion that second basemen would have been proud of, he flipped it over his shoulder into Jimmy's face, while Kate, with all the force she could muster, swung her closed fist into Stu's balls. The red backpack came around, hitting Jimmy in the head, and both Jimmy and the gun went flying. Stu fell to his knees, clutching his crotch, when the teapot hit him in the head. Both brothers were yelling and groaning, rolling on the floor as Kate and Nate went running out the front door as fast as they could.

"THE JEEP, GET IN THE JEEP!"

"Nate, the tires."

Looking across the lawn as they ran toward the Jeep they could see that the front and rear driver's side tires were flat.

"The scooters."

"I can't drive a scooter," Kate yelled as she ran.

"WHAT? Everybody can ride a scooter."

"Well not me."

"That doesn't make any sense. Can you ride a bike?"

Jimmy and Stu were out of the front door now and heading for them.

"This isn't the time for my screwed-up childhood."

"Okay, okay, get on the back of the black one."

Nate turned the key and started the scooter and floored the throttle all the way. He couldn't rip out of the driveway because it was a scooter, but he headed out onto the street in what some would call a little more than a rush.

Jimmy raced to the Jeep and stopped in his tracks, raised his gun at the backs of the departing riders. Stu's arm pushed his brother's arm back down; a group of six people were walking around the corner of the street. Jimmy tucked the gun in the back of his pants just as one of the people in the group waved to them.

"Excuse me, can you tell me if this road leads to the candle shop?"

"Yes, if you bear right at …" Jimmy slapped his brother on the side of the head and the direction-giving stopped. The group sped up past the house.

"Why are the tires flat, Stu?"

"Well, remember the time in Warrick when the same kinda thing happened? This time I thought they couldn't drive off." He tapped his temple with his finger.

"Well, you might have noticed that they have indeed driven off."

"Yeah, I should have taken the keys out of the scooters, huh?"

"You're a fucking genius, you know that, don't ya?"

"Thanks."

"Get on the back of the scooter."

If one large Italian fellow riding a purple scooter was not funny enough, two was a sight to behold. With the throttle pegged, they actually felt they were making up ground on them—that was, until an older gentleman out for a midday jog passed them.

Nate turned onto Center Street and headed up the hill to the south side of the island. He needed time. He decided to head for Southeast Light around the back side of the island.

With one hand on the scooter Jimmy hit send with the other. The voice picked up on the first ring. "What the fuck happened in there?"

"How the fuck do you know that?" Jimmy asked.

"Look, not now. He's probably heading toward the lighthouse, he goes there a lot. He'll think he's safe there. Follow Center Street to Middle Street, head west, it will lead you to the lighthouse. If he's not there, continue on that road and it will take you back to Old Harbor."

"Listen, if I don't find him, you better present yourself to me in town and have a solution to this wild-goose chase you have me on," Jimmy said and closed the phone. "This is bullshit," he said as he pulled over the scooter.

Stu got off the back and stood under the shade of an apple tree. "We need better transportation there, bro."

Across the street, up on a small hill, sat an old farmhouse where four cars were parked in the driveway. Jimmy smiled. "Let's just see how trusting these island people are."

Seconds later a car rolled backward down the driveway and the only sound was the tires on the dirt. It continued to roll backward onto the street until it was out of sight of the house. Jimmy turned the key, which had been left in the ignition, and sped off to the lighthouse.

Nate turned onto the scenic road that ran around the entire island. They traveled in silence to Southeast Light while their heartbeats told the story of the last few minutes. With the lighthouse in sight and Mohegan Bluffs to their right, Nate's pace slowed a bit. But when he heard the squeals of tires down around the corner behind them, his heart sank. Kate swung her head back and Nate was already on the throttle again. They pulled up to the dirt parking lot of Southeast Light and about forty people were milling about. He thought he saw Lou's sister, but he didn't have time to be upset; there were far more important things on his plate right now.

Sitting behind a folding table near the path that led to the lighthouse were two enterprising young kids, a brother and sister, selling lemonade for fifty cents. Quite a lofty price, but after walking or biking up to the lighthouse, most people didn't realize just how long of a way it was. Nate recognized the two kids from last year. He got off the scooter, looking behind him and taking the key out, and hurried over to the lemonade table.

"Nate, come on," Kate said, looking over her shoulder.

"Hey, guys." Nate got the kids' attention as he walked up to the table and reached into his pocket.

A car came around the bend and headed for the parking lot. They had been spotted.

Nate and Kate ran for the lighthouse. The boys from Providence were being stared at, but they didn't care—their eyes were on the prize. They ran past the lemonade stand and paid no attention to the siblings staring at a fifty-dollar bill.

Nate ran around the front of the lighthouse and down a trail heading to the cliffs.

"NATE!" Kate cried. "I'm not jumping."

He had his backpack open and pulled out his marine radio. "MIKE," he shouted, "MIKE, MIKE, answer me now."

After what seemed like a long time, Mike answered back, "Yes, Nate, what's up?"

"Listen to me, and do exactly what I say," he said as he and Kate continued toward the bluffs.

"Hey, Nate, Darren took off on his boat ..."

"Shut the fuck up and listen. Get *My Little Kitty* and go as fast as you can to Southeast Light, go now."

"Okay, are you in trouble?"

"MIKE—right now. GO!"

At the end of the path, built into the side of the bluff, was a set of wooden stairs, one hundred and fifty-five of them, that led down to a beach. The cliffs bent around the small beach, creating no access to them other than the water or back up the stairs. Kate didn't need an explanation. They both started their way down the steps to the dead end.

Stu and Jimmy made their way to the front side of the lighthouse, weaving around the tourists, trying not to look like two guys looking to hurt someone very bad. Around the front they couldn't see where Nate and the girl had gone. Then they saw a guy coming up from the cliff face, and the brothers ran over to the spot. Looking down the stairs, they saw their two little friends about three quarters of the way down. They both looked at each other and sighed.

"Here they come," Kate said, looking back.

Nate looked back to confirm. "Come on, Mike, come on."

They got to the bottom of the stairs. People were body-surfing and frolicking about. Just living a normal, uneventful life without gold and bad guys. Nate wished he were so lucky. It was obvious that it was going to take the boys a little longer than they had to reach the beach. Nate looked back again, then out to the ocean.

"Come on, damn it."

The tone had Kate worried; she didn't think they were going to get out of this.

"We can't wait," Nate said. "Come on, let's go." He took her arm and started wading out into the sea.

"What are we doing, Nate?"

"Trust me, let's go." They were about up to their necks in the water, and Nate had his backpack over his head, when the boys finally made it onto the beach.

"Where are they going?" Stu looked around.

Jimmy walked to the water's edge and shouted, "Just get back here, will you?" He laughed. "Where do you think you're going?"

Just then, around the corner of the bluff, a jet ski came bearing down on Nate and Kate, doing about seventy miles an hour. At first Jimmy thought it was going to hit them, but then it slowed down and the boy riding it helped the two onto the back of the ski. It spun on a dime, and with a rooster tail of water shooting fifteen feet in the air, headed back from where it came. The name painted on the side of the ski read *My Little Kitty*. As it started to disappear, Nate held up a finger, one that Jimmy knew very well.

"I'm going to have him eat that finger when this is through."

The boys stood in front of the stairs leading back up and sighed, a bigger one than the one they'd given on their descent—gravity, after all, was not going to be their friend on the way up. After several rest stops on the way, they reached the top and sat there for a moment, catching their breath. They finally made it back to the car and got in. Exhausted and drenched in sweat, they were still too short of breath to speak, but the expression on Jimmy's face said it all. He reached for the ignition and stopped.

"Stu, give me the key."

"I don't have it, you drove."

"Yes, I know I drove, but the key is gone."

"Jimmy I swear to God I didn't take it."

"Then where did it go?"

The two kids poured another happy customer a drink of lemonade, the person handed them fifty cents, and they put it in their money box right next to a set of keys from a car. The fifty dollars they got for playing this prank on Nate's friends would not be disclosed to their parents at the end of this day.

Jimmy sat there, his blood pressure at critical mass. Someone leaned into his window.

"Excuse me, did you know you have two flat tires?"

He looked over to his brother.

"Hey, it wasn't me this time, I swear."

The jet ski pulled into Old Harbor and up to the *Legacy*. Nate and Kate got on board and he threw his backpack into the cabin.

"How long ago did Darren leave?"

"I think he came right from your house, jumped on his boat, and took off."

"Look, tell Rebecca what just happened, and tell her I'll call her as soon as I can. Tell her to trust me and not to call the police. Go."

"What are you going to do?" Mike asked.

"I'm going after Darren."

Mike stared at Nate for a moment, then took off on the ski.

"When the friggin' hell were you going to tell me your bloody plan back there?" Kate yelled at Nate. Both of them were running out of patience.

"What plan? I don't have a plan. I'm making this shit up as we go."

"OHH, that makes me feel safe."

"How about you, with the hit-him-in-the-nuts plan back at the house?"

"Well it worked, didn't it?"

"Worked? Worked? Johnny Cash back there had a gun pointed at us."

Nate was starting the engine and turning on the electronics.

"Look, this is way out of control," he told her.

"Whoa there, fish boy, I'm coming with you, you're not leaving me here, they're looking for me, too."

"I KNOW!" He calmed himself down a bit, and repeated: "I know. I just don't want you to get hurt."

"I don't want to get hurt either."

"What about me?" Nate asked.

"Yeah, yeah, yeah, you, too."

"Ooh, you're giving me that warm and fuzzy feeling inside," Nate complained.

Kate laughed. "All right there, fish boy, let's go find Darren."

He pulled the boat out of his slip and headed out of the harbor. The closest harbor was to the north, Point Judith, about eleven miles. He'll try there first, Nate thought. But there was a chance he'd headed for Long Island, which was to the south. *Sometimes you have to play a hunch and see where it will take you, there, sunshine.*

I hope you're right, there, Lou.

Kate found some of the clothes Nate kept on the boat and changed into them, letting her wet clothes dry in the sun.

They cruised along, heading north. Kate took the wheel as Nate also changed into dry clothes. He started to arrange his clothes on the deck chairs to dry. They were about five miles north of the island. The *Legacy* was cruising about seventeen knots. He stared out to his port and saw a boat drifting as they shot by.

You're shittin' me.

He stood up straight and looked around, shocked. It was Darren; his boat appeared to be dead in the water. Rage reared its ugly head again. The man he was looking for was simply sitting there working on his engine. *You got to love hunches.*

"Turn the boat around."

"What?"

"The boat, turn it."

"Why?"

Nate grabbed the wheel and started turning it hard to his left. "Aim for that boat, and when I tell you, pull the throttle back."

The *Legacy* was closing in on Darren's boat. But he just sat there working on his engine, unaware of his approaching appointment with Nate. He got up and headed for the cockpit to try the engine one more time, and as he walked to the front of his boat, he noticed the *Legacy* heading right for him. Darren just managed a short little scream of surprise, more defensive than scared.

"THROTTLE BACK NOW!" Nate screamed as Kate slammed the throttle back, and he jumped off the side of his boat. All Kate could register of the image of Nate flying through the air was that of a flying squirrel, which she'd seen on *Animal Planet* once. Nate landed on Darren hard; they both slid to the port side of the boat. Nate was on top of him and had him by the shirt. He reared back to hit him with all he could muster, but Darren was not going down that easy, he brought his knee up into Nate's crotch. "AHHHHH." Nate lowered his arm, lowered it way down to his groin. Darren's fist got Nate on the side of the head—*third time's a charm, sunshine.*

"For the love of God, will everybody stop hitting me in the friggin' head?"

Darren managed to get out from under him and up on his feet. "Hold it right there, Nate, I can explain everything."

"It was you all along, you son of a bitch." Nate lunged for him and they both slammed down on the wet deck again. After enough rolling around on the deck, back and forth and back and forth, they both managed to get up.

"I had nothing to do with Lou's death, nothing."

"Then why are you running?"

"Look, my boat's dead. You know why—take a look, go ahead, look. Sand in the fuel filter. Sound familiar? Someone did the same thing to Lou's boat, too, right? So explain it to me, please," spreading his hands, "all of this."

"Why are you running?"

"Jesus, Nate."

"WHY ARE YOU RUNNING?"

"Man … it's complicated."

Nate grabbed Darren again, but Darren pushed him back about two feet.

"ENOUGH!" Darren's voice was starting to shake. "It's my father, I think he got Lou killed, okay? How's that one for you? Is that what you want to hear?"

"What?"

Darren bowed his head and rubbed the back of his neck. "Look, my father's in jail for being a bookie," he said, his voice cracking. "The people he dealt with are probably the two visitors that are following you. When I started visiting my father in prison, I started to get friendly with a female officer who worked behind the desk where you sign in, but who am I kidding, right? Anyways, one time about a year ago, I come in and she says, 'Hey, your dad had a visitor yesterday.' I'm shocked because there isn't anybody who would visit him except me or some of his old colleagues, and I didn't want that. She shows me the sign-in book from that day and it says Gauthier, Lou went to see my father. I thought, whatever, maybe it's because of him saving his life, shit like that. Five days ago he visited him again, and this time I asked my father about it—not an easy thing to do. But he was behind the glass and couldn't hit me. Anyway, he just smiled and said they were doing business and it was none of mine. But one of my father's major malfunctions is that he can't keep his mouth shut. So after watching him sit there unable to contain his smile, I ask him what's up and he says that if all goes well, I should be getting some money, enough to get me out of debt. None of this made any sense to me till you put that gold bar on the table, then it hit me: Lou went to my father to try to find someone to convert it to cash for him. My father has people he knows all over Rhode Island, people with means. This state is the jewelry capital of the world, after all, and there are all types here. Unfortunately, the mob is one of them."

"You think your father double-crossed Lou?"

"I don't see how he would do something like that. But I don't have a high opinion of him, so ... I need to find out."

Nate stood there staring at Darren, his wheels turning, to trust or not to trust.

"So here we are, Nate. Fifteen years later, just you and me, no Dave to muck things up between us. What do you want to do about this?"

"I don't know why you didn't just tell me back at my house."

"Telling a group of people you think your dad had Lou killed is something I'm not ready to do."

"Well then, we both need some answers. You don't seem to have a boat, so it looks like we're traveling companions for now."

Darren looked out to the horizon.

"This is the second time you didn't trust me and you were wrong." He looked back to Nate. "It ends here."

Nate nodded his head in agreement.

He'd forgotten all about Kate and spun around to look for her, hoping she hadn't drifted too far. Lo and behold, there was his boat, tied perfectly to Darren's, with Kate standing there and taking it all in.

"You guys love speeches, don't cha?" Kate said.

"How do you know how to do all of this?" Nate asked.

Kate smiled.

"You have no idea how turned on I am right now. You're a very mysterious woman."

"You men are so easy."

Looking at the lines perfectly cleated, he said, "Yes we are."

They left Darren's boat, much to the dismay of its owner, and anchored five miles outside of Point Judith harbor. They agreed—that is, Nate told him and Darren just nodded his head in bewildered agreement—to call a towboat company. Most owners had tow insurance, which was cheap money compared to the cost of the tow. Darren, however, did not have this insurance, or any other kind for that matter. So he just stood at the stern of the *Legacy* watching his boat grow smaller, like a child leaving the nest, never knowing when he would see her again.

Standing beside the stolen car, the Providence boys were at a loss about what to do next. It seemed that, in the ruckus, Jimmy had lost his cell phone. Just thinking of climbing those stairs again had his pulse quickening. *Fuck the phone, fuck all of this shit.*

They started walking down the street that led to Old Harbor, neither saying a word to the other. An old Chevy Blazer pulled up alongside them, *New Shoreham Harbor Master* stenciled in black letters on the beat-up door. "It looks like you guys could use a lift," the driver said.

"What gives you that idea?" Jimmy asked.

"Your shoes. Get in."

The one o'clock ferry left with half its capacity, because most people left on the last ferry of the day, around eight in the evening. But our special visitors were in a hurry. And let's get one thing perfectly straight, they were not leaving with their tails between their legs, but with a newfound vengeance. With their new toy in their possession, they had hope. The color screen of the handheld GPS was a sight to behold; this little baby didn't show where Jimmy and Stu's longitude and latitude was, but exactly that of Nate, more precisely that of the *Legacy*. With each update of the three-inch screen, it was starting to look like the golden boy was heading right to Jimmy and Stu's playground, the grand city of Providence, Rhode Island.

Darren took his cell phone out and made a quick call to the island to cancel his charters for the next few days, which totaled one. Nate turned to him and shrugged.

"Still don't own a cell phone, huh?" Darren asked.

"Well, I never really saw the need, till about three days ago."

Darren handed him his cell phone.

Nate dialed the number and stared at the phone.

"Hit the green button," Darren explained.

"Block Island visitor's booth, Rebecca speaking."

"It's me."

"Jesus, Nate, where the hell are you?" Rebecca yelled "I saw you take off on the *Legacy* a while ago."

"Mike hasn't come by and told you what's going on?"

"If he did, why would I ask you where you are? What the hell are you doing? Is Kate with you? What happened at the lighthouse?"

"You know, if you stop asking me questions, I'll explain." Silence engulfed the other end of the phone. He explained, with as little detail as possible so as not to upset her any more, about the run to the lighthouse and Mike's role in their escape, and about finding Darren and their destination of Providence to have a sit-down with Darren's father.

"If Darren's father is involved, then why wouldn't it involve Darren?"

"Yeah, I'm still working that part out," Nate said.

"He's standing right there, isn't he?"

"Yes."

"How sure are you about trusting him?"

"About fifty percent."

"Nate, this is scaring the hell out of me. Where do you think those guys are now?"

"I don't know. Do me a favor, get Jack and Josh to stay with you till we find out where they are, okay?

"Yeah, I'll get them right now. What about Mike?"

"I'm sure he's fine, just distracted, that's all."

"Yeah, I'll look into that also."

"I'm sure you will. Just go easy on him. I'll call you after we find out about Darren's father."

"Nate …"

"I will, I promise."

It took Rebecca all of fifteen minutes to get the word out to Jack and Josh, and within minutes of that they were in the booth listening to her story of Nate and Kate's adventure. When she was done with her story, a young, red-haired girl was at the front window.

"Excuse me, Rebecca?"

She turned to the young summer worker who worked at the ferry ticket booth across the parking lot.

"Yes, Sara?"

"Those gentlemen you described to me earlier? They just left on the ferry."

Rebecca nodded and waved her off, which the redhead heeded in a hurry; no need to feel the Queen's wrath.

Jack walked to the window and stared out to the departing ferry. "A coincidence?"

"My God, I hope so," Josh answered.

CHAPTER 14: BOXING THE COMPASS

Darren was at the wheel of the *Legacy* as they cruised under the Jamestown Bridge. Soon they would pass Prudence Island and enter the Providence River, which would take them to the heart of the city. With an hour to try and relax, Nate took a seat next to Kate, who was back in her dry clothes and trying to take a quick nap. He woke her as he took the seat next to her.

"Sorry."

"Just recharging," Kate explained.

"Sorry about all this," he said, taking a book from his backpack and opening it.

"Don't be, this is quite the time here in the States. What are you looking at?"

"Lou's family recipe book."

"What is it, exactly?"

"Well, it's latitudes and longitudes of places around the island that were discovered by my father and Lou, when they worked for the Army Corps of Engineers." He took another book out of the backpack, Lou's family photo album, and turned the pages till he came across a picture of Lou and Nate's father crouched down at the stern of a boat, holding between them a torpedo-looking thing.

"Is that what I think it is?"

"Well, if you think it's a side-scanning sonar array running at two hundred megahertz, shooting back images of the bottom of the seafloor and making it possible to navigate these waters—then yes, it is what you think it is."

"Exactly. I mean, some fools would think it's a bomb or something."

He pulled out a small chart from his pack. "This is a nautical chart of Block Island. All these depths and rocks and sandbars were made back in the forties, with mostly local knowledge. The Army Corps of Engineers actually took soundings with a hand line and weight to find some of the depths. With a large naval base in Newport and private marine electronics manufacturers in the area, there was and is a lot of testing in this area. Back in the early eighties, the Navy was experimenting with a new type of sonar that could give you an image of the seafloor. My dad did a lot of diving for the Navy, and since he was an expert in the local waters, they brought their sonar array to him and hired him to test it and get a better representation of the waters around the island. Of course my dad brought Lou in, and Lou being a self-taught engineer, he actually fixed some of the glitches with it."

Looking back over his shoulder to see if Darren was listening, he turned back and continued in a lower voice.

"When they started to find images of things down there that weren't on the charts, they decided to dive on them and see what they were. They were mostly just rocks piled up from the glacier era, but with most piles or structures, there's usually a lot of fish, so they made a decision that no one knows except for me. If the area they found was deep enough and out of the way of the bigger vessels, and if it posed no obstruction to boats traveling around the island, then Lou wrote it in this book and it became one of their secret fishing spots. But then they started to find some unexploded bombs, and then shipwrecks. They found a 1940s tugboat and a crane and a barge that was lost during a hurricane fifty years earlier. They corrected the charts and reported the ones that were important and the rock piles and reefs …" He held up his book. "They became the best fishermen on the island and even got paid for the work by the Navy."

"Do you think that wreck the gold is from is one they found?"

"It has to be, they found a shit-load of things. Most of it they turned in, but there are over a hundred sonar hits in this book, it took them years to dive on them. But my father never mentioned a wreck. My bet is they found it and never got around to diving on it, so maybe Lou dove it by himself and made the discovery."

"And never told your father or you."

"Well maybe he found it after my father died."

Nate got lost in his thoughts, he started to look through the book at the latitude and longitude numbers, but none seem to match the one he'd memorized of the wreck. The names of the locations they'd discovered were written beside the numbers. Nothing, of course, named the "Compass Rose." There were reefs and rocks and notes on where to fish, all printed out in Lou's neat, block-like writing. He turned another page, and drawn on the entire page, beautifully rendered, was a compass rose. The kind from when mapmaking was an art. He'd even used colored pencils to add colors to bring the entire drawing to life. This secret book was a part of Lou, so much so that Nate had never been given the chance to look at it. The drawing took his breath away.

"But he hid the book," Kate said. "Why?"

"Yeah, that's got me puzzled. The book must have something to do with all of this somehow. But is the reason he hid the book because of the gold? Or is the answer to his letter in this book?"

"What if it's one and the same?"

"Then we're in shit up to our necks."

"You said back in your kitchen that the letter was something you had knowledge of, that he did things like that all the time?"

"Yeah … He would teach me something by sending me on a scavenger hunt, a quest or a test, to show my readiness for what I was asking for. It usually involved me going to a library or a museum to find the answer. And if I proved myself, passed his test, then I would get the reward, which was a chance to go on a difficult dive or an offshore fishing trip with him and my dad. He would never just show me how to do something or give me an answer simply, I had to earn it. To be honest, it wore me down as I got older, these games of his, and now I feel like shit, now that he's gone."

"Well, you have his letter. Give it one more go around, make him proud. Just don't die in the process."

Nate laughed. "Is that a joke? You're one funny girl, you know that?"

"That's what they tell me."

"Who, your ex-boyfriends?"

Kate closed her eyes and turned her face up to the sun. "Yeah ..."

He stared back down to the compass rose. In small-case letters, at the bottom of the page, Lou had written, *four from the key ...*

...

"Don't just lie there getting a tan, there's work to be done," Lou shouted at a young Nate.

"Yes, sir."

"Your father will be up soon and we need to be ready to help him with his gear. You always have to be ready."

"Yes, sir."

Lou looked down at his young pupil. "What direction is the wind there, young Nathaniel?"

Nate whipped his head to the left and then the right, he looked up to the sun and turned back to Lou. "South."

"Actually southwest, but good. How many wind directions are there?"

"Four," Nate said proudly.

"Not even close, get a chart."

Nate grabbed the chart spread out on the dash of Lou's boat.

"Where's the compass rose?"

Nate knew this one. He pointed down to the four-pointed star in the bottom right of the chart.

"Now find me the wind rose."

Nate grimaced. *What the heck is the wind rose?*

"It's the same thing," Lou said.

"The compass rose is a wind rose?"

"It evolved into that from the 1300s. Originally it was used to tell the directions of the winds. Take a look at the compass on the dash there, and try to figure out all the directions of the winds. I'll give you a hint: there are thirty-two of them."

Nate turned his attention to the compass. Half an hour later bubbles appeared in the water on the port side of the boat. Nate's father was at the surface and Lou and Nate started taking his gear from him. He climbed into the boat and looked at both of them and smiled.

"What you find?"

"A rock pile about forty feet stacked like a little stone wall—another present from our glaciers."

"Turn it in?"

"Yeah, nice fish, some lobster, but nothing to get excited about."

Lou opened his leather-bound book and wrote.

"Hey, Dad, when can I start diving?"

"You ask me that every time we go out. Do you think I forget? Or are you just trying to wear me down?" Nate's dad was smiling again.

"Whatever will work, I guess," his son smiled back.

"You're about ready."

"Wait just a minute," Lou said, finishing his writing and looking up. "Like any good sailor worth his lot, you have to show that you have proved yourself."

"How do you suppose he does that, Lou?"

"Well, I asked him to name me all thirty-two wind directions."

"Boxing the compass. A great idea. Being able to name all thirty-two points would be asked of any sailor at any time, and it was called 'boxing the compass.' This picture down there in the corner of the chart has lost its meaning to most of us modern-day mariners, but the compass and the wind was all they had back in the first exploration of these waters. They had some idea of latitude, sure, but not longitude, that didn't happen till the mid-1700s, and explorers like Gosnold and Cook had just their understanding of the winds and what direction they were heading. The compass rose was their lifeline, their hope to riches."

"Why did they call it rose?"

"Well, you always show north, which early on was a point, like a spearhead. Cartographers all made their own variations of it, but it was the Portuguese who used the rose, around the time of Columbus. And it was known from that day as the fleur-de-lys."

"Your dad loves that history stuff, but the end result is that you have to prove yourself."

"Lou here, my son, believes in action and results, not to be burdened with names and dates. I believe in history, and what it teaches us is not just about ourselves but about the knowledge of others and how their knowledge will help us today understand and make our way better."

"And get us rich?" Lou asked.

"That's a whole different ballgame, Louis."

"I will learn to box the compass, and then you will teach me to dive."

"Agreed." Nate's father smiled that smile, which would burn in Nate's memory all his life.

…

The bow of the *Legacy* crashed back down into the water, waking the sleeping couple. They both got up and headed to the cockpit.

"Sorry, getting a lot of boat traffic now we're up the river," Darren said.

The port of Providence was a bustling commercial zone, an eyesore to some, or what the state liked to call a "working waterfront." The remnants of piers and wharfs sprang up along the north side of the river, just the pilings left now to show that there was once a vast area of shipping that extended all across the port, when all the city had to move its wares around the world were ships. Freighters and oil tankers now lined the south side. Farther down into the heart of Providence lay a small marina called North Pier Marina, the *Legacy's* destination, where Nate had once picked up some well-paying clients—friends of his father, if his memory served him right. The marina lay upriver a mile past the working waterfront, past the I-95, in an area where you could spit from one side of the Providence River to the other.

Nate pulled the *Legacy* into the slip assigned to them by the dock master. Once again, after names were exchanged, the dock master remembered Nate's father and the boat.

"Let's just make up a list with people you don't know," Darren told him.

"Fishing will save your soul," Nate answered.

Up from the dock to the parking lot was always an adjustment after cruising on a boat for well over two hours. It was ever so slight, but you could sense your legs thanking you for solid ground.

Darren pulled out his cell phone and walked off alone. A few minutes later he walked back. "Visiting hours isn't for another two hours."

CHAPTER 15: THE BIG HOUSE

"What do we do now?" Darren asked.

"How 'bout some food?" Kate asked.

"Yeah," Nate answered, half in the conversation. He opened up the front pocket of his backpack and started to dig for something.

"Nate?" Kate questioned.

"Yeah, umm, I know this guy, he chartered me the last couple of years, rents a house on the island. I think he owns a company here." Nate pulled out a stack of business cards held with elastic and started to thumb through it.

"Is it a restaurant?" Kate asked.

"Here it is. Costa Machinery. Bob Costa, president."

"Excellent," Kate said sarcastically.

"Bob owns a jewelry machine company, for supplying manufacturers with the things that make the things for some form of jewelry."

"What are you talking about?" Darren asked.

"Okay I'm not sure what he does, but the point is we need to find out who Lou might have contacted if he wanted to sell the gold. I've had conversations with this guy about scuba diving, and he joked, as he always does, that if I ever discovered gold to give him a call and he could take care of it for me, wink, wink."

"Is he with your mob?" Kate asked.

"No, at least I don't think so, just a guy in the gold business."

"You think my father knows him?"

"Well, I'm just thinking it might be a good place to start for finding out who could do this type of transaction. All we need is a name, plus I'm curious if you could actually do something like selling gold on the black market."

"I think you can do just about anything you want in this city," Darren stated.

"What could it hurt?" Kate replied.

"I'm thinking us," Darren said. "Or at least me."

A quick phone call and a fifteen-minute cab ride and the three of them were standing outside Costa Machinery. They walked into the side door and right onto the warehouse floor. Bulky green machines in varying sizes were arranged in the large open space. Some were actually working and extruding gold, which looked like it could be used for necklaces. Bob came down the stairs from an office up above the floor and greeted Nate with a hug.

"You son of a bitch, you fish-catching son of a bitch," he said, hugging him again.

"Bob, how are you?"

"I'm great, man. I know I've told you if you were in town … but I never thought you'd come."

"Yeah, well, I have to confess, I have an ulterior motive here."

"Strip clubs?" Bob asked.

Nate laughed. "No."

Kate faked a little cough behind Nate.

"Oh … Let me introduce you to a couple of acquaintances. This is Darren and Kate."

Bob shook their hands.

Kate turned to Darren. "Acquaintances?" she said as Darren shrugged.

"What's up, then, that made you leave that beautiful island if not strip clubs?"

"Do you remember discussing that if I ever went diving and found gold -?"

"Jesus Christ, you found gold?" Bob got very serious. Nate just stared at him, not wanting to speak it out loud, just for sheer effect. Bob motioned for them to follow him. They headed up the stairs on the far wall that led to his office. Entering the room outside his office where his secretary sat, he turned to her and told her to hold his calls. The door closed behind the four of them. His office, which had a view of the highway boasted several promotional posters of local strippers, all of them signed by the girls.

Bob sat behind his desk while Kate and Nate took two chairs in front and Darren sat on a couch toward the back of the office. Looking at the posters, Darren started to think that maybe the couch was a bad idea; he took his hands off the cushions and wiped them on his pants.

"Tell me you didn't find gold," Bob asked.

"Let's say I did discover some gold. Would it be possible to sell it outside the ..."

"Prying eyes of those who wish to diminish us of proper returns?"

"Yeah," Nate told him.

"Like I told you before, absolutely, I'll make a phone call and"— he snapped his fingers—"presto."

"Okay, look, Bob, I need to know who you would call."

"Nate, what's going on here? You wearing a wire? Because I can't tell you that." Bob leaned over his desk very serious. "What the fuck is going on here?"

Easy there, sunshine.

Nate opened his backpack and pulled out the Corona beach towel, unwrapped the bar and dropped it with a thud on Bob's desk. The look on his face gave Nate the impression that he'd been full of shit about that *if you ever find gold* story. He looked up at Nate and Kate.

"Tell me everything you know about this," he asked in the most serious tone he could muster. Nate cautiously explained that while diving he and he alone had discovered a wreck of unknown origin which contained only this one bar of gold.

Bob was sitting there the whole time turning the gold over in his hands.

"So you found this bar on a very old wreck?"

"Yes."

"Did you clean it?"

"Huh?"

"This bar has been cleaned. And whoever did it did a real professional job of it."

"So this bar hasn't been sitting down there long before I found it?"

"Absolutely not. I'm confused, Nate. If you found this, it couldn't have been there from the beginning. It was put there."

He showed all his cards then, and explained the death of Lou and the visitors chasing him.

Bob just leaned back into his chair and stared at the three of them, waiting or reading them. He slowly pulled open his side desk drawer and all three sat up a little straighter. He pulled out the biggest magnifying glass they had ever seen and started looking over the bar. He turned it over to the back and with the glass stared long and hard. He put the glass down and slumped back into his chair again.

"Spanish, probably around the mid-1800s."

"You can tell, just from looking at it?" Darren said sarcastically.

"It's how I make a living. Plus there is a date, and a Spanish symbol imprinted on the bottom."

All three said in unison, "What?"

He gestured for them to come over and picked up the glass and held it for them. Using his knife as a pointer, he said, "You have three things, first a date, 1860, then you have this Spanish cross symbol, and you have this."

Nate leaned in closer. "It's a whale, an outline of a whale."

"It's so tiny," Kate said.

"Back in the day, they would imprint the bar with a symbol, almost like a crest, to show ownership. This whale meant something to someone. At the least, the origin and destination, and more importantly the ownership."

The three stood there behind Bob's desk, staring at the bar.

"Nate, you're into some really fucking serious shit here," Bob said.

Nate explained their true destination in Providence. Bob simply nodded like he heard this story all the time.

"Now let me ask you, these guys that came after you, was one dressed in black and the other looked like he just walked off a construction site?"

All three again said, "Yes."

"Wow, you guys are like a freakin' chorus." Bob leaned back in his chair. "Look, the way I see it, you have a very large problem: you have Jimmy and Stu Ricci after you, and that is something that will not end well."

"Stu? What kind of a mob name is Stu?" Darren asked.

"So they are the mob?" Nate asked.

"That would give them too much credit. Let's say they are thugs with no conscience whatsoever when in pursuit of riches. These two are part of a local group of guys, some connected to organized crime. Not enough to have their backing, but enough to give them great latitude in pursuing an income by whatever means available. So you think somebody on your island is in on this also?"

"Yeah," Nate said. "Any idea who Lou could have contacted?"

"Look, Nate, there are about five people capable of doing this type of transaction in the area. Four of them would need me, the other is a close friend. So if the person you are going to see contacted them, I would know. Anybody else means a shit-load of trouble."

"What can we do about these Jimmy and Stu characters after us?" Nate asked.

Kate turned to Darren. "You know you're right, Stu doesn't roll off the tongue."

Bob said, "The way I see it, you have three options. Give them the gold and hope they say thank you and forget the whole thing. Two, if there is more gold, find it and use some of it to cut a deal with them. Do they know that there is actually gold?"

"They did have us at gunpoint demanding the gold bar," Nate said. "But I don't even know how they are involved, for Christ's sake. They didn't show up till after Lou's death."

"I'm afraid to ask what our third option is," Darren said.

"Run for your fucking life. Sooner or later they'll get bored looking for you and move on. But you would have to look over your shoulder for a while."

"I'm not running," Nate declared.

"That's your call. If you want, I'll give you …" Bob picked up the bar and placed it on a digital scale on the shelf behind him. "A hundred thousand, right now."

"Bullshit, it's worth more than that," Darren stated.

"You're right about that, so take it to a bank, and they'll have some forms for you to fill out—you know, for tax purposes. Oh yeah, somebody probably will check with some insurance agencies, like Lourdes of London, who might have paid off on this back in 1860."

"I'm sure it's a reasonable offer, but it's not about the money," Nate said.

"No, I wouldn't think so, at least not with you, Nate. Look, this bar is not just worth the raw gold. It's old and has history. Think of it as a work of art: it's not just worth the paint but the people involved with its story. The intrinsic value is double, maybe triple the raw gold price. Let me take a small sample and a scan of the writing and make some calls, see if I can find out anything. I'll call you with whatever answers I come up with. But keep this in mind, I can't get involved with the Ricci brothers. It took my family decades to build this balance with the real people that run this city. If I get the wrong people looking hard at me, I'm done. I'm sorry."

Darren looked at his watch. "It's just about that time."

"Can I borrow your phone to call a cab?" Nate asked.

"I have a few errands around town; I'll take you where you need to go."

I'm sure you do, Darren thought to himself as he had one final look at the posters.

Standing in the rich early afternoon sun in the middle of the parking lot of MCM Machinery, Kate turned to the boys.

"Hey listen, guys, not that you fine young gentlemen aren't showing me a wonderful time in your country, but I wonder if you mind if I skipped your correctional facilities?"

"Ah, come on, there should be a lot of those American men you came here for," Nate told her.

"I'm not sure I even want the ones I'm with."

"Now you're just being mean," Nate said. "Nobody likes a foreign smart-ass."

Darren turned to Kate and said, "I do."

"And did you think about your backpack there, fish boy? Do you want someone checking that?"

"Jesus, I've been carrying it around so much I didn't really think it through."

"I'll go back to the boat and you do what you need to do."

"Take her straight to the North Pier Marina. No strip clubs," Nate said, giving Bob his most stern voice.

"Man, you're no fun."

Bob got into his SUV and pulled up to the three. Darren leaned in to Kate. "I stashed a gun under the towels on Nate's shelf."

"My God, you think I'm in that much danger?"

"I don't know about Nate, but I have no idea what is going to happen next, so you better be prepared for all possibilities."

"Great, just great," Kate said to nobody in particular.

Before Bob drove off, he leaned out the window and said, "Nate, I need you to understand that these guys are for real—do not take them lightly. And some food for thought here, I've been involved in this business since childhood, have read and heard a lot of stories of recovered treasure, and I have never heard of anybody finding just one piece of gold before. Find the rest and buy your way out of this. That may be your only option."

Nate nodded and tapped the side of the truck as Bob and Kate drove away.

The cab picked up the boys five minutes later for their twenty-minute ride to the big house. Given the traffic on any given day in Providence and surrounding towns like Warwick and Cranston, this timeframe could vary widely.

"Can you trust Bob?" Darren asked as the cab weaved through the late-afternoon traffic.

"I'm not sure who to trust anymore. But I'll tell you one thing, I have never met anybody like her before, she has no problem handling herself. If things go bad, it's Bob that you need to worry about."

As the cab approached the Rhode Island House of Corrections, with its old granite façade, one could entertain the thought that the use of the word "house" didn't really fit a prison looking like this one; it would more aptly be named a small industrial complex of corrections.

After getting searched and worked over with a wide assortment of metal detectors, they approached the desk to sign in. Behind the desk sat a very pretty young woman, looking good in a dark blue polyester blend, which was no small task. Nate was shocked just how much this young lady looked like Rebecca. Darren walked right up to her and the smile on both their faces gave away the fact that this was the girl he'd been talking about. Nate laughed to himself, thinking about telling Rebecca of Darren liking a girl who could pass for her sister. Nate hung back to give Casanova some space. They both laughed at something that probably only they found funny, leaning in close to each other over the counter and inviting stares from the woman's coworkers. Darren finally turned to Nate to introduce him. *Even more striking up close. Way to go, Darren. It can't be easy for her to meet guys in here. After all, the visitors she meets are all here to see a family member. 'I want you to meet my dad, the four-time mass murderer.'* Nate caught himself laughing at his thought.

They were led down a corridor to a room with benches lined up in rows.

"I was expecting the glass and the phone thing," Nate said.

"Well it's our lucky day. Once a month he gets to meet family in person—go figure."

Nate's recollection of Darren's father was that he was hard to live with, that there were beatings he believed went on, though kids really never dove into that kind of talk. He was the type of guy who was too busy trying to get off the island and make it rich to care about the proper upbringing of a son. But when all was said and done, Darren was not his father, and that was a compliment. Lou told Nate that Darren's father had the ability, if he was in the right state of mind, to catch fish with the best of them. Nate remembered the old man saying that some people had the natural ability to find and catch fish, to smell them out, anticipate when and where. Lou had that power, and Nate had it to an extent. The pure talent that Darren's father possessed would get him by at times, but mostly it was lost on his passion for stupidity. So when all Darren's father's get-rich schemes or numbers-running failed, he came back to the island, tried to grab some fishing charters, and held it together for him and Darren a little longer. That ended a year ago, when he was pinched for running numbers.

Seeing him sitting, still defiant to this day, in his prison garb, Nate thought that he should be wearing a jumpsuit with the word "Dysfunctional" stenciled on the back instead of "ACI," just to cut to the chase and not waste everybody's time.

There were no hugs, no pats on the back the way fathers and sons do—no, not here—just the head-nods and *take your seat, thank you very much.*

"Wow ... West."

"Yes, sir."

Darren's father flicked his hand in that *whatever* gesture. Nate's blood pressure went quickly to simmer.

"You bring me cigarettes?"

"Well no, you don't even smoke," Darren stated warily.

"Yes, I know that, but like I told you before, others do."

"It's not that kind of visit."

"Then what kind of visit is it?"

"It's the kind to tell you Lou Gauthier is dead." Darren let this sink in for just a moment. He always treated conversations with his father as a boxing match and that was his right jab. Then bam with the left: "Nate believes he was murdered."

Not even a flinch. What a poker face, Nate thought. Then he noticed that Darren's father's eyes were welling up, not actual tears running down the cheeks, but close. He sat there not saying a word or moving a muscle. Darren wanted to start pressing him about Lou's visits, but he knew how to play him, dance around the ring a bit more, and tire him out. A few more uncomfortable minutes passed.

"How ... how did it happen?"

"It looks like he was jumped on his boat and beaten. Then somebody rigged the boat to sink," Darren said.

"Jesus Christ, it's the last thing I'd expect for Lou. He was a tough old man. I'm sure it's hard for you," he said, looking slightly at Nate. "But life is hard." He sniffed and shook his head. "You know, he came to visit me a couple of times."

"Well, that's the other reason we're here," Nate took a turn.

"Are you telling me you know he visited me? Did the old man tell you that?"

Nate shook his head no.

He turned to his son, eyes wide, head tilted.

"What?" Darren asked.

"It was business that didn't concern him, it was about our family. You had no right."

"I don't think you should lecture me on rights." Darren let this last statement linger.

All in, there, sunshine ... all in.

"We know about the gold," Nate threw in.

"Oh you do, do ya?"

"I have it. But the problem we are facing is that right now two guys, who we believe are tied to the mob from Providence, are after us. They came close to getting us on the island. Somebody sent these two goons to the island looking for the gold and they knew I had it."

Darren's father jumped up, his face red with anger—zero to pissed in 1.5 seconds. A guard came over. Darren's father put up his hand and lowered his head. The guard stood there for a moment and slowly walked back to the door and stared at them.

He tried to contain his anger. "And you think I sent them there? You think I would send somebody to hurt you and take Lou's gold? Is that what you're fucking telling me, you spoiled piece of shit?"

Nate just stared at him, wanting to reach over and grab him by the neck. *Easy, sunshine.*

"Dad, Jesus, calm down. We are trying to figure out what the fuck is going on."

"I know my reputation is shit on the island, but murder? Jesus."

"I'm sorry, Dad. Just tell us what you know, help us find who did this."

This was the first time Nate had heard Darren call his father "dad." *Darren's playing him,* he thought, *and playing him well.* If Nate had to bet that gold bar on whether or not Darren's father was directly connected to the visitors, he would bet not, but Nate had never been good at poker.

Darren's father sat back down and stared at the table. He nodded his head back and forth and looked directly at Nate.

"The business I had with the old man never got off the ground. I'll tell you what I know about it under one condition."

"Conditions," Nate said. "We are making conditions. A man is dead."

"It's just one little condition."

"Always playing the angle, huh?"

"Damn straight."

"Okay, what do you want?"

"Lou came to me with a proposition, to turn him onto someone who could cash in some gold for him for a fair price, and he would give Darren here five thousand dollars. Now Lou and I go way back, and I owe him more than I could repay. But it was his idea for the money, not mine—I mean, shit … I won't turn nuthin' down like that. Easy money, you can't beat that. Now you're sitting there with your smug little pretty-boy, smarter-than-me attitude, thinking why a guy like me wouldn't just double-cross old Lou there and have the gold all to myself … That is something you need to square with your own conscience, if you can. But I owe that man my life. I would do just about anything for a quick score, but I would never hurt Lou. So you can believe me and honor his agreement with my son here, or get the fuck out of my sight right now."

Nate was trying to read him. Lou had yelled at Nate a couple of days ago about never letting anybody make him do anything he didn't want to do. And it wasn't about the gold, not for a minute. And now Nate was trying to get over the fact that he was being shaken down for five grand from a three-time petty bookie.

"Since your angle is always about money, I'll give your son here five thousand dollars right now. I am not here to play fucking games with you. Lou is dead, that is my only angle here. So I'm asking you one more time, what do you know about this? But since you only work the angles when money gets involved … tell me, and then I'll pay your son. Don't tell me, or I find you're lying, then the deal is off and you can go get fucked." He looked around the room. "Which I'm sure is a daily occurrence around here."

Sorry, Lou, I can't be pushed around either.

Nate was positive Darren's father was about to get up and walk to the guard and back to his cell, macho bullshit being what it is and all. But he just continued to stare at Nate.

"He came to me a year ago, told me he was sick. Needed to get some things in order. Told me about the gold. Said he found it down in the Keys. I knew by his tone not to ask anything more. Wanted to sell it, I told him no problemo. I know a guy in New York, a legitimate guy who could handle something like that, hush-hush and shit like that. Lou came back a week ago and said forget it for now, complication arose. I asked what and I got his none-of-your-business look. He said he was going to give it some time to work it out. Whatever that fucking meant, but no matter what, my son would get the five large."

"Did he give you any idea who or what?"

"No."

"How about the gold, did he say how much there was?" Darren asked.

Darren's father looked at Darren and back to Nate and shook his head no.

"That's all I got. You have to understand here, boys, it never left these walls. Lou never called my guy and I never mentioned it to anybody, so you have a third party that knew what Lou knew. Don't forget, a deal's a deal." Darren's father started smiling.

Nate was not happy with the information, or more accurately, the lack of. He was getting the nagging feeling that he'd come a long way for nothing. And he was starting to miss his island. He wanted to be fishing with Kate by his side. He felt better when Kate was around. He tried to stop thinking about her for now.

The guard came over and informed them that visiting time had come to an anticlimactic end.

All three got up. "Darren, give me a minute with West here." Darren reluctantly walked out of the room, looking back to the two of them. Darren's father stood there, leaning close to Nate. "I asked the old man if Darren was the one giving him problems, because, I don't know … following in my footsteps … shit, man, I don't know. He told me that my son was a good kid, that he wished you two were still friends. Resented that Cavarlo kid for getting between you two, mucking things up and all. The old man shook his head and said it's not fair when somebody comes at you sideways. Mumbled to himself that he didn't see it coming. Look. My whole life I tried to read people, find their weakness, of course for my gain, but anyways … Somebody on the island was coming at Lou hard, and it started around a year ago. You got to start thinking that this somebody has a lot more information on this situation than you do. My question is why he mentioned Cavarlo to me. How much do you really know about your old friend?"

The guard escorted Nate to the front desk, and he signed out. The female officer told him that it was nice to meet him and he returned the compliment. As he walked out into the darkening afternoon sky the humidity hit him at an unbearable level. Darren was sitting on a bench by the busy street. Nate took a seat next to him on the bench, keeping of course his proper man-distance.

The silence lingered, hanging thick like the air.

Nate looked up at the sky. "Weather's coming in."

Thunder rumbled off in the west.

"What did my father have to say?"

"Just wanted to tell me some things that Lou said about me, you know, nice things. Which I guess your dad was embarrassed to say in front of you."

More thunder.

"You're getting better at the lying," Darren told him.

"Thanks."

"I had Simone call a cab."

"Simone?"

"Officer Ferro."

"You going to ask her out?"

"I'm sorry for my dad back there."

"Don't be."

"I can't do this anymore. I'm tired, I'm so fucking tired of it all. I'm done trying to keep up with all my father's scams and bullshit, I can't do it anymore," Darren complained.

"So you don't believe him back there?"

"The shit about not double-crossing Lou? I'm not sure. Why? Are you telling me you believe him?"

"Yeah, I think I do."

"Well isn't that just fucking great. Let's see … since you haven't seen or talked to him or me for the past fifteen years, I guess it gives you more insight into his inner workings than I have. Well it's par for the course with him, because obviously he needed to tell you something that he didn't want me to hear."

"You want to be pissed at your father, go ahead, but don't blame me for your resentment."

"What the fuck do you know about resentment, huh?"

"Is this the part where I say, I'm sorry, Darren? Do you want me to say, Poor guy, it must be tough? You play the hand that was dealt to you. You don't make excuses and you never blame someone else for your misfortune."

"What's this, is this Lou's logic? Is that what he drummed into your head over the years? Because as cool as you think you're playing it back on the island, from this side of the fence you come off as an arrogant prick.

I mean, don't get me wrong, within your little group you're the best, I'm sure. But the rest of us—you know, the ones struggling out there, the ones that put ourselves on the firing line each day trying and hoping for that one defining moment, when it starts to turn in our favor—you don't see us fighting through it all, do ya? Because all you do is fish, isn't that what you tell everybody?"

Both of them were up from the bench and facing each other a couple of feet apart, years of bickering finally coming to a head, once and for all.

"So let me get this right," Nate said. "You blame your father for all your problems instead of trying harder and keeping out of trouble. You just sit there and say, Poor me."

"Is that what you think? I'm out there every day working, trying to dig out of what my father left me in. You don't see it, do you, you built a nice little wall around yourself, no windows to the outside world. Look, you have had some tragedy in your life, I will not deny you that. So you built your walls and maybe you had to. But every single morning I wake up with a knot in my stomach, a knot put there from trying to make it work by taking chances on everything. You won't let yourself take those kinds of chances, not with friends, not with work. You're a solitary boy, Nate, I give you that, and maybe it's the way to go through life, but I'll tell you this much, I've experienced more life in a single year than you ever have, so don't preach your life lessons to me."

Rain finally started to fall. Nate looked up to the dark sky for a moment. He was at a loss for words, which was rare for him. Nobody had ever put him down like this before, and the chord Darren had struck was echoing in his ears, making it hard to think.

The cab pulled up and honked its horn and they both started for the cab. Darren stopped halfway as the rain picked up in intensity.

"This shit with my dad in there? You owe me nothing. I don't want your money."

"Then after all these years, what do you want?"

"I don't know. That's part of it, Nate—not knowing what comes next is part of it. After your parents were gone, so were you, and you never let anybody too close, other than Rebecca. But my bet now is that you've stepped outside your comfort zone, haven't you? You've taken a chance on all of this. You left the security of the island, your group of friends, you've even met a girl. So if you're starting to wake up with that knot in your stomach, then you and me will be more alike. Just like when we were kids, before all the shit got in the way."

The sky unleashed its cargo of driving summer rain, and as it fell it started to fill the senses with the smell of the earth as the steam rose from the streets. The sounds of the leaves getting pelted by the rain and the thumping of the window wipers as the cars drove by—that was the orchestra of the summer rain.

Driving in the cab they both stared out their side windows, lost in today's events. Life lessons learned the hard way. As the cab bounced along Nate kept thinking about just how the holy shit he was going to simultaneously stop being chased and find out who had murdered Lou. Darren's father mentioned David Cavarlo. Why David? He thought. His bet for not mentioning it in front of his son was that to this day David had a way of intimidating Darren, and Lou was right that the reason for the broken friendship lay squarely on David Cavarlo.

As the rain ran sideways along the windows of the cab, his memory went backwards to a time when he and David were friends, not just friends but best buds, the kind you would do anything for. They'd known each other their entire lives, Darren and David and also Rebecca. The rest of the gang came to them in their mid-teens. Rebecca was by their sides through it all, but as the boys grew and hormones started doing the thinking for them, she started to gravitate to people who didn't have parts that stuck out every time she put a bathing suit on. But every night Nate would go by the visitor's booth to say goodnight, and a brother-and-sister bond was created that would never be broken. That left the three boys. David seemed relieved to have her gone, for the most part. Life went on for the boys as it did for most boys; they occupied their day fishing and talking about snakes or boobies. Then Nate moved to Cape Cod for a year while his father did a salvage job off Wellfleet. When he returned to the island a year before the *sixty miles in a center-console for a stupid movie,* David had changed, not just in appearance—two inches higher and fifteen pounds heavier—but in his attitude toward Nate. Nate had always been the unmentioned leader; it was his ideas for the day and his destinations that the others followed. But when he came back to the island, it was David telling Nate, *Nah, let's do this instead.* Nate didn't mind, he wasn't that type of kid. The attitude toward Darren, though, was a different story. If Darren sided with Nate, the rest of the day David would *shit on … is that what we called it? No, I think it was dumped on …* Darren took it like a trooper. Until the meeting in Nate's living room with Darren the other day, he'd forgotten how much David had shit on … or dumped on … Darren. He really had driven a wedge between them, hadn't he? He could see that now, looking back. Now, with his adult thinking cap on, he believed David hadn't wanted Darren idolizing Nate. Had David actually made shit up about what the other had said when that person wasn't around? After his father's death, according to Darren, Nate withdrew and that spelled the end of the gang of three. Then the incident took place when David was accused of stealing a very expensive dive watch from Nate's father's friend. Nate agreed that David had done it, and that was the proverbial nail in the friendship coffin. Sixteen years later, sitting in a cab, he tried to comprehend that David could be involved in Lou's murder. That's one hell of a leap, from teenage egos to murder, he thought. The real danger at that moment, however, was Johnny Cash and his brother chasing them off the island. *Cut a deal,* Bob had said. Would they even be open to some sort of deal? Would one bar of gold be enough to buy the truth from them? Was there more?

CHAPTER 16: GUNS AND BOATS

Send lawyers, guns, and money, the shit has hit the fan.
—Warren Zevon

The ride with Bob back to North Pier was uneventful, at least in Kate's eyes. Bob, on the other hand, felt that just another fifteen minutes of what he called his "charming sexy talk," with things about the city, himself, and the jewelry industry, was indeed starting to work its magic, at least on a girl from South Essex, England. He dropped her off at North Pier ramp, as Nate requested, and promised to come back in about an hour to check in on her and bring her a couple of dogs from Haven Brothers. She wasn't too sure what that meant, but he seemed harmless enough. With a hundred thousand in gold slung over her shoulder, sex might actually be the second thing on Bob's mind, but then again she had seen the posters in his office.

After cleaning the boat up a bit, which always helped her feel better, she headed up to the office and grabbed a sandwich to go from the small snack shop. She settled in on one of the deck chairs, feet up on another, and once again closed her eyes and soaked in the summer sun. After a little while clouds started to fill the sky. Bored, she sat up and opened Nate's red pack, took out the family recipe book, and flipped through the pages. The numbers and drawings were lost on her, but some of the artwork, particularly the compass rose, she found beautiful. She devoured her sandwich, not realizing just how hungry she was. After going through the pages a second time, she came across a page on which Lou had used a charcoal pencil to make a rubbing of the back of the gold bar; the small whale symbol was at the bottom of the page. *So you did have the gold, didn't you?* she said to herself. But there was nothing else she could find that related to anything else to do with a bar of gold.

She replaced the notebook on her lap with the photo album of Lou's family and examined the pictures. The long-gone people who stared back at her from old photos had always mesmerized her. She examined every picture with so much interest she could almost imagine them coming back to life. Lou's letter to Nate fell out onto her lap. She read the letter a couple of times, the stanza, recited it to herself until she thought she'd put it to memory. She liked the certain charm it seemed to have … an old charm. Nobody she knew would accuse her of being artsy. Tomboy, sure, but artsy was something they did not call her at school. A raindrop fell onto the open letter.

Kate put everything back into the backpack and headed down into the cabin. It was neat and spare, twenty square feet, with a toilet off to the right. On the aft wall there was a photo of Nate—probably around fourteen or fifteen, Kate assumed—and Nate's dad, both in wet suits pulled down to their waists. Diving gear at their feet, Nate was all smiles ear to ear; even at fifteen he was a looker, in Kate's mind. And that's where Nate had been since that chance meeting, in her mind, the first boy—or man, she should say—to occupy her thoughts since … well, let's just say for long enough a time that she could forget the names of the other ones.

Lost in her thoughts, she barely registered the slight movement of the boat leaning to one side.

Jimmy and Stu had been watching her now for about an hour, waiting, very patiently, mind you, for her to go below, so that she would not see them walk down the dock. As Stu said to his brother, *So what if she does? What is one dumb broad goin' to do about it?*

The boys were standing on the *Legacy*. Jimmy turned to his brother, giving him the finger to the lip as he slowly approached the cockpit area. He reached the entryway to the cabin and turned to his brother with a wry smile and turned back to the entryway, reaching around to his back to retrieve the gun tucked into his waistband. As he peered into the cabin his forehead hit the muzzle of a gun. A Glock, German-made and cool to the touch. Jimmy started to back away to the open deck of the boat while Kate followed, holding the muzzle to his forehead. She gestured for him to take his place at the stern with his younger brother. The rain fell steadily down on them.

"Put the gun down, lady," Jimmy said.

"Lady? You don't even know my name, do you?"

"What does it matter? We just want the gold."

"I don't know what you're talking about," she calmly said.

"Look, you better--" Jimmy started to say.

"Excuse me," Kate said, pointing at the gun in her hand. "I'm the one with the gun."

The boys were not happy; the veins were all making an appearance on Jimmy's forehead. His hand lowered and slowly started to reach around to his back.

"Are you shittin' me? You think I'm that stupid? Put your sausage-fingered hands up."

He brought his arm back around and up slightly.

He was thinking about rushing her, overtaking her with his quickness of foot, which would be the first time that a two-hundred-fifty-pound man in black penny loafers would be called that. But that idea was on hold for the moment because that gun she was holding was not shaking in her hands, the grip she had on it was that of somebody who was very familiar with this weapon, and he had been around just long enough to know that a crazy broad with her back up against the wall was very dangerous, especially one schooled in small arms.

"Okay, listen up, Jimmy and Stu ... Oh, which one is Stu?"

Stu slowly raised his hand up a little higher. His brother gave him his *are you shittin' me* face.

"Good, now that we have that established, maybe you can answer a few questions."

They both stared at Kate. Her mind and pulse were racing; the adrenalin was making it hard for her not to shake. The thought coming through the adrenalin was that she should just get them off the boat, fast. That chances were they were not just going to start explaining everything to her, like Chunk from the movie *Goonies*. She knew they wanted to rush her, they did this shit for a living, and she'd only learned to shoot a few years ago and it wasn't at people. But she needed some answers, *Nate* needed answers, and she wanted to … needed to help Nate.

"How did you know where we were?"

"Fuck you!" Jimmy screamed.

"Okay, how did you know about the gold?"

"You just said you didn't know about any gold," Jimmy said.

She cocked the hammer back to its firing position.

Jimmy raised his hand. "Whoa, whoa, whoa, there, honey."

"You can leave now."

"Look, honey, we are not going anywhere, so just shoot us, if you have the sack." Jimmy smiled.

"Sack? I don't know what this sack is. But I'm guessing it's something you play with a lot."

Stu laughed a bit, which drew another look from his brother.

"Well it doesn't matter, because you're full of shit," Kate told them.

"Really?" Jimmy said.

With her arm straight out, pointing the gun at them, she backed up to the cockpit dash. She reached behind her with her free hand and fumbled for the ignition, finally found it, and started the boat. Just as the engine roared to life Jimmy made his move. With the rain coming down hard he took off like a shot at Kate. His penny loafers slipped but he kept his footing, and just at that moment Kate slammed the shifter and throttle forward. The boat jumped a foot till the dock lines tightened, held for a moment, and then the bow line snapped followed by the stern. The *Legacy* jumped forward as the boat took off from the dock, sending Kate sliding back toward the boys. She grabbed the rail mounted to the dash and looked back over her shoulder as her gun slid to the stern. The boys saw the gun heading their way at the same time their feet left the deck and their asses slammed into the stern, which sent them end over end into the Providence River.

The cab dropped Nate and Darren off at the top of the parking lot. They started running toward their dock but stopped, because it was no use, they couldn't get any wetter. There was a giant clap of thunder, which made both of them jump a foot, and then they started running again for the boat.

They reached the ramp and Nate froze in his tracks.

"My boat's gone."

"What? You serious?" Darren asked.

Nate was looking around at the rows of docks.

"Are we at the right marina?" Nate said while looking around.

"Hey, man, you know she has the gold, right?"

"No way," Nate said.

"Naaate, shit, shit, shit."

"Where the hell did she go?" Nate asked.

"Nate, we have company," Darren said as he pointed to the end of the dock where the *Legacy* had been.

"Does she even know how to drive a boat … MY boat?"

"NATE, WE HAVE COMPANY."

Stu and Jimmy were walking down the dock toward the boys. They hadn't seen them yet; the rain was so hard they were walking with their heads down.

"How the hell did they find us?" Nate asked.

"Nate!"

"Come on," Nate said as he ducked and ran into the parking lot and hid behind a couple of cars. The Providence boys were heading right for them. But they stopped just shy of the rear of the vehicle they were hiding behind.

"Don't even tell me you lost the fuckin' keys," Jimmy said while Stu was patting himself down, looking for them. Nate and Darren looked at each other, trying to show blame toward each other for picking Jimmy and Stu's car to hide behind.

"When I catch that bitch she's goin' to hurt in all sorts of places," Jimmy said as Nate closed his eyes and shook his head. Stu smiled, presenting the keys like a prize. They opened the doors just as Darren's cell phone started ringing, which he had set as a techno dance beat.

Slowly walking to the rear of the car, the boys from Providence looked down at the crouching guys with a bemused look on their faces. They looked back to each other. "Look, a little gift from heaven," Jimmy said.

Waving with his fingers, Stu responded, "Hello, boys."

Fight or flight there, sunshine.

Nate looked at Darren, tilted his head slightly to the right, and with Lou's voice echoing in his head screamed "RUN!"

At first they took off in two separate directions, but Darren, realizing this, cut right and was soon on Nate's heels. The two boys took off down the parking lot, not sure which way to go, just a blind run. The rain hadn't let up, if possible it was coming down even harder. They hit the end of the parking lot and suddenly realized the error of their decision. All they had in front of them were ramps leading to the floating docks and more boats. They could swim for it, about fifty yards to another dock on the other side of the river.

Jimmy was laughing because he had them cornered, and was making his way toward the boys in a slow strut. In the distance Nate heard something.

"What do we do, Nate?" Darren asked.

"I have no idea."

He heard it again and again, this time it registered, it was his horn on the *Legacy*, his *Legacy*, and he spun around and saw Kate at the helm of *his* boat out in the marina, about forty feet from the end of the floating dock. They exchanged a glance and Kate gave him a *what the hell are you waiting for? Run, Forrest, run look.* A gunshot rang out, which made Nate and Darren jump and look back, and Nate took off like the bullet that had just flown by them. Once again he left Darren behind to face the man in black and his brother, and when Darren turned to ask, one more time, what the fucking hell they should do, he saw Nate fifty feet down the dock, heading for the *Legacy*. Kate swung the stern of the boat around on a dime and reversed her so the swim platform was about two feet from the end of the dock. She was soaking wet, her hair clinging to the sides of her face, and there was a gun tucked into the small of her back, slightly revealing a tattoo. Nate was hauling ass, realizing he'd forgotten Darren, turning to yell back at him in time to see him right on his heels and passing him. The boys jumped off the end of the dock and flew over the stern of the *Legacy* and crashed onto the deck. Kate hit the throttle and the *Legacy* sped out of the marina and into the dark, driving rain.

The two brothers stood there in the rain, at the end of the dock, while the *Legacy's* wake moved the boats in the marina back and forth in their slips. They didn't speak. Jimmy raised his arm and fired five shots into the darkness, in the general direction of where the boat had been. Before this obsession with the gold was over, his brother thought, somebody was going to die; he saw it as clear as the veins on Jimmy's neck. Jimmy finally turned and started walking, not looking at his brother.

"Call Doc, tell him we're going to need his boat after all," Jimmy finally said. "And let's call fuck-nuts on the island."

CHAPTER 17: THE COOL TABLE

Before Nate and Kate the Beautiful (which Mike only called her to himself) left on the *Legacy* earlier that day to go after Darren, Nate had told Mike to tell Rebecca everything. He would indeed do this ... eventually, because he did everything Nate told him to do ... eventually. He had been working for him since he was eight years old. Back then he admired Nate from a safe distance; Nate was a rock star to Mike. He would watch him take out customers for fishing charters. He would overhear others wonder how, only in his early twenties, that West kid could have such a booming business. Everybody else his age was bartending, waiting tables, or running like hell off the island.

Mike made himself a fixture on the docks. He would work his way down the boats, talking nonstop to the lobstermen and the charter guys. He would think he was helping old man Verery guide the weekenders where to tie up, but in reality he just got in Verery's way. And for any tourist who needed a bucket-load of useless information, Mike was right there. Most thought of young Mike as a pest, a nuisance, a topnotch candidate for a Ritalin-type substance. He let them talk, usually to his face, because he knew that the one single thing that defined him was his passion for squid—with regards to catching them. He loved doing that so much that nobody could crush his demeanor. His pole was a relic, with a freshwater reel given to him by his grandfather, who bought it at a yard sale for two bucks. But it wasn't the fishing pole, it was the fisherman. He'd heard rock-star Nate say that once—not to him, of course, but to somebody of greater importance than a squid-catching eight-year-old.

Using the floodlights from the buildings that surrounded the docks, Mike would dance his squid rig, a glowing tube-shaped design with an upturned spiral of sharp hooks, for hours on end. The squid, attracted to the light, would go after the rig and Mike would snag them. As he grew older, with his squid-catching days behind him, he realized that the squid was the reason he now worked for and hung out with the good guys. This realization moved him so much that when he turned eighteen, he took the ferry to the mainland and got himself a tattoo, not the full ten or twelve inches that a squid could grow to, but a six-incher, with its spotted translucent skin and big eyes. *Damn straight, man, no worries,* he would say, *that's a squid.* It was his ticket to adulthood.

He would sell his squid to the New Harbor bait shop; going price was twenty-five cents a piece. He would average twenty squid a night, a sweet piece of change for a kid when all that mattered was candy and video games. One night in particular he was sitting on the dock with his yard-sale rod and reel bobbing after the squid, sun long gone, mosquitoes feasting on his bare legs, when he got himself in a pickle. His parents, who managed a restaurant down the road from the dock, trusted this boy of eight to find himself something to do that didn't involve trouble, but then most on the island and at that time (only a mere ten years ago) felt it safe enough to let boys be boys, and besides, they knew exactly where and what their son was doing. He was having a profitable night, twenty-five squid after only three hours, and he was thinking about calling it a night, when a small group of teenagers that were not indigenous to the island came strutting around the marina office. These kids were from the weekenders, and they were off running roughshod all over New Harbor as their parents helped themselves to more mudslides than they could handle. *Hey, it's an island, where can they go?* You could hear their parents declaring, hoisting another mudslide.

The teenagers, smelling out a weaker one of their species, surrounded Mike. After asking him a few innocent questions about the contents of the bucket, Mike's constant and unrelenting enthusiasm got the better of him. Leaning his pole on a piling, he jumped to his feet, reached into the bucket, and produced a nice ten-inch squid. The male teenagers of this group were at first intrigued, but when the girls, the cute girls, reared back in horror of this creature, the males turned on him. The boys didn't explain that since the girls didn't like the squid, they would have to change their initial stance on thinking the squid cool to *how dare you upset our girlfriends.* Mike, not understanding the ways of the male teenage hormone parade coursing through their bodies (in a few short years Mike would come to love the parade, no pun intended), pushed the squid closer, only to show the skin and how it changed color. One of the boys went to push it away and hit the squid, which unfortunately for Mike and the squid shot the last remnants of ink in the boy's face. First the squid was shoved down Mike's pants, then the bucket got kicked over, spilling his six-dollar-and-twenty-five-cent evening back into the harbor. Mike, not knowing when to back down, jumped up to his feet and managed to push the largest of the boys back a whole foot. The teenager's return shove moved Mike back six feet and onto his ass. The teenager was on him now, grabbing him by the New Harbor bait and tackle shop tee shirt, brought him to his feet, the arm rearing back for a punch (Mike's first), which came around with all the force of a teenage hard-on. He closed his eyes, waiting for the impact, mumbling to himself, *Not the teeth, not the teeth.* Feeling the teenager's hand clasped on his shirt, the punch was sure taking a long time, and he chanced it and opened one eye. What he saw was Nate holding the teenager's arm above his head. Two feet taller and with muscles to bring the girls in the group to a pile of giggles, Nate looked down at Mike and in his low-key voice asked if he was okay, and Mike shook his head back and forth and up and down, to cover both options. The boys could only manage grunts and shrugs and *I don't knows* when asked what was going on. Nate directed them back to their boats before he threw them off the pier, and if their parents had a problem, they could get off their drunk asses and come see him. Then the boys ran off, but not before the girls mumbled to each other and giggled, glancing back at Nate while running a few feet behind their boys. Mike had the feeling that the teenagers were not going to tell their parents shit. He slowly walked past Nate with his head down, over to his overturned bucket, and pulled from his crotch the one lonely squid remaining. *Twenty-five cents is better than nothing.* Nate laughed a bit and asked if he was okay. It was never pleasant to be picked on, and from that experience, he knew right then and there that he would never be the reason someone felt the way he did right now. All he could do to answer Nate's question was to look him in the eyes and give him the *yeah, okay* look. He shrugged and walked down the dock with his lonely squid; Nate caught up with him before he made it to the beach. They had a conversation that resulted in Mike selling every squid he could catch that summer to Nate. And if he would be interested, and it was okay with his parents, he could help out with his boat and maybe go out with some charters. Welcome to the cool table, please take a seat.

Now he needed to get to the visitor's booth to tell Rebecca everything that had transpired.

After tying up his jet ski, he managed to make it about fifteen feet down the dock by the Beach Bar. *Oh there's Tammy, I got a quick minute to say hey,* he thought. Mike was there by her side, making her laugh, asking if she'd be at South Beach tonight, some of his friends were going to have a bonfire. Then he was off again, a little farther down the dock, about another fifteen feet, and ran into a redheaded girl ... *Jerry ... no, that can't be right ... Judy?* Just to play it safe, he waved and pointed to his watch to show her the international sign for no time. *I hope she didn't notice I don't have a watch.* He made it as far as the main dock and onto the bulkhead that led to the road up to the ferry parking lot. To his right the weekenders were heading in with their boats, and it was starting to fill up early. Along the bulkhead were ten boats, tied stern to bow all along the side. A Fountain muscle boat, made to go fast, very fast was trying to dock along another boat that was already tied up. The loud colors chosen by the owner were only slightly louder than the triple engines roaring as he tried to jockey his position. He was about two minutes from causing some damage to his and the surrounding boats. Mike looked for Harbor

Master Cavarlo or old man Verery, but no luck; he took another couple of steps down the bulkhead and stopped, shook his head, and climbed down onto the first boat. There were some people on the boats that he had to walk over to get out to the muscle heads, but there was an understanding in Old Harbor that your boat would have to be walked on from time to time. Most didn't care, so much so that a half dozen people sitting on their boats weren't showing the least amount of concern that a fourth boat was about to cause some damage to their floating party.

Mike made his way out to the last boat, screaming over the rumbling of the three engines, and tried to direct the owner.

"CAPT!" he shouted. The man looked nonchalantly to Mike. "CAPT! Pull up along this boat, put your starboard engine in forward and port in reverse." The owner was confused as he looked to Mike. "Right, forward … left, reverse." A nod from the captain, for whom Mike was being polite calling him captain, since there was no way on God's green earth this back-shaven muscle head could be mistaken for a captain. As he finally accomplished this, the boat spun and the stern rotated to the boats Mike was standing on. After tying up the boat as the people on board did nothing, unless you count getting the bar set up and opening beers, Mike turned to leave.

"Yo there, guy," the back-shaver called out.

Guy … yeah, that's right, meatball. Mike smiled. "What's up, there, Captain?"

The back-shaver handed Mike two hundred dollars. Mike's attitude suddenly changed. "We're staying two nights, so if that's not enough, let me know."

"Uh … well, I'm not the harbor master; you need to go to that grey-shingled office on the dock …" Mike didn't have to finish because back-shaver had lost interest and turned around to start drinking and carrying on. Mike made his way back to the bulkhead and down to the office. *Man … maybe I'll just keep the friggin' money.*

He popped his head into the little harbor master's office. "David?" The office was empty, but David couldn't be far, since the office door was left open. Mike walked in and sat behind the desk, searching for a pencil and paper. He found a Post-it pad and wrote out where the money came from. When he finished he got up and threw the pad down onto the keyboard of the laptop on the desk. The screen was in sleep mode and popped on, and just to reassure himself that he hadn't broken anything, he glanced at the screen. He turned to leave, but then leaned back toward the computer to have another look. At first glance it appeared to be a plain old electronic nautical chart of the island, but taking a closer look, Mike noticed the chart had an icon of a boat … and this boat icon was moving … inching across the screen as if the computer were an actual GPS. Which had Mike amused, since he was relatively sure the harbor master's office was not indeed a vessel and the tiny office was not moving. But he glanced out the window to satisfy his imagination. *So it's tracking something—a boat?* Mike wondered. *That's freakin' cool.* Whatever it was tracking seemed to be heading up the Providence River. Along the bottom of the screen were latitude and longitude numbers and they kept updating as the icon cruised across the screen. Shrugging as he left the office, he walked right into David Cavarlo.

"Whoa, sorry, Chief."

"What the fuck were you doing in there?"

"I left some money those muscle-heads in the boat *Wet Dreams* gave "

David interrupted: "Do not go in my office, you piece of shit."

"Hey, Chief … I'm sorry, man. You don't have to get nasty."

"You have somewhere you have to be other than here?"

"Yeah, man." Mike slowly started to walk off to the ferry parking lot. *What the fuck got into him?*

David walked into his office and stared at his computer.

Mike let himself in through the back of the visitor's booth; luckily no summer help was there to refuse entry. (Mike's picture didn't make the wall.) Rebecca was talking to a group of people just in from the ferry about some must-see sights. They thanked her and walked off. She spun around in her chair. "Where the hell have you been?"

Mike had the sneaking suspicion that he was too late to get her up to speed about Nate. He was quick on his feet, and responded with a definitive, "What?"

"I just got off the phone with Nate."

"Oh ..."

Rebecca shook her head.

"So you know about the lighthouse chase and the thing with the ski and-- "

"Yes, Michael, I know everything."

"Where is he? Is he okay?"

"He met up with Darren and they're off to Providence to do a few things."

"Care to elaborate?"

"That's a big word there, Mike."

"I got a word calendar for Christmas."

"Well, that's all Nate told me," Rebecca said, talking down to him.

Mike slowly walked around, picking up objects on the counter and putting them back down, just nervous energy. He held the paper weight and turned it over, examining the bottom of it as an antique dealer would. "Oh look, this says that it was made in China," he sarcastically said to her.

"Look, isn't there some other place you should be?"

"You're the second person to ask me that," he said, slowly walking toward the door. As he approached the door he had a thought, not an *I have the cure for cancer* sort of thought, but a thought nevertheless ... and for Mike, that was big. But the feeling it was giving him in the pit of his stomach was a *something's not friggin' right* feeling. He shook his head, not to shake it from his thoughts but to help its emergence from the back of his head to the front, where, if he could get a hold of it, maybe he could formulate it and explain it out loud. His stomach was itching. He was so close ... *No, it doesn't make sense,* he thought. He needed more information so he wouldn't look stupid, not that he was unfamiliar with that look, he happened to wear it a lot. He stopped at the door, and with his back to Rebecca he asked her, "Did Nate say where they were going to stay in Providence?"

Still in a tone of annoyance, she replied, "Yes, North Pier Marina."

Mike continued out the door. She felt bad about being mad at Mike, but this shit with Nate was not to be taken lightly. He was somewhat of a responsible teenager, but he had his ceiling; he was seventeen years younger than the group, and she forgot that sometimes. As she watched him walk off to the ferry with his head down, she remembered she'd forgotten to tell him what Nate had said about somebody on the island that was in on all of this. But she didn't call him back, didn't tell him to stick close to Jack and Josh, because she believed he was off to look for a girl to hang with tonight. What kind of danger could that bring?

Mike's head was down, trying to move that friggin' thought around. It was the first person who asked him if he had some other place to be that got him thinking. Actually, this person's computer. *Nate's in Providence and David's computer has some sort of tracking software on it showing the Providence River. Coincidence?* And this was his dilemma; somebody would have had to put a transponder on Nate's boat. Somebody would have to have been on the *Legacy*. There was somebody on his boat the other night. He thought. But Mike remembered that it was Darren, who later claimed that he was off island. So who was on his boat, then?

He saw Kurt finishing cleaning up the cargo hold of the ferry that docked a half hour ago. Kurt looked in Mike's direction when his name was called.

"Hey, Mikey boy, where's the party tonight?"

"South Beach, bonfire, shit like that."

"Nice. Who you going with, that redhead, Gina?"

"Gina … that's right," he said, half in the conversation. "Listen. The other night, you told me you saw Darren on Nate's boat, thinking it was me."

Kurt started to laugh. "Yeah, man, it was Darren," he said, smiling way too much.

"Can I ask you a question?" Mike asked, while that shit-eating smile sat on Kurt's face. "What the fuck is so funny?" Mike's tone wiped the smile off Kurt's face in a hurry.

"Hey, man ... I thought it was a joke, that's all."

"What was a joke? Kurt, what the hell is going on?"

"That night, I thought I saw you. I was told to tell you it was Darren, that it was a prank and Nate was in on it. I mean, shit, he gave me fifty bucks and told me not to tell anybody. But if you're pissed, man ... I mean, you're my friend and all."

"Kurt, who gave you the money and told you to say it was Darren?"

Kurt paused a moment longer than Mike was willing to wait, and Mike lunged toward him.

"Cavarlo!" Kurt yelled. "It was David Cavarlo—shit, man ..."

Mike's head was really spinning now that the thought had arrived front and center and taken hold of him with a sickness in his stomach that might make him lose his lunch. He walked off the ferry and stood in the parking lot, thinking what to do next. As he stood there he couldn't see David watching him from the little window in the harbor master's office, so he couldn't see the serious look on it, but in a very short time he would.

The western sky was darkening and thunder could be heard off in the distance as Mike paced around the ferry parking lot.

I need to take a look at his computer again, make sure this isn't just my imagination.

...

People kept coming into his office to pay for the weekend or ask questions about the showers. It was making it hard to formulate a plan on what to do with Mike. Old man Verery could only do so much, being a decrepit old man, coupled with the fact that the summer help wouldn't be here until next weekend. David was the only show in town and he was starting to rip at the seams. A cute redhead came into the office and told him that a fight was about to break out on a couple of boats tied up together. On his way out he closed the door and locked it. Heading out to the boats, his marine radio went off with the report of a couple of kids drifting out of the harbor in an inflatable boat and screaming for help. *Would it be too much to ask for a bystander to help in this matter?* But it was Friday and everybody was drunk. With bitterness in his soul, he trotted down to the harbor master's boat to get the drifting kids.

Kurt handed back Mike's marine radio, freaking out over making a false report. "Relax, man," Mike said, "you didn't make it to the Coast Guard, just a harbor master. I'm sure the jail sentence isn't as bad."

"Great, man, just fucking great," said Kurt, looking down and shaking his head. "This makes us even, Mike."

"Not even close," Mike spat back.

Time was at a premium while David was being pulled in two different directions. Between the fight, which Gina (finally remembering her name) had helped with, and the distress call, which Kurt had just faked, he should be gone twenty minutes, and Mike needed ten, maybe five. He was already off across the parking lot and onto the bulkhead of the main dock. It started to rain and people were running around, as if rain was the wrath of God punishing them for their drunkenness. Mike just walked up to the door of the harbor master's office and reached up under the shingle just above the top of the door jam and removed a key. David didn't know of the existence of this key, but old man Verery, having lost his key around ten times—twice in one day—hid the key about two years ago, and the day after he hid the key, Mike knew all about it.

He didn't risk putting on the light but tried to use the little existing light that was left now that the thunderstorm had made its appearance. The laptop was closed on David's desk. He opened it and hit the space bar, but no luck. He powered it up and the password menu popped up. "Shit," he said. He closed the computer and looked around. He thought about stealing the laptop. He went as far as to pick it up. He looked down where it had been sitting on the desk, and written on a Post-it note that had been under the computer were the words "North Pier Marina, East Providence off Thurbers Ave." *Son of a bitch, this is it. He's tracking Nate somehow. David is the guy … son of a bitch.* He opened the door, and with the rain pouring down hard, closed the door behind him and walked off down the pier. David passed him, glancing back as Mike went by. He sped up to his office.

Mike's mind was in overdrive, so he didn't notice David passing, and the rain didn't help. David went to unlock his door and found that it was unlocked He swung it open wildly and looked around his small office. The computer was still there, closed, but it wasn't sitting square to the edge of the desk as he liked it, and when he lifted it, he saw that the note was gone.

Mike was hauling ass to the visitor's booth. About one step onto the parking lot, a hand grabbed him by the neck, grasped him hard. It hurt, his shoulders were hunched up, trying to relieve the strain of the grip, but it was no good, it was too strong, in a very pissed kind of way. The voice was familiar. "Keep walking or I'll blow your head off." Mike managed to look to his right and could see the gun digging into his back. He wanted to correct David and tell him he couldn't blow his head off because he was pointing his rather large gun at his kidneys, but he'd wait for a more opportune time. David led him down the short dock that ran along the side of the ferry parking lot, where the lobster boats tied up, toward the harbor master's secondary boat, a twenty-six-footer only used in a real emergency, which lay at the end of the dock. He manhandled Mike on board and instructed him to go below. Standing below, bending over slightly due to the low ceiling, he stared at David with eyes wide.

"What's going on here, David?"

"Do not pretend for a moment that you do not know *exactly* what is going on here," David said with a fearless tone.

He was standing at the top of the stairs leading topside, staring down at Mike, who was cornered like a squid in a bucket.

"Look ... David, I don't know anything ... I swear."

"What's Nate doing in Providence?"

"I don't know, I swear," Mike replied.

"So let me make sure I understand you. You are attached at the hip with Nate and his loyal gang of ass-kissers, and you can't tell me what he's up to?"

"A little harsh, don't you think?"

"I haven't got the fucking time for this!" Trying to regain his temper, David took a deep breath. "I am going to ask you one more question. And if you give me some bullshit answer, I'm going to shoot you." He didn't give time for a reply. "Is there more gold?"

Mike didn't have any training in negotiation, but he was well-versed in being a nervous kid and made a simple gesture that in any other circumstance would have been innocent. He looked up at David Cavarlo, a man he'd known his whole life, and simply shrugged.

David raised his arm at Mike and fired.

CHAPTER 18: NEW BEDFORD

"There be whales here."
—Scotty, from the movie *Star Trek IV: The Voyage Home*

Nate and Darren got up from the deck of the *Legacy* as it screamed out into the Providence River. The wind had picked up and the lightning was intense and the thunder deafening—it was obvious that the thunderstorm was right on top of them.

Wiping the water from his face, Nate ran into the cockpit. "What the hell was that? Are you a freakin' secret agent?"

"I'm fine, thanks," Kate bellowed.

"You don't know how to ride a scooter but you handle a boat like THAT?"

"I told you before, I've had a lot of jobs."

"Was one of them a secret agent?" Nate screamed.

"You know I can't tell you that," she said in a serious tone.

"HEY, can we do the vaudeville routine later?" Darren asked. "How the FUCK did they find us?"

Nate took the wheel from Kate and slowed the *Legacy* down a bit.

"I was down below and the next thing I know they're on the boat."

"Where did you get a gun?" Nate asked.

"It's mine. I told her where I hid it," Darren told him.

Kate filled them in on how she got them off the boat, and Darren finished the story with the parking lot fiasco, trying, though, to gloss over the part about the ringing cell phone.

The storm was pushing fast past them to the south. Darren came up from the cabin and handed her a towel.

"Bob?" Darren asked.

"Bob dropped me off here. He had me alone in his truck for half an hour. There were way too many opportunities for him to take it from me."

"Are we going to just call it a coincidence? We're not doing that, are we? Because there is no way they just happened on us," Darren said.

"I can't think straight," Nate said. "All this shit is coming at us too fast."

"I think you're having trouble that I saved your butt," Kate said. "You know, me being a girl and all."

"You're a girl? Really, I never noticed," Nate said, giving her a quick glance.

They drove in silence for a little while. The adrenalin-infused fear slowly drained from their bodies, leaving in its wake tired muscles, the chill of wet clothes, and for Nate and Darren, a growling stomach; neither could remember the last time they ate.

The storm passed by them now, the brilliant red of the sunset unaware of all the shit the three of them were feeling, just shining on as it met the horizon for its last act of the day.

"God … that's beautiful," Kate said, not taking her eyes off the sky.

Red sky in the morning, sailors take warning. Red sky at night, sailors' delight. The old rhyme played in Nate's head.

Prudence Island was on their starboard as the *Legacy* cut between Prudence and the coastal town of Bristol, passing under the Mount Hope Bridge.

All three had changed into dry clothes, which were starting to show the first signs of having gone from dry to wet and back a couple of times. Suddenly Darren came to the realization that he had no idea where they were going. Nate saw Darren looking around to get his bearings.

"Tiverton Basin."

Darren turned his hands up.

"Fuel, food," Nate answered.

The Standish Marina was a small family-owned marina cut out of a hill just north of the old Tiverton stone bridge, which a hurricane or two had destroyed years before the occupants of the *Legacy* were even born. With its weather-beaten roof and white-washed shingles, it gave one the impression that it hadn't changed its look for many a summer.

Tied to the fuel dock, and with the help of a half dozen burritos from a Mexican place just up the road, the situation was starting to feel somewhat manageable again. The sunset had given way to a starry night and a noticeable decline in humidity.

Nate was at the dash of the boat with Lou's notebook open, and this time he really examined each page with as much interest as he could master. Kate brushed by him as he came to the page that Kate had shown him of the rubbing of the gold bar.

"You're right," Nate said, comparing the back of the gold bar to the rubbing. "It's the same whale."

"So does that unlock some long-ago memory of a long-lost clue to all this?" Kate asked him.

He just stood there with a blank stare.

"It's time to start drinking," she stated.

She went to the cooler and took out three beers.

Taking the beer from her, he said, "Thanks."

She left him at the cockpit with the notebook and joined Darren at the stern of the boat.

Taking a beer from her, he asked, "So where did you learn to handle a boat and a gun like that?"

"The boat ... well, I have held many a job over the last, oh, ten years. One of them was a water-taxi driver on the Thames River back home. The gun, that's a perk from an old boyfriend who happened to be a gun nut."

"Didn't work out, huh?" Darren asked.

"I did mention nut, right?"

Nate joined them.

"What do we do now, Nate?" Darren asked.

"Well, let's go over what we know," Nate asked.

"We know we're being chased," Darren said.

Kate nodded and clinked beer bottles with Darren.

"Right. Why are we being chased?" Nate asked.

"The gold?" Kate asked.

It's gold, I tell ya … gold.

"Yeah, the gold. Okay, we think that Lou probably found some gold on that wreck years ago. That he might have been trying to convert it to cash before his illness took hold. But something happened with his plan. Darren's father said that Lou never got the chance to talk to the guy who could have handled that transaction for him. I think somebody else knew about the gold. Look, the Providence boys back there, as far as we can tell, didn't even *arrive* on the island till the day after Lou's death, and their only concern seems to be the gold. But they somehow knew where the wreck was, somebody obviously directed them there. It's somebody from the island, it has to be … I've been going over a conversation I overheard while Lou was on the phone the day before he was killed, and he was upset. Listen, in my entire life with this man, he never gave me the feeling that he was upset or preoccupied with something. That night, though, something just didn't feel right. Add the fact that Darren's father said he was acting different, preoccupied with something or someone the last time he visited him—once again, this is simply not Lou. Everything leads back to somebody on the island knowing about the gold and somehow starting to put pressure on Lou, and he would in no way have taken that lightly, he would have resisted this person every step of the way until he could find a way out of it. But I think he ran out of time. Maybe this person somehow brought these boneheads in from Providence for help. But who on the island is capable of murder? If he killed Lou, then he's desperate and dangerous."

"More gold," Darren said while finishing his beer. He shook his beer to see if anybody else needed one, and Nate and Kate nodded yes. Walking back from the cabin he handed out the beers.

"It's what Bob said, it seems like a lot of people are going through a hell of a lot of trouble if this is the only bar," Darren explained. "Oh— Bob called earlier during all the commotion, he left a voicemail with his number." Nate went to the dash and handed the phone to Darren. "You should take some notes on the use of this thing," Darren said.

"Just dial the number," Nate instructed.

Darren punched in the numbers and handed the phone to him, and Nate walked off to the cockpit.

"Are we not going to discuss the Ricci brothers finding us in the middle of the city?" Darren whispered to Kate. "It has to be Bob after he dropped you off."

Kate looked to Darren and shrugged.

Nate walked back to the two of them and handed the phone back to Darren. "Bob wants to be on speaker."

He took the phone from him and hit a button and placed the phone on the arm of the deck chair.

"We're all listening," Darren told him.

"All right, I started to tell Nate, but he wants you to hear it from me. I made some calls and did some research centering on the early gold trade. I believe this bar is from a legendary ship that sailed from New Bedford, Massachusetts. It isn't really known what kind of a ship or even where it sank, just that it carried a lot of gold. My research seems to lead to the conclusion that it was doing something illegal, some say the slave trade, other say whale oil."

"Well, we did find that symbol on the bar," Kate said.

"We?" Bob said. "My dear, if I recall, you have had this bar in your beautiful soft hands for a couple of days and never noticed --"

"Okay, Bob, can you continue?" Nate asked.

"Soft hands? Were you holding hands?" Darren whispered to Kate, who responded with her middle finger.

"Okay, the whale oil story seems to be the leading clue. Look, nobody knows where this ship went down. There is even a story of the captain recovering the gold, which seems unlikely, though, in the 1800s. If this is the gold from this mysterious ship, then the price of that bar and any subsequent bars is astronomical. Guys, this story of Spanish gold coming out of the New Bedford area has been told in my trade for generations—my grandfather told me about it. It's fucking legendary, with absolutely no proof. Now I know I didn't mention it to you when you were in my office, but ... I wanted to be sure. My father examined a bar just like the one you have fifty years ago."

"It's funny that you wanted to buy it for only a hundred grand, huh?" Darren said.

"I can't resist a sale. Look, guys, I also confirmed that it was the Ricci brothers that were on your island."

"Well, we just had a run-in with them at the marina," Darren told him.

"Jesus," Bob said. "Is that why you guys weren't there when I came by to give you this info in person?"

"Yeah, had to leave in a hurry," Darren said with some sarcasm.

"Well it makes a little more sense, then."

"What?" Nate asked.

"Well, it seems they made a call to bring in reinforcements, and their help owns a boat—a fast boat."

"Shit," Nate said. "Anything else?"

"No. But, Nate, if there is more gold, you need to get it to me. I can make you rich beyond your imagination."

"I'll keep that in mind."

"See ya," Bob said, and the phone went dead.

"It's Bob, it has to be," Darren stated.

"Why?" Nate asked.

"How did they find us?"

Nate shrugged.

"There is a case of the shrugs going on around here," Darren muttered to himself.

"So back to the original question: now what?" Kate asked.

"Well, we might have to take the long way around on this," Nate said.

"The letter tells us … well, actually, it tells us nothing, just the words, 'compass rose,' and that little poem."

Kate broke in, repeating the poem word for word.

"You were busy while we were gone," Nate said. Kate just smiled and shrugged, looking to Darren as she did this.

"I honestly have no idea what that refers to," Nate told them.

All three sat there and drank in silence.

Nate stood up and started to shake his head. "Bob said whale oil … Jesus Christ, listen to this. Down in Lou's basement there are artifacts from hundreds of his dives, and all of this stuff is labeled and placed on one side of his basement. But in another corner, all by itself, is a group of artifacts made up of several large kettles and long cutting tools, and they are labeled, 'New Bedford Whaling Museum.' Surer than shit, he set those artifacts aside, letting them stand out. Second, on his wall, he has a painting of a ship in a great storm off Block Island. He brought it to my attention during a debate we had over history, why some people find it important while others simply … well, never mind. He told me he had it painted over a decade ago. The story he used as an example, in our debate, was about gold, and later, when I looked at the painting, I noticed it was a whale ship. The one thing about Lou is that there is nothing, I mean *nothing* that he does that is not deliberate. He was laying out a trail for me to follow … a starting point."

"So you think a whale ship carried gold and sank off our island?" Darren asked.

"I don't know. I thought I knew every shipwreck around the island, and there is nothing in Lou's logbook about a whaling ship, just a small rubbing of the back of the bar. This once again makes it stand out. But I tell you this much, he never talked of whales or whale ships, but somehow I have just given you three examples of whales that have a possible connection to Lou. So … I'm thinking the New Bedford Whaling Museum is a place to start. At least we might find out about a whale ship called the *Compass Rose*."

"New Bedford is only a couple of hours from here by boat," Darren stated.

"Let's just say we find more gold," Kate said. "Then what? You want to make a deal with these thugs?"

"Yeah … I'll give them gold for Lou's murderer," Nate plainly stated.

"That's a lot of money," Darren said.

Nate shot Darren a look.

"It's your call," Darren said.

"So my question to both of you is, do you want to help me look for the possibility of more gold? Try to make a deal with the mob and in the process expose a murderer that's living on our island?"

"While trying not to get killed," Kate reminded them.

"Will I have to get hurt—you know, more than just emotionally?" Darren asked.

"Yeah," Nate said, "the way things are going, I would have to say yes, you will probably get hurt."

"Ah, crap. Will you buy me a boat when this is done?"

"Yeah, but we are talking grave injuries."

Nate looked to Kate.

"What, are you shittin' me? I'm a secret agent, I do this shit all the time. I'm in."

"Okay, great," Nate said, smiling.

Nate powered up the electronics and the engine and headed south up the Sakonnet River. The farther up the river they traveled the darker the shoreline got, farmland and vineyards lining the shores to the mouth of the river. When they entered Rhode Island Sound, the darkness engulfed them, with nothing but the star-strewn sky to hold their attention.

Jimmy and Stu met up with their associate who went by the name Doc, what the authorities called an alias, but what he called a nickname, given to him from his days as a medic during his tour of duty with the army during Desert Storm. Now, a gun supplier and expert for an assortment of folks who might be in need of a gun-running medic. He also happened to be the owner of a thirty-foot Fountain speedboat, *Big Booty*. Triple engines that when pushed could manage speeds of seventy-plus miles an hour. But right now the boat sat idle underneath the Mount Hope Bridge, their signal to the small tracking GPS gone, replaced with the word *searching*. It was dark, and not knowing which way they were going, they just bobbed along with the tide. Their calls to the island went unanswered, and that was not helping their mood.

"Are you sure we want to keep doing this?" Stu asked his brother. Jimmy's silence gave him his answer.

Just then their GPS beeped and located the *Legacy's* signal.

"They're heading up the Sakonnet River," Doc said.

"Well let's go, man, what are you waiting for?" Jimmy demanded.

"Well, for starters, where are they going?" Doc asked.

"How the fuck do I know? But we know where they are, and you said there is no way his lobster boat can outrun your boat here."

"That's a fact. The problem is that at the end of the Sakonnet River there are three choices and a lot of open fucking water. Head out into the sound for Block Island. Head south to Newport or east to Buzzards Bay. If it's Newport, then we are closer than they are, so we wait. If it's Block, then we go back up through Jamestown and head them off. But if it's Buzzards Bay, that's at the max of my fuel range, plus it's dark and I don't have radar, so we'd need to sit tight and find out where they are going and then catch up to them."

Jimmy was not in the mood to wait any longer. He needed to wrap this up and get back to his operations before someone else tried to take advantage of his absence. Doc sensed his impatience.

"Look, Jimmy, as long as we have this"— he pointed to the handheld GPS—"we will be able to find them. Give him his space and he'll get a false sense of security and maybe lead us to the jackpot."

"Then let's go to Newport and get drunk," Jimmy said.

"That's what I'm talking about," Doc bellowed.

The two-hour ride into Buzzards Bay was uneventful. The city of New

Bedford lit up the night sky, in stark contrast to the surrounding area. The Elizabeth Islands, twelve in all, were dark; most of them were privately owned and had only one or two houses on them, no condos or marinas. The whole eleven-mile stretch of islands was a window to the past, unlike the towns along the western shore of Buzzards Bay, towns like Westport and Dartmouth, old farm towns that had turned into larger towns with the influx of baby boomers. When the farms were all but gone, they left in their wake a lot of houses where square footage was the pedigree. And with them, the Taco Bells and Pizza Huts soon followed, creating what we have come to know as the suburbs.

The *Legacy* cruised by Butler Flats Lighthouse, which stood in the middle of the New Bedford Channel and had long ago been silenced and darkened in the world of electronics. On their right was Fort Phoenix, a revolutionary fort that had seen some action in 1812. On a grander scale was the fort of New Bedford. The south coast of New England was a bull's-eye for hurricanes, particularly during the twenties through the fifties, back before tracking them became an art form. So to combat this onslaught of hurricanes, a great wall of stone was built. Construction began in 1962 and was finished four years later, and it stood on both sides of the harbor. On the New Bedford side, the barrier ran forty-five hundred feet and twenty feet high. Since its inception, the barrier—what some called an eyesore—had never really been tested, but New Bedford was ever-ready for such an occasion.

The *Legacy* passed through the entrance to the hurricane barrier into New Bedford Harbor. As the three of them looked up at the massive gate, which was a hundred and fifty feet wide, it was like passing through a castle gate into the spectacle a city could be. The city lights made it easy to navigate their way around. There were marinas down at the end of the harbor, where it turned into the Acushnet River. But the museum was right downtown, walking distance from the State Pier.

The State Pier itself had been the epicenter of the sea trade since the whaling days; now, in its current status as the number-one fishing port in the country, hundreds of fishing boats were tied up at any given time. The State Pier stuck out into the harbor at the end of Union Street, creating two aisles on either side of the State Pier building. Nate tucked the *Legacy* down the left side of the building, just down from where the Martha's Vineyard high-speed ferries docked. At the end of the aisle, no more than six feet from the pier, the city began. As they tied up the *Legacy*, cars wiped by a mere ten feet away, while the late-night crowds stumbled by. From their vantage point on the *Legacy* they could look up the hill to the heart of the city and see the steeple of the Whaling Museum and its weathervane, a sperm whale that looked just like the little one on the gold paper weight in Nate's red backpack.

"Can we stay here?" Darren asked.

"Well, I'm hoping the harbor master is still the guy that chartered me a few years ago," Nate said. "Look, there is nothing we can do now, so let's get some sleep." He went below and hung up a hammock from one side of the cabin to the other. He pulled out a blanket and a beach towel for a pillow. Kate was standing behind him. "It's not much," Nate apologized.

"Are you kidding me, it looks comfy," Kate said.

She has aced the three-day boat test. Damn it, Lou, I wish you could have met her.

"Where are you and Darren going to sleep?"

"We'll cuddle on the chairs on the deck."

"That's not fair, I was hoping to cuddle with Darren."

"I can hear you," Darren yelled from topside.

"Sorry," Nate said. "Sleep well."

He lingered for a moment, she stared at him, studying his features, and they both stood in the small space of the cabin which was getting smaller every second. He leaned over to her and she met him halfway. The kiss was not intense, more restrained, more love than lust, but it fulfilled its meaning in letting both of them know that love was their ultimate goal, not sex, though both thought sex would be a great place to start.

"I can hear you kissing," Darren yelled from above.

Jimmy was pulling the pants off the girl he'd picked up in Newport at the Mooring Bar. He was having trouble getting them over her shoes, but then again he was drunk, the girl, too. Throw enough money around at a bar and you could attract lots of girls. It had been Jimmy's approach his whole life; he had never been known as a talker.

Doc and Stu were topside of Doc's boat drinking with the two girls Jimmy's friend had come with. The handheld GPS sitting on the dash beeped. Doc looked over to it and the word *searching* was replaced with the tracking map. He hit several buttons trying to bring up the last known bearings, but the combination of being drunk and a girl's hand down his pants made it hard (pun intended). He finally got the bearings. Pounding on the smoked glass door to the cabin, he said, "Hey, stud."

"WHAT?" Jimmy yelled from down below.

"New Bedford, they are in New Bedford," Doc yelled back, but all he could hear was moaning.

"Are we going after them now?" Stu asked while his girl talked endlessly on her cell phone.

"Only if you want to take a cab. Want to ask him?" Doc said, pointing to the cabin. The moaning got notably louder.

Shaking his head no, Stu said, "He usually falls asleep right after, probably on top of her." He looked back to the girl on the phone. When she saw him looking at her she cupped her hand over the receiver and started to laugh with the party on the other end.

"I just want to go home," Stu mumbled to himself, the only person who seemed to be listening.

CHAPTER 19: THE MUSEUM

Nate was up at the first sign of the sun, as a limited number of cars drove by and only a few people were out on the street, most of them heading early for the Vineyard ferry. Most people would tell you that sleeping outside was a pleasure, but in reality, when the temperature hit that magic number—the dew point—anything left outside would be soaking wet when morning came. Nate and Darren were no exceptions. He poked his head down below to see if he could retrieve some dry clothes without waking Kate. She was up, the hammock stowed, and she stood there brushing her blond hair.

"Hey, why are you all wet?"

"I'm glistening with the morning dew," Nate stated.

"Bummer," she said, handing him a towel.

"Sleep okay?"

"Actually, I did," Kate said. They headed up to the deck. Nate kicked the deck chair Darren was still sleeping on and Darren jumped awake, looking around.

"Morning, sunshine," Nate said, throwing a towel over Darren's head.

He got up and stretched and toweled off. "Man, I'm all out of dry clothes."

They made their way up Union Street, which ran through the center of the city. They stopped at a restaurant nestled on a cobblestone street just down from the museum. After a small breakfast and about five cups of coffee, they headed up Johnny Cake Hill, down another cobblestone street, which gave the neighborhood a nineteenth-century look. The Seaman's Bethel was on their right, with the old mariner's home next to that, which had been giving mariners a place to stay while in port since the 1700s. But sitting across the street was the brick building they hoped held some answers for them.

They paid their admissions and walked by the gift shop. As they passed it they noticed an oval bumper sticker, of the sort that was all the rage on cars and usually displayed abbreviations of towns or islands, but this one showed a sperm whale just like the one on the gold bar. Apparently it was the logo of the whaling museum. Nate nodded to the others, who looked to the sticker and back to Nate, eyes wide. They continued to walk around, taking in the sights of the city during its historic whaling days.

The whaling museum was a multi-floor building with rooms dedicated to different aspects of the whaling industry. The largest of the rooms held a half-scale version of the *Lagoda* whaling ship. The ship could be boarded and it gave a small understanding of life on a whale ship. Hanging above the ship, to the right, was a skeleton of a right whale, all hundred and twenty feet of her.

They entered a room of models of whale ships. They looked at each model, hoping that one would simply be named *Compass Rose*, but that would be too easy. Hanging on the wall behind one of the models was a hand-drawn map of the coast of New England. Dotted along the coast were drawings of tiny ships, showing the locations of where they were wrecked. The three of them leaned closer, finding Block Island on the map, and they noticed no whale ships drawn around their island. Kate saw a young man with a blue jacket and name tag walking around the room.

"Excuse me," she called to the young man. "I noticed a lot of wrecks around the coast. You wouldn't know of any around the island of Block in Rhode Island, would you?"

He shook his head. "No. But my expertise is in the local merchants of the era. Docent Saunders is quite the expert with wrecked and missing ships. Let me see if I can find him." The young docent headed out of the room and came back a few minutes later. "I'm sorry, he is about to leave for the day, but if you like you can email us and we will try to get an answer for you or check out our research department."

Nate stood there, his patience long gone, the feeling of a wild-goose chase growing in his soul. He shook his head in disagreement with the docent. "Can you try and catch Docent Saunders and tell him that we are commercial scuba divers from Rhode Island and we have found the wreck of a whale ship off the coast of Block Island?"

Darren and Kate stared at each other. The docent didn't answer but literally ran out of the room.

"I don't … we don't … have time for this," Nate said as he walked out of the exhibit room and into the *Lagoda* room.

Darren and Kate, with childhood enthusiasm, climbed aboard the ship. Nate sat down on a bench facing the ship, taking it all in. *What is it, Lou? What is the friggin' key to all of this?*

Kate leaned off the stern of the ship, looking down at Nate. "The isle is full of noises," she said. "Sounds, and sweet airs, that give delight and hurt not. Sometimes a thousand twangling instruments Will hum about mine ears; and sometimes voices, That if I then had wak'd after long sleep, Will make me sleep again, and then in dreaming, The clouds methought would open, and show riches Ready to drop upon me, that when I wak'd I cried to dream again."

Kate recited it perfectly, which sounded even richer with her English accent. This brought a smile to Nate's face.

"Shakespeare," said a gentleman dressed in the same jacket as the younger docent.

All three of them said in unison, "What?"

"Shakespeare, I believe from *The Tempest,* but I am not a hundred percent sure," he told them as he entered the great hall.

"What? You didn't know that?" Nate called up to Kate.

"What? Because I'm English I'm supposed to know Shakespeare?"

Nate nodded. "Yeah." She turned to Darren standing behind her, who was nodding in agreement with Nate.

"You, too?"

The docent walked up to Nate. "Hello there, I'm Ronald. Are you the group that thinks you discovered the *Gosnold*?" He was laughing.

"Is that funny?" Darren asked.

"The *Gosnold* is an enigma. People have spent their lives trying to find out its story."

"So there was a whale ship called the *Gosnold*," Kate said. "Did it sink off Block Island? We didn't see it on that map in the room with the ship models."

"Well the *Gosnold* ... was a ship with a lot of controversy, and most think that it was sunk on purpose, so you don't see it a lot in the books and maps. Plus most people think it's the byproduct of an overactive imagination. But don't let that scare you off. Tell me what you think you found."

"We're just some divers who might have discovered a wreck off our island. I'm Nate and the two up in the rigging are Kate and Darren." They both raised a hand when they heard their names. "Well ... actually, it was a family member we believe found the wreck years ago and never told anybody. We've recently stumbled on it ourselves. And now we're just trying to fill in the missing pieces."

The docent simply opened his hands palms up. Nate stared at him and let a smile stretch across his face.

"What makes you think it is the mysterious ship the *Gosnold*?"

"We found some artifacts that lead us to believe this," Nate explained.

"Dear God." Ron started to pace around the hall. "What kind of artifacts?"

Don't show him the gold, sunshine. Nate just smiled.

After a short silence Ron turned to the three of them. "The *Gosnold*, a one-hundred-fifty-foot, two-hundred-forty-ton whaler, it was the last great ship of its day. It sank during a hurricane in the 1800s, but it was never really clear where."

Kate and Darren joined Nate and Ronald in the middle of the great hall. He started walking from the great hall into the model-exhibit room.

"From what we know, which is mostly folklore with a bit of speculation thrown in, the *Gosnold* was at the end of a profitable career. It was 1856. The *Gosnold*, like most whale ships at this time, had to travel to the Pacific for whales. The journey would have lasted three to five years. They'd been stopping in the Tortola in the Virgin Isles for years on their way back to New Bedford. In 1860, upon leaving Tortola, they just missed a hurricane coming off the coast of Africa, but it caught up with them off Long Island. Hoping to outrun it, they tried to make it to Point Judith, Rhode Island, but off Block Island something happened and she caught fire and sank. The captain's name was Jacob Mayhew. He stated that it was a fire from an overturned lantern he accidentally kept burning in his cabin during the storm." Ron looked to the three of them.

"If you don't mind me saying, this ship seems to garnish a lot of your attention for what on the surface seems uneventful," Kate said while looking at a wall of photographs of whale men standing on the New Bedford State Pier with whale carcasses surrounding them.

Ronald laughed. "The folklore portion of my little uneventful story is the part you might really be interested in. After the sinking, the captain, part of a very influential family here in the city, left whaling and lived a very rich life, buying vast amounts of real estate and even donating money to this very museum for its construction. The second mate started a textile mill that became the biggest in the city. It seemed that every crew member came out of this mishap financially better off. But the interesting part is that the family of the captain depended on the success of this last trip to get them out of debt. Like most whaling families, they stayed in the business a couple of years too long and were on the verge of bankruptcy. The ship, by its own captain's account, was sunk due to his error, the insurance policy was voided, and there was the loss of the oil; one would speculate that this would be the end of the Mayhew family fortune. But like the rest of the crew, they seem to have come out of this situation very well indeed. So just how did they do so well when all was lost? Now I come to the last portion of my uneventful little story, which is the pure folklore, but I believe it still resonates throughout this city today. One member of the crew wasn't as secret with his upturn, financially speaking.

Christopher was his name, and after his return he fell madly in love with a girl from a very powerful and rich family. After every attempt to attract her admiration failed, he tried to buy the respect of her father. And he told the matriarch a story … a story of years of selling the whale oil the *Gosnold* got on the black market outside of industry regulators, converting this black market oil to gold and building a power base that would give them an edge when the industry finally crashed."

"They must have gotten the gold off the ship before it sank," Darren added.

"If they hit Southwest Ledge, they were going down fast," Nate said. "No way I'm buying that. That gold went down with the *Gosnold*."

"So people survived the sinking?" Kate asked.

"Every single one of the crew made it to shore in their long boats, and nobody from the ship ever spoke of the sinking again."

"Well you seem to know quite a bit about the *Gosnold*," Kate said. "It doesn't sound like much of an enigma."

"This story I just told you was told to me by a volunteer here, and it took him ten years to research it. Nobody has ever spoken of it, not of the sinking or anything of their fortune. Captain Mayhew told of the *Gosnold* floundering and being blown out to sea for miles until it finally burned and sank beyond their sight."

"Well that's convenient," Kate said.

"Jesus … it's the burning ghost ship," Darren whispered to himself as he turned to Nate, who partially nodded in agreement.

Ron's tone became very serious. "Now … you didn't find gold down there, did you, son?"

Nate, without pausing or showing any sign of lying, looked into his eyes and said, "No." *You are getting better at lying, sunshine.*

"Well, then, what did you find?"

"Tools and kettles and the such," Nate explained.

"Anything with the ship's name?"

Nate shook his head.

"Well, my guess is you found one of thousands of ships lost or sunk on purpose after their usefulness was gone. Where did you get the idea of the *Gosnold* to begin with?"

"From an old family friend who recently passed," Nate told him.

Ron's eyes welled up and he stared off to the side for a split second. It was ever so slight; you would have to have been looking for it to have caught it.

The docent looked back to Nate.

"I never mentioned the name of the ship," Nate calmly said.

Ron was sweating a bit, and it was obvious that he wanted them the hell out of there, but he continued nevertheless: "Well, somebody's fooling with you. But feel free to continue this folly, there, sunshine."

Nate froze in his spot. "What did you just call me?"

Ron smiled. "If you want more info on the whaling era, please see our research assistant, Laura, in back of the auditorium. I'm late for a meeting. It was a pleasure to meet all of you, but if you would excuse me." They shook hands and he left them in the room surrounded by pictures of dead whale men.

"We're being set up," Nate said.

"By who?" Darren asked skeptically.

"Lou ..." Nate said as he headed for the research department.

Kate and Darren looked at each other. "He's losing it," Darren said, and Kate shrugged.

They caught up to Nate in a room that was made up of nothing but photos and portraits. Kate was mesmerized by the pictures. Slowly she walked around the room, looking at every picture with intense interest. They entered a room of nothing but black and white pictures from floor to ceiling, portraits of everything from ships to dead whales; Kate was staring at each and every picture.

"Kate? Kate?" Nate called out to her.

"Pictures just fascinate me to no end. Something about a moment caught in time. What were they thinking? Who were they? What did they make of their lives? It seems to me that we owe it to them, to take time and look at them."

Nate and Darren were taken in by her passion and started to look around.

Kate was slowly walking around the room. "So what's this fire ship you mentioned back there?"

"Well, Nate knows it better; I'm just the guy who believes it."

"I want you to tell me." She smiled at Darren.

"Well, back in the early history of Block, when the area wasn't really civilized yet, there was a small group of people called wreckers who gave false signals to passing ships, or just set traps for them, and they'd rob the ships when they wrecked. One ship in particular came by the island, it was in trouble to begin with—something about the captain being murdered at sea and the weather battering them hard. These wreckers went out to remove them, along with any items they wanted. But an old lady who'd apparently gone mad on the journey from Europe refused to leave. So they set the ship on fire to get her off. She didn't leave. The ship blew back out to sea, and they could hear the screams of the burning woman. And witnesses for years said that once a year they saw the fire ship and heard the screaming of the woman."

"And you believe this?"

Darren smiled and shrugged.

"That's kind of cute that you do."

"Hey, what if the *Gosnold* when burning was mistaken for one of the sightings of the fire ship?" Darren asked.

"That would legitimize the story Ronald just told us," Nate said. "I guess."

"Oh my dear God," Kate mumbled.

"What is it, Kate?" Nate walked over to her.

"Gentlemen, I give you Captain Jacob Mayhew."

It seemed that most whale captains and especially the ships' owners were vain men. Their portraits were large and imposing—four feet tall with large wooden frames, the men with stoic looks on their bearded faces. The portrait of the captain of the *Gosnold* was a lot smaller than the others, a simple eight-by-ten with a plain wooden frame, and he was smiling. Nate examined the painting and the name Jacob Mayhew etched on the nameplate fixed to the frame.

"What's your secret, Captain? What is your connection to Lou?"

Kate, standing behind Nate, blew on his neck, making him jump a foot.

"Funny," he told her.

"Hey, guys?" Darren said. "I found the *Gosnold* and you're not going to believe what else."

When Kate and Nate leaned in to take a closer look at what had attracted Darren's attention, Nate stopped breathing for a moment. The old eight-by-ten black and white photograph was of three men, and behind them a ship tied to the dock.

"How can you be sure?" Nate asked him.

"Take a closer look, first the ship. You can't make out the name on the stern, but three letters are visible."

Nate leaned in closer. "G O S," he spelled out. This brought Kate closer. "Okay, I'm with you so far."

"Okay, now take a look at the flag that's on the rail at the stern."

"Oh my dear God," Kate said.

"Exactly."

The little white flag wasn't any bigger than two-by-two and was frozen in the wind that must have been blowing that day. The imprint on the flag was a simple outline of a whale, just like the one that had brought them here.

"The three men, the guy in the middle," Kate said, "the tall one, look at the confidence in his face, how he's standing there. Now look at his portrait again. That's Captain Mayhew all right. And the other two I don't know, but I wonder if it's the mate who was in love."

"We're close," Darren said from behind them.

They all stared at the photo.

"I'm not the kind of guy who believes in coincidences," Darren said, "never have."

"Oh I'm getting goose bumps all over my body," Kate said as Darren, like a little boy trying to sneak a peek, glanced at her body then looked back at the picture.

"Let's go to the research department," Nate said with that smile of his.

They followed the signs to the research room in the back of the auditorium. A young woman was roaming the room like a grade-school teacher, stopping here and there to see if anybody needed help. She looked up as they entered the room and she practically ran over to them—more of a hop than a run, Kate thought. She approached the group, telling them her name—Tina—as she pointed to her nametag, which was decorated with little drawn flowers and smiley faces. It took a unique individual to put that much attention into a little thing like a nametag.

"Laura's off today, but whatever you need, I'm your girl," she said.

Kate shook her head, trying to clear the enthusiasm out of it. But before any of them could ask a question, Tina ramped up: "This research facility has over ten thousand books, which can be searched with our online database." Her voice seemed to get higher as she finished a sentence. All three nodded their heads in acknowledgement. "Most of the books were donations of our fantastic members, whose names are on the great wall when you enter," the girl said, with a few giggles thrown in.

Darren leaned over to Kate's ear and whispered, "I think she's a robot." They both tried to hold in a laugh.

"Well shucks, Tina, how do we get started?" said Kate, faking her attitude. Nate gave her a raised eyebrow.

"Wow, are you from England?" Before Kate could answer, Tina was off and running again. "One of my Facebook friends is from England, Judy Everheart." Tina stopped and stared wide-eyed at Kate, giving her the *do you know her* look.

Kate just stared back, smiling.

"Anyways … You have to be a member of the museum to have access to the database or check out any books," she said, again laughing.

Nobody could see what was so funny, but they went with it for now.

"Well, Tina, if we're not?" Kate asked.

"Not what?"

"Members," all three answered.

"You guys aren't members?"

Darren busted out laughing and tried to hide it by coughing and walking away.

"No we are not, Tina," Nate said, keeping the only straight face of the three.

"Well that's super easy to fix. Go to the front desk and for a small annual donation you can be a member—so what are you waiting for? Go sign up. It's wicked easy."

"Wicked easy?" Kate said.

"Wicked easy," Tina said, laughing.

"Okay then, thank you, Tina," Nate said.

"That's what I'm here for, so if you need anything, I'm your girl."

"Yes you are," Nate replied, and after Tina hopped out of the research room Kate and Darren were in tears, leaning on each other.

"Everybody just calm down," Nate said with a smile, laughing. "I'll go to the front desk and sign up, because apparently it's wicked easy. Why don't you two knuckleheads have a look around, but don't touch anything till I get back."

They both laughed at Nate as he headed out of the room.

They slowly walked around the room, glancing at books and some artifacts hanging on the wall. Kate found her way to a whiteboard and took a marker from the tray. Darren found a comfy armchair and plopped down in it.

"What does he need to find out?" Kate asked, uncapping the marker.

"Well, more about the *Gosnold* or what is the *Gosnold* or who is the *Gosnold* ... oh, and don't forget, the compass rose, with the same questions applying."

Kate wrote *Gosnold* and compass rose on the board. "What else?" she asked.

"The captain, maybe he has a connection to Block."

Kate wrote *the captain*. "Oh," she said, and wrote *The Tempest*. "Ronald says that thing I recited from Lou's letter was from that." She turned to face Darren and saw Nate standing in the doorway, all the color gone from his face. "Nate? My God."

Darren spun in his chair, reacting to Kate. "Jesus, Nate," Darren said.

"Nate, what's wrong?" Kate asked as she headed for him.

"Lou."

"What, what do you mean Lou?" she asked, by his side now. "What about Lou?"

"It's Lou," Nate mumbled again.

"Nate? Did you see Lou's ghost?" Darren asked in his scared voice as he stood up.

"Sort of."

"What?" Kate said. "Come on … you're scaring Darren."

"I went to sign up. It seems that I'm already a member, a lifetime member."

"What?" the two said, in perfect sync.

"About a year ago somebody made me a lifetime member, paid in full. I told her that wasn't possible, so she looked it up. Louis Gauthier, she said."

"Now I've got goose bumps all over my body," Darren stated.

Nate looked around the room; he stopped at the whiteboard. "Please tell me you wrote that."

Darren and Kate both gave a little snort of laughter.

"Well, the good news is that if we find nothing, at least they gave me three Whaling Museum tee shirts." He threw them each a shirt. Darren opened up the shirt and saw the whale logo staring right at him.

"I told you we were close," Darren said. "The old man definitely wanted you here."

"It goes way beyond that. According to the older volunteer behind the desk, Rita, Lou has been coming here for fifteen years. At first he was involved heavily in some research, then as the years passed he helped with building and organizing exhibits. Then his visits were less frequent --"

"Let me guess, till about one year ago?" Kate asked.

"And for the past year, guess who he went to lunch with every time?"

"Rita," Darren stated proudly.

Nate and Kate laughed. "Ron Saunders," Nate said.

"Yeah," Darren said. "That's who I meant."

"You think he was researching the *Gosnold*?" Kate asked.

"I think the discussion with Ron the Docent is proof of that," Nate said, looking at the computer on the long oak table. He stared at it for a moment. "They gave me a login number and password," he said, but didn't move any closer to the terminal.

"You never worked a computer, have you?" Kate asked. Nate shook his head no. She turned to Darren.

"I can search for porn," Darren said.

"Jesus, it's like you guys live on Gilligan's Island."

"I have a cell phone," Darren said defensively.

Kate sat down at the terminal. "What do we look for first?" Kate asked.

"Try *Gosnold*," Nate told her. Kate typed the word in the search box and clicked the mouse. In a few seconds it had one thousand search hits, which displayed the corresponding books below.

"Crap, that's a lot of books to start looking through," Darren said.

"We have too much information," Nate said. "If I was to follow Lou's clues, it would only be from the information in his letter to me. But there must have been something we missed, something I haven't found yet, or maybe he just never got around to what was supposed to guide me here. But this is where I'm supposed to be," he said, looking up at the whiteboard. "*The Tempest*, start with *The Tempest*."

Once again, with a very high level of speed, she typed *The Tempest*.

"Let me guess, you were a typist, too," Nate asked as Kate just smiled.

The search revealed one hit.

"There is only one book pertaining to *The Tempest* in this room," Kate said.

After a few minutes of searching, it was no surprise that Kate was the one to find it. She handed the hardcover book to Nate. "This is your little family mystery, you're the only one who would know it if you see it," she said. She headed back to the computer with Darren by her side. "We'll *try compass rose next*," she said, already typing.

Nate sat there staring at the cover of the book titled *People and Culture in Southeastern Massachusetts.* He slowly opened it as if it were a magical book and the answer would be right there, smack dab on the first page. *No such luck, sunshine, I'm not going to make it that easy.* The book was a byproduct of the Works Progress Administration, created by President Roosevelt to put people to work during the Depression. The WPA paid people to pave roads, build government buildings, and in this occasion, write essays. This book in particular had come from the Federal Writers' Project, which paid local writers for stories and essays about their areas.

Kate was up looking for a book while Darren was doing the hunt-and-peck on the keyboard. Just as she was returning with a book, SLAM, the book Nate was reading hit the desk hard, and everyone in the room jumped.

"SON OF A BITCH," Nate cried. "You son of a bitch. You laid it all out for me ... every clue, right there for me to see."

Tina popped her head into the room. "Is everything all right?"

"Yes, Tina, everything is fine," Darren said, staring at Nate.

Both of them were by his side now. "What, what did you find?" Kate asked.

Nate was not really talking to the two of them, more to himself; he got up and started pacing the room. "Lou has been laying all this out for me over the years, baiting me. I mean from the whale ship painting in his house, to my interest in the early New England explorers, to the places where he taught me to fish—all of this has been laid out before me."

Nate walked over to the book and opened it up. "It's all right here. This is the story of Bartholomew Gosnold, and it's the story I've been telling all my life. Growing up I learned about Bart from my father. Bart sailed into these waters in 1602, eighteen years before the pilgrims up there in Plymouth. He sailed up the Acushnet River, the very route we took to get here today. He set up a camp, fished for cod. Took sassafras trees, and made very good friends with the local natives, the Wampanoags. After a summer of great delight, he decided not to stay. The cargo he and his crew loaded on their ship, the *Concord*, was worth a small fortune back in England. So he left, with one hell of a map of Cape Cod and the islands ... my God ... he was the one who named it Cape Cod and Buzzards Bay. And that chain of islands we passed last night, he called them 'Elizabeth Islands.'"

"After his queen," Kate added.

"After his queen. He even named Martha's Vineyard. This was the guy I wanted to be, to see all of this land for the first time. To witness so much fish that you could not sail into the bay without them getting in the way. To have the sky filled with so many birds that it darkened the sky for hours. This is the soul I wanted to have, to become. Knowing my love for Bart, Lou used this to get my attention, but he needed to get me to an exact location. And Bart roamed all of Buzzards Bay. Which brings us to this book. This research was done during the Depression, but it was never published until about sixteen years ago, so I never would have seen it growing up. By the time it was finally published, girls and fish were more important to me than good Bart here. It seems," he said, looking down at the book, "that Bart's first mate, John Brenton, loved a certain island so much that it was all he talked about when they got home, especially in the company of Bart and his patron, the Earl of Southampton, who was also a patron of Mr. William Shakespeare. The theory goes that Brenton's description and Shakespeare's description of the island from *The Tempest* sound a lot alike. Lou is using the lines from *The Tempest* to tell me where to go next. It's the island that Gosnold and Brenton fell in love with that summer in 1602. It's where they set up camp.

Darren said it first: "Cuttyhunk Island."

"New England in the summer, you got to love it," Nate said with a smile on his face.

"I take it we're going to this Cuttyhunk place?" Kate asked.

"Those Elizabeth Islands we talked about, it's the last one in the chain of twelve, and it's only about a half an hour away," Nate explained.

"What about the compass rose?" Kate asked. She looked down at the computer. "We have one thousand two hundred and five search hits."

"It's not here. The first clue was the lines from *The Tempest*, which leads us to Cuttyhunk. Then he gives the compass rose. That answer, I believe, is somewhere on that island."

Before Nate closed the book he noticed that someone had drawn, in a corner of the page, a small compass rose. *Damn it, Lou, stop screwing with me …*

CHAPTER 20: A CALL FROM HOME

They made their way down Water Street back across Route 6, running against the traffic. Kate saw the potential problem before the two boys did. "We've got company," she said.

Nate's and Darren's heads jerked so hard to the floating dock to which the *Legacy* was tied that it made Kate jump herself.

The New Bedford harbor master's boat and a state police boat were tied up to Nate's.

"Jesus, Kate, I thought it was the boys from Providence," Nate told her.

"Sorry, but this can't be good either, can it?" she said, trying to defend her position.

They walked down the ramp and onto their boat. The harbor master put down his cell phone and turned to the three of them.

"Hi, is there a problem?" Nate asked.

"I take it this is your boat?" the harbor master asked, even though he knew the answer.

"Yes, sir, Capt," Nate said, smiling. Calling anyone behind the wheel of a boat "Capt"—short for captain—was a maritime tradition, but mainly just served to boost the ego of that person. The harbor master's chest seemed to have puffed out a few inches. Nate put out his hand for the harbor master to shake. "Nate West," he said. When it was obvious that this hand was not going to be shaken, he lowered it and tried a different tack, because playing the dumb card—*What, you can't tie up here?*—wasn't going to get him anywhere.

"Is there a problem?" Nate asked in a serious, *I belong here* tone.

"What makes you think that tying up to a restricted dock and going sightseeing is permitted?" the harbor master asked.

"Look, I've tied up here before without a problem, and for the record, we had dire circumstances for doing this."

"Dire circumstances, huh?" the harbor master said, shaking his head.

Kate leaned into Nate and whispered in his ear, "Hey, mate, we are wearing matching New Bedford Whaling Museum tee shirts. And yours still has the price tag."

"I told you we would look silly," Nate shot back.

"I think Darren and I look great."

Nate jumped on the harbor master's boat and walked over to him. He was writing something on his clipboard.

"Is James Potvin still running things for you guys?" Nate asked.

"Well, he stopped running things around here right about the time we stopped people from tying up to this dock. You should know that since 9/11 the State Pier is under a restricted policy."

"Look, I'm sorry I didn't follow procedure, and I hope I didn't cause too much trouble. I didn't know this would be a problem. So I'll just be on my way now."

"No, Mr. West, there is no problem. You see, this is my job. And part of my job is to impound illegal vessels. You see there is no problem with any of this."

Nate stared at the harbor master, trying to think of a way out of this, fast.

On the opposite side of the State Pier was a parking lot, which had another fifty or so fishing vessels tied up to its docks. Beside this lot stood the Wharfinger Building, which had been an office for the whaling trade a hundred years ago and was now a small visitor's museum. To the far left of the parking lot was the Global Oil Company, which supplied fuel for the fishing fleet and any recreational vessel that needed it. That was where the *Big Booty* was fueling as Nate and the gang were getting a shakedown from the Harbor Master from Hell.

Jimmy and Stu were standing just to the left of the museum, hiding around the ticket booth for the Cuttyhunk Island ferry.

"It's got to be in his red backpack," Stu said. "We went through that boat, top to bottom."

"I am going to strangle him with it."

"I would wait until the police are gone," Stu advised.

Jimmy closed his eyes and slightly shook his head. "When the cops are done with him he is ours, there is no fucking way he can get out of this one," Jimmy said as he turned and headed back to Doc and his *Big Booty*.

"A towboat will be here shortly to bring your boat to our impound mooring, and that's where it will stay until you pay your fine and appear in court on trespassing charges."

"I'm sorry, I didn't get your name," Nate asked.

"Harbor Master Corriea."

"Captain Corriea, just let me pay the fine and I will be on my way."

"Why does he keep saying 'I'?" Darren whispered to Kate. "There are three of us up to here in shit."

"He needs the company of a woman to let him see the error of his ways," she whispered back.

"There is no way you're walking out on this violation," the harbor master stated.

"Nate West, right?" asked the state trooper, who finally put down his phone.

"Yes, sir," Nate answered.

The trooper went from his boat to the harbor master's to Nate's. He put out his hand.

"I don't know if you remember me, I'm John Holden—last year? Me and four other troopers chartered you for a fish derby out of Connecticut and you got us a fifty-two-pound striper."

"Absolutely, I didn't recognize you with your uniform. You came with your dad … Barry. Right?"

"That's us," the trooper said, smiling ear to ear.

Thanks, Lou.

Seizing on his good fortune, Nate was not going to let it go. "How is your dad handling retirement?"

Still smiling, the trooper said, "Great. Fishing every day."

"Well, tell him if he needs any hot spots to give me a call."

"I will, but he will call you every day," the trooper said, laughing.

"Jesus," the harbor master said, "can we break up the love fest? Here comes the towboat."

"Let them go, Manny," Trooper Holden told him.

"WHAT?"

"Let them go."

Manny, the harbor master, who had a chip on his shoulder the size of a small rodent, grabbed Trooper Holden's arm and turned him away from the other three. "They are in violation—*violation*. If you just let everybody go who violates our policies, the harbor will be in anarchy."

"Anarchy, Manny? Don't you think you're overstating it a bit?"

"NO, I DON'T."

"Okay, Manny, three things. First, hold it down, you're embarrassing me. Second, listen carefully, let them go. He is a friend, and we all need friends, Manny, especially one that can fish like him. Third --"

Manny interrupted, "You can't tell me what to do. I am the New Bedford harbor master."

"And I'm a Massachusetts state trooper, assigned to New Bedford harbor, and that trumps a city harbor master. Always has, always will."

Trooper Holden was like most Massachusetts state troopers, tall and intimidating. Standing a foot taller than Manny, his stare alone would have made most people pee their pants. Finally, the intimidation seeping through his pores, Manny got it and stared down at his feet. "What's the third thing?" he asked.

"Let go of my arm before I shoot you."

Darren and Kate slowly got on the *Legacy* and slid over to the dock lines as Trooper Holden talked Harbor Master Manny down from the ledge. Trooper Holden leaned over to Nate's boat. "Nate, you can leave. Next time just call me and it won't be a problem to tie up here." He handed Nate his business card.

"Thanks, John. I mean it about your dad, too."

With a small laugh, Trooper Holden said, "Great, that will mean a lot to him."

Nate started the engine and turned on the electronics. Kate and Darren stood with him in the cockpit. "You're the friggin' luckiest person I know," Darren said.

"Fishing will save your soul."

"I am starting to believe that," Darren replied.

As all three boats started to untie from each other Trooper Holden shouted, "Oh, Nate, I almost forgot. Your friends were here when we arrived. They said they didn't know where you were. But they told me to tell you what's up. And they will be catching up to you real soon."

Nate's stomach did a three-sixty as Kate and Darren bolted upright from their untying and all three glanced at each other.

"I'm not sure who you're talking about. Can you describe them?"

"Muscle boat—formula, I believe, blue and orange—a driver, and two others ... mid-thirties, one dressed in all black. Ring any bells?"

"Oh yeah," Nate answered.

Kate walked over to the side of the boat to talk to Trooper Holden. "Actually it's an old boyfriend of mine, been kind of bugging us," Kate told him. At this the harbor master's ears perked up.

Nate turned to Kate with a wry smile creeping across his face. "Hey, John, we were wondering if you two could do us a little favor," Nate asked.

Kate looked to Darren and shrugged. "Now it's 'us,'" Darren smiled and finished untying the boat.

"They're moving," Doc said, turning to Stu, who was pumping fuel. Jimmy looked over to the alleyway that Nate was in and with a smile waited for the *Legacy* to come out behind the towboat. The towboat emerged from the State Pier first, then the harbor master's boat and then the trooper's boat, and they turned north, heading deeper into the harbor toward the Fairhaven-New Bedford Bridge.

"What the fuck is this shit?" Jimmy yelled out to the harbor. When the *Legacy* came out last it took all of three seconds before the engine roared and headed south toward the hurricane barrier entrance as fast as she could.

"Let's go, let's go—NOW!" Jimmy yelled. Doc was up throwing money at the attendant and Stu was untying the boat. The loud thunder of the engines as they came to life backed the attendant away from the edge of the fuel dock.

"Come on!" Jimmy yelled again.

"Jimmy, we can track them," Doc yelled over the roar of the engines. "I am not comfortable screaming off after them."

Jimmy gave Doc a stare that brought Doc's hands down to the throttles so fast that a second look was not necessary. The boat planed up in the water and the thousand-yard gap was closing fast. Within five seconds of the Big Booty's takeoff, the trooper's and harbor master's boats spun on a dime and with sirens blaring took off after the Providence boys. It seemed to the boys that they knew they were going to fly after them. As Doc throttled back, he looked over his shoulder to the blue lights. Jimmy watched the ever-shrinking Legacy and with his ever-aging eyes he couldn't be sure, but he believed Nate was giving him that finger again.

"How the HELL did they find us?" Kate screamed.

Darren was standing at the stern watching the *Big Booty* being sandwiched with the authorities. "If you even suggest that I had anything to do with this ..."

"I am not even thinking about it," Nate said. "So relax."

"That is getting increasingly harder to do around here," Darren said, finally turning around to face them. His phone went off with that silly ringtone and all three jumped a little. He walked past Kate and Nate to get his phone from down below. He popped back up, flipping it open. "Jesus, I have ten missed calls and four voicemails." He put the phone to his ear. "Jesus Christ—Nate? The calls are from Rebecca. You need to call her right now, she sounds frantic."

Nate didn't get rattled easily. But if his friends—Rebecca in particular—were in trouble, that was a different story. When Rebecca and Nate were sixteen, Charlie Graber tried to get to third base with her, and when she wouldn't have it, after a raging argument between the two, he sent her home crying. After Nate found out, the Graber kid came to school with two black eyes, and when they went away, he came back with two new ones. Nate was biting the inside of his cheek now as he made the call home. On the first ring, Rebecca answered.

"Beck?"

"Nate, Mike's missing." She just blurted it out. No easy way to break into this.

"What? My God … Beck, what happened?"

"Nobody has seen him since last night. When he didn't come this morning, I checked around. He was supposed to go to a beach party last night … never showed. I called his mother, just being casual, and she said he told her he was going to be out fishing with you all night. That was yesterday afternoon. It's my fault, I didn't tell him to be careful, to stick close to Jack and Josh." Rebecca started to cry. It was only the third time Nate had heard her cry, including the incident with Graber.

"Beck, call the police, tell them everything, and then tell Sergeant Cofflin to call me. Okay?" He could hear her snort a cry of acknowledgement. "Where's Jack and Josh?"

"They went to check your house. Oh wait, here they come now."

They entered the visitor's booth and headed straight for Rebecca. Josh said, "Is that Nate?" He put out his hand for the phone and Rebecca's shaking hand gave it to him. "Nate, they got Mike."

Nate's mind started spinning, no need to ask what or how, he heard it right the first time, no need to repeat. He could hear Rebecca scream in the background.

"I don't know who, but there was a note pinned to your office door. It says, 'I have something you're missing and you have what I want. Call the cops and it will remain missing.' They left a phone number."

He gave Nate the number.

"Listen very carefully," Nate said. "I told Rebecca to call the police. Obviously, do not do that. I have to hang up right now ... no time to explain. I will call back shortly." Nate hung up.

Jack walked over to Rebecca, and she collapsed in his arms. A young redhead with an Irish accent knocked and entered the visitor's booth. Josh went over to her and explained it was not a good time. "But I found Kurt," the redhead said, and Rebecca jumped up and ran over to her.

Nate gave the other end of the conversation to Darren and Kate as he pulled Trooper Holden's business card out of his wallet. He was frantic trying to punch in the numbers. Darren and Kate just stared at each other; Darren sighed and ran his hand through his hair.

The three boats were all tied together. Jimmy and Stu were sitting at the helm, avoiding the trooper's eyes. The harbor master was on the phone with someone reading off Doc's registration numbers for the third time; either the person on the other end was deaf or Harbor Master Manny kept screwing up. Whichever one it was, it was making everybody very nervous. The trooper was just sitting there, staring at boats idling by, the people in them gawking, probably relieved it was not them who'd been stopped by the police. Trooper Holden made a mental note of one of the boats, thinking maybe he'd pull it over later, just for shits and giggles, whatever that meant.

Stu leaned over to his brother. "If they search us, will they find anything ... you know?"

"WHAT ...?" Jimmy tried again, a little softer. "What the fuck you think he does for a living?" he said, gesturing to Doc.

Stu shrugged. "I never asked him."

"There are probably enough illegal guns below to overthrow a small Central American country."

Stu, his eyes bugging out, stole a sideways glance at the harbor master.

The harbor master handed Doc his paperwork back. "Do you mind if we come aboard and check you for safety equipment?"

"Actually we are in a rush, but thanks."

"I'm sorry I worded it as a question. Prepare to be boarded," Manny advised.

Doc looked over to the boys, who slowly started to stand a little straighter. Jimmy thought about the gun at the small of his back. He was not going to be taken down like this, not from the likes of these guys—no way.

The trooper, who smiled when Manny told them to prepare to be boarded, answered his phone on the second ring. He listened for a minute or so. "You got it. No problem, really I will actually enjoy it." He hung up his phone, swung his feet off the side of the boat, and got up from his captain's chair.

With one leg on the *Big Booty* and the three Providence boys backed up against the cabin door, Trooper Holden turned to the harbor master.

"Let them go, Manny."

Manny didn't turn to face Trooper Holden, but picked his head up and stared out to the harbor. He didn't move, didn't utter a word. With one leg on the deck of his boat and the other on the rail of Doc's, he looked like the Captain Morgan pirate on the rum bottle. Manny just stepped off the boys' boat and walked to his helm, threw his clipboard on the dash, and started his engine. Doc and Stu were untying their boat as fast as humanly possible.

"Call this number and thank them for this," Trooper Holden said. "Oh, and slow the fuck down in my harbor."

Doc took the card and handed it to Jimmy. Their boat slowly pulled away from the other two and throttled up just a bit and headed out through the hurricane barrier.

"My harbor?" Manny turned to Trooper Holden.

"Prepare to be boarded?" Holden shot back.

The *Legacy* was sitting in the middle of Butler Flats, using the lighthouse as a shield from the exit of the harbor a half mile away.

"What are you doing, you're letting them go? We had them," Darren argued.

"Somebody kidnapped Mike, and it can't be them. The timeline from Providence to New Bedford doesn't give them the time to get Mike late yesterday afternoon. So somebody on the island has him. If everybody is involved with each other, having them busted is not going to help resolve this shit in a good way."

"Somebody has Mike," Kate gasped. "My God."

Darren's cell phone started to ring. Nate looked down at it and flipped it open. Put it to his ear and didn't speak.

The voice on the other end said, "I guess I have you to thank for getting us out of that potential problem," Jimmy said.

"Where's my friend?"

"I'm your friend, Nate."

"Fuck off, asshole. I'll give you the gold, right now. Just tell me where Mike is."

After a short pause, Jimmy said, "I have no idea what you're talking about." A serious tone had taken over his voice.

Nate rubbed his hand over his head. "Whoever you are working for has my friend. I think you need to get on the same page here, Jimmy. Murder and now kidnapping? Jesus, that's a lot of jail time. Oh, I'm thinking federal charges, you'll get the feds involved on this one."

"I need to make a phone call."

"You do that and call me back." Nate hung up the phone and he headed down into the cabin. "They're tracking us somehow."

"What makes you so sure?" Kate asked.

"Somebody was on my boat, and now everywhere we go they turn up. I had Mike ask around. He came back with Darren, and after the discussion in my living room the day of Lou's funeral, I told him to ask around again to double-check Darren's story." Nate was taking off the access panel to the circuit panel that controlled the *Legacy's* electronics.

"Thanks, buddy."

Nate tilted his head. "Anyways, somebody must have found out he was onto him. It's my fault, I got all of you into this, and now Mike is in trouble."

"Jesus, Nate, I think we are all in trouble," Kate said.

"Got it," Nate yelled.

All three of them crammed into the front cabin.

"I mean I'm not an electronics expert … but Lou and I installed all these electronics ourselves. I spent a week in this panel." He was pointing to a small black box, about the size of an iPod, that was attached with clamps and wires to the boat's GPS. "This is not part of it."

"Can you really do something like this?" Darren asked.

"You two really need to get cable TV," Kate said. "They can track cars with this type of technology. They have chips in cell phones and even in pets. It's a GPS world, it's really no big deal to do."

"Thank you, Professor Honeydew," Nate said.

Darren went to unplug it. "No, wait," Nate said. "Let them track us for a moment longer." Kate and Darren looked at the transmitter and back to Nate.

Darren's phone went off. Nate reached up out of the cabin and felt around the dash and brought the phone back down.

"Papa Gino's," Nate answered.

"Funny, Nate," Jimmy answered.

"What did you find out?"

"Well, we are having trouble getting in touch with our associate right now, so what do you suggest?"

"The way I figure it, Jimmy, I don't think you are aware that someone kidnapped my friend, so maybe I'll just call my state trooper friend back to search your boat." Nate let this sink in.

"All I want is what's due to me. I want the gold."

"Why do you think you're due the gold?"

"Long story. Maybe we should meet and I'll tell you all about it."

"You know that's not a bad idea," Nate said. "But two things. First, can you give me the name of the person on my island that you're dealing with?"

"Fuck you."

"Okay, I'll help you out a bit here." Nate read the phone number that Jack had given him from the note left on Nate's office door. There was a long pause on Jimmy's end. "I'm taking that silence to mean that this is the number you've been calling. I'll let you know where we're going to meet when I'm ready."

"What makes you sure I'll wait?"

"That brings us to number two. Now you see me … now you don't." Nate nodded at Darren, who pulled the clips off the electronics wiring. He ran up to the helm and took off down Buzzards Bay.

At that exact moment Doc's handheld GPS beeped and entered into search mode.

"We lost them," Doc announced.

CHAPTER 21:
MAD MAX AND MENEMSHA POND

Nate took the *Legacy* through Woods Hole, which was one of three ways to get from Buzzards Bay through to Vineyard Sound. A very tricky maneuver, some would have said, if you caught it on the wrong tide. With Falmouth to their left and the beginning of the Elizabeth Islands, with Hadley's Harbor, to their right, Nate pulled the boat off to the right of the channel, with a clear shot to see anybody approaching.

Kate and Darren stared at Nate, who was violently biting the inside of his mouth. "Give me a few more minutes here," he said, "and I'll try to explain my reasoning."

"You're not in this alone," Kate said.

"It's my fault Mike is missing—*my* fault." He opened the phone and dialed the visitor's booth. It didn't even ring and Jack answered. "Jack, how's Rebecca?"

"Lying down. She's pretty upset. Nate, listen … Rebecca has every girl under her control running around the island asking questions. Something came up, maybe you can make sense of it. Mike's friend Kurt, the kid who works on the ferry, got into it with Mike yesterday afternoon. According to one of Rebecca's spies, it was over a prank that he played on Mike. The night Kurt saw Darren on your boat was a lie; it was David Cavarlo on your boat that night. David convinced Kurt it was a joke and gave him fifty bucks to tell Mike that it was Darren."

This was the second time David's name had been brought up in this; Nate had been denying it to himself since Darren's father mentioned his

name. He didn't want to believe it, couldn't believe it. David Cavarlo,
lifelong friend. He knew Lou, for God's sake. He couldn't be capable of
murder.

Gold, I tell ya ... gold.

"You still there, Nate?"

"Yeah ..."

"What's David got to do with this?"

"I'm starting to think everything. Where is he now?"

"Well that's the part that scares me. He's missing, too. The town's
emergency boat is gone also."

"Great, just great. Okay. Take care of Rebecca; I'll try to call you later."

"Nate, there's a storm coming and I don't mean metaphorically. The
remnants of Hurricane Beal, big seas, high winds, a lot of rain, should be
here tonight, late. It's fast moving, should be gone by morning."

"Jesus, is it too much to ask for a simple break?"

"Nate?"

"Yeah?"

"You know ..."

"Yeah, I will, just take care of Rebecca."

Nate left the cockpit and started pacing around the stern of the boat.
Kate and Darren were leaning at the back wall of the cockpit, watching
him try to reason this hole steaming pile of shit out. The boat drifted
close to shore; Darren steered back to the middle of the cove and turned
back to Nate, who finally filled in the missing gaps of the conversations
he'd had with Jimmy and Jack.

"David? How can that be? We're talking about murder here. He is
... was a friend. One of us. My God, Nate. It can't be."

"We're missing a big part to this story," Nate said. "There's got to be
something big that got him into this mess. Your dad mentioned David
when he wanted to talk to me alone."

"That's what he told you? Why wouldn't he just tell me that?"

"Well, I think your father felt that David could manipulate you to
believe him --"

"Well, shit. Aren't I the fucking fool, then?" Darren stared out to Woods Hole. Kate leaned over to Darren and kissed him on the forehead. She turned back to Nate and said, "You need to call that number."

Nate took a deep breath and, once again, like a veteran cell phone user, dialed the number that was left on his office door.

"You're wasting all my minutes," Darren told him.

Kate gave a little chuckle, for both the joke and the probability that Nate didn't know what it meant.

On the third ring, someone answered. The person on the other end didn't say anything, but Nate could hear a dog barking in the background.

He decided to take a leap of faith. If it was indeed David, then he needed to get him upset, move him back a few steps. David was always a bit shaky when pushed. He might be able to control Darren, but Nate knew what button to press with him. The difference was that he'd never seen a reason before to press it.

"David, this has gone far enough." He let this sink in. The phone went dead. *Bingo, it's David.* He stared down at the phone. It rang after a couple minutes.

Kate turned to Darren. "For the love of all that's fair in the world, change the friggin' ringtone."

"You're so dramatic," Darren said.

This time Nate didn't say anything.

"Hello, Nate. I didn't give you enough credit to figure out it was me."

"What the hell are you doing? Did you kill Lou?"

"I'm doing the talking," David explained. "You have something I need, so if you want your friend back, then let's get this over with."

The blood in Nate's body was boiling away with anger, seeping, steaming anger that he'd never felt before. There hadn't been enough time to digest the involvement of David and the death of Lou. Just not enough time.

Nate took a deep breath and started to scream into the phone: "You listen to me, motherfucker. I am going to track you down and fucking kill you. You come back into my life and do this—murder, David? Jesus

Christ … it was Lou. He loved you like he loved everybody. You son of
a bitch. Mike better be okay. Because it's over, David, it's over, you can't
make believe we don't know --"

David cut him off and started screaming on his end: "SHUT UP.
Shut the fuck up, you piece of shit! I don't care about Lou, Mike, or you.
Just give me the fucking gold, and I mean all of it. I know the old man
left you the whereabouts of more, so I want it now or so help me Mike is
dead, and then"—he whispered—"then I'm coming after your beloved
Becky, and then you're going to wish you were dead."

Nate regained some control of his temper, he needed to for Rebecca's
sake. He would rather die at the hands of David than bring Rebecca
deeper into this.

"Okay, David, let's finish this. I'll give you the gold, and I'm on my
way to find the rest. Meet me at Quint's boat. You remember that, don't
you, David? From when we were friends?"

"Yeah, I know where it is. But listen to me, Nate. You always thought
I was predictable. I hope you see things differently now."

"Oh I see things differently now, David. But let me leave you with
this. You're blind right now … lost our signal around Butler Flats. Right?"
Silence on David's end. "My bet, once you took off with the harbor patrol
boat with Mike, you headed for Point Judith harbor, and you're sitting
at the west end of the fuel dock. So tell George and his golden retriever
Ted I said hi. It's going to take you about three and a half hours to get to
us; seas are building. No matter what you think, you're still predictable.
Let me talk to Mike."

"FUCK YOU."

"David, things are unraveling for you. You're leaving Jimmy and Stu
out in the cold here. I think they're getting angry …"

"You know something, Nate? You think I'm a monster, but you
threatened to kill me earlier. It's amazing what somebody's capable of
when pushed to their limit."

"See you at Quint's boat, Chief." Nate hung up.

"Well, that went well," Kate told the boys. "I think you have him right where you need him."

"Where do we need him, exactly?" Darren asked.

Nate took the helm and throttled up the boat through Woods Hole and into Vineyard Sound. It would take about half an hour to get to Menemsha Harbor on the south side of Martha's Vineyard, but he needed a few more answers before they could meet.

"Why Menemsha?" Darren asked.

"Somehow David found out about Lou's gold bar, but the thing is, he is pretty confident there is more. I'm getting a wicked bad freakin' feeling, though, the longer I go over Lou's game in my head, that the only thing Lou is hiding from me is his two-hundred-year-old bottle of Captain Kidd rum. I mean, that would be classic Lou. We need to find out if that gold was still down there when he discovered the *Gosnold*."

"So you think that Captain Mayhew managed to recover the gold?" Darren asked.

"It seems that he did, according to Ron's—I mean Lou's—story at the museum," Kate said.

"If anyone would know if it was possible to recover gold at the depth of seventy feet in 1860, it's this guy Max, an old friend—actually an acquaintance of Lou's and my father's. I don't think Max has any friends, to be truthful. But this guy is the greatest historian on scuba diving and wreck recovery. If anybody in the world knows if it's possible, it would be Max."

"And if it *was* possible?" Kate asked.

"Then we have nothing to exchange for Mike that could end this, because just one bar of gold that four people are intent on possessing is in no way going to end well. So we need a plan that doesn't involve the gold to get Mike back. Because there is no way I'm going to Cuttyhunk, with Mike's life on the line, to uncover a bottle of rum. I think it would send David off the deep end. And then I think we all might be in deep shit."

"I'm all for not dying," Darren declared.

"David's three hours away, if not longer with this storm front moving in, and our friends back there in New Bedford won't know where we are till we let them. So let's go try and figure this out," Nate said.

They headed south through Vineyard Sound, with Naushon, the largest of the Elizabeth Islands, to their starboard and Martha's Vineyard to their port. For the first time all day, they traveled along in silence.

Kate was the first to break it. "Where are we going again? Menemsha, Quint's boat thing, Cuttyhunky ... I am quite confused."

"Martha's Vineyard, we're going to Martha's Vineyard," Darren explained.

"Cool, can I get one of those Black Dog tee shirts?" she asked.

"We are after millions in gold, with the mob on our heels, loved ones in mortal peril, and all you want is a tee shirt?"

"I'm on vacation," Kate said, smiling.

The harbor of Menemsha had been an active fishing harbor for a century. The difference in this particular harbor from that of Edgartown or Vineyard Haven was that it still looked like one. It was the least commercialized of the four harbors, and the smallest. To find it from out in the middle of Vineyard Sound, you looked for the lowest point working from Gay Head Lighthouse. When you entered between the two breakwater jetties you banged a right, and if you continued straight down the channel, you would enter Menemsha Pond and pass Quint's boat. But first things first.

Just like he had years ago, after traveling sixty miles in a center-console to see a stupid movie, Nate found a spot at the end of the harbor where the charter captain's dock lay. Nate talked to the harbor master, who was just a young twenty-something, a summer helper. After dropping a few names he got the okay for a quick stay and returned to the boat to see Kate holding a lobster roll and a Coke, fresh from Larsen's fish market, which sat a mere ten feet from the *Legacy*.

"This is my first time here since the movie," Darren tried to say with a mouthful of lobster. After saying it, though, he remembered that it was also the date of Nate's father's death. He quickly turned away from Nate and tried to look busy with something other than that memory.

There were rows of cottages overlooking the end of the harbor. Once fishermen had lived here, but now the houses were occupied by the rich and famous, like Ted Danson, and Jim Belushi, and Lenny Clarke. Nate, Kate, and Darren continued past these well-maintained cottages. They reached Max's house, and if you were to play Which One of These Things Don't Belong, all fingers would point here. The white picket fence that lined the house was overgrown with sea tomato bushes, which in several places had busted off the pickets, on their way to becoming out-of-control shrubbery. The yard was not immune to Max's neglect, either, littered with junk recovered from fifty years of diving. Barnacle-encrusted portholes, giant anchors. And for some reason, a lot of old tires.

Nate had come here once with his father when he was five, but because of what Nate's dad said was Max's foul mouth and perverted mind, Nate had been forced to stay in the yard. Now he was standing with Kate and Darren on the same spot.

"Okay, a few rules and a warning before we enter," he started to explain. "This guy Max is around eighty years old, but he's built like somebody in his fifties. He is huge. He was the first commercial diver out there, before there was even a name for it. He was the first to dive on the *Andrea Doria* back in the fifties, days after she sank. He is certifiably crazy … to say the least. He is also, though unsubstantiated, a freaking pervert, so if you want to stay outside, I'll understand." Nate pointed to Kate.

"Uh, I don't think so. I'm a big girl."

"That's what I'm afraid of; you have boobs, so he's going to be gunning for you. If we can get through his bullshit, his knowledge on diving is incredible, so the hope I have is that we can solve this *what is Lou hiding* shit before we have our meet-and-greet later tonight."

Nate turned up the walkway and pounded on the weathered door.

Kate leaned into Darren. "There is no way this guy is going to live up to Nate's hype. He's probably not even home."

"Hey, little miss doubty pants, I'm just telling you what Lou has told me over the years," Nate said. "I was also told that he hasn't left his house in over five years. And for the record, Lou doesn't exaggerate, so there's that." Nate grinned at her and then banged on the door again. This time footsteps could be heard approaching the door, loud footsteps.

"Hey … I think of you more as a little miss nosy pants than a doubty pants," Darren told Kate.

"Keep laughing, guys."

The door flew open and the frame was filled top to bottom with Max. Kate and Darren took a step back, almost falling off the front steps. Nate didn't move a muscle.

"I'm not fucking buying nothing," Max said. Then, looking down at them: "Oh … sorry. I didn't know there was a dame present." He looked past Nate, directly at Kate, actually her boobs.

"Who says 'dame' anymore?" Darren said, leaning into Kate.

"Max?" Nate yelled. "Max," he yelled again, this time waving his hand in front of Max's face, trying to break his stare off Kate's chest. "MAX! Nate West. Jonathan's son and Lou Gauthier's friend." Hoping for a sign of acknowledgement, Nate was surprised when Max scooped him up in his arms in a bear hug.

"Oh my God, little Nate West! I'm so sorry for Lou. I wanted to go to the island for his funeral, but … Fuck it, I thought, I don't travel well these days."

"Ah, that's all right, you were at my dad's," Nate said, still trapped in Max's bear hug.

"Damn right, great fucking man, your dad," he said, dropping Nate back onto his feet. "What the fuck do you want?" His tone went from *nice to see you* to *get out* in mere seconds.

"We're interested in some info on the possibility of recovering something at the depth of seventy feet back in 1860."

"Would this something be shiny?"

"Yes it would."

"Then you came to the right man. Come in, come in, I haven't talked business in years, especially with a real diving family like yours." Max held out his arm to make room for them to enter, but managed to sweep Nate and Darren behind him to allow Kate to walk in first. As she squeezed by, Max's hand fell to her ass, and Kate looked back over her shoulder and smiled at him.

Darren looked to Nate as he entered the house. "Game on."

Nate shook his head and went in.

The interior was the exact opposite from the mess outside. Every square inch of wall was taken up with an artifact or a framed photo. There were model ships and submarines and skeletons of fish. The dining room had been turned into a mini-library. All three looked around the room; they could have spent hours in there looking around Max's version of the Smithsonian. Max fell into his chair and flipped the lever which shot his feet up. Kate pictured a cleaning lady dressed up in a French maid's outfit cleaning and dusting everything while Max the giant stared.

"Please have a seat." Talking directly to Kate, he pointed to a chair two feet from him. Kate thanked him and sat.

"You're English."

"Yes."

"Was there in World War II. They bombed the shit out of your country."

"Yes, sir, I might have heard a thing or two about that."

"Ah, a smart one … You a virgin?"

"Whoa, whoa, whoa, there, cowboy." Nate jumped up from the couch, with Darren just behind him.

"No, it's okay, Nate," Kate assured him. She turned to Max. "Lost it to Miles Doughtry in his family's barn. I was sixteen."

The room was silent. Max was smiling, though.

"Max, we are a little short on time, we need you to focus," Nate said.

He had been thinking of a way to tell Max the story without all the details. But the only way to get to the bottom of this with someone like Max was to be blunt and straightforward; if he sensed a lie, you were done.

"So what did you find and where did you find it?"

"It's not that easy." Nate decided to lay it all out. The guy hadn't left his house in years, he thought, and was one good crap away from a major stroke.

"Our working theory here, Max, is that Lou discovered a wreck off Southwest Ledge, we think about fifteen years ago. We also have come to believe that it was the whale ship *Gosnold,* which sank after catching fire in seventy feet of water during a hurricane in the 1800s. Lou never told anybody about this wreck. But, Max, we think Lou was murdered. I found him on his boat beaten to death. His boat was rigged to sink. I dove on it to prove just that, and he was anchored up on a wreck. We later determined that it was the *Gosnold,* and while down there I discovered a bar of gold." Nate opened his backpack and handed Max the gold bar. "As you can see, this bar has been cleaned, it seems it wasn't down there for very long."

Max just held it, turning it over in his large hands. "Fifty years of diving, never found anything as beautiful as this." He shook his head and handed it to Kate and wiped his hands on his pants, as if the gold were dirty. "What makes you think Lou put it there?"

"Where would you put it if someone was after it?" Nate asked.

"Is there more?"

"We have been following some leads and think the *Gosnold* was carrying a lot of this gold when she went down. The story leads us to believe they might have recovered it then."

"Well, just do a survey of the wreck, bring in some equipment for searching for more."

"I believe Lou did all of that. Look, Max, somebody on Block knew about this gold and killed Lou and kidnapped our friend and is holding him until we discover where Lou hid the rest of the gold."

Max stared at Nate for the first time. Nate sensed his confusion, and continued.

"Lou left me some clues, one of his wild-goose chases he loved to test me on. People, Max, people who are chasing us right now, really believe that there is more gold. I can't get there and find out that there is none.

Lives are in danger. Do you think the gold could have been recovered back then?"

"If you want my help finding the gold, just ask. Handing me a load of bullshit was not your father's style—or Lou's style, for that matter."

"It's not about the gold," Nate told Max.

Max flipped the lever and stood up like a forty-year-old. He took the gold from Kate and thrust it into Nate's face. "BULLSHIT. People have been searching for sunken treasure since the first ship ever sank. Thousands of people have died in the pursuit of it. But now ... now treasure hunting's gone corporate, you can actually invest in treasure hunting, with historians and electronics experts, unmanned subs on the payroll, it takes years before an actual person hits the water. The days of Mel Fisher and Lou Gauthier are long gone. But you see, however it's done, and whoever does it, it's always been about the gold. Look at it, smell it, feel its pulse. It's alive. It has power, a power that cannot be comprehended. It has called to us, all of us, since the discovery of it. There is no controlling it, no asking it for mercy. You're after the fucking gold, Nate, just admit it. You're a diver. This shit is in your blood."

"FUCK YOU!" Nate cried. "You know what I want. I want Lou back. If this gold got him killed, then FUCK IT and you, too. I'm getting our friend back; the gold is only a tool. So once again I'm asking you to go FUCK yourself!"

Nate turned to leave, with Max still holding the bar of gold in the middle of the room. Kate and Darren were close on his heels.

"What about the gold?" Max asked, a little subdued.

"Stick it up your ass."

All three walked out into the front lawn and stood by the broken gate. Kate and Darren stared at Nate for a sign on how to handle this mess.

"Nate, the gold," Kate pleaded. "We need it for Mike."

Nate stared at the road in front of him. "Fuck." He turned back to the house. Max was standing in the doorway.

"Please, all of you, come back in, please."

They came again into the living room. The gold was sitting on the

chair where Kate had been sitting. Max walked into another room, and
when he returned, he looked all of his eighty years. He motioned for them
to join him at a large oak desk in the corner of the room.

There were no apologies from someone like Max.

Move on, there, sunshine.

Max had his fists clenched and was using them for support as he
stood over his desk. In front of him, he placed a coffee-table-size book,
the kind with large glossy photos. It was on the history of scuba diving.
He turned each page slowly, allowing them to watch the history pass by
them. He stopped at a page that showed a canvas suit with a big brass
helmet, equipment from an earlier era of man's attempts at conquering
the underwater world, which was cutting edge for its time and also very
dangerous.

"The earliest record of diving dates back to three thousand B.C.
Aristotle wrote about the diving bell in the fourth century. By the late
1700s, hand-operated air compressors and the diving helmet and suit were
starting to make it easier. It continued with this setup until the 1960s. In
1860, this would have been the type of suit used. Heavy lead shoes would
allow you to sink. The suit would fill with air, allowing your leg to rise,
then leaning your head back would trigger a lever that would purge the
air out as you stepped forward. Brutal and fucking dangerous, and most
did not survive the attempt. Now the thing is, only a few people had this
equipment and knew how to use it. There would have been some sort of
trail, a story in the local papers or something. If they dove on a wreck
around here, it would have been news, and I would have found something
about it over my fifty years of searching for this type of thing."

"To this day, nobody knows if there was even gold on the *Gosnold*
when she went down," Nate explained. "They tell us that this family
whose gold it was would have gotten themselves into a lot of trouble if
anybody knew of its existence."

Max turned to the bookshelves behind him. Nate noticed that the
entire wall at the back of the dining room was a library, and each book
on the shelves was in alphabetical order. As rough and tough as Max

appeared on the outside, order was the way of life on the inside. After a few seconds of searching he plopped down a book on the desk on top of the picture book. This one was more of a logbook, bound in old, worn leather. Inside, some of the sections were handwritten, in a neat longhand, others printed, along with rough drawings of ships. Some pages contained sketches of wrecks. Max fell into his worn desk chair, which let out a groan on impact.

"You have something that looks a lot like this, huh, Nate?" Max asked, tapping his finger on the book.

Nate just turned to Max and gave him a look of surprise.

"It's your family's dirty little secret," Max said, staring back at Nate. After a minute of uncomfortable silence, Max turned his attention back to the notebook on his desk. "The Lafrance brothers. These two brothers, Roger and Anatole, dove on wrecks all over the east coast. They were mavericks, sometimes hired guns. I found their logbook decades ago in a freaking flea market of all places. These guys were local, New York. Nothing in their logbook about whale ships or Block Island. But these are the guys, I'm positive. It would have been the Lafrance brothers who pulled this off."

Kate picked up the logbook and walked around the room, staring intently at the hundred-year-old words from long-gone brothers.

"My problem is how they could have found the wreck," Darren said. "I mean, it went down in the middle of a storm. Even today it would take days, even weeks, to locate that needle. With all our technology."

"How would you find her, Nate?" Max asked. "Your father was the best. What does your instinct tell you to look for? If you were this captain?"

"Oil."

Max laughed, tilting his head back. "No flies on your shit, boy."

Kate looked up from the log and stared at the back of Max's large head and shook hers as she looked back to the log.

"The oil left on board would have left a streak in the water for days," Nate said. "Whale oil is thick, nasty stuff, even if it all burned in the fire when she went down. My bet is that the captain probably looked for it from on top of Mohegan Bluffs on a clear day. He would have been able to follow the slick."

Kate walked over to the three of them. "Photographs tell the truth when all around us is a lie—the truth is in the photographs … There is no more gold, Nate, and for that I am truly sorry. This was in the logbook."

She placed a four-by-six black and white photograph on the desk. It was the same photo as the one in the whaling museum, the one of Captain Mayhew and what was believed to be two crew members.

"The back of this photo says that on the right is Anatole and on the left is Roger Lafrance, and in the center …"

Nate finished: "Captain Jacob Mayhew." He sighed and walked away from the desk and sat on the couch, defeated, covered in fear for Mike and Rebecca, for Lou, for this plague that one single bar of gold could bring.

Darren stared at the photo and rubbed his hand over his forehead and eyes. Kate joined Nate on the couch and took his hands in hers.

"What do I do, Kate? How can I help Mike now?"

She didn't know how to answer him. She kept thinking nobody was going to get hurt, that everything was a game, which as long as Nate stayed positive seemed true. But now, with Nate sitting there far worse than just doubting himself, but truly scared—now Kate had a whole new perspective on this adventure, a darker outlook than she'd had even moments earlier.

"Do you play poker, Nate?" Max asked, walking back into the room from a backroom of the house.

Nate shook his head no.

"But you understand the concept of bluffing … right?"

Nate nodded.

"Well then, look them straight in the eye and tell them you found the gold."

"And when they call my bluff?"

"Then give them the gold." Max threw two bars of gold onto the couch. They bounced a foot off the cushions and back down again. All three of them turned to the chair that held the original bar of gold and it still sat there on Kate's original seat.

"I knew it," Darren said, pointing at Max, "you have the gold! Don't you see, guys? He was probably partners with Lou."

Max bellowed out a laugh that echoed through the house.

"It's fake, hotshot, a prop from a movie. Some dildos from Hollyweird filmed a movie off Edgartown twenty years ago. Something about lost Inca gold or some horseshit. Anyways, these movie people left the gold in about twenty feet of water off South Beach. After a storm, months later, some of it washed up on shore. It set off a fucking feeding frenzy—you know, thinking it was real. I was brought in to clean it up from the sea floor, and I kept it for ... hell, I don't know ... I guess I like the way it looks."

Nate picked a bar up from the sofa. It looked real enough. Not like the other one a few feet away, but close enough, he thought.

"How much do you have?"

"About twenty bars."

Nate turned the bar over in his hands, much the way Bob had back in his office. It was definitely lighter than the real one, but just maybe.

"I'm going to need all your fake bars and a shovel, if you don't mind, Max."

"You got it, just hurt this fucker hard, will ya?"

CHAPTER 22:
QUINT'S BOAT AND MR. SPOCK

They climbed back on the *Legacy* and fired up the engine. "Time to call our Providence friends," Nate said as he turned on his GPS, and Darren went back to the access panel and put the clips back on the wiring. They untied the boat and headed out to the channel and turned north. This smaller channel, lined with beach to the starboard and a pier to the port, would lead them into Menemsha Pond. Although very shallow in spots, Nate's boat could find shelter there and wait out Jimmy and Stu. As they got to the end of the channel, right before it opened to the pond, Nate nodded his head in the direction of the beach. Sitting there, the hull of a boat, most of it gone, buried in the sand, the wood whitewashed from years of sun and salt. But no mistake, it was Quint's boat. Darren stared at the boat as they slowly passed. Kate looked to the two boys for an explanation, and when none came, she decided to wait it out. Boys and the silly things they cling to …

The *Big Booty* was hauling ass, seventy-plus. The boys from Providence were finding it hard to breathe—dogs might have liked to stick their faces out car windows, but humans didn't care for it much, go figure—but time was of the essence. They had lost touch with that little shit David from the island and they needed to get the gold before this two-timing piece of shit could get a hold of it. This folly they were on was wearing the brothers thin. But the gold was calling to them. Something about the search and the possession of it kept them going.

The water in Vineyard Sound was strangely calm even though the storm racing toward them was now only a few hours away. The storm was coming from the south, so the waters surrounding the islands were protected from the building sea that was starting to rage in Rhode Island Sound.

After fueling up at Georges in Point Judith, just as Nate had told him he was doing, David went below to check on his companion. Mike had been shot in the chest with a Taser gun, which would make anyone feel like shit for a good part of the day. His eyes were bloodshot, his hands and feet numb from the tie wraps. David reached over and ripped the duct tape off Mike's mouth. "No need for this now. I'm going to ask you again: what is Nate up to on Martha's Vineyard?"

"Look, David." Mike swallowed hard, trying to get his voice back; hoarse and low he tried again: "David, I don't know what he is up to, you have to believe me."

"No, I don't, Mike, I don't have to believe a word you say. That's the way it works. We are going to meet up with them shortly, and if he fucks with me, I'm going to kill you. Do you believe me?" David asked in a sarcastic tone.

"Yes," Mike answered. He turned back up to the cockpit. "Hey, Chief." David stopped and slightly turned his head in Mike's direction. "I heard a lot of yelling up there earlier. You need to keep in mind Nate is smarter than you. He always has been."

David slammed the cabin door. Seconds later the boat took off at full speed, sending Mike off the front v-berth onto the floor of the cabin. He screamed and lay there in a heap, unable to get back on the bed since he'd been hogtied with tie raps.

They anchored the *Legacy* in three feet of water, the closest the boat could get without hitting bottom. The three of them walked through the waist-deep water with two black duffel bags filled with fake gold bars, a red backpack with one legitimate gold bar, and one Army-issue green shovel, the kind that folded in half, split between the three of them. They made their way onto the beach and along the shore to the old hull of a long-ago movie boat. They dropped their cargo onto the sand and leaned against the hull for a rest.

"Now what?" Kate asked.

"Well, I figure the Providence boys, the way that boat can haul ass, will be here first, then David. I'm guessing half an hour, so we need to bury the gold."

"Bury?" Darren asked.

"We need to buy some time to get to Cuttyhunk." Nate picked up the shovel and duffel bags and headed over to a small dune.

"Nate?" Darren called to him.

"Yeah?"

"Something's been bothering me since Max's house—this dirty little secret he talked about. This notebook thing, what has it got to do with the gold?"

"Kate will tell you. Sit tight, I'll be right back."

"That's what they say in all those *Friday the 13th* movies," Darren told him.

"Well, if you hear something over the dune, don't worry, it's only the wind," Nate said from the top of the dune as he slowly walked down out of sight.

Darren turned to Kate and raised his eyebrows.

She told him about Lou's notebook and how they had come about the spots. Darren just leaned against the boat and shook his head. She decided to change the subject: "Well then, what's the story on this Quint's boat thing?"

"See, you are a Little Miss Nosy Pants," Darren told her, and she punched him in the arm.

He looked at the old hull they were resting on. "She's looked better."

Kate turned and looked herself.

"Have you seen the movie *Jaws*?" Darren asked.

"Of course."

"Well, this is the Orca that they chased the shark on. Captain Quint's boat. Actually, there were two boats, I believe. Anyways, after the movie finished filming, they left the boat in the pond, and after a storm it washed up here and it's been rotting in this place for thirty years."

"Well that's interesting. But I want to know why every time either one of you mention it you sigh and stare off into space."

Darren sighed.

"See, like that," Kate said.

"Fifteen years ago Nate, myself, and David Cavarlo took Nate's twenty-one-foot boat the sixty miles here to see the movie; we heard about the boat being here. But when we got back to Menemsha, the weather turned on us, and it took us hours to get home. The whole island was out looking for us. How much did he tell you about his parents?"

"Rebecca told me the night we found Lou that his parents were dead. And I was there when he had an argument with Rebecca about his father dying in a diving accident."

"Well … his father was killed the day we came here for the movie. That's why they were looking for us." Darren was walking around the beach now, picking shells up and throwing them. "I've been thinking about that day a lot these last couple of days. You know, that incident was the last time all three of us hung out together. From that moment on, we split apart."

"Nate changed?"

"We all changed. That was just the exact moment for us."

They heard the engines of the *Big Booty* roaring before they could see her. Standing on the beach that ran along the channel in and out of the pond, they had a clear shot of the entrance to the harbor. Minutes later the boys from Providence entered the harbor slightly faster than they should, just as Nate had predicted. The occupants were pointing down the channel to the pond. Nate had left the GPS on in order to direct the Providence boys to Menemsha. Darren looked back over the dune, looking for Nate, then back to the boys.

"Looks like you have the con, Mr. Sulu."

"That's your contribution? Star Trek jokes?" Darren, slightly panicked, asked her.

The boys headed down the ever-shallower channel and saw Kate and Darren standing on the beach a mere forty feet away.

"Shit, shit, shit," Darren said, looking back over his shoulder again, "here they come."

"What do we do?" Kate asked.

"Well I don't know, I'm just Mr. Sulu. You couldn't make me Mr. Spock? Mr. Spock would know what to do."

After a few attempts at getting close to the beach, Doc realized the only way to get to shore was to have Jimmy and Stu jump into the waist-deep water and for him to bring the boat over to the pier on the opposite side of the channel and wait it out. After several minutes of Doc pointing to the water and to the stern of the boat and again to the shore and back over his shoulder to the pier, it became clear to Jimmy that his black jeans were going to get wet. The look on Jimmy's face as he waded through the water toward the beach removed any doubt that Jimmy was one pissed off individual. Darren once again looked over his shoulder. The boys had finally made it out of the water and were pushing through the sand toward them. It took Darren a full minute to comprehend that Jimmy already had a gun pointed at them.

"Do not fucking move. Where is your friend Nate?"

"We were just thinking the same thing ourselves," Darren told him.

"Oh were you?" Jimmy gave a quick glance around the beach and returned his stare to Kate and Darren.

"Oh shit," Darren exhaled, looking past Jimmy and Stu to the harbor entrance.

"What is it, Stu?" Jimmy asked, keeping an eye—both eyes, that is—on Kate and Darren.

Stu turned around. "A boat?"

"A boat. Care to elaborate?"

"What?"

"Do you know who the fuck it is?"

"Umm, it says 'New Shoreham Harbor Patrol,'" Stu explained.

"What?"

"Block Island. It's David Cavarlo," Darren said.

"Well, well, well. Nate has put together a nice little party. But our master of ceremonies is missing, huh? Maybe that gold he's been carrying around has gotten the best of him ... maybe he is off to leave you two to clean up his shit."

"I believe it's your shit that we have here," Kate said.

"Shut up, BITCH!" Jimmy screamed, walking closer to her and bringing the gun a foot away from her head. But in doing so he'd momentarily taken his eyes off Darren, and with a speed that actually impressed himself, Darren pulled out his gun and put it a foot from Jimmy's head.

"Watch the way you speak to the lady, meatball."

Stu was slowly walking toward the group.

"Stu, don't take another step." Stu froze on hearing Darren's instructions.

"Look, buddy, you don't want to be doing this," Jimmy said. "This is the big time here ... understand me?"

"Shut up, bitch," Darren whispered in his ear.

The early evening sky was much darker than it should have been. The approaching storm front, just a few miles away, had sucked all the energy out of the air, and it had grown calm. The humidity hung in the air, and the sense that at any moment the storm would just explode like a fireworks display. The soft glow of the beach was on its way out.

"Just back over there with your brother and we'll keep the playing field even," Darren instructed Jimmy, who looked down to his gun and nodded and slowly backed over to his brother.

Kate could see that Darren's hands were slightly shaking. In the background David's boat approached. With twin outboard motors, David simply brought the engines up out of the water and the bow came to rest on the soft sand. He manhandled Mike out of the cabin and pushed him overboard. Kate screamed and made a movement toward him, but she was rebuffed by Jimmy's gun. Mike landed in two feet of water and struggled to get to his feet. His hands still tied behind his back made this very difficult. Only after David took the anchor off the bow and brought it onto the beach and set it did he return to get Mike out of the shallow water. Mike was coughing up saltwater as he was dragged onto the beach.

"Well, we have quite the party taking shape here, don't we?" Jimmy said. "Except for Nate."

David walked Mike over to the group and threw him on the sand. Kate fell to him and held him in her arms. "Are you okay?"

Looking up to Kate the Beautiful, he said, "I am now."

She ran her hand through his hair to get it out of his eyes.

"Where's Nate?" Mike asked.

Kate shrugged.

"Where's my money, David?" Jimmy said, turning his gun to him, while Darren kept his aimed at Jimmy.

"Where's Nate? He has it."

"I'm right here," Nate said, walking down from the dune. He looked to Kate and Mike on the ground. "You okay, Mike?"

"He shot me with a Taser gun ... I peed my pants."

"I'm sorry I got you into this, Mike."

"Don't be. Nobody saw this coming. I'm just pissed I peed my pants, to be honest."

Stu laughed at Mike's attempt at humor. Jimmy turned to his brother and gave him the look, and Stu stopped laughing.

Slowly David pulled out a gun and with his arm lowered put the muzzle to the back of Mike's head. "Give me the gold now," he said.

"And if I don't?" Nate responded.

"Then I'll shoot Mike. I have nothing to lose now. If I don't pay these guys here, they're going to kill me."

Nate turned to Jimmy and Stu, who were both nodding in agreement.

"What the hell is going on, David?" Nate asked.

"I think he's embarrassed to tell you, so I will," Jimmy said. "Your friend here is into us for ... what is it up to today, Stu?"

"Umm, one hundred thirty-five thousand, give or take."

"Always good with numbers, bro," Jimmy said, turning to Nate. "A complete and total moron ... but a genius with numbers."

Jimmy started walking around, way too confident for Nate's liking. "You see, Nate, Mr. Cavarlo here has a gambling problem, a big gambling problem. It first started with high school sports, what, about five years ago? Then college ... then pro sports ... the big kahuna. You went on a bad losing streak, there, David. You just didn't know when to quit. But what am I saying? We've been over all this already."

"Nate has the gold. Just take it from him and be done with it."

"I still have the floor, Mr. Cavarlo. Then you came to me with this little story of sunken treasure. I was at first skeptical, but with these three here running all over New England, I'm starting to think you might be telling the truth." He walked over to David. "But I'm not going to be party to kidnapping, that's not how I play."

"But you'd kill me, that's murder."

"But that would be on my terms, and it's only murder if they find the body. How many bodies have they linked to us, bro?"

"Umm, zero."

Jimmy shook his head. "Great with numbers." He picked Mike up from the ground. "I will be taking him from you now, and if that gun so much as raises an inch ... murder will be my only option." He turned Mike so his back was facing him and took out a knife and cut the zip ties binding his hands. He and Kate walked over to Quint's boat and stood behind Darren and his gun.

Nate slowly turned to David and Jimmy.

Still staring at David, Jimmy said, "We have a deal."

"I don't know what you're talking about," David said.

"I'm not talking to you, Mr. Cavarlo."

"Yeah, we have a deal," Nate responded.

"WHAT?" David said, stunned.

Nate opened up his backpack and threw the bar of gold at Jimmy's feet. David, eyes wide and mouth open, made a gurgling sound.

Jimmy picked up the bar and turned it over in his hand, which seemed to be the thing to do with a gold bar. "You see, Mr. Cavarlo, you've caused me quite a lot of trouble here. I thought I was going to take a nice ferry ride to your island and be given bars of gold—enough gold, mind you, to get you out of your debt. But instead I got flat tires and scooter chases and a swim in the Providence River. So I'm thinking to myself that there is a chance I'm not going to get paid. Then when I enter this harbor my phone rings and it's Nate here, and he tells me that if I get their friend back from your evil clutches, he will give me the bar of gold. So here we are, but the problem now is that you still owe me." He pointed to Stu.

"One hundred thirty-five thousand ... give or take."

"No, no, no, you can't do this. Look, there's more gold, I'm sure of it. I heard Nate talking about a letter that the old man left telling him where the gold is."

"How the hell do you know that?" Nate said. "Do you have my house bugged, David?"

"You're such a FUCKING BOY SCOUT. DO YOU HAVE ANY CLUE WHAT'S GOING ON AROUND YOU? FUCK!"

"Like gambling and murder, David?" Nate asked in a low, calm voice.

"FUCK YOU!"

David raised his gun at Nate, who was only a few feet away.

"DON'T DO IT, CHIEF. POINT IT DOWN NOW!" Darren yelled, walking closer to Nate and David, his gun aimed at David's head.

"You don't understand, I am a dead man. So why not take you with me?"

"Put the gun down," Jimmy instructed.

"WHY? TELL ME WHY," David yelled, spit flying out of his mouth.

Jimmy just walked up to David and with the butt of his gun smacked him on the head. As his knees buckled under him Jimmy grabbed the gun from his hand in one swift motion.

"Because I'm in charge. I'm calling the shots."

Darren lowered his gun. David managed to get back up; his eyes were watering and spit ran down his chin. *He's a first-class mess,* as Lou used to say. He looked to Jimmy, and with all the self-pity he could muster, said, "There's more gold."

The storm was just about on them now. The wind had started very slowly, but now it was blowing at thirty knots and the waves out of the southwest were crashing onto the jetty that protected the harbor, creating a thunderous noise, the spray reaching ten feet in the air.

"You know, David, I actually believe you," Jimmy said. "Can you beat that? The way I figure it, you went to great lengths, I mean you went off the deep end trying to secure the gold. Let's see … You had some smalltime bookie from your island framed and sent to prison, just to cut off the old man's means of getting rid of the gold. Then you have murder—oh, that's right, you murdered him, didn't you? And let's see …" Jimmy looked around and saw Mike slowly raise his hand. "Oh yeah, almost forgot: kidnapping. So the way I see it, there has to be more gold."

Darren stared at David, who was staring down at the sand. "You had my father framed just because he was going to help Lou?" Darren's move on David was so quick nobody had time to react. He bent over and hit David with his head and wrapped his arms around his waist as if he were a New England Patriot. David's feet came off the sand and they both hit the beach hard. Darren was screaming and punching him as he sat on top of him. Stu grabbed Darren's shoulder and spun him off, and that's when Nate made his move. He tackled Jimmy, whose gun flew off into the sand. Jimmy managed to kick Nate in the chest and send him back five feet. They both got to their feet, and it was at this time that the much-too-quiet Stu hit Nate with his own impressive tackle, sending him back down onto the sand while Stu stared down at him. Mike ran and picked up Darren's gun, which had gone flying during his initial attack, and pointed it at Stu, who brought his hands up in the "I surrender" position.

The sand around them erupted, it was exploding all around them, missing them by the smallest of margins. There was no sound but the whipping of bullets. All went quiet; everyone on the beach was frozen. Jimmy jumped up from the sand and walked over to the water's edge.

"IT'S ABOUT FUCKING TIME. WHAT WERE YOU WAITING FOR?"

The group slowly turned and noticed Doc and his *Big Booty* tied up across the channel fifty yards away. In his hand was a high-powered rifle with a muzzle and a very impressive scope. Doc waved to the group.

"It's always smart to have a gun dealer on your payroll," Jimmy said. He walked over to Mike and took the gun from his frozen hand. "Thank you." He continued over to Nate, who was standing, and punched him in the stomach. Nate bent over, the wind in his lungs gone. Then he continued over to David and pointed the gun in his face. David started to cry and closed his eyes. Jimmy slammed the gun upside his head, knocking him out this time. "Still might need you yet," he said. "Okay. Now where's the gold? Tell me RIGHT now or all I have to do is raise my hand and my friend will open fire."

"The gold is buried over the dune behind you," Nate said. "It's marked with an X made out of driftwood, and there are twenty bars in two black duffel bags."

Jimmy stared at Nate as he raised Darren's gun. "You're coming with me to see."

"No, I'm not."

Mike, Darren, and Kate stared at each other with a growing unease; they didn't know what he was trying to prove.

"What gives you the balls to think you have a say in this?"

"Because any minute a Coast Guard boat will be coming around the pier and head over to us ... and all I have to do is raise my hand."

"You're bluffing."

Thirty seconds later an orange, twenty-foot Coast Guard boat came around the pier and headed right toward them. The look on Nate's face, for a brief moment, was shock; nobody caught it except for Kate.

"Stu, start heading for the other side of the dune and look for some Xs."

Stu slowly headed over the dune as the Coast Guard approached.

A guardsman came to the side of the boat and yelled over the increasing wind, "Is one of you Nate West?"

Nate raised his hand. Behind the Coast Guard the *Big Booty* had untied, and as quickly as possible, without attracting attention, was leaving the harbor and heading into the rolling seas.

With his arm still raised, he turned to Jimmy. "Your gun-running friend seems to have somewhere to be."

"Is everything okay here? What's wrong with that guy?" the Coast Guard officer said, pointing to David lying on the sand. Nate turned back to Jimmy. He looked over his shoulder and saw Stu standing on the dune and nodding yes to Jimmy.

"Are we good here, Jimmy?"

It was apparent that the appearance of the Coast Guard boat right when Nate had said it would come had spooked the shit out of Jimmy.

"Yeah, we're fine," Nate said. "Our friend here has had too much to drink, that's all."

"Okay," the officer said. "Look, Petty Officer Betsy Farrell wanted me to check on you, but you need to seek shelter. The storm is just about on us." Another guardsman, who had been on the marine radio, tapped him on his shoulder and made circles in the air with his finger to tell him they had to fly. The boat turned on a dime and sped out of the harbor into the darkness. Nate started backing up down the beach toward the *Legacy,* Kate and Darren and Mike walking backward with him, as Jimmy started his own backward walk toward Stu up on the dune.

"GO, GO, GO," Nate cried and the four of them started off in an all-out run. They rounded the corner and pushed through the waist-deep water out to the anchored *Legacy.* They climbed on board, Nate and Darren first helping the other two on.

"Jesus Christ, how the hell did you pull the Coast Guard out of your ass like that?" Darren asked.

"When I was burying the gold, I had an idea to cut a deal with Jimmy, but I needed a backup plan to get us out of here, so I doubled back to the boat and called Betsy back on Block and she made a call. The timing, that was just freaky … a gift from Lou." Nate started the boat. "Darren, just cut the anchor line, no time to play games." He turned to Mike. "Are you okay?" He put his arm around Mike's neck.

"Yeah. Thanks for getting me back. He's playing the outfield without a glove … you know?"

Nate nodded in agreement.

The *Legacy* started out of the pond and into the channel. The wind was pushing her all over the place, making it hard for Nate to keep her in the middle of the channel. As she pushed past Quint's boat, Darren noticed something.

"Hey guys, the beach is empty. David's gone."

Nate pushed the throttle high.

Just over the dune Jimmy and Stu were kneeling over the shallow hole Stu had dug in the sand. Stu pulled the two duffel bags out.

"Jesus, I can't believe he gave all this up," Jimmy said.

"Maybe he kept some?"

"Who gives a shit? This will do us just fine." Jimmy picked up a bar and examined it closely. "It looks different than the one he gave us for his friend."

Stu picked up his own bar. "But looks real, I mean, where would he get fake gold bars like this?"

Jimmy nodded his head in agreement. Upon being right for a change, Stu, in a fit of overconfidence, flipped the bar up in the air a foot or so, watching it spin end over end, and held his hand out to catch it. But the bar missed his hand badly and slammed onto the rest of the bars in the bag.

"Hey, you dickhead, you broke it in two."

"Sorry, bro …" Stu picked up the two pieces. "Umm, bro …" He turned both pieces to his brother, showing him the inside of the bar, which was white, just like plaster.

Jimmy's face started to go all contorted, his body started to shake violently like he might be having a seizure. Spit flew from his mouth as he collapsed onto the sand face first.

"BRO!" Stu jumped to his side, went to turn him over. That's when he noticed it: two small wires attached to his back like little darts. He spun on his knees and followed the wires to a Taser gun. The last second before a green army shovel came in contact with his head, he saw David Cavarlo.

David rolled Jimmy off the duffel bags and knelt down beside the gold and started to laugh—a hardy laugh, the kind that told people you had finally done it, after all your hard work and perseverance. But the hardy laugh turned to cries of anger when he noticed the broken bar of gold plaster.

The *Legacy* was about to leave the harbor when Mike looked back down the channel to the beach and just made out a figure on the dune running for David's boat.

"Jesus—Nate? Somebody's coming." They all turned and could just make out somebody on the boat. "Shit, it's him … it's David."

"Can he catch us?" Kate asked as the boat started to hit some big waves.

"In these conditions?" Nate said. "I don't know."

"You're a better captain," Mike told him. Which brought a small smile to Nate's face.

"Okay listen, everybody needs to put on lifejackets. It's going to get very ugly in the next half hour. I'm going to try and lose him and make it to Cuttyhunk before the height of the storm."

They all put on lifejackets except for Nate, who put his on the dash. He needed all the mobility he could get.

"I'll never put a lifejacket on again," said Darren, quoting Quint from a scene in *Jaws*.

"Mike, work the spotlight, turn it on and give me a scan of the front of us about every thirty seconds. Everybody else hang on."

The boat was starting to take a beating, the seas easily six to eight feet and that was only because the wind was coming out of the west and the Elizabeth Islands were blocking the wind. But to enter Cuttyhunk Harbor they were going to need to head to the north side of the islands and out of their protection.

CHAPTER 23: CUTTYHUNK

"The isle is full of noises, Sounds, and sweet airs, that give delight and hurt not. Sometimes a thousand twangling instruments Will hum about mine ears; and sometimes voices, that if I then had wak'd after long sleep, Will make me sleep again, and then in dreaming, The clouds methought would open, and show riches Ready to drop upon me, that when I wak'd I cried to dream again."

—Caliban, from *The Tempest*

Darren saw the blip on the radar screen before Nate did. Nate was very busy at that moment trying to keep the boat from pitchpoling and capsizing in the giant waves, standing at the wheel, one hand on the throttle, trying to judge the distance of the next wave with relation to the one they were on and either throttling up or down to control the distance of that all-important next wave. Kate was just trying not to throw up.

"There it is again," Darren yelled over the wind and engine noise. "He's following us."

"Is he following us or trying to get us?" Mike asked.

"HANG ON!" Nate screamed. The boat was in midair, the wave they were on just dropped out from under them. The *Legacy* fell six feet straight down and hit the water with a boom. Kate fell on her ass and slid toward the stern of the boat. "GRAB HER!" Nate yelled, fighting the urge to let go of the wheel and go for her himself, which would have gone under the heading of Bad Idea. Darren, hanging onto the doorframe, grabbed her ankles and pulled her back into the cockpit as a wave crashed over the side of the boat and filled it with about two feet of water.

"Should we close the cockpit door?" Darren asked, getting up. "This is getting crazy."

"If we close the door and we do go down we're trapped," Nate explained. Nobody brought that idea up again.

Their one shot at Cuttyhunk would be by going through a channel between two of the Elizabeth Islands, Pasque and Naushawena. The opening, known as Quick's Hole, was about a thousand yards wide. The problem was that if the tide was running against the wind direction, a lot of water would be pushed into the opening of the channel, creating a wall of water that would be just about impossible to get through. Nate had fished Quick's Hole over the years and seen it in some tough conditions, but this would be a first—or a last, he thought to himself—in these condition. His approach was plotted out in his head—*make for the south side of the opening, where the wind would be blocked the most from Naushawena Island.* He knew from his years fishing that the GPS reading wasn't always accurate. It showed water depth at one to two feet but he knew it was more like ten, plenty of water to cut across into the middle of the hole and bypass the wall of water facing the opening.

"Nate, he's getting closer," Darren said, staring at the radar screen.

"I thought you were a better captain," Kate said.

"Well yeah ... but he's gone insane and lucky to be moving that fast in this."

"You know I'm starting to believe you make stuff up just to shut me up."

"I would never try to shut you up. Give you a false sense of security, sure."

"HANG ON!" he cried, and the boat slammed down from another wave and the group took the hit by bending at the knees. They all stood back up.

Twenty-five very long minutes later they approached Quick's Hole.

Nate headed for the south side. "Mike, leave the light off, I'm going in with just the electronics," Nate said. "I don't want to give him any help."

"Can you do this without looking?" Kate asked.

"Absolutely," Nate said.

"You're doing it again. Aren't you?"

Nate just smiled and looked down to the electronics. After a few minutes the waves were diminishing in height. There was still not really any rain, but the wind was making up for any lack of dramatic effect.

The *Legacy* entered Quick's Hole. Nate slowed the boat down a bit to catch his breath. The wind was whipping wildly around Quick's but without waves there were no complaints.

"Can we just sit here till the storm passes?" Kate asked.

"Nate, I can't get a hit on the radar, the waves are higher than us, they're blocking anything behind them."

"I don't think he can get in here. Mike, hit the spotlight behind us for a second."

Mike moved the little joystick and spun the light behind.

David's boat came off the wave around six feet, the high-pitched whine of the twin Yamaha engines screaming now that they were out of the water. The boat came down and headed right for them. When it landed it was pushed to the right of the *Legacy,* missing it by about a foot. Nate slammed the throttle of his single diesel engine, making everybody clamor for something to hold on to.

"He's trying to ram us!" Darren screamed.

"YOU THINK?" Mike screamed back.

In the relatively calm water of Quick's Hole the harbor patrol boat was closing fast on the *Legacy.* Nate cut back to their port; his only advantage over the other boat was his turn radius. As they headed back past the harbor master's boat, David ran to the side and started to fire Darren's gun at them. They all ducked, not being able to hear the gun shots over the wind and engine roar—all except for Darren, who just stood there.

"GET DOWN, DARREN!" Kate yelled at him.

"He's got my gun. There are no bullets in it. I never loaded it."

"WHAT?" Kate, Mike, and Nate all screamed at the same time. Each of them had threatened somebody with it over the last couple of days.

"What?" Darren said. "Like any one of you were actually going to shoot somebody."

David's wider turn was complete and he was back on them again. Realizing that the gun was not loaded, he decided to ram the Legacy, and himself included, to end all of this forever.

Nate was not going to go down that easy.

"HERE HE COMES," Mike shouted. "JESUS, HE'S HEADING RIGHT FOR US."

"I KNOW," Nate yelled. "Look, we are going to head back out into Vineyard Sound, I can outmaneuver him out there, I'm sure of it."

"It sounds like you're convincing yourself more than us."

Nate looked at Kate and with a lowered voice said, "Yeah … a little bit."

Back out into the storm. They made their way along the last remaining shoreline of Pasque Island. As one island descended into the next—which was Cuttyhunk—the seas became a mess, what they called a *confused sea*. No rhyme or reason. The rhythm of the ocean was replaced with a wave from the port and then one from the starboard. They were a toy in a bathtub, a very large, angry bathtub. At times they could hear the engines of David's boat; having to turn on the light every so often was giving him their position. They headed along the backside of Cuttyhunk Island, the houses giving off a glow from their windows, and they tried not to think of the people sitting in there, warm and dry …

Focus, there, sunshine.

President Roosevelt used to come to Cuttyhunk for the striper fishing. The blessing of this last island was the fact that it sat out in the middle of Buzzards Bay, and at the end of the island lay a reef called Sow and Pigs, which extended out another quarter mile. The striper fishing was legendary, along with a reputation for claiming so many ships over the last two hundred years that people stopped counting. The surrounding water around the reef was deep but the reef at low tide stuck out of the water. When the seas were large, the waves crashing over the reef could grow two stories high. Nate was gunning for the Sow and her Pigs.

The *Legacy* was taking a pounding, the four of them being beaten to death by the sea. But Nate still felt their chances were better out here than at the hands of David Cavarlo. As they cleared the last part of Cuttyhunk the thunder of the crashing waves was mind-blowing. Nate bore down over the wheel.

"Nate, what are you doing?" Darren asked. "We can't be exposed to this. We're going to swamp and go down."

"I'm going to draw him into us and then I'm going to punch her through the cut."

"WHAT?" both Mike and Darren screamed.

"I won't go through the cut on a good day," Darren pleaded.

Shaking his head back and forth, all Mike could say was, "Nate …"

"I'll draw him into it with us, but he's behind us," Nate said. "His timing is not our timing."

Darren and Mike looked to each other. They both knew that the small opening around the halfway mark of the reef drew about fourteen feet of water, when the seas were running around the same height; the trough of that wave would expose the reef. Fourteen feet at the top of the wave, zero at the bottom. Timing—it was all about the timing.

Kate grabbed Darren's shirt at the neck and pulled him close to her. "What the fuck is the cut?"

"It's a small opening in the reef. He thinks if he times it right, David would get hit with the next wave coming through the cut, probably sinking him."

"What about us?"

"Umm … what?" Darren said.

Nate slowed down the boat, trying to get a read of the waves. They were heading right into them now. The bow of the *Legacy* got buried into a wave, the front windows under water for what seemed like an eternity. Then the bow slowly raised up, pushing the water over the cockpit roof and creating a waterfall behind them. The water was pouring in a bit faster than pouring out. Nate slowed a bit more. The back window of the cockpit exploded, sending glass all over them.

"WHAT WAS THAT?" Mike yelled.

The dashboard to Nate's right had exploded, too, and there was a small hole in the fiberglass, a bullet hole.

"Jesus, I think he found some bullets," Darren told the rest of them.

Nate pushed the throttle up a bit and started to head back up the reef. Watching his GPS, he turned slightly to Mike. "SPOTLIGHT STRAIGHT AHEAD." Without hesitation Mike hit the spotlight, but it was still facing behind them, and they all spun to look when the light went on. Fifteen feet behind them was the bow of David's boat, the front window blown in, his radar dome gone, just wires flapping around. His arm was stuck out the window firing a gun. They could just make out the flash of the muzzle. "MIKE! THE LIGHT!"

Mike rotated the light to the bow. A wave lifted them up as Nate pulled the throttle back into reverse for a brief second, keeping them on top of the wave, and when the light finally shined on the next wave coming through the cut, Nate slammed the throttle forward and the *Legacy* responded with a jump.

"KILL THE LIGHT."

The boat flew off the top of the wave. The next wave was about five feet ahead. The *Legacy* landed on top of it, and coming off it Nate started spinning the wheel hard to starboard. They were through the reef. Mike spun the light back behind them and turned it on.

All four of them turned around. It took a second or so to register, because the hull was what they were staring at … the bottom of David's boat, painted blue, riding the next wave up and then down. The next wave after that engulfed the hull, and the entire boat was swallowed by the sea. They all turned back around and glanced at Nate for a reaction. He just stared forward.

They cruised behind Penikese Island and into Cuttyhunk Pond, which in itself seemed easy compared to what they had all just gone through. As they slowly entered the pond, the rain finally arrived. Nate pulled into an empty boat slip. Mike and Darren rushed around the boat, tying her off.

"Follow me," Nate screamed through the rain. He led them up the hill into the very small town. A small hill rose up through the center of the cottages. The second to last house on the right sat in darkness. He led them up the porch, where Nate searched the top of the doorjamb for a key. He slammed the key into the lock and entered the dark house, the group on his heels. He turned on a light to reveal a small but tidy kitchen. Mike closed the door behind him.

Nate realized everybody was staring at him.

"An acquaintance of mine owns this house," he said. "She said if I was ever in need ..."

"In need of what?" Kate asked Darren under her breath, but just loud enough for Nate to hear.

"Who cares?" Darren responded. "I need a towel."

Nate came back into the kitchen with towels and passed them out, then he grabbed the phone on the wall and dialed Josh's cell phone.

Josh answered on the first ring.

"It's me," Nate said.

"Are you okay? Betsy told me her friend saw you on the beach with a group of people. Is everybody okay?"

"Yeah. We're on Cutty. I got Mike, he's fine."

"Thank God."

Nate could hear Josh tell his brother and Rebecca.

"What about our friends?" Josh continued.

"Listen ... it's a long story. We met up with the boys from Providence. And David ... David killed Lou."

"Oh my God. Where is he now?"

"I left him with the boys, he's in deep with the mob, but let's keep that to ourselves. Tell Rebecca all is fine and I'll call tomorrow."

"David ... Nate, really?"

"I know. I think it's over, though."

"No more David?"

"I don't think so. I'll call tomorrow," Nate said and hung up.

The boys let Kate take a hot shower first. They were staring at Nate, not really understanding why he'd told Josh what he did, but not feeling uncomfortable about it one bit.

Darren started to open every cabinet, looking for anything with booze in it; at this point mouthwash would do. But after a ten-minute search, two bottles of wine and half a bottle of rum was his total take. When Kate came back into the kitchen after her shower, the boys were standing around drinking wine in their underwear, their clothes in the small dryer in the back closet.

Kate didn't seem to notice or care about the boys' apparel.

"Shower's free."

"I'm next. I got Tasered," Mike shouted, running down the hall toward the bathroom. The bathroom door closed and the shower turned on.

"I'll never forgive myself for what I got him into," Nate said.

"It wasn't you, it was David, and that fucking bar of gold," Darren said.

Kate was staring out the dark kitchen window, the rain pelting hard against the glass.

"Is everything all right?" Nate asked her.

"We caused somebody's death out there tonight, and we're sitting around drinking, making jokes. Shouldn't we at least call somebody, for Christ's sake?"

"He caused his own death; we just got out of the way."

"Is that how you see it, Nate? That we were innocent bystanders out there? How about back on the beach, guns pointed at each other? Whose way were we getting out of there? Our own?"

"Is there a problem with what happened out there, Kate? Because I don't have one. David killed Lou and almost killed Mike."

"And us, for that matter," Darren butted in.

"I don't think my life will ever be the same because of what he caused, so I'm sorry if I don't show any remorse. He killed himself, Kate, that's the way I see it."

"Are you sure he killed Lou? What's your proof? The word of a mobster? But I guess we'll never know, will we?"

"Hey, look, I'm sorry you feel this way. We all made the decision not to call the cops, we're all adults here. You could have made the decision to stay back on Block."

"Well I didn't, did I? And saying that doesn't mean shit. You can't un-ring a bell."

Nate just stared at her—the one, she was the one. Now, with this adventure coming to an end, reality was starting to sink in, the ache and pains had begun, and the bitter taste of the last few days would linger in the air until it broke them apart, sending her away from him.

"So now what?" she asked.

"You and Mike go with Darren back to Block on my boat."

Kate laughed off to the side, the kind of laugh that told Nate she considered what he'd said to be stupid. "So you can go off and find your buried treasure and satisfy your curiosity?"

"Is that what you think all this has been about?" Nate was mad now, his voice amped up a notch. "You think I would put my friends' lives in danger over my curiosity? If that's what you think, then go to hell."

So there it is, this is the end of her with me, he thought.

She looked right at Nate with eyes wet. "I think we might all be going there." She turned and walked out of the room.

Nate turned to Darren, who was still sitting at the kitchen table. Darren finished off his glass of wine, grabbed the bottle off the table, and shrugged to Nate as he shuffled off to the living room.

Mike walked into the kitchen. "Where did everybody go?"

Nate walked by him, headed for the bathroom. He turned on the shower and got in. Standing there, wet again, he closed his eyes and leaned against the back shower wall.

He was just a boy again. His father was sitting on the stern of a boat, the sun so bright it was hard to keep his eyes open. He looked to his boy and smiled. God, he loved his dad's smile. They both just stared at each other and continued to smile. The love they held for each other was unbreakable. Finally he looked away from his dad. "Why does everybody have to die?" the boy said.

"Well that's easy. Love. We all die because we love."

"I don't understand."

"Most don't."

"What do I do now?"

"Lou loves you as much as I do."

"What does Lou want me to find?"

"Love," the father told his son.

Nate opened his eyes when the water shut off. The bathroom was engulfed in darkness. He stumbled out of the tub and felt around for confirmation that the sink was not going to catch him in the jewels. A knock on the door, and Mike told him the power was out and that he'd left a lantern in the hallway for him. Nate dressed by lantern and then made his way to the room Kate was in. Gently he knocked on the door.

"Kate? It's me."

No response. He stood there for a moment, an inch from the door, willing her to answer. He heard the old wooden floor creak; she was right on the other side of the door.

He whispered, "Kate."

The door slowly opened. Her room was lit by candles, about five of them, some on the nightstand and dresser, and it gave the room a dream-like glow. She walked over to a rocking chair and sat, her legs folded up to her body.

She didn't say a word.

Nate walked over to the foot of the bed and sat, keeping a six-foot distance from her in the tiny bedroom.

"My whole life, since I could remember, I've played it safe, all business. It was the way my father was, it's the way Lou is … was, no questions asked. You see, all I do is fish. No complicated relationships, a small group of great friends, that's it. And I actually had myself convinced that this is the way it should be. Safe. I decided to never let anybody close and at all times stay in control. I'm not trying to make excuses for the way I am. I just honestly thought that I needed to do all of this for Lou, that nobody, I mean nobody, would have gotten to the bottom of any of this, at least not to the extent that I would have accepted."

"So you're telling me this is just business for you, a job?" Kate asked in a soft voice.

"No … that's the problem. I mean at first, I convinced myself it was, but as the whole thing started to unfold, it felt like for the first time in my life I was living and I wasn't playing it safe. Then here you are and you got me all turned about, and now you are all I can think of. But because of this … because of my decisions, somebody's dead, and the truth is I don't care, he took something from me and he deserved to die for it."

"So if you didn't come here to apologize, then what? Just to confirm what you said downstairs, that you're not sorry?"

"I came in here to tell you … that I have fallen in love with you. And if what happened out on the reef tonight ruined it, then I am truly sorry." Nate got up and turned to the door.

"Nate."

His hand on the door knob, he paused.

"You're not going to tell me you complete me, are you?" Kate asked.

"Jesus, you're tough. You're not going to make this easy, are you?"

"You ever been in love?" she asked.

"No," he said, without hesitation.

His back was still to her. She placed her hand on his shoulder and he turned around.

"Love is a tricky thing," she said. "I thought I was in love before, actually a few times. It's not something I take lightly. I have never met anybody like you before. And I mean that in a good way. The thing is … not everybody thinks like you, so you might have to adjust your perspective, or at the least give me time to catch up with your way of thinking."

"Yeah, I'm really starting to see that now," Nate said.

"We all have a turning point in our lives that sets us on a new course, uncharted waters. How we handle ourselves when that moment arrives defines us from that time on."

"You're going to just leave me declaring my love for you hanging out there?" Nate asked.

"You're not listening to me, are you?" she responded.

"I love you."

"We've only known each other for a few days."

"Defining moment."

"Don't use my words against me."

"I love you."

"Still want me to go to hell?"

"Well if I'm going there, too ... yeah."

She wrapped her arms around his neck. "I hope I don't come off too preachy."

"No, no. I loved the uncharted waters part."

She pulled him close into a tight embrace. "You smell like fish."

"I always do."

"You complete me," Kate whispered in his ear. Nate pushed her backward, collapsing on the bed. They both started to laugh. She wrangled herself on top of him, sitting on his chest. She grabbed a pillow and put it over his face. "Can you hear me?"

Nate nodded his head yes, from under the pillow.

"I love you, too. Now if you get me hurt, I'll kill you in your sleep. Got it?"

Yes from under the pillow. She removed it and kissed him smack on the lips.

Gold, I tell ya ... gold.

CHAPTER 24: THE WRECK PART III

From their vantage point on the bluffs it looked like everything was working in their favor. But now, now it looked like the ship had come about and just missed the reef. Wait, she's listing to the port, listing badly. That's it, she hit it all right, but damn they're making a run at it. She'll flounder; the tide will push her back to the reef. *Wait, what is this, it's on fire, they set her on fire. They're in boats … wait … longboats, oh my God, we wrecked a whale boat.*

"Put out the fire, everybody listen, this isn't what it appears. Everybody down to the beach! Help them get to shore! NOW!"

The old lady hunched over and grabbed his arm. "Let them go down, let's get what we need."

"It's a whale ship, you evil creature, they have been at sea for years, they have nothing in their pockets and nothing in her belly. So let's try to save our souls and help them get to shore."

He looked back out to sea in the driving rain and wind. For a moment it looked like the fire was burning underwater, a glow could be seen after she went down. This was the end of the ten-year reign of the *Gosnold*, one of the most successful whale ships of her era.

CHAPTER 25:
BART AND THE COMPASS ROSE

"He that dies pays all debts."
—William Shakespeare, *The Tempest*

The bright morning sunshine was screaming through the two small bedroom windows. Kate and Nate were spooning on the bed, on top of the covers, fully dressed. Kate was the first to smell the coffee and sat up and smacked Nate on the ass.

"Get up, there, sunshine, it's coffee time."

He rolled over, rubbing his eyes. "You just call me sunshine?" he said, getting up to follow her out of the bedroom.

So there it was, with David Cavarlo dead, Nate, Kate, Darren, and Mike sat at a small green linoleum table from the 1950s and sipped their coffee. Through the windows they could see people walking up and down the street. It was summer, after all, and a tropical storm would not deter New Englanders from their boating. And Cuttyhunk Harbor in the summer could hold upwards of a hundred boats, so people were milling about, taking it all in on this little island.

"So now what?" Mike was the first to ask.

"What's the chance that you three take my boat back to Block and let me waste my time with this Lou thing?"

"Uh, let's see," Darren said. "Take the five, carry the one ... oh yeah: zero chance, from my calculations."

"Okay, then let's go find a compass rose," Nate told the group.

"Oh, like an *X marks the spot* kind of thing?" Mike asked.

"I wish it was that easy. I'm open for suggestions."

They all sipped their coffee.

"Right, let's go for a walk around the island and just see what comes up," Kate blurted out.

"Brilliant," Mike yelled and jumped up, heading for the door.

They all followed suit and started for the door as Nate left a note for the owner.

Darren turned to Mike. "A walk around the island, that will take all of ten minutes." Mike shrugged and headed out into the street.

Kate walked up behind Nate as he was writing. "You better not be signing it love and kisses."

"Well to be honest with you, Mrs. Bousquet is about eighty years old, so I better not get her all hot and bothered."

"Oh," Kate said with a relieved smile stretching across her face.

"Let me guess, you're the jealous type," Nate asked.

"Vicious."

They headed out the door into the middle of the street.

There were leaves and twigs littering the street, but the sun and sky gave no other clue of the storm that had ripped through the islands last night.

"Which way?" Kate asked.

"This way, we'll head up to the lookout up there," Nate said, pointing. "It's the highest point on the island. We'll have a look around."

They walked by a small church and a small cemetery, up another hilled street that led to an old World War II lookout tower. Now that the threat of a German or Japanese attack was long gone, all that was left of the tower was its cement base. Before they reached the tower road, Kate noticed a small, white-shingled building, which long ago had been a one-room schoolhouse but was now home to the Museum of the Elizabeth Island-Cuttyhunk Historical Society.

"Hey look, a museum," Kate enthusiastically said.

"OOO, really," Mike said with the same enthusiasm, but with a touch of sarcasm thrown in.

"Why not?" Nate said.

They all entered the small museum. It was full of pictures and displays of the island and its fishing community from days gone by. A man and a woman were repairing a broken pane of glass on a small back window. "Hi, please look around," the woman said. "Just cleaning up from the storm. If you have any questions, my name is Lori." They all nodded, walking around. Nate recognized the guy as Captain Revene, a charter boat fisherman from Cuttyhunk. He tried not to make eye contact with him, mainly because Lou wasn't a big fan of this captain. Something about cheating at the Martha's Vineyard Bass and Bluefish Tournament, a decade back. Lou never liked a cheater.

Mike got bored in about five minutes and walked back outside.

The three of them repeated their act from the whaling museum, looking at the pictures and artifacts. Lori left the captain to finish the window himself.

"Okay, you three have spent more time in here than any other person in the past three years," Lori said, and added, with earnest enthusiasm, "Please tell me you have questions, I just love questions."

"Okay," Nate said. "We are on a kind of historical scavenger hunt, traveling around New England looking for things."

"Things?" Kate whispered to Darren.

Nate turned to both of them. "Can you two please stop the running commentary that you have been doing since this whole thing started? It's quite annoying." He shook his head with just a hint of a smile and turned back to Lori.

Darren whispered to Kate, "Annoying? I don't think you're annoying."

"You either, mate," she said, and pointing to Nate, "Him, on the other hand …"

"As I was saying, Lori, do the words 'compass rose' stand out to you at all with regards to something on this island?"

Lori took the question very seriously and thought for a moment before answering no.

"Okay, thanks."

"Anything else, just ask."

They started milling about again, and just like in the whaling museum, it was Kate who found the clue.

"Nate, you have this picture in Lou's photo album."

"What?" Nate and Darren joined Kate at the picture in question. It was the picture of three guys standing in front of a stone wall. Just as in Lou's photo, the wall extended up and out on all sides of the photo, giving the impression that it was big, whatever it was. Nate stood straight up and noticed the pictures were grouped together with regards to certain times and themes from the history of the island. The other photos surrounding the twin of Lou's were from the building of the Bartholomew Gosnold Monument, which sat at the far end of the island, by West End Pond.

"Jesus, these are Lou's uncles. They were masons, from Block."

Lori was standing behind them. "That's a group of workers who built the Gosnold monument back in 1902."

"We're from Block Island. These guys are related to a close family friend. He actually has this photo in his family album." Nate turned to the others. "This has to be it." He turned back to Lori. "What can you tell us about this monument?"

Lori smiled from ear to ear. "Do any of you know who Bartholomew Gosnold was?"

All three nodded in unison.

"Really? Okay, good. So you know when he explored these waters, this was where he made camp for that summer in 1602. The Dartmouth Historical Society had this built in 1902 to commemorate the tercentenary of his and his thirty-plus crew's landing here on June 4, 1602."

Nate stopped breathing and he stopped hearing anything else. The room spun for a moment as all the blood drained from his face. *Jesus, Lou … How do you do this? You continually amaze me.*

It took Darren a few moments longer to put it together. Lori finished talking about the monument and told them something about a book, and walked off.

"Jesus, Nate. The date, am I wrong?"

"No you're not. It's the same date."

"What about the date?" Kate asked the boys.

Nate was still trying to wrap his mind around it, so Darren was the one to explain.

"June 4 is the date Nate's father died, the day we went to the Vineyard to see *Jaws*."

"Whoa, that's not a coincidence, is it?" she said, turning to Nate, who held up his finger as he paced around the room, figuring out the last details of his thought. Lori came back with a book about Cuttyhunk and handed it to Darren, who handed her ten bucks and thanked her.

"Can I ask a question?" Lori asked, not waiting for an answer. "Who are these three guys in the picture? We don't have any names for the workers. It would be great if they were local, and maybe you have more pictures you could donate?"

"Gauthier, the three guys in the photo are related to Louis Gauthier from Block Island," Nate explained. This brought Captain Revene's head up from his window repair and he strutted over to the group.

"You're West."

"Nate West."

"Yeah … that's right, Jonathan's boy. I read something that old man Lou died recently?"

"Yes, a few days ago." Nate paused, trying to think how long it had been, then returned his attention to Captain Revene.

"Strange guy, no disrespect or nothing, but he used to come here once a year, same time every year, and head over to the monument."

Nate looked at the captain. "If I had to guess, he came sometime in June."

"Yeah, that sounds about right."

The three of them left the museum and joined Mike, who was sitting on a stone wall across the street, talking to a couple of girls. Mike jumped up. "I'll come by after," he told the girls as they laughed and continued down the hill. They all walked into the small street. "Where we off to now?" Mike asked.

"Can you keep it in your pants?" Nate asked.

"Sometimes," Mike answered.

"Gosnold monument. I'll explain on the way."

They headed up the rest of the hill to the highest point on the island, where the lookout tower once stood. From this vantage point they could see all of Buzzards Bay to their right and Vineyard Sound, with the Gay Head Lighthouse, to their left. At the very end of the Island and the Gosnold monument, Sow and Pigs Reef stood out like a darkened branch surrounded by green Atlantic water, and off to the west stood the monument. The terrain leading out to it was full of hills and valleys lined with sea tomato bushes and wild blueberry and raspberry plants.

"You're shittin' me, right?" Kate asked. "Can one thing be easy?"

"Um ... no," Darren told her.

"Always the optimist," Kate said, looking at Darren.

"Okay, everybody, buddy up," Nate said and started down the first of many sandy slopes to the monument.

Darren turned to Mike, who was last in line, and handed him the Cuttyhunk book. "Find out what you can about the monument." Mike started to flip through the book.

"Okay, here's the way I see it," Nate started to explain. "And let's just take the gold out of the equation, for now. Lou wants me to get to the New Bedford Whaling Museum, which we do, in a roundabout kind of way. Once at the museum, though, he directs us to Cuttyhunk. And even though we haven't found anything about the compass rose yet, we discover that Lou's family built the Gosnold monument and that Bartholomew Gosnold landed on the same date that my father died. And for some reason, Lou visited the site once a year."

Mike looked up on hearing this and returned to his book. Kate slipped down a small hill. She got up and checked her legs. "Ah, shit. I got a tick on me."

They all started checking their legs.

"All right, so," Nate continued. "Lou never told me much about his feelings about the death of my father, but I know this much: he was very upset that he wasn't with him the day he got killed, visibly shaken. Although he never told me directly, I got the feeling that he was supposed to be with him that day. Something to do with my father's death and bringing me here are related. It's that date, June 4."

"I know you don't want to bring the gold into this discussion," Darren said, "but I'm having a hard time separating the whale ship being named *Gosnold* and the very monument we're traversing the barrens of Cutty to get to."

"Yeah, I know," Nate sighed. *Gold, I tell ya ... gold.*

The thundering noise of a Coast Guard helicopter brought all four of them looking upward as it screamed overhead. They all stared out to Sow and Pigs Reef.

"Anybody see a wrecked boat out there?" Darren asked.

"The tide was going out along with the wind. That boat should have been blown miles out to sea," Nate said, trying to convince them.

"You're doing it again, aren't you?"

Nate turned to Kate and gave her a weak smile.

"Hey, since we're on the subject, does anybody worry how David got away from those guys from Providence?" Darren asked. "I mean if he killed them—and now with the chance that his body could wash up on a beach around here—I'm just saying ... you know ... We were the last ones seen with all of them alive. Seen by the Coast Guard—you know, the ones that know us."

They all stopped walking and stared at one another. The helicopter hovered a mile away over Vineyard Sound.

"One freakin' problem at a time," Nate pleaded, heading down the hillside.

They made it to the beach with just a few scratches. The beach, however, was not really a beach, in the sense that there was not one grain of sand to be found on this side of the island, only millions of ocean-smoothed stones for as far as the eye could see. The sand over the years had been washed out to the sea surrounding the island, revealing the rocks that lay beneath it. This was the reason Cuttyhunk still had its isolated feel after all these decades, with just a few houses scattered about. If it was beautiful Cape Cod sand, some developer probably would have turned it into a haven for condos and billon-dollar houses. The west side of the island also was empty of people; on occasion you might find a hardcore fisherman casting out into the fish-laden water. But today the four of them were the only ones standing on the rocks.

The monument itself sat up on a patch of land clear of the rocks that inhabited the beach. It took a little while to get to the foot of the monument, dodging the marsh and brush that surrounded it.

When they all finally made it, they touched the monument, connecting with it if for no other reason than the bitch of a time it took them to get there. *Tag, you're it*, they all said to themselves.

"Mike, what you find out?" Darren asked.

"Well, it's made of native fieldstone. Sixty feet tall, and, like, eighteen feet around, and it's solid, no access. Just those fake-looking indents to make it look like a door and windows, that's what the book says, at least."

The monument was built like a tower, round and tapering as it rose. It almost looked like a smokestack from a long-gone building. The four of them walked around the tower several times, running their hands over it, looking for the mythical stone that would push in and open a door, but all they found was stone and cement.

"Maybe we have to scream *compass rose*, you know, like *open sesame?*" Kate said.

"Brilliant," Mike said, and he screamed, "OPEN SESAME!"

"Mike," Kate said. "Compass rose."

"COMPASS ROSE!" Kate and Mike screamed.

Nothing happened. Mike looked disappointed, as if he actually thought it would work. "Damn it," he said. "I got to take a piss."

"Do you always announce your bathroom regiment to the general public?" Kate asked.

"What?"

"Go piss behind the monument, but not on it. This is sacred ground," Nate joked.

"Oh, like Bart didn't piss all over this place," Mike said as he headed around the opposite side.

"Does anything resemble a compass rose? Anything looking like it's pointing to north?" Nate pleaded with them as he looked at the stones.

"HEY GUYS?" Mike said, coming back around. "GUYS!"

"What?" Nate yelled as all three turned their attention to Mike.

Mike was there with a gun pointed at his head. David was grabbing Mike's neck and walking him closer to the group. His shorts were torn, his legs scraped and bloody, his eyes red and swollen.

Kate gasped while Nate and Darren just stared into David's mad eyes.

"I'm fine, thanks," David told them. "What? What are you looking at? How did I survive? You stupid bastards, I may have only spent a year at the Coast Guard Academy, but in that short time they trained me well. Don't get me wrong, I almost died out there. I thought I was going to make it in the boat, but you are the better captain, Nate, I give you that. But that's all I'll give you. It took me most the night to get back over to the harbor side, but then I searched a few houses, and boom, there was Darren sitting on a couch all warm and dry. I could have killed all of you in your sleep."

"It's over, David," Nate insisted.

"IT'S NOT OVER! There is gold somewhere on this island and you're going to find it for me."

"There's no gold, David. All Lou wanted to do was to get me here for my father's sake. This is the place Lou went to grieve for my father."

"BULLSHIT!"

Nate walked over to the keystone of the monument. "LOOK!" he shouted. "Look at the date on the keystone, June 4, 1602. June 4, the same day my father died. That's the quest Lou wanted to send me on. To let him and I pay our respects to my father together." Nate stared at the keystone, lost in a sudden thought. *Four from the key.*

"NO, NO, NO!" David screamed.

"THEN WHAT? What's the secret to all of this shit, then, because I DON'T KNOW WHAT YOU ARE DOING." Nate walked a little closer to David and Mike, his voice toned down. "How did we get here, Chief? How is it Lou is dead and you're standing there with a gun pointed at Mike, which I wish you would put down."

"Fine, I'll point it at you."

"I would like that better."

"Always the hero. Well I guess this is the part of the story, Nate, where I tell you that you were right, years ago when you turned me into your father's friend, that you knew I stole his dive watch, that, as always, you were right. Since the age of thirteen I had a dirty little secret. When you were gone to live on the Cape I got bored and started to break into people's houses. Actually I didn't have to break, nobody ever locked their doors. I took watches, electronics, money. This went on for years, just a bored kid on a nothing island. But this one particular day, something extraordinary happened. Right after your father died, I went for Lou's house, figured some of those artifacts in his basement could be worth something. When I went into his office, sitting right there, I mean right on his desk, was a gold bar. I froze. I knew he was diving on something every time you and your dad weren't around, but gold ... I guess you guys weren't too close after all. Anyways, I was going to take it and run. But he walked in the front door just as I reached for it. So I ran out the back, leaving it. But he must have known. He started locking his doors, and every time I did manage to get in, I never saw that bar again. So as years went by, I obsessed about it. As the technology got cheaper and easier I bought listening devices online, I bugged his house—yours, too. You live one boring life, Nate, let me tell ya. I tapped phones—you name it, I had it covered. But no fucking bar of gold. Then ... then a sudden turn of luck, for me, not Lou, the old man got cancer, his number came up, and he started making calls to get the bar cashed in. I think you know who he tried to use. Darren, how's your dad?"

"FUCK YOU," Darren screamed, heading for David, but Nate grabbed him.

"No, no, no, there, old friend," David said, pressing the gun harder to Mike's temple.

He continued: "This is the part you guys know, I got into a little bit of trouble with some people from Providence, and they were coming at me pretty hard, so I confronted Lou one day at his house, told him if he didn't cut me in I would tell anybody who would listen, I would tell about the gold, he would have lost it all, so he told me that there was more, a lot more, that if I let him take care of some unfinished business, he would take care of me. Well, that day never came, so the other day I pressed him a little harder and he told me he got rid of the bar, gave it back to the sea, and that he'd lied about there being more gold."

"So you killed him."

"I sabotaged his boat and pulled up alongside him, and that old French asshole punched me in the face, almost got the best of me … almost."

Upon hearing about the final minutes of Lou's life, the color ran out of Nate's face. "Look around, David, it's over. What are you going to do, shoot all of us? Look at it, it's solid rock, no hidden treasure here … nothing. David, Lou was leading you on, he played you. You killed him over nothing."

"NOTHING! What was that gold bar you gave the Ricci brothers, huh? Where did that come from?"

"David, it was the same bar you saw on his desk years ago. When he knew you were coming after him he put it back on the wreck. I dove on Lou's boat after you sank it. It came to rest on the wreck, it was just sitting there where he found it years ago, and all of this letter shit was just a gesture from an old man giving me one last adventure … one that involves my father."

"It was the same bar?" David asked himself, his voice lower. He seemed to have lost some of his energy. He pushed Mike to the ground and started to pace around with his hands to his head.

"It's over, Chief. Come on, give me the gun," Darren pleaded, walking over to him.

David raised the gun and fired at Darren, and Darren grabbed his stomach and collapsed to the ground. Kate screamed and rushed over to him along with Nate.

"Jesus—Darren," Nate said.

There was blood all over him. "Put pressure on it, here," Nate told Kate. She pushed down on the wound, trying to stop the flowing blood.

David raised the gun to Nate, who was kneeling by Darren. Mike, who was still on the ground a foot or so from David, swung his leg around and kicked him in the groin. He backpedaled for a moment and fired at Mike, just missing him.

Nate leapt up and headed toward David at a fast clip, the gun went up again, this time he aimed it at Nate, and another shot rang out. Nate stopped in his tracks. Kate screamed once again and Mike's eyes went wide.

David fell to his knees, the gun still in his hand. He slowly tried to raise it again. Another shot, and he fell in a heap on top of Mike.

Mike screamed and kicked David Cavarlo's lifeless body off of him. Nate spun around and saw Jimmy and Stu on top of a pile of rocks a thousand yards down the beach. To their left, on the ground, lay Doc with a sniper rifle on a tripod. Jimmy and Stu started heading over to them after they said something to Doc, who took off down the hill to the water's edge.

Kate was still putting pressure on Darren's stomach. Nate joined Kate by his side. "We're going to get you help," Nate said.

Darren looked around the beach. "How?" His breathing was very fast.

Jimmy and Stu came up alongside them. Stu looked at the wound. "Doc's coming with a med kit," he said. "He was a medic in Desert Storm, before he joined the dark side," he assured Kate with a smile.

Doc came running and jumped to Darren's side. He rolled him over and started to wash the wound.

Turning to Nate, he said, "Sorry, I didn't think he was going to shoot. I would have taken him earlier."

Nate and Kate stood back up as Doc continued to work on Darren.

Kate ran over to David's body. "YOU SON OF A BITCH! HAPPY NOW? You're fucking dead, you stupid bastard—you're DEAD! AND I DON'T GIVE A SHIT!"

Nate took her in his arms. He turned to Jimmy and said, "I thought he was dead, and you, too, for that matter."

"Well, he was never really cut out for this line of work. He left loose ends. I was pretty pissed that you gave me a couple of bags of fake gold, but then you did give me a real one, too. So I figured we were even. But then you left your GPS tracking thing on, so I figured, what the hell, let's see if there's more gold. And maybe I could run into this asshole again," he said, pointing to David's body. "We pulled in this morning, saw your boat. Tracked you to the path that led here. Our boat is anchored out there a bit. But David?"

"He chased us through the storm and sank out there." Nate pointed toward the reef. "What are you going to do about him?"

"I'll take him for a boat ride ... no more David. You have a problem with that?"

"Nooooo," Kate, Nate, and Mike all answered.

Darren moaned and grunted.

They all gathered around Doc.

"Look, it's a through-and-through, I don't think it hit anything major. The bleeding has already stopped." He looked up to Kate. "I need a hand here."

"Why, because I'm the girl?"

"Yes, because you're the girl," he answered.

He stitched the wound up with Kate's help.

"Let me guess, you were a nurse, too?" Darren asked in a weak voice.

"Never a nurse."

"Great ... that makes me feel better."

They brought Darren over to the monument and leaned him up against the stones.

"How are you feeling?" Kate asked.

"Not too bad."

Doc turned to Nate. "I've got him pumped up with quite a bit of pharmaceuticals, so don't let him fool ya: when they wear off, you better have him in a hospital."

Doc and Stu brought the body to a dingy they'd liberated from some unsuspecting owner in the harbor and pulled up onto the stones. They threw him in and covered him with a beach blanket and joined the rest of them at the monument.

"So there's more gold?" Jimmy asked.

"Actually, I think there is," Nate stated.

"You told David …" Kate began to say, but Nate cut her off.

"Everything I told him was a lie. Lou wants me here because he hid something in this monument."

"The whole speech about the dates on the monument and your father, I had a freakin' tear in my eye—and it was all a lie?" Kate screamed.

"Well Lou had it played out to give me multiple meanings, but there is something hidden here."

"It's solid stone and cement," Mike said.

"Exactly, stone and cement, that's what Lou told me about his past. Told me it was made up of stone and cement. His family made their cement with byproducts from the islands, but he told me that too much salt made it tough to keep the cement together. Did you ever take a look at his stone wall?"

"Yeah, it's a piece of shit, falling apart in places, the cement was no good, keeps crumbling," Darren weakly tried to add to the conversation.

"Keeps crumbling. But not all of it. Some of it holds together just fine. In his logbook he wrote in the corner of the page with the compass rose on it, '*four from the key*.'" Nate walked to the keystone of the monument, which read *1902*. "Four from the key," he said as he counted four stones. He examined the fourth stone, then he looked around, took the water bottle Doc had given Darren, and sprayed a little bit of water over the stone. There, worn away by time and the sea, a very faint outline of a compass rose appeared, a simple circle with notches to represent the four directions. "Does anybody have a knife?" Nate asked.

Stu, Jimmy, and Doc all displayed several and varying knives for his perusal. He took the multi-tool from Doc. He opened it and held it to the cement just above the etched stone.

He ran the point of the pliers along the cement that held the fieldstones together. All that happened was a white scratch appeared on the cement. He moved his arm down to the compass rose stone and did the same thing, and this time the cement gave up its hold and crumbled down the monument.

"Lou has been coming here to fix the cement around this stone," Nate explained. "His wall back home was just an indicator of how the cement was holding out."

He continued to scrape along the stone as everybody crept closer to him.

All the cement was gone after ten minutes of scraping. The stone wiggled like a loose tooth, slowly coming out with every wiggle. It finally fell to the ground, revealing a small opening into the monument. "His family built this, he must have known about this hiding spot."

They all stood there waiting for Nate to reach into the hole, to bring an end to this quest the old man had started them on.

Nate slid his hand into the hole and fished around for something, anything that would legitimize all this trouble the letter had caused.

"Ah, shit," Nate exhorted as his hand came out with a bar of gold.

"Crap ... more gold," Kate said.

He reached back in three more times with the same result, three more bars. A fifth time into the hole produced a bottle of rum wrapped in burlap, and the last thing retrieved from the hole was a book, just like the leather-bound book with Lou's notes in it, this one wrapped in wax cloth for preservation. Nate sat at the base of the monument as everyone else looked at the gold, and simply thumbed through the book. A letter fell out of the back with Lou's handwriting on it. He read it to himself.

Standing up, Nate said, "Guys." They all turned to Nate. "A letter from Lou," he said.

Nathaniel:

If you're reading this, I must be dead. (I always wanted to say that.)

The gold that you have found here is all that is left from the whale ship Gosnold. You hopefully already know this. I could never figure out what happened to the rest. There is no more and should be no more. This gold has brought me nothing but pain. I discovered the wreck from one of our spots; I dove on it one day when you and your father were away. When I found the gold I kept it to myself. I waited for a day when your dad was not around to bring the gold up; I should have been with him that day. I am sorry for that, and I hope you can forgive me, because I never forgave myself. So do what you will with it, but there's blood on it. I hope it brings you some joy in your life, because it never did for me.

Love, Lou.

P.S.: The rum is Captain Kidd's, don't let Jack and Josh tell you otherwise.

Nate, Kate, Mike, and Darren, along with Jimmy, Stu, and Doc the gun-dealing medic, all stood around the Bartholomew Gosnold Monument on the island of Cuttyhunk in Buzzards Bay in the southeastern part of New England with hundreds of thousands of dollars in gold at their feet, and nobody knew what to do or what to say.

It ended up being Nate.

"Screw it." He turned to Jimmy. "You can have the gold."

The rest of the crew exchanged glances. Darren got to his feet with the help of Kate.

"Lou's right," Nate said, "this gold is tainted. Take it."

Jimmy stood there and stared at Nate. "What makes you think I won't just shoot all of you and take all the gold, huh?"

A smirk crept across Nate's face. "Well, first of all, I told someone back on Block that if they don't hear from us by noon today, they are to call the authorities. I gave this person all your names and the make and registration numbers on your boat. So there's that. Also, as fucked up as you are—and you are one fucked up individual, Mr. Ricci—we made a deal, I know that must mean something to you."

"You're pretty smart, there, Nate," Jimmy said, giving him his own demented smirk. "If you ever need work …"

"There are a couple of things I need from you."

"Oh, here it is," Jimmy said, laughing.

"First, I keep one gold bar for Lou's niece. That's how all this shit started."

"Is that it?"

"The second thing, stay off my island."

Jimmy just laughed and headed off down to the beach, the other two following like loyal pets. When they reached the stolen dingy, they threw the three gold bars on top of the beach blanket and rowed out to the *Big Booty*, like the gold was no more important than a picnic basket.

"The chief's got his gold," Mike said. "Being dead, he probably doesn't know it, though."

"Can you make it back?" Nate asked Darren.

"No … I got shot, and I'm—I'm starting to realize—really high. What am I going to tell Doctor Spencer?"

"Tell him you shot yourself," Nate said.

Darren nodded. "Yeah, he'd believe that, it was my gun, after all."

"Mike, can you go back and get the *Legacy* and bring her around?" Nate asked.

"Okay, boss." Mike was up and off around the monument. "I can't believe we gave away all that money," he said as he hiked up the hill.

Nate walked around the back of the monument and yelled to Mike, who was already halfway up the hill, "Hey, meatball, talk to those girls *after* you get us. Us first, girls second."

Mike gave the thumbs-up and headed down the opposite side of the hill.

Nate walked back to Kate and Darren.

"He's going to find the girls first, you know that, don't you?" Darren said.

"So you're okay giving that gold to the mob?" Kate asked.

"The mob, no. But getting them off our backs? Yes. The gold's tainted." He smiled. "But what if we could find gold that wasn't tainted?"

"What are you talking about, Nate?" Kate asked.

He pulled out the notebook. "Nobody asked me about this. All too busy with the gold, huh?"

"What's that?" Darren asked.

Nate opened up the book and showed it to Darren. "You recognize these latitudes and longitudes?"

Darren stared intently at them. "Jesus, those are small numbers. That's the Caribbean."

"Right you are. Lou spent a year down there with my dad the year before he died, spent it with that sonar array."

"Do you have any idea how many ships over the last five hundred years carrying gold sank down there?" Darren asked.

"I know that they have only found one percent of them. I'm thinking with these sonar hits and the extensive notes in here"—he held up the book—"it should be a great head start on finding our own gold."

Darren managed to get to his feet.

"Anybody for Christmas in the Caribbean?" Nate asked.

Kate and Darren raised their hands and smiled.

EPILOGUE

"The ocean knows no favorites. Her bounty is reserved for those who have the wit to learn her secrets, the courage to bear her buffets, and the will to persist, through good fortune or ill, in her rugged service."
—Samuel Eliot Morison, *The Maritime History of Massachusetts*

The bright turquoise of the Gulf Stream water poured around the hull of the boat as it headed north to the harbor of Islamorada, Florida. It took the *Legacy II* one month to make it from Block Island, because of what Kate called romantic areas of interest and a great deal of shopping all along the eastern seaboard. Nate thought they were lucky it only took a month.

The new *Legacy* was a forty-five-foot Cabo Express, with twin diesels that gave it more than one thousand horsepower. It had two tuna towers and a custom hull color of light blue (Kate's choice). This was a hardcore fishing and cruising battlewagon.

As the *Legacy II* maneuvered at the dock, Mike ran from bow to stern, preparing the lines. As if Nate had been handling this boat his whole life, he docked her with ease. The three of them stood on the dock admiring the boat, something they had been doing since they left.

Two beautiful girls around Mike's age walked by and could be heard whispering to each other, *Nice boat.* Mike took off after them and thanked them. He turned back to Kate and Nate and shouted, "Thanks, guys, go ahead and wash my boat down and fuel up. I'll be back."

Nate looked at his watch and yelled back, "Two hours or I'm freakin' leaving you, got it?"

Mike gave the thumbs-up and caught up with the girls.

"How long will it take to head back down to Key West?" Kate asked.

"A couple of hours. Their flight doesn't get in till morning."

They took a cab for a twenty-minute ride to their true destination in Islamorada. The house was simple, terracotta, a shingled roof, yellow shutters, and a Toyota Prism in the driveway. In the yard Annie was watering some newly planted ferns. Which she stopped doing when Nate opened the gate to her yard. She ran up to him and hugged him hard.

Sitting on her back deck, she stared at Nate's old red backpack full of hundred-dollar bills.

"Tell me again how much."

"Five hundred thousand."

"Dollars."

"Dollars," Nate said, laughing.

"How?"

"Well, that's complicated. You need to tell me right now if you have a problem with hiding this? I'm going to give you a number of a guy in Rhode Island, his name is Bob Costa. He will give you a game plan for … let's just say he can give you some guidelines in this sort of thing. Do you have a problem with any of this?"

"I don't have a problem with anything right now."

"Lou loved you a great deal and wanted you to have this. It just took a while to get it to you."

Annie hugged Kate and Nate for ten minutes, wiping her eyes with the back of her hand. She was still wiping her eyes as the cab pulled away from her house, and she was still standing there as the cab disappeared from her street.

"She has a lot to tell her husband," Kate joked to Nate.

Standing at the dock, fueling the *Legacy II* up, Nate glanced at his watch. A half hour late, Mike came running down the dock and climbed onto the boat.

"What, she punch you? You have a bruise on your neck," Nate said.

Mike rubbed his neck, smiling. "I hope Tortola is this friendly."

Nate entered the office to pay for the ungodly amount of fuel a vessel this size held and used. He opened his wallet and handed the attendant an MCM Machinery corporate card. He signed it and headed out to the boat.

The plan was working like a dream. It started back on Cuttyhunk. Once Mike finally made it back to the Gosnold monument and picked up Kate, Darren, and Nate on the *Legacy*, they headed back to New Bedford. Darren's drugs started to wear off and he started to do a lot of whining. While he was being seen by actual doctors, and of course the police, Nate started his first in a series of phone calls. First to Rebecca and the guys on Block, skipping over the part about Darren getting shot (she'd blame Nate for that, so he'd just tell her that tidbit at a more suitable time). The second call to Bob at MCM Machinery, to tell him about the gold and who had it. That was when it all started to come together.

The gold, with the help of Bob's friends in the business, would be purchased from the Providence boys for the standard gold price, and no matter who made the initial purchase, after some favors cashed in, it would end up in Bob's hands.

Jimmy and Stu would get around five hundred thousand cash and be on their merry way, congratulating each other for a fine score. Through his connections, this Spanish, nineteenth century, *Gosnold* whale gold would fetch Bob around five million. If the Ricci brothers only knew …

This money, Nate would explain, was only the tip of the iceberg. With Lou's sonar hits in the Caribbean, which could mean the potential of millions more lying on the bottom of the Caribbean Sea, Bob would be a fool not to be a part of this. Nate explained that he didn't want the money, except for Annie's share, the rest was all Bob's, with one stipulation. Nate asked to be funded by Bob—a new boat, dive gear, sonar equipment, computers, anything and everything to help find this new, untainted gold. And this gold he would keep, of course, minus Bob's share. So created from tainted gold was The Block Island Research Institute, or BIRI for short. They even made tee shirts.

The next morning, sitting on the stern of the boat and drinking coffee, Mike, Nate, and Kate watched the tourists stroll by. At the end of the dock they recognized the people they had been waiting for. Darren, Josh, and Jack, along with Rebecca, came strolling and smiling up to the boat.

"Why do we live in New England again?" Rebecca asked.

"Cold back home?" Nate asked.

They all nodded.

"Well, for the next four months you will be warm and wet, so no complaining."

As Darren got on board, Nate turned to him. "How's my boat running?"

"You mean my boat, and it's running fine. Had a good fall run of stripers, made some good money."

"Fishing will save your soul."

"I think it has … thanks," Darren said as he slapped him on the back.

Rebecca turned to Nate. "You missed David's memorial last week."

"Yeah, well, big turnout?"

"Surprisingly, no." She shook her head and left it at that.

After David Cavarlo's sudden disappearance from the island, rumors started to fly. Somehow it was discovered that he had a large gambling problem and speculation arose that he'd fled to save his ass. Although Rebecca would never admit to it, her network of workers had the ears of a lot of influential people on the island, so probably no one would find out who actually started the rumor. Then, a month after his disappearance, the wrecked stern of a vessel washed up on a Nantucket shore. It was registered to the town of New Shoreham on the island of Block.

Cavarlo Senior would never admit the possibility of David dying out there, but he was overruled by his wife and a makeshift memorial was held. Lou once said that sending out enough bad karma would one day smack you on the ass. That it did, it smacked David right on the ass. If karma had a name, Nate believed it would be called Louis Gauthier.

With a course laid out to the island of Tortola in the chain of the British Virgin Islands, discovered not by Bartholomew Gosnold but by Columbus over five hundred years ago, the *Legacy II* and its seven occupants started off on their own journey of discovery. An adventure that for hundreds of years people from around the world had been a part of. Fortunes lost and found, lives claimed by it. Just the stories of gold had brought countries to war and wiped out entire civilizations. But these seven were New Englanders; adventure was in their blood, in their souls … along with the sea. New Englanders had traversed some of the greatest hardships imaginable and they had prevailed. Do not forsake these New Englanders, because what they set their minds to, they will conquer.

Gold, I tell ya … gold …

THE END

ABOUT THE AUTHOR

Kevin Saulnier lives in Westport, Ma. With his wife Anne and two daughters, Emma and Lily. When he is not busy fishing and cruising Buzzards Bay and Rhode Island Sound on his boat the Billou, he is writing and looking for shipwrecks.